B.

Black Water

A Place of No Hope

Neil Millar

To order additional copies, please contact us.
BookSurge, LLC
www.booksurge.com
1-866-308-6235
orders@booksurge.com

Black Water

Neil was born in 1968. Aged 25, he was involved in an accident that made him realise how precious life is. Since this time his aim has been to find greater meaning and direction life. Black Water is his first novel.

Acknowledgements

A book is never written by one person alone. Every writer needs help, support and input. Here I'd like to thank the people who have helped me. First of all, my parents, my children and Jo for their support, patience and belief in me, without which my dream of writing would have remained impossible.

I'd like to thank Drew for being as honest as a writer needs his best friend to be, Beryl for the first germ of an idea; the Munro clan for their background of Black Water; Chris for the healing, Holly for the questions...all of them, especially the ones on the phone at unearthly hours! And thanks also too to the editing team at Cornerstones.

To those who gave me the inspiration and support, especially Mum and Dad

THE CONSPIRACY

I was crouching on a playground of deadly spiders and snakes. Head down, eyes covered, waiting. It was only 10:34 local time and already the temperature was pushing ninety degrees. A gale-force wind whipped powdery dust from the parched plain into a swirl. It sand-blasted my face until it stung like salt rubbed into a wound. With gritted teeth I waited it out, knowing that when the bluster died away I would be straining for every breath.

Whumph, whumph, whumph...the earth trembled to the helicopter downwash as it lifted off the ground. A moment later it tipped its nose and was heading away. As the dust settled I stood up and looked beyond the scrawny bushes that littered the parched plain. In the distance was an awesome sight: the Himalayas — two hundred and fifty thousand square miles of parallel converging mountain ranges with some of the highest peaks in the world.

The freezing precipices, howling winds, avalanches and slopes had claimed the lives of better climbers than me, but I was the Patrol Commander leading Britain's first operational military unit inside India since Ghandi's silence sent the Raj home, and if I needed to lead my unit into the Himalayas, I would.

Standing next to me was Doug Cooper, my 2 I/C, 2nd in command. Muscle-bound, with abnormally large forearms plastered with tattoos, Doug was also known as 'Popeye'. He was a toughened professional with an exemplary record and as solid as they come.

'Looks like the welcome committee's on its way,' he said. He pointed across to a shield of dust rising on the horizon.

It was large, fast-moving and heading for us. I assumed it was a convoy of small vehicles or at least an armoured personnel carrier; so as it drew closer I was surprised to see one jeep manned by two people.

Six minutes late for our rendezvous, Rajit Ramjit, the Indian Military Liaison, stepped down from his jeep. He was probably the least attractive man I'd ever met. With broken yellow teeth and a long lower face that swaggled with fat from his jaw line he reminded me of a hippo. I could almost imagine his stout figure rising from the water with his prey clamped between his rotting jowls.

'A thousand welcomes to India,' he said, pumping the living daylights out of our arms. 'Your help is plenty, plenty appreciated. India and Robert family is plenty, plenty grateful to have most elite fighting force from Britain helping. A thousand thank yous and a thousand more welcomes.'

Tall and gangly, Greg 'Spaghetti' Fielding, came to my side. He was grinning and smacking his lips as he turned a Bon Bon around in his mouth like clothes in a tumble drier. He leaned into my ear. 'That was a welcome worthy of a politician. I feel I should be discussing the tea-bag trade with him, or at least the price of a cuppa.'

I smiled, slapped him on the shoulder and nodded at Macca, Steve McNamara, that he should climb aboard the jeep first. The ginger-haired Scot threw his Bergen into the foot-well and climbed in.

From the front of the jeep Ramjit was beaming a broken-toothed grin at us. 'Police do not know girl's whereabouts. We will go to her home and very, very wait for news.'

The driver crunched the jeep into gear, let out the clutch and launched us into the kind of journey across bumpy terrain that a soldier's arse was made for.

It was now thirty-six hours since twenty-four year-old, Anglo-Indian, Shreela Robert, had been snatched from the streets of a mountainside village outside her parents' home.

Based on intel from the Kremlin, SAS in-house intelligence, our assumption was that the abduction was somehow politically motivated. Top of the suspect list was former KGB General, Oleg Koslov—the same Koslov I had failed to take-out in the Philippines two years earlier. US intelligence sources had monitored his movements between Calcutta and a group of islands in the Bay of Bengal three days before the abduction took place. He had vanished the morning prior to Shreela Robert's disappearance and had not been seen anywhere since.

The abducted woman's home was in a village located on a hillside plateau. The road towards it was steep with many twists and turns and for several minutes our jeep whined up the track, but when we reached the perimeter we came to an abrupt halt.

Our driver honked his horn. It had little affect, in fact, I was having more success swiping away flies than he was having shifting bullock carts, rickshaws and the people in once-white clothing that were walking mindlessly in front of our vehicle.

Fortunately the Roberts' home was close to the village edge; a vast property behind an eight-foot wall and iron gates. A cobbled courtyard ringed a small chapel in the heart of the entrance and behind it ran a long, white, curved building.

As we pulled up the front doors of the house burst open. A wave of brown faces with huge toothy smiles surged into the courtyard, jabbering greetings. They patted us on our backs, took hold of our hands and shook them as though we were already heroes.

Suddenly they fell silent and parted to reveal a woman standing on the steps. She advanced sedately, moving stiffly from the hips, and held out her hand to offer the gentlest of handshakes. 'I am Manisha Robert, Shreela's mother,' she said. 'My servants will take your colleagues so they may freshen themselves. I would like you to follow me.'

She led me to the back of the house, to a veranda that looked down onto a garden with tall, stooping trees and patchy, scorched grass. It was a peaceful place, where birds sang and a gardener scratched rhythmically at the lawn with a rake. We sat down at a table and were cooled by a servant boy fanning us with a giant leaf.

Manisha Robert looked at me with a pensive frown.

'Today is the second day since Shreela was taken from us. My daughter is a spirited child. She greets the storms we have here with much enthusiasm. Sometimes she says it is as if she has become at one with them. It was a stormy night when she disappeared.'

She leaned forward and bowed her head for a few moments. When she looked up again her eyelids were wet and a tear was rolling over her cheek.

'Are you a family man?' she asked, dabbing her eyes with a handkerchief.

'Family is difficult for me,' I said, not wanting to broach a subject that was sore for me.

She gazed out into the garden, nodding and forcing a sad smile.

'For all of this my husband blames me. He has stopped listening to me. All he is concerned about is blaming me for the evening that Shreela was taken.'

I waited for her to continue.

'My sons and I were playing Carrams, a board game we play in India. I had not seen Shreela since prayers. It was ten o'clock when my husband came home, and this is when things began to dawn.

'He asked where his Shreela was. I sent my sons to check her room. When they found she was not there they checked for the servant boy Kalid. "Where is my Shreela?" my husband stormed. He shouted at me and told me I should have forbidden her to go out into the streets with the servant. He told me they should never have been allowed to speak.'

'They were friends, right?' I asked.

'Yes, but they should not have been. Our class should not be courted by the lower classes.'

'So, was your daughter courting the servant boy?'

'No. My daughter was only a friend to him. This is the kind of girl she is — she has no time for class, race or snobbery. To her, all are humanity — all are equal. But Kalid...well, I believe the poor boy had become infatuated. I told my husband to let them be. "Trust our daughter's highest intentions," I told him. But he forgets that our baby girl is already making her own way in this world. I reminded him that she is only returned home to briefly visit us after meeting government ministers.'

She paused as a servant brought tea and poured it. As I took a sip Mrs Robert slid a small photograph across the table to me.

'Shreela is my eldest,' she continued. 'This picture was taken many years ago.'

It was a black and white picture, faded around the edges, of a young girl standing on a wall. Perhaps it was the way she pointed at the camera, or the way her feet pointed at each other, or maybe it was the way her hair was all tied up in pigtails...there was something about the girl. I stared at the picture for I don't know how long, and only stirred from it when Mrs Robert spoke.

'Why is it that you are smiling?' she asked.

'She looks like trouble,' I said, 'and a very pretty young girl.'

'She is her father's darling and he worries about her. Not just because of the men who chase her, but because of her work.'

'What concerns your husband about her work?'

'My husband has contacts in the government. It is through these people that my daughter's work was first arranged.'

'What does she do?'

'She nurtures the native tribes of Kali Pani into civilisation under the guise of religion.'

I thought for a moment. 'You mean she's a missionary?'

'Yes, but recently she learnt that the government have changed their policy and now wish to remove the natives that she helps. She feels for them. She says they are being evicted from a homeland that has belonged to them and their ancestors for more than a thousand years. You see, there is money to be made from the land and the government say that the natives must now either accept civilisation or perish. My daughter views this policy as unacceptable and had begun to campaign against it. But the officials who helped her get this post as a missionary say she has stabbed them in the back.

'My husband is a very proud man. He is hurt by our daughter's behaviour. He wishes she would conform to normal womanly behaviour.'

She paused for a moment and narrowed her eyes, then, keeping her voice low, she said: 'I believe my daughter's disappearance has been arranged to shut her up, but my husband will not entertain my thoughts.'

She slid another photograph to me and watched me closely. 'This is a more recent picture. She is very pretty here.'

I held the picture and looked at it without focusing on it—the implications of Manisha Robert's theory were too far-reaching to dismiss instantly. 'I'm not exactly clear why they need to shut her up,' I said.

'I only know she met government officials just a few days before she disappeared. She told me they were very displeased with her. She said there were things—confidential things—that she would not discuss with me.'

Immediately questions began buzzing around in my head. Surely if the government wanted to shut her up they would just bump her off? Did she serve another purpose? If Mrs Robert was right, then I couldn't see the sense in the Indian government asking for British support to retrieve someone that they had arranged to kidnap.

I drew the conclusion quickly that this was a crazy theory; that she was mad and that perhaps her husband was right to ignore her. I held the pictures out across the table, intent on giving them back to her.

She shook her head and pushed my hand away. 'Please keep,' she said.

'I can't take pictures with me once I move on,' I said. 'If I was caught by the men who took your daughter and I was carrying a picture of her with me it's likely to cause us both a problem.'

She straightened her back. 'Then please take the older picture,' she said. 'This picture is your guide to my daughter.

Keep it by your heart and it will lead you to her. I will pray that this will be so.'

I looked at the mother and then at the girl in the picture. I could see resemblances; the round cheeks, dark hair, almond-shaped eyes and the full lips. For me, the picture would have little use, but if it helped Manisha Robert to believe in something...

I took the picture intending to chuck it away later. Just then one of the servants announced that food was waiting for us.

The Roberts' servants laid out curried vegetables, Bombay potatoes, naan bread, rice and chutney. Popeye, Spaghetti and Macca had filled their plates to overflowing by the time I reached the hall.

'Who knows when we're gonna get fresh again,' Spaghetti said, taking the middle seat at the long wooden table and tucking in as though he had never been fed.

Manisha Robert guided me to a place near the head of the table. 'Please sit here. My husband will wish to talk with you. Take as much food as you require.'

By the time I had filled a plate with the vegetables John Robert had joined us. He was a tall man with a purposeful stride and a grinding handshake. With a name like his I had expected that he would be more fair-skinned, but he was swarthy and spoke with a slight accent.

'When will you look for my daughter?' he asked as he sat down opposite me.

'First we need some direction. Our liaison is in contact with the police. As soon as he knows where your daughter is we will move.'

A servant brought a plate of food for John Robert. He reached for the salt pot, shook some out into his hand and sprinkled it across his plate.

'You have done this before?' he asked.

'Many times.'

'And how many successes?' His voice was raised—

strained—and I noticed all other conversation around the table had stopped and everyone was looking at me.

I guessed the purpose of his questions was to work out the odds of us finding his daughter. 'If your daughter can be found, we will recover her. We are well trained, experienced soldiers.'

He mixed the rice and the curry together with his hands then began eating with his fingers. He added more salt and cast his dark eyes around the room. 'Where is Kalid?' he said.

Manisha Robert raised her head. 'We are searching for him, my husband, but...'

Robert banged the table and glared at his wife. 'I want that boy found. Why are you sitting down eating when he is missing?'

Without a word Manisha Robert rose from the table and left the dining room.

∾

After we had eaten I went into the courtyard. The afternoon was scorching hot. I looked at the chapel and decided to go inside, not for religious reasons, but because I imagined it might be cooler in there.

Manisha Robert sat on a mat. I stood still a moment and then tried to back out without disturbing her, but she heard me. 'Please,' she said, calling me forward. 'Two prayers are always greater than the one.'

'I have no idea what to say,' I said. I hoped she would let me off the hook.

She took my hand and encouraged me to sit with her. 'It is easy. Just say what you feel and feel what you say. Open up your heart and speak with your soul.'

I forced a grin and closed my eyes. To begin with, the words flowed surprisingly easily through my mind. I asked that I would find Shreela safe and return her to her family. I asked that she would be unharmed and that she would remain strong at this time in her life. But then for some reason the words just dried up. As I tried to think of other things to say, something I would rather have shut out slipped into my mind.

I didn't want to hear her voice. Not now. I didn't want to hear her snarling, angry words going around in my head. I didn't want to see her face or the images of her waving that empty brandy bottle before my eyes.

I scrunched up my face, doubled my fists and tried to make the images of my wife disappear. 'Show me how to find peace,' I begged.

The shock of hearing my own voice startled me. I squinted out of one eye, hoping that I had just imagined speaking the words out aloud, or that maybe, by some miracle, Mrs Robert had failed to hear me.

She was staring at me and suddenly I felt like a right bastard. How could I sit next to her, with all she was going through, and pray out loud about my own troubles?

She studied me, biting her lip. 'Accept it, honour it, then let it go,' she said.

'Honour...honour what?' I frowned at her.

'Honour the pain that you feel. It is the positive acceptance of these feelings that will help you grow beyond them.'

'I don't know what you're talking about. And what do you know about my life anyway?'

She was about to reply when the door behind us crashed open. John Robert stood in the shaft of light. 'Why are you praying?' he bellowed. 'Prayers will not find that boy. I want him found.'

I staggered to my feet and headed to the door, staring deeper into Robert's dark eyes than I had ever looked into anyone's eyes before. It was the strangest feeling, as though I was within his soul. It occurred to me then that he did not wish to find Kalid for the boy's own safety and protection. There was something else—another reason—a darker reason.

I stumbled past him into the courtyard only to be blinded by the brilliant sunshine and deafened by the voices echoing the name of the servant boy, Kalid.

A PLACE OF NO HOPE

As we stood in the place Shreela had been taken from I knew the answer to the question even before I asked it. The lack of a crime scene cordon and the lack of even one forensic expert looking for evidence made it quite clear; but even so I just had to ask.

'Did you find any clues?'

The Police Chief shook his head and walked on.

Ramjit swung his arms. 'Plenty, plenty people disappear in India. Plenty, plenty people impossible to find, but Mr John Robert wants daughter. Why bother? We don't know. Such a big, big fuss over just one more missing girl.'

I paused for a moment, wondering if Ramjit was displaying a cultural attitude or just a personal one; whatever the case, it didn't seem to be a moral one. I knew if it was my child who had been abducted I'd want all the stops pulled out to find them, and I'd be on everybody's case making sure that happened.

At the police station we were taken into a small back room with a ceiling fan. The Police Chief scraped chairs across the floor from all directions to form a circle around his desk. 'Thank you, please sit,' he said, before opening the thin file on his desk. 'At Kidderpore truck is found.'

'What's Kidderpore?' I asked.

'Thank you, please, Kidderpore in Calcutta is a dock. Please, the boat is gone now.'

'What boat?'

'Please, yes, a boat.'

I took a deep breath and tried to get to grips with the language barrier. 'The boat,' I said calmly, 'was it stolen?'

He ignored my words and passed me a picture from the file. 'This is picture of man on boat. Oleg Koslov,' he said. 'For three days he is at the docks. Then we don't know where he is gone.'

I passed the picture to Doug. He raised an eyebrow.

I knew instinctively what was on his mind, he was thinking back—remembering a memory that I didn't want to face it. I swivelled in my chair and turned my back. Facing the Police Chief I said, 'You know where he took her?'

'Kali Pani.'

He pulled a map off the shelf behind him and unrolled it on the table. He drew a line down a river with his finger and then jabbed it right in the heart of the Bay of Bengal. 'Please, Kali Pani means Black Water. It is group of islands one thousand kilometres into Bay of Bengal. It is worst place on earth.'

'Beats freezing your bollocks off on the peaks of the Himalayas,' Spaghetti said, laughing like twenty rounds of machine-gun fire.

The Chief drew himself up tall. 'Happening there is bad, bad shit. Please, these islands are surrounded by sharks.'

Macca leaned forward, suddenly interested. 'Oh, really, what type?'

'Please, in Kali Pani, you say shark and shark will appear. This is the legend of Kali Pani—it is place of no hope.'

'I don't see why sharks are such bad, bad shit,' Doug said.

'The legend of Kali Pani is –'

I cut in. 'I'm not interested in legends. If we were operating in Sherwood Forest, tales of Robin Hood would have nothing to do with the task at hand. I want specifics. How can we be sure Koslov has taken the girl to this place?'

'Because Mr Oleg Koslov is in operation there.'

'Tell me about his operation.'

'He deals in arms. Kali Pani is strategic place for this.'

I paused for a moment as my brain tried to process the revelation. 'Correct me if I'm wrong, but it sounds like you're telling me that the Indian government allow Koslov to deal in arms on their territory.'

Ramjit eyed the Police Chief and then threw his arms up in the air. 'All dealings are lawful and confirmed with our government. Please, you are not here to question our authority. You are here only to assist us with girl.'

In disbelief I looked at Doug. He was shaking his head and puffing up his cheeks. Spaghetti was scratching his head; Macca had his hand over his mouth and seemed to be a million miles away.

'Fine,' I said, 'but I assume that he's proved he is acting in accordance with your law by showing you evidence: locations, warehouses, etcetera...that's where I want to start.'

'This is not very possible.'

'What does that mean?'

'Please, Mr Oleg Koslov does not have any such location.'

'I don't understand. You just told me he works out of Kali Pani in a legal operation and for that to happen you must know his sites.'

Ramjit was shaking his head and drawing a circle around the islands with a finger. 'Please, three hundred islands, two hundred and fifty where no one lives. Jungles, swamps, streams, rivers, mosquitoes; no one wishes to go and look and make inspections.'

'Tiny islands,' Macca said.

'Yes,' Ramjit said. 'Mr Oleg Koslov is everywhere and nowhere—he is like a ghost.'

Spaghetti took Bon Bons out of his belt kit and laughed. 'This is starting to sound like a joke. You're telling us we're hunting a man who's like a ghost, on a group of two hundred and fifty islands that you call the worst place on earth?'

The Chief wobbled his head. 'Thank you, please, it is like looking for invisible needle in a haystack.'

'Or a shag without complications,' Spaghetti mumbled.

'Please,' the Chief said, 'what is shag without complications?'

I'd heard enough. 'We'll report this back to the CO, get kitted out and get cracking,' I said.

The return journey to the Roberts' house involved a steep incline and I marched the lads up it.

Doug was by my side. 'We should have finished Koslov in the Philippines,' he said.

I paused and eyeballed him, but no words came. His reference to the previous mission hit a nerve. The images of that night had remained vivid and clear in my memory. I swung back and marched a little harder up the hill.

Even before the first snaps of gunfire echoed that night the place had stunk of death. It suffocated the senses in the same way the blanket of fog smothered the ground beneath the gangling trees.

The screaming had started again, in the same way it started every night, with a horrific, fearsome screech that tore through the jungle. As quickly as it began it was stifled, and all that remained was a series of shivering whimpers.

Silently I inched forward and poked my M-16 rifle through the edge of the elephant grass. It took no more than a second to locate the disturbance and, as usual, my Primary Target was the cause. A slimy man, with leathery features and a hooked nose, Oleg Koslov loomed over his latest victim. He groped and slapped her with an agile hand, like she was the cheapest whore in the world. But it was not the hand molesting the woman that made her writhe with fear. In one violent, stabbing motion he drove the hypodermic needle through her flesh.

A sudden wave of hatred surged up inside me. My heart thump, thump, thumped against the ground like a rhythmic mortar attack. I wanted to pull the trigger immediately. I wanted to take him out, to end the numb days of waiting and watching. I wanted to take the strike now, put him to ground immediately for the way he abused life.

But I couldn't.

I couldn't take the shot.

The range and angle were all wrong, and to fire a round off now would not only put a bullet in my target, it would embed one in the hostage. I gritted my teeth and cursed Koslov as I released my trigger finger once again and resolved to wait for a better shot.

But here was my dilemma. Hostages were being grilled alive daily in a hundred and twenty degrees of sunlight, shrivelling up without water, being drugged and raped repeatedly. And the dead were piling up, thrown on the outskirts of the camp, bloated corpses with rotting flesh that teemed with flies. And while I could wait forever and a day to get that shot on a target that was always shrouded by human shields and seldom came into the open, they couldn't.

As I watched the drugs take effect on the woman, I knew another day would bring one more innocent death—a death I could prevent.

I lowered my head. I scrunched up my eyes. My breath rasped through my flaring nostrils and a small voice inside my mind screamed out, 'Forget Kolsov, save the hostages.'

With a deep, dry swallow I held up a fist and waved it three times, the signal to my unit to go.

With a blinding flash and a bang the first of the stun grenades went in. The whole place erupted; gunfire snapped and cracked overhead, whooshing and pinging off the trees.

I punched a pair of rounds into the throat of one of the men holding the woman. His voice box exited the back of his neck and splattered the foliage red. I swung back to the Primary Target. He had grabbed the woman around the neck. With his head down behind her back he was pulling her backwards and retreating into the trees.

I whipped round in time to see another target closing on my position. He pulled the pin on a grenade and was about to toss it in my direction. I jabbed two rounds into his brain. He stared at me with vacant eyes as his body crumpled in slow motion. The palm of his hand opened. The grenade dropped and bounced by his feet.

I buried my head in the dirt and waited for the explosion. Boom!

A deadened thud shook the ground. Mud, stone and damp human fragments pelted down like heavy rain. When I raised my head the target had been reduced to smouldering, charred remains.

For several long minutes we peppered the camp with fire. When return fire became sporadic we moved in—fire and manoeuvre, fire and manoeuvre. We spanned the camp, mopping up the remnants of resistance.

Four of us broke away into the jungle, pursuing the Primary Target, but it was too late: he had vanished.

The two lives that I despatched that night were the most lucid of the three killings of my career. The men's deaths were at such close proximity that their dying moments were clearly etched on my mind.

Oleg Koslov had slipped through the elephant grass that night. And it didn't matter what anyone tried to tell me, because I knew the simple truth of matter was that he had only been able to go on and amass an empire of arms dealing that fed terror across the globe because I had failed to take him down that night.

I was drenched in sweat when I reached the gates at the Roberts' home. Macca was a few paces behind.

'You know, back there, when they said about saying 'shark' and sharks appearing, it's really no surprise—there are about three hundred and fifty different species of fish that come together under the heading of shark.'

Spaghetti sniggered. 'There's a big difference between Gordon the Goldfish and Sid the Shark, Macca.'

'Aye, I agree, but the sort of shark that is going to nibble our undies off isn't a cold water fish, it's one that likes temperate or tropical waters, like the great white or the hammerhead.'

Doug threw his head back and roared with laughter. 'Sometimes I wish you would keep your knowledge to yourself, Macca.'

Macca furrowed a brow at him like he didn't understand and continued. 'You know, the shark is very interesting fish, it hunts by smell, sight, taste, touch and electrical perception, so once it has you in its radar you're as good as –'

'Fucked!' Spaghetti cut in.

Still Macca persisted. 'It's the hammerheads that cause the most problems. Generally they hunt sting-ray, bony fish and invertebrates, but they are known for aggressive, unprovoked attacks on humans.'

Doug was still laughing and Spaghetti was clapping his hands. 'Champion, just prize bloody champion,' he hooted. 'Just remind me will you, Macca: why did you give up school teaching?'

'I decided I couldn't stand the little sods.'

'So you swung the career pendulum from teaching kids to life in the army.'

'Aye,' he said, as though there had been no other options open to him.

I smiled, though the hilarity did not divert my attention from the opportunity to right my wrong with Koslov. 'Sharks aren't anything for us to bother about,' I said dryly. 'Miss Robert's most probably being held inland.'

'Some sharks are known to swim up rivers,' Macca persisted.

At that moment a servant unlocked the gate and led us back into the Roberts' estate. I asked him if they had a map we could look at, an encyclopaedia and a telephone we could use. He took us through to the library. Macca got busy looking up Kali Pani, Spaghetti looked at the map and Doug got to work on an inventory list.

I followed the servant down the hallway to the telephone. The first call I was going to make was home, to Jodie. As I thought about speaking to her I wondered why I was bothering. At that moment I really didn't want to speak to her. I really didn't want to hear her voice. I just felt, rather numbly, that I should.

It was a blessing for me that my son, Christian, answered the phone.

'Where are you?' he asked.

At six he had little concept of distance and travel, so I kept it simple. I told him I was a long way from home. 'I hope I'll be back in a few days' time,' I said.

'I got a Hercules colouring book today, Daddy. It's got Hercules, Hercules and Pegasus, Hercules and Zeus.' I could hear him turning the pages. 'I'm Hercules; who do you want to be in my book?'

'Well, if you're Hercules then I guess I'll be...'

He jumped in before me. 'I'm colouring you in now.'

'Am I Zeus?' I asked, 'Hercules' dad?'

'No, not Zeus. Hold on.' His voice faded as he whispered to Jodie, 'Mummy, what's this one's name again?' His mother said something. I didn't catch it. 'Hades,' Christian said, returning to the phone. 'You are Hades.'

'Good,' I said, trying to remember who Hades was.

'God of Death and the Underworld,' he said.

'Great...thanks...lovely,' I said, gracefully accepting the kick in the nuts.

'I love you, Daddy,' he fired at me.

I choked. 'I love you too and I can't wait to get home and play football with you.'

'Can we play Hercules football, then Hercules cricket?'

'Yeah, sure, just as soon as I get home.'

'Will that be before I go to bed?'

My mind flashed back to the morning I left for India. It had begun with a hangover. I was lying on the floor, resting my head on the fold of my elbow, aware in my semi-conscious state that the sound of my son's naked feet pattering across the wooden floor was not a good sign.

His feet came to a standstill by the crown of my head.

He shook my shoulder.

Play dead, I told myself. Stay still.

My shoulder was shaken again.

I ignored it and continued to be dead as I tried to figure out where I was.

There was a pause, the briefest of respites, and then he dropped to his knees to inspect me. His breathing was faint and shallow and he was so close I could feel his breath on my scalp. Under normal circumstances I would have reached up and grabbed him, scared the living daylights out of him and then tickled him to death while he screamed. But these were not normal circumstances: my blood system was poisoned, my head was throbbing and I was fending off nausea.

But in Christian I was dealing with an expert at finding the Achilles Heel, and while I was trying to kick a fuddled and hung-over brain into gear, my hair, short and cropped almost to the scalp, was pinched and pulled.

In a flash, I raised my head. I was up on my knees. My heart was pounding. My arms were flailing, thrashing at thin air. I stared at the little figure with a heaving chest and eyes that bulged at me with fear.

Jesus! My head hurt!

With a growl, I collapsed back into the heap I had risen from and wrapped my arms around my head in the hope that it would hold together.

A second of silence, then: 'Daddy, the telephone is for you'.

Despite the fact that he had been warned countless times that the telephone was not a toy, he still persisted.

'Very funny. Now put it back and leave me alone,' I said.

He dropped the handset onto my back and using his mother's pet name for me, 'Stupid idiot', he padded out of the room and headed upstairs. 'Mummy, Daddy's drunk again,' he called out.

I wondered if I had let the last opportunity to play with my son as his father in our home together slip by. I wondered if things would ever be the same again. In my heart, I knew our days together were numbered, and as I longed to have them back the person I blamed for that destruction was coming onto the phone.

I could hear her cackling with laughter as she took the phone from Chrisian. 'God of Death and the Underworld,' she said. 'I see he's got you summed up.'

I gritted my teeth.

'How long are you away for this time?' she snapped when I didn't bite at her comment.

'Couple of weeks. I guess you'll be happy to get me out from under your feet.'

There was a pause on the line. 'Look, don't start bitching, Mike. It's because you're always away that I started having this affair. Time and again I've asked you to get discharged...get a normal job...get a nine to five...get something that gets you home for more than a few months of the year. I wanted you to be at home. I wanted a normal family, but you couldn't do that. So don't start blaming me for finding someone else.'

I took a deep breath.

I scratched my head and bit my lip. I looked up at the ceiling and closed my eyes.

I didn't know what to say.

I certainly didn't know what to do.

One thing I did know: I was glad I was thousands of miles away from the mess that was my personal life.

Jodie and I had one of those weird marital arrangements where we were living separate lives under the same roof. It had been that way for the last eight months, since I discovered that she and the local policeman had been romping in my bed while I was on tour with the Regiment. I refused to move out, so they decided he would move in, and they now played out their affair right before my snarling face.

Like a pair of B-52 bombers dropping ordnance on the enemy, they pounded the mattress in the room above me night after night, while below them I stressed like an enemy in a trench, clinging onto to a bottle of brandy. It was a tortured existence, but I was determined to see it out. A c c o r d i n g to my solicitor, a former SAS sergeant, I could get a better financial settlement and access to Christian if I stayed in the house and kept my cool. So night after night, I drank and drank to keep my cool.

And I couldn't see what she saw in him. On the morning I left for India Jodie was just taking me to task again for drinking when he shuffled into my lounge.

Because he was a bobby and because he was a slob and

because I would gladly drive over him at 60 mph and knacker my suspension, I had nicknamed him the sleeping policeman.

'Cuppa tea, babe,' he yawned, like he had just entered a café.

Sporting a pair of faded Mickey Mouse shorts, he dropped onto my sofa and stretched out his hairy legs.

I glared up at him from the floor as he scratched his balls, sniffed his hand, snatched up the TV remote and flicked through the channels. This scruffy bastard end of law enforcement, with the head of hair that looked like a flock of birds had stopped over for a nest-warming orgy...his days were numbered. No smug stranger was going to swagger into my home, turf me out, claim my possessions as his own and then treat the booty like a bag of shit. Stuff the financial settlement. I was prepared to do time for this arse-hole.

I couldn't fathom it. How the hell could she be serious about such a sorry-looking sod? And why couldn't she see that letting him stop over and parading him first thing in the morning made her look stupid? Was it to tease me? Was it to make me jealous or make me realise what a great woman I was missing out on? What a load of bollocks! And what the hell did he have that I didn't, except the Disney shorts and the sexually molested hair?

Were the two of us in some sort of competition without my knowledge? Was his presence in my home somehow announcing that he was the victor? Christ, if that was true I really had to start facing facts, because that had to make me the sorriest shit on the planet. I might as well just go down to our base at Stirling Lines, book myself a .45 out and blow myself away.

'I'll get your tea in a minute, just as soon as I sort this loser out,' Jodie said. But as she spoke her eyes clamped onto the brandy bottle. She picked it up and wagged it in front of my face. 'I want you out of here. I want your arse out of my house today.'

My best assassin's smile crept across my face. 'Fine.'

Jodie stared at me for a moment. It seemed she didn't

understand the expression and didn't know quite how to react. She made a grab for Christian. To his credit, he wriggled free and ran around me. He grabbed the telephone up from the floor. 'It's for you, Daddy,' he said, putting the receiver in my hand.

'I'll sort you out later,' Jodie snarled at me. She seized Christian again. This time there was no escape for him. 'How many times do I have to tell you that the phone is not a toy?' She dragged him out into the hallway and started up the stairs. 'Now don't you ever touch,' Smack! 'the phone again.' Smack!

I looked long and hard at the doorway. Something wasn't right about smacking Christian for playing with the telephone: telling him off, yes, but repeated smacking, no. But before I could give any more thought to what was wrong with it, a smug voice that shouldn't have been in my lounge spoke.

'You know why she hates her life with you, Mike? It's because you're a lazy, screwed-up bastard,' the sleeping policeman said.

I swallowed hard. 'Then I guess it's out of the frying pan into the fire for an opportunist slob who can't even make his own brew in the morning.'

At that moment his face was saved from a date with my fist by the sound of a lung-bursting roar from inside the telephone handset.

'Hello,' I said.

'At fucking last,' my Commanding Officer spluttered. 'Get your sorry, domestically fucked-up arse down to fucking base right fucking now.'

'Are you still there, Mike?' Jodie was saying. 'Mike?'

She was sniffling. How much of the conversation had I shut out? Had I missed her saying something important?

'Did you hear me?' she asked.

'What was that?'

'I said I miss you.'

There was a lengthy pause. I was convinced my imagination was playing tricks on me.

'I want to apologize for everything. I know all this must

have hurt you. I'm sorry. I want to make it up to you. I mean I want to try again...with you. How do you feel about that? Can we try and sort things out?'

I leaned my head back against the wall and closed my eyes. In my mind's eye I saw a daisy and heard the words 'she loves me, she loves me not' that was exactly what life with Jodie had become, never knowing from one minute to the next what she was thinking or feeling, never knowing whether she would throw her arms round me for a hug or hurl crockery at my head.

'What d'you say, Mike?'

Despite it all, I knew that I didn't want to bypass an opportunity to gain access to Christian whenever I was home from tour, and it was that fact that made me agree to her crazy idea. 'We can try,' I said, grabbing the moment before it slipped away.

'You don't sound sure.'

I wasn't sure, but I lied. 'I'm fine with that. You know it's what I want.' I wanted to avoid more talk on the subject until I had figured things out in my own mind. 'I need to go. I have to speak to the CO about things over here. I'll speak to you as soon as I can.'

When I put the phone down my head was buzzing. It was the same every time I spoke to Jodie. It was like a whirlwind of confusion that just enveloped me.

I dialled for the CO and waited for him to come to the phone.

Robert Jackson-Wright was a thickset man with a menacing smile and quick, searching eyes that seemed to sum up people and situations in seconds. He had various nicknames that we all called him behind his back: Jacko, Eagle Eyed Action Man and my favourite, Antenna, because of the two strands of grey hair sticking up from his bald head and the fact that he seemed to know everything about everybody without seemingly being told anything by anyone.

I needed to give him our sitrep, situation report.

I filled him in on the details of Shreela's whereabouts and

relevant info on Kali Pani. I then went on to Manisha Robert's theory surrounding the abduction.

'Load of bollocks,' he barked.

'Sir, with respect, I've spoken with the authorities over here. It's quite clear that Koslov is working with the government's approval.'

'Edwards, you were sent to India to find and free a woman, not to listen to fucking hearsay and get involved in politics.'

'Sir, I know that, sir, but –'

'Edwards! Do you need a fucking reminder of what is expected from you?'

He meant that I was required to follow orders without question: an invaluable rule in combat, but this was one of those situations when I felt I was better informed than he was. How could I make him listen? 'Sir, you have to understand that –'

'Edwards, I don't have to understand anything. You need to get to grips with the chat we had before you left. The threat of RTUing your arse was not an idle one. Now follow fucking orders, find the fucking girl and get the fuck out. I expect a sitrep at 18:00 daily. 18:00 tomorrow I will supply info from the Kremlin. Are we clear?'

'Yes, sir.'

I waited for the CO to disconnect then slammed the receiver down at my end.

I cursed myself. 'What an idiot!' I had not only questioned the CO once, but three times. Did I really want to get myself RTU'd, returned to unit?

What a dickhead.

Shaking my head and pissed off with myself I headed back to the library.

Macca rocked back in his chair as I entered. 'Aye,' he said, 'Kali Pani is the worst place on earth. At least it was when it was discovered by Ptolemy. He called the islands "Islands of Cannibals."'

'Go on, read the bit about Marco Polo,' Spaghetti urged him. 'Go on, let's hear all that again.'

Macca cleared his throat. 'Marco Polo called it the island of head-hunters.'

Still smarting after my conversation with the CO, and bewildered by the one with Jodie, I didn't feel like joining in with the guys. I headed over to the window and stood with my back to everybody.

Macca said, 'There's a great picture here, a group of men circling a naked guy while the cannibals tear him to pieces.'

'Well, at least there are no cannibals anywhere these days,' Doug said.

'What makes you so sure?' Macca asked.

'Well, this is the twenty-first century. Ptolemy was a Roman—look, it says as much underneath, BC..."Before Cannibal" thousands of years ago!'

'It means Before Christ,' Macca corrected him, skipping Doug's dry humour.

'Look,' Doug went on, 'further down it says Marco Polo never even went there.'

Spaghetti laughed. 'Well you can't exactly blame him, can you?'

It was at that moment that I took out the photograph Manisha Robert had given me. 'She says it will be our guide,' I said, tongue in cheek.

'Did she draw a map on the back of it or something?' Doug said as he took the picture from me. He held it up and laughed. 'Christ, how are we supposed to recognise her from that picture? She must have been all of two years old when it was taken.'

Macca took the snap from Doug. 'She's a bonny lass, there's no doubt about that,' he said. 'Look at her eyes and the expression in her brows...And her lips won't have changed shape. We'll know this girl when we see her.'

'I'm not so confident,' Doug said.

'Me neither,' I said. 'I only took the picture to humour the woman.'

'Christ, you're a bunch of doughnuts sometimes,' Spaghetti piped up as he eyed up another Bon Bon. 'We'll recognise the woman because she'll be the one chained up inside a cage surrounded by guards.'

At that moment a horn beeping repeatedly and a sudden cacophony of raised voices came from outside. I threw open the door and headed into the courtyard. Ramjit stood up in the jeep on the other side of the entrance gates. 'Please,' he shouted, 'I have plenty, plenty bad news of Miss Shreela.'

SILENCING THE SERVANT

Ramjit and the Police Chief got out of the jeep. Mrs Robert appeared at the chapel door. Her husband strode across the courtyard. 'What is it? What news have you brought about my daughter?' he shouted.

We all crammed inside the library. 'In Kali Pani Miss Shreela has been seen for certain,' the Police Chief said. 'At Port St. Peter, I am told she is arriving at docks.'

'Who saw her? Why did your people not stop her? What is wrong with your people over there?' Robert said.

'Please, in Kali Pani they are not knowing of kidnap. Fax machine is buggered. Please, only when we call to speak to police officer he says he has seen Miss Shreela.'

Manisha Robert turned to me. 'This is where my daughter was working until she fell out with the government. She is loved by the locals and loathed by the parasites that make their trade off the island.'

'Was Koslov seen with her?' I asked.'

'Oh yes, yes, we are understanding that walking with Miss Shreela was Mr Oleg Koslov.'

Robert swung towards the outer door and shouted to the servants outside. 'Where is Kalid? What is it with this boy? Why has he not come to me? I will whip him for this disobedience. I will whip all of you, for you are failing to find him.' He slammed the door behind him and rejoined us. Mrs Robert placed her hand on her husband's forearm and tried to calm him.

John Robert removed it.

He said, 'This is the boy who led my daughter into the

village on the night she was taken and now see how he avoids talking to the men who will rescue her.'

Manisha's voice was barely audible as she looked up to her husband's dark eyes. 'He is but a boy and very frightened, my husband.'

'And you think our daughter is not frightened? This boy tried to court my daughter like a man and look after her in the streets of India without my permission and without a chaperone.'

'And he knows he has wronged you, my husband. He is no doubt fearful of your retribution.'

Ramjit indicated that he wanted to talk so I followed him to the corner of the room. He kept his voice low. 'Please, what is the chance that you will find Miss Robert?'

'Locating her is the hardest thing we have to do.'

'Please, ten days is psychological breaking point. If we have not found her by then...'

'Then what?'

He leaned forward as though bowing to me, 'Then, well... perhaps we must leave her and call this search off.'

'I won't pull out until I receive orders from my CO to do so, and this ten days is bollocks. I've seen some of the toughest soldiers crumble into wrecks within hours of being captured. I imagine this woman was broken the minute she was taken. I would imagine by now she's already been badly humiliated by Koslov.'

He came back at me. 'We're not talking about interrogation.'

'Ramjt,' I said, trying to restrain my temper and keep my voice low, 'she's been torn away from her family, bound and gagged and had a real gun pointed at her head for the first time in her life. It's likely she's been drugged and she's probably being raped. Would you leave a child of yours to that kind of humiliation?'

He looked down at the floor for a moment then raised his head. 'I am sorry, we are close to war with Pakistan. I have to understand if we are wasting our resources on this woman.'

Doug came over and stood beside me.

'Is this the inventory list?' I asked him.

He nodded and passed it to me. I glanced over it and handed it to Ramjit. Still annoyed at him I said, 'I can't believe how cheaply you look at life.'

Ramjit narrowed his eyes. 'My first son was lost in a Hindu and Muslim riot. My third son was taken from me. He was gone for a week then one morning I woke to find his carcass lying at my doorstep. In those days I had neither the money nor authority to seek revenge or search for my son. No one—no one—came to the aid of my son. Do not accuse me of cheapness when it comes to life. I will fax your inventory through. It can be loaded onto a plane while we travel to the air base. We should leave while it is being prepared.'

Ramjit nodded at me and left.

I looked at Doug. He patted my shoulder. 'Sounds like someone with an axe to grind.'

At that moment the library door burst open. Gasping for breath, a servant said, 'Mr Robert, Mr Robert, come, come. We have found him. We have found Kalid.'

Robert spun on his heel and marched out of the library.

⚜

Across the courtyard and through an archway we followed a narrow path that ran steeply downhill. I was caught up in a jabbering crowd, hemmed in on either side by high walls and had no option but to go with the flow.

As the pathway levelled out we surged into another courtyard, circular and smaller than the one at the front of the main house. It was flanked by barn-like buildings with laundry strung up everywhere and people hanging over a balcony like it was the upper tier of a football stadium.

'Stinks of piss, shit and spices,' Spaghetti observed.

We were ushered forward into the middle of the huddle. The chattering subsided and an expectant hush filled the courtyard.

John Robert loomed over the boy. 'Why did you not come to the British soldiers when I sent for you?' he shouted.

'Please, Boss, I did not know, Boss.'

'Three times I sent for you.'

'Please, Boss, yes, Boss, I did not know, Boss.'

Robert struck the servant across the side of the face with the flat of his hand. Kalid screamed, an exaggerated, girlish scream. Two servants rushed forward and hauled him back onto his knees.

'You are a liar,' Robert shouted. 'My daughter is taken; you are the only person who saw what

happened and you do not come when I asked.'

Kalid looked up at his boss like a pleading beggar. 'Please, Boss, it is only that I did not know, Boss.'

Robert beckoned us all forward. We were standing close to the servant when a voice from the upper tier shouted, 'Beat him.'

A cheer spread through the crowd.

Kalid said something. I could not hear him as his voice was lost amongst the mass. He repeated it, shouting, his throat straining, his eyes wide open, desperate.

Robert held up his hand to quieten the rabble.

'Miss Robert is loving storms,' Kalid said. 'Village is covered in cloud and thunder is up above. Lightning is flashing. I am only going with her. I am only protecting her from the storm.'

'You were seen arm-in-arm with my daughter,' Robert shouted, 'Like you were making her go somewhere she did not wish to go.'

'She told me where it was she wanted to go. '

A woman in the front row of the crowd shouted, 'Liar.'

More shouts spread through the crowd. 'Beat him. Kill him. Liar!'

'You are mistaken,' Kalid squealed. 'I love her. I love Miss Shreela.'

Robert stepped forward and raised his hand to crack the boy in the face again, but Macca stepped across and blocked his way. About a foot in height separated the two men and Robert, the smaller of the two, backed away.

The woman in the front row shouted again. 'He was dragging her along the street.'

Instantly, the noise from the horde rose louder than before.

'It is only that she wanted different view of the thunderstorm. I wanted her to come with me. I wanted her to see my view.'

'Did you drag her?' I asked.

'I only promised her we would go to other view a little later. Miss Shreela is saying if view is very, very bad she will never go into storms with me again.'

'You hurt her. She called out at you,' the woman shouted.

'Is this true?' Robert bellowed. 'Is it true that you hurt my daughter?'

The noise of the crowd rose again, louder and longer than before, more restless.

Kalid continued, 'Please, Boss, five men took her, Boss. I am the one who came to tell you.'

'Did you know the men?'

There was a long pause between Robert's question and Kalid's answer. 'No, Boss,' he said, looking down at the cobblestones.

Robert drew the woman who had been calling out from the crowd. He stood her in front of Kalid. 'Did this boy fight off the men?' he shouted.

'I did not see,' the woman said, 'I only heard Miss Shreela screaming out above the thunder. She said she did not want to go with him.'

'They came in a truck,' Kalid shouted. 'I was pushed on ground. A foot was pushed on back. Men pointed gun at head.'

'Can you describe the men?' I asked.

'No, all was very dark. Face was pushed to ground and I am seeing nothing.'

'How then do you know there were five of them?' Robert said.

'I counted feet.'

'You already said you could see nothing. How then is it that you can now count feet in the darkness with your face pushed on the floor?'

'I am telling truth, Boss. I counted feet. Please believe me, Boss.'

'Describe their shoes.' Robert said.

'I...I...'

'This boy is a coward,' Robert shouted to the crowd, 'a liar and a coward. My daughter has been taken. Kalid is the last to see her alive. He did not come when I asked him to come to me.'

'Kill him,' a single voice cried.

A moment later, a hundred voters cast a unanimous verdict. Bumping and jostling, they closed in around us.

I bent over the servant. Doug, Spaghetti and Macca formed a ring around us. 'There's something you're not telling us,' I said to the servant.

'No, Boss. I help you, Boss.'

'These people will kill you unless you speak up now.'

The boy stared at me for a few seconds then grabbed out at me as I started to rise up. 'They will very, very kill me if they know the truth.'

'They'll kill you if they don't. So if you have something to say get on with it.'

'Two days before Miss Robert is taken I came to the village store. A man is offering me more rupees than ever I earn. He is telling me if I am letting him down he will kill me. I must make choice, money I never had or die.'

'What did he ask you to do?'

'He is only asking me to bring Miss Shreela to the village—this is all he asked. I did not know any more than this. I did not know he would take her away.'

John Robert was standing above me and heard what I was being told. Once again he made to strike the boy. Macca caught his wrist with one of his big hands and shook his head. 'Why did you not say this before? You are a trouble-maker and a liar. I cannot trust you,' Robert shrieked at the boy.

'Boss, I will take you to man who made me do this.'

Robert stepped back as though he had just been struck by lightning. Slowly he nodded. 'Then lead us to him,' he said.

Macca, Doug, Spaghetti, Mrs Robert, myself and what seemed like a hundred employees followed Kalid and John Robert out of the courtyard and through the gates. Big-eyed and long-limbed, Kalid walked at the front of our procession. He reminded me of King Louis from Disney's Jungle Book, a character I remembered as not being the most genuine monkey in the jungle.

As we reached the village, a raspy motor bike shot up and down our procession several times as though it was orchestrating something, but it had disappeared by the time we reached the local store.

I followed Kalid and John Robert into the shop. Doug, Macca and Spaghetti stood at the entrance.

'You know this boy?' John Robert said.

The store-owner frowned. 'Yes, of course. Kalid is your servant.'

'I understand he is also your servant. You arranged the kidnapping of my daughter along with Kalid and some other men.'

'Why for are you saying this? You are wrong. I did no such thing. I am your friend. Your daughter is my customer. I am very sorry, very, very sorry for what happened to Miss Shreela, but I had nothing to do with kidnapping.'

'You paid Kalid.'

'Why for are you saying this? I did nothing.'

'You are a liar.'

'Men came here and ask to talk to Kalid. I was asked only to bring Kalid here. I know nothing more. I do not know if these men are the men that took your daughter.'

'Liar. You work for these people.'

'Why for are you saying this? For myself I work, you have been wrong informed.'

Robert walked from the shop. He gestured to some of his workers. They immediately picked up anything they could lay their hands on and threw it at the window of the shop. Within seconds the whole crowd had followed suit and a mixture of glass and stones were flying past my ears. I covered my head, ducked and got the hell out as quickly as possible.

Kalid had escaped. I twisted, bumped, banged and pushed my way through the unyielding mob and broke beyond them, stumbling into a muted world—the remainder of the village square.

At that moment the motorbike engine engaged and shot in his direction. I began running after the servant, but my legs were heavy and slow, like they were running through knee-deep water, and all too quickly the motorcycle had shot beyond me. A glint of metal in the rider's hand caught my attention, a blade that he swung in the air as he cried like a warrior.

Kalid turned to look behind him as he continued to run. He fell and recovered his footing only to stumble again and then again, his skinny, panicked legs were no longer coordinating. Captured in the village square, Kalid's only escape now was a row of doorways in front of him. He reached the first one with no more than a few seconds to spare.

It was locked.

He rushed towards a second door, but even as he reached out to shake the handle it was too late. As Kalid screamed with his last lungful of air I heard the hiss of the blade cutting through the air before it sliced through his flesh and bone.

He looked up at me and for a second seemed to smile. The blade had been so sharp and quick and the cut so fine that perhaps, for one deluded moment, the servant believed he had not been cut. But then blood began to seep through the wound, his body lost its balance and he reeled backwards.

Slowly his head peeled away from his body, and from the exposed stump of his neck blood burst upwards, like a spewing volcano.

The bike skidded to a halt and its rider leapt back towards the kill. Standing over the twitching corpse he hacked at it repeatedly until the head came clean away from the neck and the servant's carcass sprawled on the town square.

My heart beat out of control. Paralysed, I was pinned to the spot, numbed into stunned silence, staring through burning eyes at the revolting reality of the scene. But it was my name that I heard being called now, not the servant boy's. 'Mike! Mike!' voices behind me were shouting. 'Mike!'

And at that moment, as hands grabbed me and hauled me across the back seat of the jeep, the village square erupted into a ball of flames.

.

THE WORST PLACE ON EARTH

You expect to see death when you sign up for the army. You expect to put a bullet in the enemy, see them blown backwards or torn to shreds by your gunfire. You're told what to expect, you hear stories from those who have killed and then eventually, if you see some action, you might have your own stories to pass on to the guys who haven't spilled blood yet.

And you might think it's all glory, you're out there all gung-ho and killing week in, week out, but it's not like that. It's not like that at all. In ten years I had killed three people, one in a riot and the two back-to-back in the Philippines.

I got to see the first guy. I got to see him fumbling with his weapon, knowing it was me or him, knowing I was already looking down my sights, telling him to put down his weapon. But the stubborn bastard wouldn't give up. He couldn't accept that I had won, that he should just surrender his weapon and take a step back with his hands in the air. In a fraction of a second, as he brought his gun up with the intent to mow me down, I put all of my training into practice and took him down with one body-thudding squeeze of the trigger.

And you need to control the rush of adrenaline in the moments after your kill. And you have to shut it out. You have to be clear why you pulled the trigger, why that man is now dead, and you have to focus. You have to focus for your own sake. You have to focus for the guys in your unit. You have to focus for all the people relying on you for protection.

Some hours later, sitting alone in a toilet cubicle back at the barracks, taking the longest shit of my life, I learned how to shut the killing out so it didn't exist. I learned how to move on. You have to shut it out. You have to shut out any thoughts that you have just taken a man down who might have a wife and a kid waiting for him at home. You have to believe he was a sad, lonely bastard operating without anyone who gave a toss about him, because if you let any other thoughts in they would just screw you up.

You tell yourself you did the right thing. You tell yourself that in the same circumstances you would do the same thing over and over again. You tell yourself that what you did was right, that it was just, you pick up your coat and you go for a few beers with the lads. You laugh it off. You joke and you convince yourself and everyone around you that nothing has changed.

But in all my years in the army, in all my years saving victims from guerrillas, storming buildings and aiding bomb victims, I had never seen anything as cold-blooded and sickening as I had in that mountainside village. Had the bloodshed happened in combat perhaps I would have understood it better, perhaps it would have sat right with me. Perhaps then it would have been different. Perhaps then it would have been okay.

But it wasn't okay. It had all happened in a tranquil mountainside village, and it was *very* not okay.

'What the fuck happened back there?' Spaghetti said, as the jeep bumped along the road towards the helicopter rendezvous.

'Where the hell did the Police Chief go?' Doug said.

'There was just no law and order. It was a free-for-all,' Macca said.

From the front passenger seat Ramjit said, 'Please, in India law is taken very much into own hands. Kalid and store owner are disloyal men to Mr Robert and Mr Robert has sought retribution. Please, village will riot—now will be many, many hours of violence and looting. Tomorrow all will be calm.'

Spaghetti chuckled to himself. 'Tomorrow they'll all wake up wanting tea-bags and rice. It's going to be a hell of a shock for them when they realise the consequences of torching the old corner shop.'

The conversation continued, but I did not participate.

❧

An hour later a helicopter put us down at the wheels of a military transporter plane. A man in a combats spoke to Ramjit, who in turn came over to me. 'Munitions, supplies and vehicle are very, very ready. We leave immediately. It is two-hour flight. We arrive before midnight. We have hotel booked and begin tomorrow. Now you can have plenty, plenty rest and very good breakfast.'

'We'll rest in flight,' I said, 'unload, and plan our mission tonight with our guide.'

'Oh, no, no, this is not very possible. Guide will be sleeping.'

I stared at him in disbelief. I wasn't going to waste time while Ramjit took forty winks in a nice hotel. 'Then we wake him up, Ramjit.'

'Oh, no, no, no. I disagree. This is not done in Kali Pani.'

'I don't give a damn what you agree with. My orders are to find Shreela Robert. I intend to do that as quickly and efficiently as possible. Now, you either cooperate or I get on the blower to my CO and discuss why we're leaving you to sort your own shit out. Do you get the picture?'

An hour into the flight Spaghetti was still listening to his Walkman, Macca was restless, Ramjit was reading. Only Doug looked to have found any real peace. My mind was alive, my thoughts taking on three strands: the events of the last few hours, the things I had learned about Kali Pani, and the opposition—Koslov.

Of the three, Koslov was the easiest to get my head round. I was trained to fight the likes of him in a jungle environment: I'd had the experience of doing it before and I was confident my unit could fulfil the assignment. The reputation of the islands recounted by the Police Chief and Ramjit gave me little cause for worry—as far I was concerned, they were locals trying to impress us with how scary their island could be. Thus far the evidence didn't support the reputation.

Having sorted out two of my thoughts I hoped the third would just disappear and that I would be able to settle into sleep. But every time I closed my eyes the images of Kalid's death replayed in my mind. I tried to let the thoughts go, concentrating on my breathing, sheep jumping a fence, a pond of still water...

I must have drifted off to sleep, because the hand on my shoulder startled me.

'Landing, landing,' Ramjit told me.

I took a quick look out of the window. It was dark, but I could make out the shoreline and some lights just up ahead.

I buckled my belt and felt the plane's approach as the pilot throttled back and raised the flaps. A few minutes later I felt the bump of the runway, the power of reverse thrust and the plane slowing.

We came to a standstill.

'Kali Pani,' Ramjit said, jumping up with far too much enthusiasm for my liking.

Doug was first at the cargo door, with his sleeves rolled up, ready to go. Macca stretched.

'Excrement,' Spaghetti said, sticking his Walkman away in his Bergen and stifling a yawn. 'The place of no hope, a road to nowhere and an extinct tribe of cannibals,' he said, making light of the task ahead.

Ramjit stopped what he was doing and looked at Spaghetti. 'Who told you the cannibals were extinct?'

'I did,' I said.

Ramjit gripped my arm. 'Mr Michael, do not be fooled about extinct cannibals. In Kali Pani jungle the cannibals are very much alive. Kali Pani is the worst place on earth.'

A chilling north-westerly blew across the airfield as we shifted our equipment into a disused aircraft hangar. Within minutes the military transporter was back in the sky, the runway lights were out and we were plunged into ghostly darkness.

Ramjit had already left to find our guide, and while we

waited for him to return we pulled the big roller doors across the entrance and closed ourselves in. We lit our burners and made a brew, but in the murky light of the hangar, sitting on the upturned boxes, I began to feel restless. It was difficult for me to finger any one thing for that unease — it was everywhere. It was in the cold, damp air that turned every breath to vapour, every noise that echoed and every movement that made my skin tingle. At one point I checked over both shoulders because I believed that someone was standing behind me.

Macca got to his feet, clutching his mug and shivering. He turned a three sixty and checked the depths of the hangar as though he was looking for something. 'They say a lot of the old Scottish castles are haunted.'

'They also say Bonnie Prince Charlie was straight,' Spaghetti said.

'What's that got to do with anything?' Macca replied.

Spaghetti shrugged — 'I thought we were having a 'Did You Know' moment of irrelevant Scottish facts.'

'Did you know they feed Italian ghosts on spooketti?' Doug said, without grinning.

'What the hell are you going on about?'

Doug yawned and stretched. 'It seemed relevant.'

We drank our brew in the silence of the hangar and waited for Ramjit to return with the guide.

Ali was a small dark skinned man who didn't smile. He passed a cigarette to Ramjit, lit it up, unrolled a map and spread it out on the concrete floor. Running his finger across the narrow strip of islands he said, 'This is Kali Pani. South Kali Pani is where you are now. What do you want to see?'

Ali's English was good, heavily accented, but slow and clear and precise.

'We need to see places where someone would hide,' I said.

He nodded slowly as if waiting for me to add something else. When I said nothing, he snatched up the map and folded it away. 'Kali Pani is one big hiding-place. Many men come here to hide. To help you may endanger my life.'

'I want to find a woman. She was kidnapped from the mainland.'

He looked at me, narrowing his eyes then unfolding the map again. 'I will try to help you.'

I turned to Ramjit, 'We need air surveillance and navy patrols. We need questions asked of anyone who moves on and off the islands by boat.'

'Please, the Indian navy already patrols like this. There can be no more cooperation,' Ramjit said, shaking his head and waving his arms.

'Are you serious about getting this girl back?' I fired at him.

'No, no, I will try for you. I will try for you. But please, please, I am making no promises. I do not know what can be done. I can only ask and then see what is happening.'

Ali said, 'If you intend to go into the jungle you need a bucket and a brush.'

'For what?' I said, trying not to laugh at something that sounded more like a requirement for a Boy Scout outing that an SAS op.

'I'll tell you about the bucket and brush,' he said, with a dramatic nod of his head. 'Scorpions...you need the bucket and brush to sweep up the scorpions.'

'Scorpions!' Spaghetti said. 'What the fuck do we want to sweep scorpions up for?'

'At night-time the islands are covered in scorpions. You will need to keep watch for them wherever you camp.'

Calm and knowledgeable, Macca reassured us. 'Scorpions mostly feed on spiders, holding their victims in their claws and stinging with the venom in their tails. There are over fourteen hundred varieties and not all are venomous. Those that are venomous are only harmful to children and animals.'

Ali grunted. 'In Kali Pani *all* scorpions are poisonous and there have been many deaths. Not all deaths have been children. You will also find our snakes deadly poisonous. In Kali Pani we do not go into the jungle and say the word snake.'

'Why not?'

'Because if you say 'snake' then a snake will appear. This is the legend of Kali Pani, it is a place of –'

'No hope. I think we've got that one,' Doug said, without a hint of humour.

Ali pointed at the map. 'Here we have an island that we call Venom Island.'

'And is it a place where someone might hide?'

Ali shrugged. 'This depends.'

'On what?'

'If their wish is to die of snake bite,' Ali said flatly.

'I need helicopters,' I said, looking at Ramjit.

'I have ordered for you, but will take two days.'

Ali said, 'I can arrange this for you sooner.'

Ramjit shot him a look.

Ali said, 'But it is unwise to use helicopters, landing is a big problem as the terrain is mostly jungle, on other islands much land is jagged and volcanic.'

'I just want to check the area out from the air. I won't need to land anywhere.'

'Also it is monsoon season. Occasionally we have freak storms. At this time of year helicopters have been known not to stay in the sky very well.'

'Are you trying to hamper us?' I asked.

Ali shook his head. 'This is not my intention. I only want you not to crash-land in the jungle. If that happened we would all be lucky to continue living.'

'Are the snakes and scorpions really that bad here?' Macca asked.

Ali looked at Ramjit. 'You have not told them?'

'Told them what?' I asked.

'About the Jarawa.'

'What about the Jarawa?'

'They are a tribe of cannibals.'

'Yeah, we heard about cannibals, but Ramjit was just kidding, right?'

Ali said, 'I'll tell you about the Jarawa. The Jarawa refuse to integrate with settlers. They object to any intrusion onto their lands. Last month a group of jungle clearance workers were attacked by the Jarawa. There were five of them. Three died with poisoned arrows shot through their throats. Two survived...with body parts missing. These men were not attacked for cutting down trees. They were attacked because they were trespassing.'

'If they were trespassing that suggests that some boundary exists and if that's the case –'

Ali cut me off. 'Civilized people make boundaries. The Jarawa are not at all very civilised. They consider that both Kali Pani islands are their territory and they do not tolerate trespassers. Now you are also a trespasser.'

There was a moment's silence as Ali's words sunk in, and, as was often the case, Spaghetti was first to react. 'So what I'm hearing is this: if we can avoid being eaten by jaws, stop the scorpions from stinging us, make sure we don't get hugged to shit by a snake or gummed to death by the bottom end of the fucking food chain, then we might—just might—find Miss Robert and prise her away from the man referred to as a ghost that is everywhere and nowhere. Am I right?'

Ramjit nodded.

Spaghetti picked up his M-16, took off the safety and stood up. 'Game on then. When do we start?'

SCREAMS OF DEATH

Ali, Macca and I drove away from the airport hangar at 01:00. Our aim was to speak to an associate of Ali's who had a helicopter.

We had to wait at the airport gate while our driver went to find a member of the security staff to undo the padlock on the gate for us. While we waited Ali turned and looked me directly in the eye. 'What have they told you about spirits on this island?'

For a moment I thought he was going to warn me off about some local brew, but the look on his face told me he wasn't about to get sociable and discuss alcohol. 'No-one has told me anything,' I said.

'I'll tell you about the spirits. Kali Pani has a hellish history. In the nineteenth century the British invaded the islands, murdering thousands of indigenous people as they settled. In 1858 a penal colony began here and thousands of the restless from India were sent—freedom fighters, criminals, lawless people. Poor diet, rampant disease, floggings and being hung from the gallows were the most usual ways that a prisoner held in Kali Pani would die. Also, there were many martyrs amongst the prisoners, many hunger strikers. At one time during the early nineteen hundreds as many as four hundred and fifty men refused to eat.

'In 1937 the British returned all the freedom fighters to India. It was then that something worse happened, Japanese rule.

'During the eight years of Japanese rule the pain and cruelty of these islands peaked. Women were taken out into the bay kicking and screaming and dumped into the waters around Port St. Peter. There were three ways to die for these women, by shark attack, by snake bite or by Japanese gun if they swam back to the boat and begged for their lives.

'For other women death was even uglier. They were taken out onto the jetty, slit open from top to bottom and left where they stood as they tried to hold in their intestines.'

'When the Japanese left in 1945, they handed over more than fifty thousand prisoners and a capital city that had become one huge graveyard. It was during this time that the islands were named Kali Pani. It was said that being sent here was as good as a death sentence. Sometimes prisoners did escape from the British, but they never escaped death. In the jungles the cannibals ate them, in the sea the sharks attacked them.'

'So what's all this got to do with spirits?' Macca asked.

Ali pointed his finger at Macca. 'I'll tell you about the spirits. As you can see many people were sent to early deaths on the islands. Because of what I told you, the deaths to Indians and the indigenous tribes –'

There was something Ali had said that I wanted to clarify. I cut in. 'Tribes...you've mentioned tribes a couple of times, as in more than one. Earlier you only mentioned the Jarawa.'

He looked at me as though I had missed the point. 'This is because the Jarawa are the local threat. Other cannibal tribes live on the islands surrounding Kali Pani. Many more were murdered or wiped out by measles, syphilis and flu that the British brought with them. Some tribes integrated into civilization; even some Jarawa are friendly now. All tribes except the Coralenese have been contacted. The Coralenese are the least friendly of all.'

'What's their story?'

'They live on an island ten miles out of Port St. Peter. Every few years contact parties are sent with gifts of food and animals and every time the contact parties arrive they are showered by arrows.'

'Tell me about the Jarawa,' Macca asked. 'How can you tell the friendly ones from the not so friendly ones?'

Ali looked at us. 'Unfriendly Jarawa fire poisoned blow darts and arrows at you, friendly ones don't. This is the only difference. Now shall I continue telling you about the spirits? The people of Kali Pani say that for many spirits it was not their time to die. They say they are angry that their lives were cut short and because of this they have not gone on to the next life—they have decided to stay behind and haunt the island, especially Port St. Peter. You can feel them around you sometimes, they make you will feel uncomfortable. '

'You mean like someone's watching you?' Macca said.

'That's bollocks,' I said. 'What are you trying to do, Ali, scare the hell out of us?'

Ali shrugged. 'You will change your mind,' he said. He turned back to face the front as our driver got back in and we drove out into the darkness.

We were soon in a town area and screwed-up litter was skipped across the street on the breeze. Our headlights picked up a rickshaw dumped under a palm tree, a battered Austin auto bumped up onto a broken pavement, torn and broken fences, and walls of graffiti with words I didn't understand.

There seemed to be a lot that I didn't understand, all of the stuff Ali was saying for one thing. Spirits and ghosts were all alien subjects that I'd heard and read about over the years, but certainly didn't believe in. As far as I was concerned if you couldn't see it, you couldn't shoot it, and that meant it didn't exist.

Macca leaned over the front seat and spoke to Ali. 'Are these ghosts supposed to be from the penal colony times or the Japanese occupation?'

'For all time. Kali Pani has much anger in its spirit.'

I laughed out loud. Ali shot me a glance. 'This is the second time you have suggested that this island has a spirit,' I said.

He furrowed his brow and spoke to me indignantly. 'You have a spirit, your friend has one, I have one, the driver has one, together we make up the spirit in this jeep. Add the past spirit and another two hundred thousand people and you have the spirit of this modern-day island.'

'What do you mean, modern-day island?' Macca asked.

'The spirit of the past and the present, the energy that governs these islands today, making the future as we speak.'

'So what you're saying is Kali Pani has anger in its past and its present.'

'No, it has anger in the past and this causes unrest in the present. It is an island that never sleeps. People here are always restless, restless attracts restless and this attracts the less desirable people who come here to trade. The Indian government are foolish to try to prosper the islands while this feeling exists.' He paused a moment. 'A woman has come to Kali Pani who has the foresight to realise that the islands need healing, she comes with a higher consciousness, but she is a woman before her time and not liked by some. I believe her work will be stopped.'

'Do you know the woman?' Macca asked. 'Is her name Shreela Robert?'

Ali pointed across the driver's vision. 'Pull over here,' he said. Ignoring Macca's question he jumped from the jeep.

'He knows his history,' Macca said, as we got out and followed him.

'I'm not totally sure that I trust him.'

'Why not?' Macca asked.

'Lack of eye contact—I never trust people who don't look me in the eye. He's too still and deep thinking to trust...and I didn't like the look that passed between him and Ramjit over the helicopter.'

'Ali encouraged this helicopter thing to happen.'

'He's probably getting a cut of the profits. The look on Ramjit's face suggested he didn't like him suggesting it.'

Macca shrugged. 'It might be nothing.'

'Did you notice the way Ali offered Ramjit a fag earlier? Without looking, casual, like he knew him well?'

'Are you sure you're not just making something out of nothing?'

'I don't trust either of them.'

Macca thought for a moment. 'Maybe it's important that

we don't push incidents like the helicopter discussion aside and ignore them.'

'No, Macca, it's more than that. We need to face up to something—this island is not the most affluent place in the world. People here are definitely susceptible to corruption. Take Ali for example, he's a guide, he knows people and places and he's perfectly placed to enjoy any extra trade from people like Koslov who want to hide here. I mean, think about it, he's a guide in a place that's pretty well billed as hell on earth. Who in their right mind is going to visit a place like this? I bet Ali doesn't work more than a couple of weeks a year.'

Macca was deep in thought for a moment. 'When I saw the abduction on the news that morning I never thought we'd end up in a place like this.'

'You saw it on the news?'

'Aye, but that was awful weird. I saw it around seven o'clock and waited to hear more at seven thirty, then eight, but it never came back on again.'

'Really?' I said. 'I saw it at seven and never had the chance to see it again.'

'It was like they took it off the air.'

We reached Ali's friend's house and stood behind Ali. He had knocked on the door and was waiting. A few seconds passed before an overhead window opened. Ali and his pal exchanged Indian dialect. The upshot of the conversation was that the following day we were leaving at 07:00 and flying until 17:00.

Heading back to the airfield I felt fidgety. I noticed Macca shifting in his seat too. 'What did you say?' he asked, looking at me as though I had spoken.

'Nothing,' I replied, shaking my head.

'I could have sworn...'

Ali turned to us with wide eyes. 'They are with us,' he said. 'They are watching us.'

I was about to ask what the hell he was talking about when the most inhuman scream pierced the night.

All of us jumped at once. The driver swerved across the

road and bumped up the kerb. I swivelled round and looked behind. There was nothing there. 'What the...' I shouted.

'Faster, faster, faster,' Ali said, grabbing the wheel and pulling the jeep back onto the road.

'Where the hell did that come from?' Macca shouted.

'More like what the fuck is it,' I shouted back, looking out the back of the jeep, first over one shoulder then the other.

'It is what I told you before,' Ali panted. 'It is the spirits. It is Kali Pani's anger.'

The driver floored the accelerator pedal. We bounced harder and faster along the road.

I could hear screams all around me, constant and shrill.

Out of nowhere a brick flew through the air towards us.

Thunk! It bounced across the bonnet and under the wheels, rocking the jeep.

'Shit,' Macca shouted, 'They can throw things?'

Bang! Another brick smashed into the wing and bounced between Macca and me. I cupped my hands over my head and bent down with my head between my knees.

The jeep roared along the empty roads, bouncing us over one pothole after another, shaking and throwing us about like rag dolls.

Still the screaming followed us.

Only when we shot through the open security gates at the airport did it stop. The jeep screeched to a halt outside the hangar. I raised my head from between my legs. Nervously I looked around.

Silence.

Macca looked at me.

Spaghetti hauled open the hangar door and took one look at us. 'What's wrong with you lot? You look like you've just seen a ghost.'

'Fucking right,' Macca spluttered. 'We just fucking did.'

Spaghetti's laugh echoed across the desolate airfield and died somewhere in the cold night air. It was then that the screaming started for a second time.

A NIGHT IN HELL

The screaming stopped as we rolled the door closed and backed inside the hangar, but it was only the briefest of respites before the rhythmic whispering started.

'Jesus, what is this?' Macca asked, cowering.

'It sounds like the wind,' Doug said, unmoved and unemotional.

'How can that be? The door's closed,' Macca said.

'It's howling around the hangar.'

'Are you deaf? That's no howl, and besides the wind doesn't throw bricks at you.'

'That must have been someone hiding; maybe kids, a local gang or something,' Doug said.

Ramjit was close by, eyes flitting from one side of the hangar to the other. Ali stood upright, his head cocked to one side as though listening to something. 'The chant is tribal,' he said. 'They are the native spirits.'

'You mean the cannibals?'

'Yes. Try to relax.'

Macca cracked. 'Relax? I've just had bricks thrown at me by the Invisible Man and had some unseen creature shrieking in my ear. Now you're telling me our camp is haunted by dead cannibals. How the hell am I going to relax?'

Ali ignored him and walked across the hangar to sit on one of the upturned boxes we had used as seats earlier. He sat on one, crossed his legs and closed his eyes.

Doug persevered, 'There must be another explanation.'

Ali said, 'Calm your soul, still your thoughts and communicate with the spirits through your mind, but beware of your thoughts or you will allow low entities to feed from your energy field.'

Macca followed Ali's example. Ramjit headed over and joined them. 'What a load of horse- shit,' Spaghetti said.

Moments later the hangar fell silent.

Macca stretched. Ali took a minute, coming round slowly and taking in some deep breaths. 'All gone,' he said, getting up and dusting down the back of his trousers.

Doug was still standing in the same spot he had been standing in when the screaming started. He glanced around the hangar and pulled a face, 'Macca, you tart. I can't believe you're taken in by this crap. Look for stereo speakers around the hangar perimeter.'

Ali lit a cigarette. 'We were just visited by good spirits who are trying to protect you, but they struggle against a dark spirit.'

'So your forte is obviously horror trips, Ali,' I said. 'I have no idea how you created that illusion with the brick or the voices and the screams, but hey, well done.'

Ali stared at me for a few seconds then shrugged. 'It is not my problem if spirits scare you.'

'I'm not scared by them,' I said. 'I just refuse to be taken in by your attempts to put the shits up us before we even start looking for this woman. I'm a soldier for Christ's sake, I'm bloody sure I'm not going to be manipulated by your bull-shit illusions.'

Ali shrugged. 'Suit yourself.'

Spaghetti changed the subject. He had something far more important on his mind. 'I hope you're not going to keep that up all night, Ali. I want to get some kip.'

Ali flicked his cigarette ash onto the floor, 'There are over two hundred thousand people living in Port St. Peter, if they manage to sleep at night so can you.'

'Hey, we got rid of them once,' Macca said, 'we can certainly do it again.'

'We need to focus on the job we came here to do,' Doug said coolly.

'Oh yeah, right,' Spaghetti said, 'I came here to get a woman who had been kidnapped, now it seems we're playing fucking Ghostbusters in a horror house.'

'You all need to get a grip,' Ali said, glancing in my direction. 'You all need to stop arguing. The dark spirits will feed from this negative energy.'

'I'm going to stay awake tonight,' Spaghetti announced, 'just to make sure there's no more weird shit.'

Trying to regain some control I said, 'Let's get some rest until 06:30. At 07:00 we go sight-seeing in the helicopter. Seems like Spaghetti's just volunteered himself for stag, everyone cool with that?'

As I threw out my sleeping gear I was aware that we were all on edge, but I was unaware that Ramjit was standing right next to me. I jumped and almost knocked into him as he spoke. 'It is not too late to turn back,' he said.

I stopped laying my bedding out. 'I can't leave another human being in the hands of Koslov,' I said.

He slapped me on the shoulder. 'Please, I'm with you, Michael, I am plenty, plenty with you. Believe we can win, that is the spirit. It is important that we believe.'

It was the first positive thing Ramjit had said. That in itself made me curious. It just didn't seem right to be hearing any kind of reassuring words from anyone right now.

I tied up my hammock. Ramjit wandered away and Ali came over to me. 'Kali Pani is a strange place during the day, but at night it is worse. I have come to warn you that you carry much negative energy with you. Also, I want to tell you that one of the spirits does not like you. I warn you that you must not trust anything you might see, hear or feel tonight. I warn you that in Kali Pani your dreams may seem more real than normal.'

Stretched out on the hammock a few minutes later I began to feel more alone than I had ever felt. A smile from Christian would have gone down a treat. I'd have loved to have been with him at home, reading a bedtime story: Peter Pan, Aladdin, Robin Hood—he loved the tales with the nasty villains, and the more fighting and the nastier the villain, the better. Often, when the story was finished and the light was out, he'd roll over and flop his arm around my neck and say, 'Do you believe in the story, Daddy?'

Thinking he'd be frightened by the villain if I said yes, I always said no. Once he said to me, 'Stop pretending the baddies don't exist, Daddy. Just because you can't see or hear, it doesn't mean stuff's not there.'

A drink would have been nice, but as there wasn't one I curled up and shut my eyelids tightly. I could taste the brandy, the tingling sensation as it passed over my tongue and throat. I pictured the lounge floor, me with a bottle in my hand, and turned over in my hammock. The sleeping policeman underneath Jodie, them screwing in my bed; I turned onto my back. Him sitting on my sofa, watching my TV with his feet up, playing with my son, building up a relationship with him that I should have been building; I rolled over again. The brandy bottle slipped out of my hand, rolling across the floor and *he* was looking down at me, lying on the floor. 'Jodie just wants you out,' he said.

Anger snapped inside me, not at Jodie or the policeman, but at me. What had I been thinking about when I said to Jodie that we could give it another shot? What a mug. The way she was…what she did…it affected everything. It had been her behaviour that had forced me to drink, it was the drink that had kept me out of the gym. It was that which had ruined my fitness, which could put my life in jeopardy, which could jeopardise the lives of my unit, which had nearly got me thrown out of the Regiment. It was her…all her. She was ruining me and I was just letting it happen.

I rolled over again and this time I smiled and felt a tumbling sensation. I was tickling and fighting and laughing, chasing and screaming with Christian. Jodie flashed through my mind again, her long legs, slim and shapely as she breezed through the bedroom naked. I was reaching out to her and felt myself falling over.

Suddenly I felt as though I had been transported to another world. It was deep and hypnotic, amazingly familiar and warm.

I was back at school, my old school, but it was slightly different; there were no boys. It was full of young women, not schoolgirls, but women in their twenties and thirties. One woman was on the floor gathering up her books. I went over and helped her. She seemed familiar...an old girlfriend, her long hair, tied in a pony tail, her eyes blue and alive. I offered my hand to help her up and she took it and asked if I would take her out on a date.

'Sure,' I said.

But she laughed at me. 'What makes you think I'd date you?'

'Suit yourself,' I replied, backing away. I was at a door, pushing it open.

She called to me, 'Seriously, will you take me out?'

I looked at her legs. 'Yeah why not?' I said.

Next I was in a classroom on an L-shaped bed. The girl was on top of me; her blouse fell open and her breast fell out. I took it in my mouth and sucked on it and we rolled over and over. We made love and I felt warmer and more contented than I had ever felt about anything in my life...ever.

She took my hand and led me from the bed. I was walking, but my eyes were closed. 'Shush,' she was saying, 'shush, it's a surprise.'

'I'm scared,' I whispered.

'Don't worry,' she giggled. She passed me something and told me to hold it.

'What's this?' I asked, opening my eyes.

Gently, she kissed me on the lips and inched away. 'You know what it is,' she said, 'show me how you use it.' My body felt drugged as I looked down at my handgun. Suddenly I was aware the scenery had changed. I was no longer in my old school; I was back in the hangar. There was no bed, just my hammock.

But she was there, standing in front of me. 'Show me how you use it,' she breathed into my ear.

I stood back and pointed the gun at her. She giggled again. 'Not at me, silly, at you.'

I raised the gun to my head. I knew it was wrong, I knew I shouldn't be doing this, but her suggestion was too powerful for me to ignore.

'Show me,' she said.

I heard a bang. I jolted and shook. I heard shouts and then I heard the screaming again.

I had not blown a hole in my head. I was not dead. And yet someone was trying to take the gun out of my hand. I pulled away from them and fought them off. More people joined in. I was wrestling someone on the ground and then I recognised the faces around me: Spaghetti, Doug, Macca, Ali and Ramjit.

Everything was in a haze and their voices were muted. 'Mike?' Spaghetti said, shaking me. 'Mike?'

Ali was there in front of me. 'He's not with us,' he said, 'his spirit is not altogether in his body. He needs to come back down to earth.'

They sat me down. I watched them through a haze as they paced around me. My ears were ringing. My temperature was high and I felt sick. I held my head in my hands until the feeling went away.

'You okay, Boss?' Doug asked me after a while.

'I...I have v-vague r-recollections of the m-most amazing s-sex,' I replied, with a stammer I had never had before.

'And damn nearly shot yourself afterwards,' he added.

'I...I d-did?'

'Seriously,' Doug said. 'Spaghetti just got to your gun as you squeezed the trigger. You were pointing it at your head.'

I looked at Spaghetti. The expression on his face told me that Doug was not joking. 'I v-vaguely r-remember it,' I slurred. 'Th-thanks.'

'It was the spirits,' Ali said. 'I warned you not to trust the night-time. These spirits lure you into things. They come to you and look human. I warned you. You must let all negativity pass or you will die on this island.' He turned to Doug. 'You will have to watch out for him. They see his weakness and his weakness is now yours.'

THE ECHO WITHIN

My body was numbed, but my brain was wired as I lay on my hammock in the shadowy, dimly- lit hangar, getting really worked up over Ali's outburst. Weaknesses? Bollocks, I didn't have any, and who was he, after only knowing me for a maximum of three hours, to speak with any kind of authority about me?

In the morning Ali and I were going to have a chat. He was going to be put right on a few things and he was never going to talk to me like that again in front of my unit. It was bad enough that I had pointed a gun at my head, but to have some stranger refer to me as having a weakness was beyond fair. And what made it even worse was that minutes later the guys had all wondered off to their beds, to be alone with their thoughts and the images of their Patrol Commander behaving like a circus clown. I sensed it now as they tossed and turned, sniffing and scratching in their hammocks: they were wondering if I really had the balls for the job.

What Ali had obviously overlooked was the fact that I was a solider, and therefore by right I didn't have weaknesses, and if I did, then I made them disappear. I was a wheel, a cog in a dispassionate war machine and I acted like one at all times. No way could I give the impression that I had ever had or would ever have a weakness.

So why was I worrying about what my unit was thinking?

Clearly I had demonstrated enough stupidity in one incident.

I had to change something. I had to stop the stuff that just kept echoing within me.

I began by reviewing the most recent past, what Ali called

'spirits' and I called 'ghosts'. A few hours ago I had not believed in them, and I still didn't, but I had to admit that there was growing evidence to support his theory.

It didn't sit well with me—ghosts didn't fit my reality, in fact they messed it up, big time. They were not physical and they were impossible to kill, so they couldn't exist, would never exist. But if they didn't exist, then I had to find something else to blame for driving me to the point of aiming a gun at my own head during my sleep.

Nothing.

But there had to be something; if ghosts didn't exist there had to be something else that made me stick a gun to my head.

Stress?

Tiredness?

Exhaustion?

A trip to madness?

None of these were right. I was in a stupid, fucked up cul-de-sac of questions. I wasn't stressed, tired, exhausted or mad and I knew it, but I had to find something to blame, so that in the morning I could justify it all and be cured of this weakness tag.

I was sweating and uncomfortable, and I felt like my head was going to explode when Spaghetti came and stood next to me.

'Still awake, shit-legs?' he grinned.

'No, I always sleep with my eyes open,' I replied.

'Yeah, course you do.' He shifted from foot to foot. He offered me one of his Bon Bons and hung around like he wanted to chat. 'That was weird; you got out of your hammock and leaned forward like you were kissing someone. You looked like you were in a trance, you know, like you were sleepwalking. I just knew I had to get that gun off you.'

'Thank fuck for small miracles,' I said.

I didn't mean the sarcasm. I didn't mean to be hostile towards him, it just came out that way. I watched him wander back across the hangar and didn't feel an ounce of gratitude towards him for saving my life. In fact, I blamed him for putting me in the predicament where I looked like a tosser.

At least the stammer had gone.

And where had that come from? I'd never had one of those before. But as I thought about it I remembered I had stuttered before. As a kid, when my parents ranted and raved at each other or at me, I had been unable to talk properly for hours. And then at school, I had stuttered in front of the headmaster after I kicked some kid in the gonads because he was sitting in front of my peg and wouldn't move. And then there was the time when I was a spotty teenager and I had been caught by the police etching obscenities into a mate's car bonnet. It had just been for a laugh, but the Old Bill really put the shits up me that night and I stuttered like a jackhammer on the pavement, 'D-d-d-d-d-don't t-t-t-tell m-me d-d-d-dad.'

What was that all about?

As I closed my eyes for a second I was suddenly transported back several hours to the CO's office. Standing in front of his desk he got straight into discussion. 'Not interested in the details of your fucked-up merry-go-round home life, Edwards, just need to know if your professional judgement is turning to rat-shit.'

'No, sir, I'm fine, sir. Just a few maritals, sir –'

He eyeballed me and screamed into my face. 'So explain the fuck to me why you have been slacking on your training and how the fuck half the regiment became drunk and disorderly just by coming within ten fucking paces of your alcohol-stinking breath.'

'S-sir, I have b-been d-drinking, sir, and my t-training has suffered, sir, but not b-badly, sir. I can still o-o-operate.'

'I'll be the fucking judge of that, you lazy arsed, fucked-up bastard.'

'S-sir, y-yes, sir.'

He walked away from me, pacing his office. 'If a man in my regiment breaks his leg, I think it's appropriate to break his arm to numb the thoughts about his leg, so I'm going to numb your troubles, Edwards. I'm going to send you on a mission and get you away from your marriage problems.'

It was then that he went on to tell me about the mission. 'You are to find and free Miss Shreela Robert from her kidnapper. If Koslov is involved he will be the Indian's responsibility, not ours.'

'S-sir, to be h-honest th-that –'

'I don't want your fucking stuttering thoughts,' he snapped. He returned to the front of his desk and sitting on the edge of it he proceeded to give me his version of a fatherly chat. 'Edwards, I'll be frank, after what I heard over the telephone this morning I would prefer to send someone else in your place, simply because I now view you as a fuck-up, but you cause me a problem: you *are* experienced in hostage situations, you *have* opposed Koslov and you *are* available to go. Now I can justify not sending you because you're slapdash in training and stink to high heaven from a night on the piss, but what I cannot then justify is having a waste of time tosser in my Regiment. Wake up and smell the shit, sunshine—you are part of an elite regiment and you are expected to behave accordingly. I have no room for screw-ups. You have a long flight to India. Sort your head out and do your job or you and your fucking luggage will be on the platform and heading back to the Paras. Now get your shit together and get the fuck out of here,' he ordered.

My God, the stutter...

I was under so much strain, and I hadn't even realised: the marriage, the sleeping policeman, my career, the screw-up with Koslov years ago, and now this mission. But none of it was a weakness. It was just stuff, and I had to deal with it.

In the twilight hours my mind continued to run riot. It replayed memories: making love to Jodie at sunrise on the beach, Kalid's death, Koslov's escape and the two of his men that I had put to ground; Jodie hurling every dish and item of cutlery at me from the draining board in the kitchen during a row...

As I replayed those memories I must have slipped back to

sleep. Suddenly Spaghetti was rolling back the hangar door and sunlight was bursting in. 'Holy shit,' he shouted.

I leapt from my hammock and jogged across the hangar to the door, wondering if the ghosts had trashed the jeep overnight or torched the terminal building.

'Tell me this isn't true,' he said. 'Tell me this just ain't fucking happening.'

THE DEATH TRAP

First there was Belize, then Ireland, CRW Ops (Counter Revolutionary Warfare Operations) and then the removal of a sultan.

Sultan Sa'id was viewed as a tyrant oppressor who liked his countrymen to pay homage to him. He ruled over a country rich in oil and strategically important to the West. His armed forces were led by the British Special Forces and his enemy were the guerrillas infiltrating from Iraq and stirring up trouble amongst the tribes in the Musandam Peninsula. Prior to the British withdrawal Sultan Sa'id was removed by senior British officers and replaced by his son, Qaboos. Under Qaboos a plan grew to encourage the rebels to come down from the mountains and surrender, but while some of the rebels obliged, others did not.

In a desperate attempt to overthrow the new ruler the rebels hatched a plan to take the palace while Qaboos was in residence. Unbeknown to the guerrillas though, Qaboos had a last minute change of plan. When the rebels stormed the palace they missed the bait and ended up with an uncle, two wives and three sons.

Forty-eight hours into the siege I became part of the assault team that retook the palace in the dark. Four teams hit it at ground level while another four went in from the roofs. The guerrillas were totally taken by surprise. They had been enjoying the hospitality of a negotiator right up to the moment we blew in the front door. Few shots were fired, and those that came from the guerrillas all ended up in the elegantly decorated palace walls.

As I remembered back to that op, I remembered the

immaculate RAF helicopters, the way the pilots and engineers loved those clean, well-kept machines like babies. And as I thought about all the other times the RAF had provided us with transport I realised that I had assumed that all pilots everywhere had that same love for those machines that could float in the air.

But as I looked out across the tarmac from the hangar door that morning in Kali Pani I realised I was wrong. Standing before me was the dirtiest, most neglected machine I had ever seen.

'If that's what the outside looks like, makes you wonder what the engine's like.' Spaghetti said.

'I'm sure it's fine,' Macca said, 'they'll have regulations, all aircraft have to have them.'

We made ourselves ready, filling our Bergens and belt kits with enough supplies for a day's flying—water, fruit, biscuits, salt tablets and spare magazines...just in case.

Headgear, as Spaghetti nicknamed the pilot because of his turban, smiled and waved as we headed out towards him. He shook our hands enthusiastically and gave several small bows and then, opening the door to the death-trap with rotors, he crossed himself.

Inside the helicopter Ali explained where we wanted to fly while Headgear made the pre-flight preparations with an absent-minded chatter that did nothing to instil confidence in his flying ability. Just as I was getting used to going nowhere fast there was a judder and a rattle. The rotors had begun to turn.

'Ha-har, very good, very good,' Headgear said. He grinned over the seats at me with dancing eyes that suggested he'd forgotten to take his medication.

'A fucking dodo that found wings,' Spaghetti spluttered at me.

Was I really going to let this happen? Was searching for Shreela in rickety old bird with the pilot who had uninstalled the confidence programme, the right thing to do? It was a risk, a dumb risk, a risk brought on by desperation to get us searching against the odds, craziness caused by trying to force the speed of an operation.

It was stupid, it was mad, but we were going to do it.

On a north-easterly heading, we were soon over a two-kilometre stretch of ocean that fed between the north and south islands. North Kali Pani was the greater landmass and appeared as a continuous horizon of green treetops.

'They could be anywhere amongst this,' Spaghetti shouted in my ear.

'It's likely to be no more than a slight clearing, a tent, a discoloured patch where a camp fire might have been lit,' I shouted back.

We had been over north Kali Pani for about ten minutes when Ali leaned over the seats and pointed down. 'Jarawa,' he shouted.

I looked down, but saw nothing among the trees. 'Where?' I asked.

Ali tapped Headgear on the shoulder and made a circling gesture. Headgear swung the death- trap around. Ali pointed down again.

Through the trees I saw two small, skinny, dark men looking up at us, holding something in front of their faces. And then I saw two sticks coming towards us. 'Arrows!' Ali said. 'They always like to try their luck. Jarawa never miss a chance of fresh meat.'

Headgear pulled away and continued on our heading north. I was now feeling like I was baking in an oven. Sweat was running down my forehead, making rivers over my stomach and back. My shirt was sticking to me.

Five minutes passed and there was another call from Ali. More Jarawa. This time I saw them darting through the trees, bare-arsed men, and women with their breasts dangling.

'We scared them,' Ali shouted.

But they weren't running and tripping like scared people did, they were dispersing in pairs, like they were working a plan.

Ali grabbed Headgear's arm and pointed down. Again Headgear swung the helicopter for a better view.

'Clever buggers,' Ali shouted as we hovered above the treetops.

Looking from tree to tree, I saw dozens of dark legs dangling over the branches, almost hidden within the foliage. I felt an intense urge to move on. 'Let's go,' I called across the seat to Headgear.

Ignoring me, Headgear eased the control stick to one side and tilted the heli as he tried to get a better view.

'Let's go. Hanging in the sky's just threatening these people.'

Still Headgear held us steady.

'Let's move!'

Suddenly the helicopter swayed violently. I grabbed at a handle above my head. Doug, Macca and Spaghetti splayed all over the seats and slipped downwards, grabbing at the backs of seats, each other, anything solid. Through Doug's window, which was now more or less below me, I could see the Jarawa in the trees firing up towards us. I could hear the tap of the arrows as they hit the heli windows. 'Level it,' shouted Spaghetti. 'Level it up.'

We levelled out a little, but something wasn't right. The heli nose was dropping. Something was wrong up in front.

Headgear started screaming. I grabbed the back of the seats in front of me and leaned forward into the cockpit. An arrow was sticking out of Headgear's chest and blood had already blotted his sweaty shirt.

'We're losing altitude,' someone shouted from behind me.

There was now little or no distance between us and the treetops.

'Up, up,' Ali shouted. 'Pull up, pull up.'

I threw myself over the seat and reached across Headgear. 'I'm dead,' I heard him saying to himself. 'I'm dead.'

Shoving Headgear out of the way I grabbed the stick and hauled it to the right and back. The nose rose sharply, throwing me back into the seats. The stick slipped from my grasp. It shifted on its own now while the heli performed like a like a runaway cart in a house of horrors roller-coaster ride.

I grabbed at the stick again only this time I forced it down and left and in a second, trees were rushing towards us.

'Up, up.'

Already the skids underneath us were skimming the treetops, juddering and banging. Then suddenly we were heading down into darkness and chopping our way through foliage.

We halted.

Smack! I hit the windscreen.

The heli groaned.

Macca moved.

The heli slid, crashing and snapping until it jammed between the branches of a several thousand year-old tree.

'Sit still, you fat bastard,' Spaghetti spluttered.

'Screw you,' Macca replied.

'Calm down,' I roared.

The story of the tree workers flashed through my mind. We needed to get organised and get moved out. I checked Headgear for a pulse. 'He's dead,' I said to Ali.

He nodded like he knew.

'Could have been the impact of the crash or the poison arrow he was shouting about,' Macca said.

At that moment I really didn't care how he'd died. The fact was he had and we had to move on.

'The radio,' I said to Ali, 'tell someone where we are.'

'I'll tell you about the radio,' Ali said. 'The radio does not work.'

'What, you mean it just broke?'

'Yes, that is what I mean. It just broke two weeks ago.'

Macca said, 'Everything will be fine, they'll be able to pick up our last position on the airport radar.'

'Airport radar is also dead,' Ali said, flatly.

I glared at him. 'Spaghetti, the Satcom—tell me the Satcom is intact.'

Spaghetti had already eased open a door and I could see

from the look on his face he was contemplating the jump down
to the ground. 'You really think we should hang here and set
it up while Jungle Jim of the Jarawa is out hunting brunch? I
love sausage rolls, but I'm fucked if I'm ready to play the star
attraction in a mid-morning snack. It's about eight to ten feet,'
he said.

Spaghetti went first, then me and Maeca. Ali came next
then Doug.

On the ground, I said, 'Right where are we?'

'Kali Pani,' Ali said with a frown. My temper was still
simmering. His smart answers were no longer endearing. I took
him by the throat. 'You know what I mean. Where the fucking
hell are we?'

'West of the island,' Ali wheezed.

I let him go.

Doug pointed at the map in his hand. 'So we just head
south and get out of here ASAP.'

'No,' Ali said, massaging his neck. 'You cannot go that way.
That goes right through the heart of a known settlement. The
Jarawa will ambush us without any trouble at all. We must move
away from them and turn a wide arch back to Port St Peter.'

'And how long will that take?'

'Two days. But if you have your radio and Mr Ramjit has
navy helicopters perhaps you can arrange something.'

In front of me, to my sides and behind were tall, skinny
trees. They seemed to grow at whatever angle they wanted to
and bushed out near the top. Lower to the ground were smaller
versions of the same, growing like thick hedges. And in the trees
was the sound of a hundred birds singing tunes I'd never heard
before. It was hotter, clammier, muggier than it had been in the
heli and already I wanted air, and a damn good lungful of it.

I raised my hand to scratch my chest and felt the stiff
card in my pocket. I took the picture out and looked at it for a
second. What kind of a crazy woman was Manisha Robert that
she believed a bloody photo would guide me?

A voice at my shoulder startled me. 'Maybe she's close by
or something,' Spaghetti shrugged. He whipped a Bon Bon out

of his belt kit and looked up into the trees as he shoved it in his tumble-drier mouth. 'Weirder shit's happened and we are in the weirdest place in the world.'

'Cut the crap talk,' I said, screwing the picture up. 'You think I'm going soft or something?' I picked up a fist-sized stone and scuffed out some earth to make a small hole for it, then stuffed the picture under it and replaced it.

Spaghetti laughed. 'I was just kinda hoping there might be a short cut to the woman that would get us off the island quicker.'

'Sometimes, Spaghetti, you're a real dickhead,' I said. Turning to everyone else I said, 'Be on the lookout for the Jarawa. Let's move out.'

Ali said, 'They will be hiding behind trees, you won't see them before their arrows hit you. They have survived for thousands of years on an island where other men have perished. They have proved themselves smarter than the British, the Japanese and Indians rulers. They will follow your scent as you move.'

'Then I hope they like the smell of shit,' Spaghetti said, 'because I'm so scared right now that I've just filled me pants.'

'In that case, you bring up the rear,' I said. 'Let's see if your shitty little arse will put them off having us for brunch.'

ENEMY CONTACT

The terrain was uneven, littered with volcanic boulders and mosquito-infested bogs, streams and swamps. Often we were forced to crouch and weave through thick jungle growth that was so dense in parts we were in danger of losing each other. Flies buzzed around our heads, leeches crawled up our clothing and slipped sensationlessly onto our skin. Birds whistled the same calls over and over and over again until I wanted to scream, and all the time the heat sucked the moisture from every pore.

I had to keep all my powers of concentration wired to the max and I had to make sure every man in my unit was doing the same. Every rustle in the bushes, every movement of a leaf, every twig snap could have been the Jarawa, and had we lost our concentration for even a moment they could have been down on us with a shower of arrows. Failure to react at lightning speed to any enemy contact in any regiment in the world could lead to your death, but with the nature of our work in the SAS, behind-the-lines missions, surveillance, laying up for days on end, those skills were tuned to the finest frequency. Kali Pani jungle was a place that would test our skills like no other place.

Already it was plain to me that with such thick foliage our enemy could get so close to us that they could take us out before we even knew they were there, and while Koslov's lot might have been noisy or clumsy I was sure that the Jarawa could move up on their prey in silence.

We had no idea if they had found the helicopter, picked up our scent and followed us. I assumed they had and they would, so I set our pace accordingly, moving for long periods, taking short rests and limiting our water intake so our supply lasted.

Each time we broke we agreed a new rendezvous point. This was done so that we had a meeting point if we were compromised or if one of us got lost in the foliage. I always set the RV as the point I intended us to rest next.

'Last two days have been sunshine,' Ali said, when we stopped to get our bearings. 'Before this we had only rain for one week. The monsoon season is starting any day. In the coming weeks the streams will widen and this ground will become boggy and difficult to cross.'

'No sweat,' Spaghetti said.

'Mosquitoes will be everywhere, your boots will be heavy with mud, humidity will be higher, but at least your search will be narrowed.'

'Why's that?' I asked.

'Because if your man has a camp in the jungle he will be wise to find higher ground.'

In nine hours, heading north then east, we covered around sixteen clicks, kilometres.

'We are one hour from the trunk road,' Ali announced.

'Excellent,' Macca said, 'surely we can use that to get up a head of steam and get to wherever we're heading quicker.'

'I'm up for getting out of this jungle,' Spaghetti said, 'too many creepy crawlies for me.'

Ali stepped forward. 'I'll tell you about the trunk road,' he said, 'it is risky.'

'The Jarawa are known to wait along the trunk road. They fire arrows at passing vehicles. In Kali Pani even passenger buses need armed escorts. On foot we would make easy targets, even after dark'

Doug said, 'Why not just set up the Satcom here and agree an RV with Ramjit now?'

'No point,' I said, 'Ramjit doesn't have helicopters until tomorrow. We have a sitrep to make with Antenna at 23:00 local time, 18:00 GMT. I don't see the sense in wasting time setting up comms twice. '

'Okay,' said Doug, 'but I don't like this travelling along the trunk road. It's risky and could lead to unnecessary compromise.'

I agreed with Doug. 'We'll stay under cover and move until we make our sitrep with Antenna.' I pointed at the map and looked at Ali. 'What's this town like?'

'Tugagat is small—a few houses and a store.'

'Right, well we're going to head there. We'll aim to lie up a click north of the town around dusk, get some rest and then go on to Tugagat. We'll spend the day doing a recce on the town. Hopefully Ramjit will have the helis in place by tomorrow evening to get us an airlift out of here.'

'Tell the pilot to keep his windows shut,' Spaghetti added dryly. He bent down to pick up his Bergen from the ground. 'Awe, shit!' he shouted. 'Something just bit me neck.'

I rushed over to him. Ali stood next to me. Neither of us could see anything bigger than a pin-prick, just a dot of blood and a slight redness. 'It could be a spider,' Ali said.

'You mean it might have just bitten me and fell off?'

'That is one possibility,' Ali said.

'What do you mean, one possibility, what else could it be?'

'Spiders sometimes use people to make nests.'

Spaghetti frowned. 'You're joking, right?'

Ali shrugged and walked away.

'Hey, you are joking, aren't you?'

Ali swung back towards him. 'I mean what I said. Humans are sometimes used for nesting.'

'Can't we stop it?'

'Yes.'

'How?'

Emotionless, Ali stared at him. 'First we have to let the nest grow then you will need a small operation to cut it out.'

'Why can't we just do it now?'

'It is too small. It must grow first.'

Leaning on a tree next to me, Macca changed the subject. 'I suppose those ghosts will be back tonight.'

'Let's just hope they're city dwellers,' I joked.

I replaced the cap on my water bottle and prepared my Bergen to move off, but Macca continued, 'Perhaps it's Jarawa black magic, they don't like civilization so maybe they make spells and send them into the city at night.'

Ali overheard him. 'The ghosts are spirits from the past. There is no Jarawa black magic,' he said with a tone of indignation.

Spaghetti scratched his neck and managed a little chuckle. 'I'll never forget the look on your face last night, Boss, shock and ecstasy in one go—like shagging the missus and being caught by your mum.'

'I must admit, when I came to I was relieved my pants were intact,' I said.

'Only because we put them back on you,' Doug sniggered.

Though I felt sure I was being wound up, there was that element of doubt in the mind, like when you've had a few beers too many and someone tells you that you pulled your trousers down on the dance floor the previous night: you can remember going to the dance floor and unbuckling your belt but the rest is a haze. It was like that.

The light was fading and we had another hour of foliage to get through in order to reach the trunk road, so, ignoring the guys, I announced it was time to make tracks again.

As we headed on I thought about the dream I'd had the previous night. It bothered me that the same thing could happen again. Suddenly Ali's comments about the negativity came back to me and I remembered that I still hadn't had that conversation with him yet.

He was in front of me now. He pushed back a branch and turned to me. 'They prey on your weaknesses. They poison your mind by using images familiar to you, things that will attract you.'

'Yeah,' I said, 'I wanna talk to you about that.'

He stopped dead in his tracks and looked me directly in the eye. 'You have demons that you carry with you, dark shadows from hell that have attached to you. You must exorcise them.'

'Right, Ali,' I said. 'This bullshit has to stop. There are

no demons, no negatives and no weaknesses. I don't want you talking like that again in front of my unit and I don't appreciate _'

He started walking on, then stopped again and turned back. 'Tell me about your dream.'

'Did you hear me or what?'

'Yes, I heard you. Now tell me about the dream.'

'You're not getting it are you? Did you hear what I said about not talking in front of my unit like that again?'

'Yes. Now please tell me about the dream. I believe I can help you.'

'You don't fucking let up, do you?'

Without thinking about it I started telling him. I couldn't stop myself, it just came out of its own free will and my mouth just wouldn't shut up, even though I told it to. It was like some higher force had overridden my brain and said, 'You will talk.' 'There was a girl. Like an old girlfriend. I couldn't see her face clearly,' I said.

Ali cut in, 'It's important that you distinguish that it was not an old girlfriend, you do understand that, don't you?'

'Yeah, course I do. I know it was just a dream.'

He swung back towards me again, almost knocking me over. 'Understand also that it was not just a dream. These spirits can make themselves very real. They know situations close to your heart and they will use that to help you hurt yourself.' I must have given him a look of confusion or a look of doubt or something. 'They pick up this information from your energy field,' he said, as though trying to clarify it for me. I looked at Ali, pulled a face and shook my head. He turned away and carried on walking. Speaking over his shoulder he added, 'I believe the spirits came as your old girlfriend because you seek a purity in love that you found in adolescence and want to revive.'

'Bollocks,' I laughed. It all sounded ridiculous. I expected Ali to turn and argue with me, or at least I hoped he would so I could prove he was talking rubbish. There was no way what he was saying was credible. In the silence he allowed me by not arguing I wondered about this 'purity in love' he spoke of. What did he mean? What was 'purity in love' anyway? Was it that flutter of excitement caused by simply holding a girl's hand in the playground, the rush caused by necking with her on the street corner by the shop and thinking I was in love while not having the vocabulary to describe the feeling, wanting nothing more than to feel close, to be close, thinking about her all day long?

Leaves brushed my face, a small boulder on the ground pressed into the arch of my foot. I winced, but did not falter from my step.

I remembered that girl, my first girlfriend, the girl who I snogged for the first time, and I remembered the way she had dumped me—she had met someone else, an older lad with a car. It really hurt me, especially when I got home and looked in the mirror and realised that my raging teenage hormones had turned my face into a beans on toast feature with a dash of Cornish cream. And then I remembered my next girlfriend, the one who got drunk, smoked weed and slept with a guy at a rock concert. And the one I lived in a bed-sit with, who told me the guy she was going out with was on the same college course as her and that they were 'just good friends'.

A branch snapped back and a leaf smacked me in the face.

Suddenly I was aware of a pattern: a lack of pure love and a whole lot of shagging going on behind my back!

Ali turned again. 'Accept your difficulties, stop struggling and do what you must do,' he said.

His words stayed with me. I thought about them as we continued through the jungle in the late afternoon drowsiness. I related them to what I had been thinking about my past relationships. I did want that feeling of pure love back in my life, the one I had felt in school. It was the best feeling I could remember; it made me smile even now as I thought about it, it sent tingles and a rush of excitement down my spine.

I was never going to feel like that with Jodie.

The realisation came as such a shock that it sank like a

boulder inside me. I stopped walking and the guys behind me walked into me.

'We're here,' Ali said.

His map reading was perfect and we reached the trunk road in just under an hour. For the first time that day we ate: it may have only been dried biscuits, but I was so hungry they might as well have been steak and chips.

As we rested I used the time to get a better grasp of our circumstances. I was confident we could make Tugagat in the seven hours before dawn, but I wasn't confident we had shrugged the Jarawa off. Their ability to follow our scent sounded far-fetched to me, but without any evidence to the contrary I had to trust what my guide was telling me.

Our ultimate enemy was Koslov, and we still had no real idea about his strength on the islands. I also had to bear in mind that other gunrunners and smugglers could disrupt our mission if we crossed their path.

I knew in Doug I had a solid 2 I/C. Greg, despite his humorous moaning and groaning, was a tough soldier, while Macca, an unknown entity to me at the beginning of the mission, had impressed me with his handling of John Robert when he had tried to beat Kalid. Macca's one flaw was his ability to spout misinformation in a credible way. I had made the decision not to trust what he told me as early on as the plane from the UK to India.

Ali had dealt with the spirits in the hangar when I was at a loss what to do. He led us to the trunk road without a hitch. His local knowledge had proved invaluable, and though I was still annoyed about the radar and radio I knew that anger wouldn't serve any purpose.

The most worrying factor regarding personnel was the lack of support we were getting from the Indians. The two extra soldiers Ramjit had promised had turned out to be no more than a driver for the jeep and a communications guy to keep tabs on our movements from the base at the hangar. I was concerned that when we were ready to make our move on

Koslov we would be going in alone. I could only hope Ramjit's promise of support at six hours' notice turned out to be kosher.

We moved through the foliage, close to the road edge. At times I could see the road through the leaves, lit by the moon. The night sky was clear, not necessarily what you'd want in a covert operation, but at least we didn't have a full moon shining down on us. I rested Ali at the front of the line. Night movement required something different, and I knew that Spaghetti's ability to feel out disagreeable situations was far more finely tuned than the rest of ours. In the first two hours we travelled three clicks and in the third hour we rested and set up the Satcom.

My conversation with Ramjit was brief. The helicopters being loaned by the navy would arrive at Port St. Peter the following afternoon. We agreed an RV on the trunk road as this was the widest area of open space available. We agreed on a grid reference and a time for our extraction.

Next was the call to Hereford. Antenna was waiting. I told him our situation, including the heli crash, but excluded the ghost stories. 'Kremlin tells me that Kali Pani is now a strategic point for gunrunning and drug-smuggling. Always knew there was some trade, but the lines are now busy. Theory is that the trade increase is due to Koslov's connections through Asia.

'US intel advise Koslov has a base in Mayishmagar. Satellite pictures show an increase in shipping and storage facilities over the last six months. The Americans also decided to take a closer look. They flew recon over the island and sent in Secret Service agents. This confirmed arms caches, mostly AK-47's and some SAM launchers. Koslov is believed to have several bases on the island, but they did not investigate further. They say they passed their info to the Indian authorities eight weeks ago.'

'Funny no one's mentioned that to us since we've been here,' I said, building on the picture that the Indian military liaison couldn't be trusted.

We wrapped up the call, squared away the Satcom equipment and got moving again. Less than an hour passed before Spaghetti gave our signal for danger, three low whistles. He made a hand signal for me to move forward.

Crouching down, I waddled up to him. We perched on the edge of the jungle where it met the road. There was a noise in the distance, a low droning sound. 'Heading this way?' I asked him.

He nodded.

'What do you think it is?'

'Vehicle of some description,' he said.

'Just one?'

He nodded again.

'See any lights?'

He shook his head. 'Could be obscured by a bend in the road and tree coverage,' he suggested.

I disagreed. 'I would still expect to see a glow in the sky somewhere above the trees. The lack of light coming towards us suggests that this is not a bunch of lads on their way home from a club. It couldn't be Jarawa because they don't drive.'

I passed the info along the line.

From the noise I guessed that the oncoming vehicle was a jeep or a Land Rover, which meant five to seven blokes. We waited on the cusp of the jungle for almost five minutes as the engine whined closer.

The jungle noises evaporated.

The moon, though not full, illuminated the Road to Nowhere, and every eye in the unit focused on it. I released the safety of my M-16 with a soft double click and then heard the same noise travel alone the line of my unit.

I swallowed.

The engine revved as the driver changed down the gears and accelerated up the hill. And then I caught the reflection of the vehicle's metalwork in the moonlight. I had been right, it was a jeep, with an open top. I saw the driver and a front-seat passenger and then two others in the rear. I saw what looked like a weapon in the front passenger's lap. The guys in the rear had bags on their laps. It was impossible to see if they were armed.

I thought about what they might have in the bags and assumed it was probably a night run for food to a sympathetic grocer. Although it was most likely that they were transporting rice, bread and other food basics, I was conjuring up the smell and taste of sausage rolls, pizzas and pasty, and with my stomach running on empty I wished I was back home.

I could have taken the jeep out with the grenade launcher on my rifle, seized anyone who survived the blast for questioning, captured their weapons and kept the food. The initial excitement of a sighting always makes you consider the quick strike, but I had to think about the mission.

We were there to get Shreela out, not engage the enemy at will. Taking out the jeep would almost certainly prove detrimental; it would have consequences. If these were Koslov's men, and we took them out, their failure to return would ring alarm bells at their camp. The destroyed jeep and the burn-marks would be impossible to conceal properly, not to mention the blast and flames that could be heard and seen for miles. Another consideration was that if these men belonged to another band of troublemakers then we might just be giving ourselves another enemy we didn't need. We were lightly equipped too, out for a day of observation, not a gun battle. If we engaged them the battle could spiral and in no time at all we could find ourselves high-tailing it through the jungle without ammunition.

I waved at the guys to stand down and we let them pass. I stayed put in the foliage for a few minutes. I would have waited longer but Ali pointed out to me that I had a scorpion crawling around behind me. I flicked it away with the butt of my rifle.

'These smugglers and gunrunners, how many groups of them are there?' I asked.

He shrugged like he didn't know.

'Ali, I don't give a shit about the gun trade in general. All I want to do is hit the right operation. If I get it wrong I could have a whole band of ugly guys after me. All I'm trying to do is work out who those guys in the jeep were so I can consider them or ignore them. Were those men who passed gunrunners? And how many groups are there on this island?'

'Many groups,' he said. 'Most are from Thailand, some Sri Lanka and Indian.' He shook his head. 'I don't know them all. I just know there could be many.'

Doug was at my side, listening. I looked at him and said, 'We might have just had our first visual of Koslov's guys.' I turned away from Ali and lowered my voice. 'I'm thinking that we should concentrate our search in the north of the islands when we get the helis from the navy.' I told him about my conversation with Antenna, about the base at Mayishmigar and that the Indians knew about this and failed to mention it.

Doug made sure Ali was out of earshot. 'I don't trust him or Ramjit. The fact neither one mentioned Mayishmagar to us just makes me even more suspicious about them. We need to watch them closely,' he said.

THE JARAWA

'Right,' I said, as I concluded my briefing after our rest, *'we'll* use this LUP as a fall-back position if anything goes wrong. Otherwise we go out there, recce Tugagat until 17:00 then fall back here. Macca will be with me, Ali you will go with Doug and Spaghetti, but stay ten yards behind them. Any questions?'

There were none.

We left the LUP, an area no greater than eight feet by six, and headed to Tugagat. Doug, Spaghetti and Ali took the north side of the town, Macca and I worked the south. We stopped for a mouthful of water before we headed in closer. Macca said, 'You think we might end up in a gun battle with Koslov?'

'Highly probable,' I said.

He sighed and looked away.

'What's the problem, Macca?'

'I have a bairn on the way. The way I feel about enemy contact's changed.'

I looked at him and clapped him on the back. 'Keep your mind focused while you're out here and going home to see your kid won't be a problem.'

'It's not the bairn,' he said. 'It's the wife. She's gone back to her parents in Aberdeen to have the baby. I wanted to be with her.'

'And maybe you will be. Get this gig out the way and you never know, the timing might just work out.'

'I don't feel sure that'll happen. All day yesterday...even before the crash and in the jungle, and again this morning I've had this feeling...'

'Forget it, Macca. Put it out of your mind for a bit.'

He shook his head and bit his lip for a second. 'I don't want a gun battle. I just don't want one.'

'I prefer not to engage Koslov too. I have my own family, but if we have to do that then we will. It's part and parcel of our job.' I was telling him what he already knew, trying to remind him, trying to get him to pull himself together.

'I know,' he said. 'I've always been fine about all that, but something's changed in me over the last few days and I didn't see it coming.'

'Look, I can understand where you're at with your wife and kid and all that. We're in the same boat, but right now we have a job to do. We have to be professional here, put away our personal lives and do what we have to do, right?'

He nodded, 'That's fine. Fine. Yeah, fine, we'll just do that.'

I wasn't convinced. I could see he wasn't in the right frame of mind. I just hoped if it came to it that his training would pull him through.

The recce of Tugagat was a long day in the heat watching a shop, a petrol pump, a guest house and an array of grass huts. I watched kids kicking a punctured football, playing cricket with a flat tennis ball and as I looked at them I thought about the times I had played in the garden with Christian during the summer before I left for India, trying to teach him football and cricket, only instead of Liverpool and Man United, or Northants and Essex we played as Pan versus Hook, or Aladdin against Jafar, and usually we ended up rolling on the grass and tickling each other until his mother called out of the window to us to tell us that we might get grass stains.

Back at the LUP we had four hours to kill before the RV. We rested in shifts, two sleeping, three watching for Jarawa or Koslov. Bedding down on the hard earth, dead foliage and stones was not the most pleasant experience, but I was so exhausted that the discomfort really didn't last for long. I slipped into a heavy sleep—a sleep that I'm happy to say came without dreams!

When I woke I noticed how fidgety everyone was. It had

been a long hot day, with little food and drink and it was made all the more frustrating by the leeches, mosquitoes and flies that buzzed around our heads. It was during this time that I became aware that Spaghetti and Doug were covered in ticks as well as leeches. 'You too, mate,' Doug said, lifting up my shirt to check my back.

Ali said, 'They slip under your clothing. As they crawl up you they suck your blood.' He flicked a leech off the shoulder of my jacket with a stick as it arched its back to slither towards my neck.

Spaghetti twisted up his nose. 'Slippery buggers. What about these?' he said, pointing at something else that had attached itself to me.

'Tick,' Ali said.

'As in dog tick?'

'No, jungle tick.'

'What's the difference?'

He shrugged nonchalantly. 'Dog tick is for a dog...jungle tick for everything that passes.'

Macca said, 'Ticks...now they have backward-facing claws that dig into your skin.'

'And they fall off when they are full,' Ali said.

'Full of what?'

'Your blood.'

To stop them we tucked every item of clothing in tightly—trousers into socks, jacket into trousers. We did a body check on each other every ten minutes to make sure none of them were crawling anywhere they shouldn't be.

We were all scratching. It was very uncomfortable. We were just into the second hour when our discomfort spilled over. Spaghetti was the most irritable one amongst us. I had noticed earlier that the skin on his neck was raw and beginning to look very sore. Spaghetti's agitation hit its peak when Macca dozed off. Macca was snoring too loudly and Spaghetti shook him. In a whisper loud enough to carry to me, he said, 'Are you actually snoring or have a couple of pigs crawled up your arse?'

Even though his words lacked his usual humorous tone

Doug and I couldn't help a chuckle. Macca wasn't so amused. 'Fuck off, you stringy piece of pasta,' he bit back at him.

'Hit a touchy spot, did we? Christ, now I'm not sure if you've taken in a pig or a grizzly bear.'

They continued to take whispered digs at each other for the next few minutes until the pressure of being picked on by superior wit got to Macca. I saw his temper flare and got up just in time to get between him and Spaghetti and keep them at arm's length. Macca was determined to have the last word. 'One more comment from you, Spaghetti boy, and I'll make mincemeat out of you, you bastard.'

It was then that Doug lost control and laughed out loud, 'You think they have any Bolognaise sauce and Parmesan cheese in that store in Tugagat, Mike? We can rustle up a half-decent Italian.'

'And if you could just stop tossing all the spinach down your fat neck for five minutes, Mr Popeye, we could add a decent source of iron,' Spaghetti retorted.

'Come on, lads,' I said. 'Let's keep it down. We don't want to be found by the Jarawa.'

At 21:00 I set Doug and Macca to sterilizing our area, making sure there was no dropped kit, disturbed foliage or footprints behind us for anyone to know we had been there. Spaghetti and I recce'd the area for the RV with the helicopter, making a slow sweep of the area for several hundred metres on either side of the trunk road.

At 22:30 we heard the heli coming in. Doug stepped forward into the trunk road to give the signal. As we had never anticipated the crash landing it was fortunate that Doug had a torch in his Bergen, but out on the trunk road, with the noise of the helicopter, he would quite vulnerable, especially if the Jarawa showed up. With their arrows, he could be taken down before we knew it. I hoped the landing would be over quickly.

He had the torch on, giving the signal.

The helicopter came straight in. The noise overhead was thunderous as it dropped. The trees were taking a battering from the downwash of the blades, dead foliage was being thrown up all around us and my vision was narrowed to a squint.

I had estimated that a tight landing between the trees was possible, but now, as the big beast hung just over the treetops, the gap looked too small.

If the heli could not settle down we would need to be winched up: more precious moments of exposure, more time for the Jarawa to line up their poisoned arrows. More risk.

But it was more than that, more than just the Jarawa. Tugagat was close. The heli noise would carry to the town. It wasn't inconceivable that someone, perhaps someone on a gunrunner's payroll, would hear the noise and come and take a look. That could compromise the whole mission.

It seemed like several heart-stopping minutes before the heli eased down far enough for us to see that it was going to make it. As it came in the treetops were bending with the force of its blades, clearing the trees above me by no more than five or six feet. Suddenly it was down.

We waited for our signal to board. When a helicopter lands in the British services the loadmaster is in charge from the moment it touches down and we have to wait for him to ID us and then follow him one at a time and board. So when we saw the Indian loadie at the loading door, brightly lit up by a light shining through from the interior of the craft, we expected him to come to us, but he didn't; he just beckoned us forward without even bothering to check.

First up was Ali. He parted the trees and started across to the transport when I saw the loadie lurch forward, clutching his leg and hopping.

Ali was aboard.

But still the loadie was hopping around.

Doug had his head down and was going for the heli.

The loadie fell onto the deck.

Doug was home. For a second he and Ali seemed to scuffle with the injured loadie before dragging him inside the heli. As they moved him the moonlight light caught him and I could see something sticking out of his leg.

An arrow!

Shit, the Jarawa were around. Without another thought I slipped the M-16 off my shoulder and took the safety off as I looked wild-eyed into the darkness. By now Spaghetti had joined the men at the helicopter and Macca was following on.

I was the last man. I rose up, hoping I could make it without being hit by an arrow, but as I stood I was halted.

My heart stopped. My way forward was blocked.

Out on the road I heard the heli blades quicken and I knew the crew were preparing for take-off.

I had no way through to them.

I looked on in horror and at the same time as the increased downwash hit me so did the panic: if I didn't make it to the heli before take-off I was Jarawa food for sure.

Blocking my way was a dark figure that stood no more that four feet tall. At that precise second he might as well have been ten feet.

I gawped into his face, with its toothless mouth and hollow-eyed stare, and I swallowed hard on a parched throat, half-expecting a blow-dart in the back of my neck at any second.

Out on the road the heli blade rotation increased and I sensed I was about to be left behind.

Think! Think quickly! What do I do? Do I put a bullet in him and take a run for it? Surely the lads knew I was missing. Surely they would come and get me. Surely they would hold the pilot back.

Desperately trying to control my fear of being left behind I moved my hands slowly and gestured. 'Me...go...there...to helicopter...then me go in sky.' I bowed with my hands in a prayer position to humble myself before him and thanked God that Doug and the other guys had not returned fire—that would have sealed my fate for sure.

The load doors were closing. The heli was off the ground. The trap door was shutting on my life.

But at that moment, to my utter amazement, the little Jarawa stepped aside and let me go. I bowed, took one step forward and sprinted like never before.

Already the helicopter must have been two maybe three feet in the air. What was happening? Why weren't they waiting?

With downwash thwarting the momentum of my legs and forcing back every breath from my lungs I lunged forward. I hit the loading doors with everything I had and knocked the last drops of wind from my guts.

Sheltered from the rotor wind I gulped in short, sharp, frenzied breaths as the heli continued to rise. My legs were no longer on the ground, but dangling out of the doors, and looking down I saw we were already above the trees.

Two strong hands grabbed me, then another pair and suddenly I was being dragged in to safety.

Doug slapped me on the shoulder. I looked up at him and saw his grin. 'What took you so long, shit-legs?'

'Jarawa,' I said.

The Indian loadie, who was bleeding all over the deck, got my attention. 'Hit a vein,' Doug said, nodding down at him.

Ali was down at the loadie's side. 'He needs hospital, very, very quickly. He must have the antidote or he will die. He has only minutes.'

Doug headed through to the pilot and told him what we needed to do. We flew directly to the hospital. By the time the loadie reached the doctor's care he was already slipping in and out of consciousness. As we raised him onto the hospital stretcher a doctor was already preparing a hypodermic syringe loaded with the antidote.

We left him there, hoping he would be okay, and headed back to the helicopter. Doug said, 'You know, you had a lucky escape, Mike.'

'I did?'

'Yeah, look at your Bergen.'

I slipped it off my back and thanked my lucky stars. Stuck through the material was a Jarawa arrow.

Back at the airport in Port St Peter our hangar had begun to look like an ops centre. Ramjit had been busy. For the first time so far in the operation we actually looked something like a military outfit in theatre. Looking around I suddenly had a greater level of confidence: we had maps, we had radio, we had vehicles and most importantly we had three navy helicopters sitting outside on the tarmac.

Ramjit had been listening in on the radio and already knew we had come under fire from the Jarawa. He had contacted the hospital and been able to tell them about the arrow the loadie had taken. It was his action that bought the vital seconds that saved the loadie's life.

'What did you find in the north?' I asked Ramjit.

'Yet we find nothing.'

'Where have you looked?' I asked, moving to stand in front of the map.

'Today we have had much equipment coming and there has been so little time we could look.'

'Okay, so where did you look with the time you had?'

'Actually, we could look nowhere.'

I glared at him. 'You blew off an afternoon of searching to move equipment in.'

'I don't understand,' he said. 'What is blowing off?'

'You bloody well know what I mean.'

'Oh no, no, why for bloody bloody now?'

I felt he was playing me for an idiot. I lost my cool and had him against the door. 'Dawn tomorrow, those three helicopter had better be up in the sky searching for Shreela Robert or your arse will be nailed to the rotor and your limbs will be gesturing on the blades, do you understand why for bloody, bloody now?'

WHAT HAD WE DONE?

I gave the guys every moment of sleep possible. I knew the trek through the jungle had taken it out of them. In the morning they looked better, having drunk, eaten and slept. As for me, I had slept little.

The memory of the previous night in the hangar dogged me, and our lack of progress gave me something to occupy my mind with during the night hours. Standing by the map at 03:00 I marked the areas we had covered on our way to the RV at Tugagat.

While I was plotting on the map I recalled Spaghetti's flippant comment about the helicopter crash being close to Koslov's camp. Out in the jungle I had swept away any thoughts of coincidence simply because I didn't believe in that sort of thing, but as I studied the map I was subconsciously drawing a line from our crash site to Tugagat, from Tugagat along the trunk road to Mayishmagar and from Mayishmagar back to the crash site. Without realizing what I had actually done I had drawn a triangle in blue permanent ink right across Ramjit's map.

I stood back and looked at the triangle. It took me little more than a few seconds to rubbish the idea—in general my luck in life wasn't that good, things never fell into place that easily.

I thought about the Jarawa: Ali had mentioned in the helicopter that they 'never missed an opportunity', but climbing trees and firing arrows seemed to me to be pretty extreme behaviour. I recalled that when we flew over them I didn't feel they were frightened, but organised, and obviously pretty motivated to shoot us down.

In the morning Ali was sitting outside in the jeep, shirt off, enjoying the blazing early morning sunshine and sharpening a stick with a penknife. He grunted good morning.

'I've decided to send two of the helicopters into the north of the islands. I'm going to go off myself and survey a couple of islands near the coast. I want to check the surrounding islands in case Koslov is using one of them. What do you think?'

He looked up briefly, squinting against of the sun. 'Okay,' he said.

I watched him carving the stick for a few moments then asked another question. 'If you were Koslov, and you hit the end of the trunk road and then took a boat out to another island, which island would you set up camp on?'

He paused his carving. 'Haven Island.'

'Why?'

'Only the south-west third is civilized, the rest is wild. It is not so thick with trees. I think it would be a better place to camp.'

'Are there any tribes on that island?'

He examined the stick. 'Only Bengali settlers.'

I was about to head back into the hangar, but I stopped and turned back with one last question. 'Do the Jarawa always climb trees and fire arrows at you when you're guiding people over the island?'

He lifted his head and looked across the airport towards the jungle. 'For some time now, yes.'

Macca came towards us from the hangar; Doug and Spaghetti followed. Spaghetti complained of a headache and sickness as he scratched at his neck. I suspected he either had mild sunstroke or was very dehydrated.

Ali looked up. 'Your neck,' he said, pointing at Spaghetti. 'It is time to take a look at it.'

'It's itching like crabs this morning.'

Ali got out of the jeep and examined the lump. It had grown since the day before and it looked red, raw and nasty.

He touched it and Spaghetti winced. 'I think this is a spider for sure,' he said, prodding it a little more and looking in my direction. As casually as a car mechanic offering repairs, he said, 'I can cut it out for you, with no problems, in a couple of minutes.'

'Like hell you will!' Spaghetti said.

'The nest is getting established,' Ali said, ignoring him. 'I'd say a big spider laid many eggs under your skin. Come. It is only a very small cut that is needed.' He headed off towards the hangar.

Spaghetti stood staring at me.

'Come on,' I said, starting towards the hangar.

He stood his ground, shaking his head. 'You know, in some countries they have spiders that hide under toilet seats and bite your bollocks off while you take a shit.'

'Spaghetti, if a spider could survive the stink you make then it deserves whatever little goodies your scrawny bollocks have to offer. Now get your arse into the hangar and let's get the job done.'

We walked to the hangar in silence. Up ahead the flame of Ali's burner roared into action. Ali waved us over. 'I am really very good at this,' he said, puffing his chest out like a kid bragging he was the world champion of Scalextrics. He was now standing over the burner with his knife, turning the blade over in the glow. 'I will sterilize my knife and then you will be all right,' he called. 'Infection is not very usual when I inflict first aid.'

'Inflict?' Spaghetti swallowed.

'I'm sure he means administer.' I clapped him on the shoulder, turning away to laugh.

'Look,' Spaghetti said into my ear, 'I'm not sure I'm explaining myself very well –'

'What the hell is there to explain?'

I walked on, shaking my head, leading him closer to Ali. Turning back to him I said, 'What would you rather have, spiders nesting under your skin, growing into great big motherfuckers that chew through your eardrums and wander out of your gob while you're serving tea to your future mother-in-law? It's not polite, mate. It's a fucking conversation stopper, I can tell you. And women won't find it attractive.'

'I dunno,' Doug said, 'Spiderman's back in fashion again.'

'Yeah,' Macca said with a guffaw, 'some chicks are hot for that. I mean look at M.J...she was well up for it.'

'Fuck you,' Spaghetti snapped. 'Fuck all of you.'

Impervious to our taunting, Ali pulled the knife out from under the heat. 'I have done this operation before. I am really not very bad at it at all.'

Spaghetti frowned at me with the passion of a defiant kid. I nodded to Macca and Doug. They took hold of him and pulled him onto the side of a table. 'Don't you have anaesthetics or something?' Spaghetti said.

Ali shook his head. 'I am not a doctor and I do not have such drugs, but you are a tough British soldier and that is anaesthetic enough.'

'Surely I can just go to hospital and get this done properly?'

'I need you, Greg. I can't have you in a hospital. There's only four of us and anaesthetics can make you sluggish for days. I need you. It's tough. Sorry.'

Peering over the tip of the blade and wobbling his head, Ali said, 'In Kali Pani hospital, in this condition, you will wait days for treatment, but if my knife slips and all goes wrong...well, I just hope that I have made you bleed badly enough so that the doctors will treat you today.' He cleared his throat. 'I will operate now.'

Spaghetti turned his head away as Ali, with the precision of a surgeon, slit open the flesh on his neck. The incision was fine and took several seconds to bleed; Spaghetti wouldn't even have felt a thing for a few moments.

Blood oozed from the lip of the cut and trickled down his neck and over his shoulders. Ali looked at me and raised an eyebrow as though he was waiting for something that hadn't happened.

'What is it?' Spaghetti said.

With the edge of his blade Ali raised the fold of skin he had cut open. 'Looks like the Ganges,' he remarked as the rivers of blood flowed down Spaghetti's neck.

Doug laughed.

Spaghetti shot him a glance.

'Please be still,' Ali said, still holding the skin with the point of the blade.

At that moment several dozen tiny white objects scuttled from the wound.

'What's going on?' Spaghetti asked. 'It feels like furry legs going down my back.'

I wouldn't have said anything to him, but then again I didn't need to, because Macca was there. 'The spiders have been released and are running out of the wound with all your blood.'

Spaghetti was on his feet dancing about like a man possessed. 'What have you done? What have you done? What kind of fucking spiders are they?'

'Tarantulas,' Doug said, laughing hard.

'Get your arse back on the table. Let Ali get the rest of them before they stick their fangs in you,' I said, pulling him back down.

Doug started laughing. 'Pasta man, pasta man, does whatever a pasta can.'

'He could spin spaghetti webs,' Macca added.

Spaghetti was getting more and more worked up, so I told the lads to make breakfast while Ali finished off and I dressed the wound.

A while later we all sat for breakfast. Forcing himself to be cheerful and attempting to be conversational, Spaghetti said, 'I reckon I'm here because I upset the Sergeant Major.'

'How'd you do that?' Doug asked.

'I buggered his office. He had this tape of jungle music and kept playing it, over and over. I put mosquito netting up around his desk and played his music over the tanoy system. He went ape, threatening us all if someone didn't own up. Course I owned up to it and next thing I knew I was in Northolt waiting for you and watching the news about some poor kidnap victim in India and hell...here I am.' He stopped and laughed inwardly. 'You know, I only saw that story once. I watched TV for almost three hours while I was waiting for you and I never saw it again.'

'Macca and me were the same.'

Doug said, 'I was in the mess hall all morning with the TV news on. I never saw it at all.'

'Makes you wonder, doesn't it?' Spaghetti said.

'Wonder what?'

'Well, if it was blacked out...because the only other news stories that morning weren't that grabbing, some bollocks about a guy called Hamilton who made half a billion on the stock-market in one day, something about milk being cheaper at the supermarket than delivered to the doorstep and who's shagged who after the latest glitzy party in Hollywood. Not exactly gripping stuff when you consider that a rich and wealthy Anglo-Indian who is trying to save the planet has been grabbed by a notorious trouble maker and is being held captive on Shit Island during monsoon season.'

'I screwed up too,' Doug said. 'Me and the missus decided to part before I went on a tour. To make myself feel better I went straight out and nabbed the first girl who would have me, a Borneo prostitute, as it happened. One night after we'd done the whole Kama Sutra she asked me about my home life. I told her about the split with the wife. Anyway next time I saw her she told me she had fallen in love with me and, well...she was so hot in bed...'

'You mean her performance impaired your logical judgement,' Spaghetti said sincerely, 'Happens to me all the time. So, what happened next?'

'Next she tells me she's pregnant and I have to marry her and bring her back to England. I told her no way was that going to happen. It was then that she came down to the barracks with her old man. Both were shouting their mouths off at the stag. Next the Sergeant Major, had them dragged in to see him. That's when the shit really hit the fan. The SM listened to their story and sent them home in a chauffer-driven jeep. Next, he pulled me in and told me I was an idiot and if he ever had to put up with a gobby prossy and her pimp father again on my account I'd be on the next flight home.'

'So was that the end of it?'

'No. When the guys trained they used to jog into the village. For weeks afterwards they said they could hear her wailing and calling my name as they jogged by her home.'

'They were just taking the piss though, right?'

'That's the thing, couple of times the guys brought love letters back. Course, I got the piss ripped out of me mercilessly. Every day someone would start wailing or calling my name and shouting "Marry me". Luckily, I could see the funny side, well...at least for a while.'

'The lads can be cruel sometimes,' I said, without much sympathy.

'Don't I know it?

'So were you sent home?'

'I waited for all the piss-taking to die down. The letters stopped coming, so I began jogging into the village with the lads again. Second or third time I went she came out and started screaming and clawing at me and trying to rip me clothes off. You got to imagine the scene: there's me holding onto me shorts, her pawing at them and eight or ten guys trying to bend her fingers back and prise her off. Then we all fall on the floor, and they're still holding her down while I'm sprinting out of the village with me kecks torn to shit, a bare arse hanging out and the lads rolling around in the road, laughing their heads off like a pack of shagging hyenas.'

'I bet that was a right sight,' I said.

'Yeah, very bloody funny. You can imagine the laughter I mustered up when I heard her bloody father or pimp or whatever he was shrieking his bollocks off at our red-faced SM. I tell you, the guys who can out-shout a Sergeant Major are few and far between. I was out of there pronto—next flight home.'

'Was she really pregnant?' I asked.

'Course not. It was just a ploy to get me to marry her and bring her back to the UK.'

'Here,' Spaghetti said, 'I heard the CO got stuck into you about something else.'

Doug winced then stared at Spaghetti, like it was a closed subject.

'Come on,' Spaghetti pushed. 'We're all mates here. I told you my story, Macca's going next, aren't you?'

'Aye.'

'Go on.'

Doug sighed. 'The missus and me began seeing each other again.' He stopped like that was it, but Spaghetti pushed him for more. 'It was crap,' he continued. 'I stayed there for a few weeks then left. When I left the ex-wife she got hysterical. She was shouting and screaming at me in the street, begging me not to go, and as quick as I was shoving my stuff in the car she was pulling it out and taking it back in the house. In the end, in desperation, I pushed her away. She ended up on her arse in the road. A neighbour reported the incident to the police. Course you know the CO and the Chief Constable...thick as thieves. Anyway, obviously he knew what had happened in Borneo. He called me in and told in no uncertain terms to zip me pants up, sort my shit out or get RTU'd.'

We were all silent for a second then Spaghetti said, 'You're a knobhead, you know, Doug. If you had married that prossy and brought her home it would have been like printing money. I reckon that without reciprocal foreplay she could have banged them out at two an hour. Jesus, with a line of sex-hungry guys waiting for satisfaction and cash-in-hand payments, I reckon that next time you returned from a tour you could have been travelling home from Stirling Lines in a brand new Beemer with the soft top down.'

Doug sighed and raised his eyebrows.

I scraped up the remains of breakfast from my bowl. 'So I reckon we all ended up on this mission because we messed up in some way,' I said. 'I got drunk and failed to train, what did you do, Macca?'

He stared at me blankly and shook his head, 'Nothing,' he said.

Spaghetti laughed. 'I like you, Macca, but I get the impression you could fuck up with a nuclear weapon and not realise the harm you'd caused.'

I looked at Macca and couldn't disagree with Spaghetti. He was a harmless looking guy, an unusual characteristic for a soldier.

Doug said, 'What if you're right though? What if we are all here because we screwed up?'

'You think too much,' I said.

'But what if it was true?'

'It can't be.'

'Why not? It's a shit mission...why not send some trouble makers, some dispensable guys?'

'Doug, you're talking shit. You're starting to sound like Macca.'

'Oh well, in that case then I'll shut my mouth.'

Macca extended his middle finger.

◈

We flew out over Port St. Peter at a greater altitude than the previous day. The scene from a thousand feet was the kind you'd pick out in a postcard shop and send to your relatives back home to make them jealous of where you were. It was absolutely breathtaking, turquoise waters breaking onto white sandy beaches, flanked by the greenest palm trees.

Fifteen minutes out and I could see Haven Island on the horizon, a few minutes later I could see the coral reef that surrounded it. The pilot tapped me on the arm and pointed down; he was almost out of his seat, looking below. 'Dolphins,' he said through the headset.

He dropped our altitude a hundred feet or so to get a better look at them. Grey-backed, leaping out of the water, they were a wonderful sight to see. A few minutes later we swung into the south-western tip of the island and my attention was taken by the sight of people snorkelling in the sea.

'I thought these waters were full of sharks,' I said to the pilot.

'They are, but I am told the sharks stay away from Haven Island because of the dolphins. The dolphins hunt them in packs and kill them. Also, the dolphins come to swim with the divers. All are very friendly.'

Over land, and we saw people on bikes and then further along we saw a group riding elephants. The pilot laughed. 'First time I climbed an elephant I had no idea how to mount. I climbed up its bum and I found a foothold. It was only then that I lost my leg knee-deep in its arsehole.'

I cringed and turned back to look down from the helicopter window. I saw a boat docking and we hovered while the passengers disembarked. There was a mixture of dark and fair-skinned people getting off. From their luggage, including oxygen tanks and fins, I assumed they were day trippers there to see the coral and to swim with the dolphins.

'This is one of the few places on Kali Pani that is recommended to foreign visitors. Haven Island has no cannibal tribes and is very pretty. The Bengalis make them welcome and sell them trinkets. Australians come here mostly, some British, some Americans and rich Indians who can afford vacations.'

As we moved on I noticed the foliage cover was not as thick as it was on Kali Pani, and I began to feel that Koslov would never make a camp in such a place. An hour flying over the rest of the island confirmed my feelings were correct.

We headed back to Port St. Peter to refuel and I checked in with Macca. He had been out all morning and was just heading back out after refuelling. He hadn't seen a thing. I spoke to Doug and got a disappointing result from him too.

We were halfway through day six. Our only breakthrough had been seeing the jeep heading north on the main trunk road the night before, and even that was not a confirmed ID. I began to feel annoyed and wondered what I was doing wrong.

Suddenly my mind teemed with images again. I was lying on the floor of my lounge at home. I looked drunk. The image changed. Jodie...a man...Her lover. Christian pushed between them. He was saying something. 'Stop pretending things don't exist. Just because you can't see or hear or because you don't believe, it doesn't mean stuff's not there.'

Still in a reminiscing semi-trance I picked up the radio and spoke to Macca again. 'Where are you?' I asked.

'Just flown over our helicopter wreckage from yesterday,' he reported.

'Roger that, humour me, just follow the route we took out of the jungle, but around five clicks north.'

'Roger that. Any reason?'

'As they say in the police force, I have a hunch.'

I felt like an idiot, going on gut feeling: that was the kind of rubbish you got in cheesy TV detective stories or in real life when people who wanted to impress you said things like, 'I just knew that was going to happen.'

I had Port St Peter in visual. The streets were busy with people and cars and up ahead

I could see the airport runway. I breathed a deep, frustrated sigh and had just leaned my head back when the radio crackled and Macca came back. 'I've found something,' he said.

I almost dropped the handset. 'Roger that, confirm what you see.'

'There's movement, white bodies, looks like some sort of small structure has been built.'

Thirty minutes later we all stood outside the hangar. I held down the map over the jeep bonnet and Macca showed me where he had seen the camp.

'Did it look settled?' I asked.

'Hard to tell from five hundred feet with jungle coverage below.'

I turned to Ali. 'Tell me, do you know of any people who have a camp in this area?'

He shrugged, then said no.

I turned to Ramjit. 'I want a drop off for Doug and myself about five clicks south of here at 22:00 tonight.'

Ramjit turned away and lit a cigarette. 'Too noisy,' he said.

'They must have heard the helicopters today. More tonight and they will run away.'

'So what do you suggest?'

'Beach landing by boat, just here,' he said, pointing at an area around thirty clicks off our mark.

'No good. If we left now it would take us till first light to travel through the jungle. We don't have that much time, plus I really don't fancy another run in with the Jarawa. We need to get in close, do our job and get out.'

'But my way retains the element of surprise,' Ramjit persisted. 'Your move is too aggressive.'

'There's nothing aggressive in my move. I don't want to surprise anyone. We do this sort of thing often. I want it to happen.'

Ramjit held my stare then bowed his head. Stepping away, he said. 'Then I will arrange it for you.'

Ali held out his hand for me to shake. 'You are going to be in the Jarawa settlement again. Good luck, my friend. May the angels in heaven look down upon you and grant you life.'

KOSLOV

Koslov was an enigma who played cat and mouse almost perfectly and the fact that he was a former KGB General worried the West. While the Soviets claimed he had defected at the time the Berlin wall came down and the KGB underwent changes, US intelligence maintained he had departed with the Soviets' blessing.

He now shipped arms, an occupation not deemed as illegal, even when the arms were shipped to highly questionable buyers. And although Oleg Koslov appeared high on the CIA and British Intelligence Service most wanted lists it had nothing to do with him having any front line connection with terrorism. If he had committed some act of mass terror in the Western world, hijacked a plane, shot a politician, even blown up a car, then a case could have been built for pursuing him. But the fact was that he was a Soviet, former KGB and that his hands were only dirtied in Asia, where he was thought to have supported governments in tidy-up operations in return for a safe haven, made him difficult to touch.

But his organisation was expanding and what bothered the Americans and the British was the fact that every terrorist group or state needed a supplier if they were to advance their arsenal, and Koslov was fast cornering that market.

Though nothing had ever been viewed as concrete evidence, he was linked to rebels Iraq, Algeria and Palestine. It was thought that he had the respect of many Asian and Arab leaders, but probably not the trust of one of them. It was a curious quirk in the nature of what he did and who he worked for was that no one could trust anyone, especially if you were deemed an outsider.

But by far the greatest concern for the intelligence services was the fact that Koslov was believed to have been the KGB representative involved with the Russian chemical and biological warfare team. No one was too clear how deep the connection had really been. No one was too clear how deep the connection still was.

What was known was that what he had done in the Philippines was just a desperate attempt to raise funds after the Italian Secret Service pounced on twenty million pounds' worth of stock floating from Algeria to Syria. It was believed to have been a sample cache to sweeten a growing relationship with Syria, but the Italian's coup ensured that the Syrians never looked at Koslov again and had never allowed him passage through their territory since. Meanwhile, the Algerians were believed to have given him thirty days, notice to leave.

Although what happened with the Syrians and Algerians must have been a disappointment, Koslov's business grew and, following a Western 'after sales service' type of policy, he began making more money from the training camps he provided. This was the only solid evidence the Americans had obtained to date, when one of their Secret Service agents infiltrated Koslov's circle for a time. It was reported that that agent encountered quite a horrible end. He was compromised while on a routine drop to a dead letter box. He immediately contacted his superior, but before he could be extracted he was hacked up into small pieces, placed in a three by two box and couriered to the US Embassy in Australia.

Needless to say my greatest fear in going after Koslov was that I might get caught and end up suffering the same fate as the US agent.

Heading back into the jungle to watch Koslov was, in itself no more than a bread and butter surveillance mission for us, but I did have one major concern.

'Those Jarawa could seriously mess things up,' I said to Doug. 'They avoided us when we recce'd the landing zone, they probably followed us from the time we crashed and I don't see what we can do about them while we're watching Koslov.'

'You mean while we watch Koslov, the Jarawa watch us?'

'Yeah, and that would be okay if they were vegetarians.'

'We could take Macca or Spaghetti to watch our backs while we watch Koslov.'

I thought about it. 'I'm not convinced that would offer us any kind of reassurance. These little buggers just crept up on us at Tugagat. They could take out Spaghetti and Macca and we wouldn't know they had been there. We'll leave them behind, extra bodies just add more to the risk of compromise.'

During the afternoon Doug and I focussed on planning our recce. We marked the drop zone on the map. We marked Koslov's camp and a fall back RV in case we were compromised and lost each other.

Our experience of the Philippines had taught us that Koslov was organised. My assumption was that during the two years since my last contact with him he had expanded his organisation and improved the way he defended his camps. Another assumption was that whatever the structure of his camp, our target would be centrally located and therefore difficult to extract. And while getting in to her would be difficult, getting out with her was going to be even harder. I was also certain that some form of engagement with Koslov's men would take place and because of that a casualty or two had to be expected.

We packed our Bergens and belt kits with supplies for the next forty-eight hours: sweets, biscuits, water, spare magazines. Ramjit was to arrange support troops who we would RV with and pick up fresh supplies for the next two days. We would then proceed to the target area, complete a final recce then make a move for Shreela. How we attacked the camp couldn't be decided yet—we needed to look at its structure, how they worked their stag, the number of men and weapons.

I gave Spaghetti instructions to speak to Hereford. I told him to report that we had an unconfirmed ID on Koslov and that we were moving up to recce the target area.

During the rest of the day I ate plenty of fresh food, especially mangoes' as there seemed to be such a massive supply of them. I was used to cutting off the skin and then eating it to the bone, but Ali showed me a new way, opening one end and sucking out the juice from under the skin.

Having hardly slept in three nights and aware that I was going to be awake through this one, I slept until an hour before the off. As the clock ticked down, Doug and I ran through our plan once more. When we had finished we chatted over a brew.

'Have you been thinking about home much?' he asked.

'Couple of times. When you're being stalked by a cannibal tribe or being scared out of your wits by your dreams thoughts of my home-life seem almost comforting.' I told Doug what Jodie had said about wanting to make another go of it when I got back. 'I was just getting used to the idea of moving back into the Barracks then she goes and says that.'

'Did you give her an answer?'

'I said yes.' He was staring at me. 'You think I'm a wrong?'

He shook his head. 'It's not my life, how can I judge what's best for you?'

'That's the hard thing—I'd really love to spend the rest of my life with my son's mother and see him grow up and have a happy family, but...' My words tailed off.

'Do you feel like your heart's not in it or like you're going against the grain?'

'Yeah, I do.'

'I noticed something during my separation—when you go against the grain you really notice when things feel bad. I find shit happens less often now if I feel the rub of the grain.'

'What would you do if you were me?' I asked him.

'Years ago I'd probably have gone back and tried at the relationship, but now...with a divorce and the deal in Borneo under my belt...I'd say just check the rub of the grain.'

Outside, the rotors of the helicopter started to turn. Normally pre-flight checks took around twenty minutes, so I felt no compulsion to rush out and get a numb arse aboard the heli. I sipped my tea. 'When I think of life with Jodie I feel like all my strength just drains away,' I said.

He laughed. 'Jesus I can relate to that. Every day when we finished at the barracks and I headed home, I felt exactly the same thing. I just turned into my street and suddenly I felt flat.'

'Really?'

'Yeah. In fact thinking about it, even when I was in Borneo and I jogged up to that prossy place my energy drained, then suddenly when I had passed it all came surging back. You know, I hadn't given that a thought until now. I'll watch out for that in the future.'

Doug got up and slapped me on the shoulder, 'I think you'll know what to do when you get home.'

'I think I already know what to do—it's actually doing it that's the problem.'

'Perhaps that's because the time hasn't arrived for you to leave yet,' he said.

I got on with smoothing my face in Camouflage Cream and a dose of mosquito repellent for good measure: we'd both been bitten to hell the previous day.

The pilots had been briefed and already knew our drop zone and by the time we headed over to them they were ready to take us straight up.

As we got closer to the drop zone I pushed all thoughts of home and a Jarawa compromise out of my mind. It was a critical time, and for the next twenty-four hours I had to remain totally focused.

Because of the terrain the heli was not able to place us on the ground. It was going to hover just above the top of the tree-line and we were going to exit by fast rope, through the treetops.

In the dark, with trees close together and thick foliage to contend with, it wasn't going to be a quiet or painless drop down to the jungle floor, but whatever happened it needed to be quick—we were only going to be five clicks away from Koslov and we already knew that the Jarawa frequented the area. A helicopter hovering was sure to arouse unwanted suspicion.

The loadie signalled for us to be ready. I gave Doug the 'OK' signal and he returned it. I got to the fast rope and took hold of it in both hands with the rest of it dangling around my boot. A minute later the loadie gave us the green light.

Out went the rope and me with it. My eyes were unaccustomed to the darkness and my vision was initially restricted to a distance about the length of my body.

I slipped down the rope. Crash! I hit the roof of the trees, leaves and small branches breaking underneath me. Snap! A branch broke below my feet. My face got whipped by the leaves and twigs. Crack! Bigger branches. I kept my legs together; no way was I crushing my nuts on a fat horizontal branch. My feet hit something solid. Another branch. I pushed myself away and continued the descent. Thud. I hit the ground.

I released the rope, slipped my night-vision goggles on and found Doug less than six feet away. The whole drop had taken less then twenty seconds and already our ropes were slipping back through the trees and the heli was moving on.

We got the compass and map out as the heli thudded into the distance and the night time noises returned to the jungle. Even with all the insect sounds, the place seemed creepier without the rest of the guys there for company.

We began heading north. The moonlight cast ghost-like shadows everywhere and the still trees watched us with suspicion.

When we crash-landed a couple of days earlier we had headed through the jungle as quickly as we could, but we had also been careful not to leave obvious signs of our passage. Now that we knew we were within striking distance of Koslov it meant we had to take extra care. We moved forward cautiously now, replacing foliage as we passed.

The going was slow. Painfully slow. We stopped to check our bearing regularly because with such thick jungle coverage we could easily walk within a metre of Koslov's camp and miss it. I had to remain sharp; concentration was vital. I kept running words through my head to stay focused: vigilance, care, focus, but all the time I was on the look-out for little dark faces in the darkness, wondering if the Jarawa knew we were back, wondering if they were watching us, following us, waiting to pounce on us, fire a poisoned dart or an arrow.

After two hours my thoughts started to waver and I started to think of Jodie. Could I really face going back to her? Was she serious about making a go of it with me? Could I ever be sure things would work out? Was my desire to see Christian grow up in a stable home ever going to happen?

As soon as I realized my focus was slipping I tapped Doug on the shoulder and told him I needed a break. We drank, not too much as once we got to the target we didn't want to be bursting to urinate. There was nowhere to sit and with scorpions scuttling around we set off again pretty quickly. This time I led, hoping it might help me to concentrate better.

My plan had been to find Koslov's camp during the fourth hour, but well into the fifth hour we were still searching. 'Shit,' I said, as we came to a small clearing with a steep bank. 'That must be a good thirty feet down.'

Doug peered over my shoulder. Down in the valley we could see the silver shimmer of the moon reflecting off the water. 'My guess is that fills up during the monsoon season,' Doug said. 'The curvature of the banks shows erosion.'

I looked to my left, following the stream. Not too far in the distance was the dark shadow of a mountain. 'I bet it feeds from there,' I said. 'The bank slopes away more naturally down there. That's where we'll cross.'

We negotiated the downward slope in the moonlight, but at the bottom something caught between a couple of stones in the stream grabbed my attention. I tapped Doug on the arm. 'Hold on,' I said. As I stepped across to retrieve it I was thinking to myself, paper in the jungle, that's weird. I picked it out and shook it, then carefully unfolded it. 'Oh my God!' I said.

I showed Doug. 'I buried this picture under a stone when the heli crashed.'

He shrugged. 'Maybe the Jarawa found it.'

We began up the other side of the river basin. It was thigh-knackeringly steep and both of us were grabbing at grass and tree roots to haul ourselves up.

Dawn was just breaking when we moved on again and in less than five minutes I almost stumbled right out of the trees and into a clearing.

I stopped dead in my tracks. I couldn't believe I had just set foot in their camp before I even realized it was there. I withdrew slowly and dropped to my haunches. I gestured to Doug, telling him to back up and go five paces to my right.

I dropped down on my belly. I closed my eyes and took a deep breath, relieved that I had just stepped into the enemy camp and lived to tell the tale.

Wriggling forward I peered out from underneath the foliage. There was a tree to my left that obscured everything on that side of my vision, though it was a little more open on my right. I could see for about ten yards.

The primary objective of the recce was to spot Shreela Robert and her location within the compound. Our secondary objective was to see how many men Koslov had, the structure of his camp and the kind of weapons he had at his disposal.

They didn't appear to have a stag, but I knew there would be one somewhere in the camp; no way on earth was anyone going to make a camp in this location and not put someone on watch, even if it was just to keep an eye out for the scorpions.

As I tuned in to my surroundings the jungle noises seemed to escalate and then the birds kicked off their dawn chorus, but it was a noise in the scrub that concerned me.

Somewhere behind me I could hear something working its way through the undergrowth. I knew it couldn't have been Jarawa or human in any way as it was too small and couldn't have cared less about how much noise it was making. Whatever it was I hoped it would go away.

In the camp I could hear someone breathing, heavy breathing with the occasional snore. I also thought I saw a movement.

'Taking a piss?' someone said. The voice came from the

other side of the tree. It was heavily accented. It could have been Russian, Polish, Yugoslav any one of those former Iron Curtain countries.

The noise in the undergrowth was closer now, about level with my left hip.

'Yeah,' came the reply, grunted, as though he had just woken up. The person on the move coughed, clearing his throat.

The scratching in the undergrowth had stopped, but now something was climbing my leg, crawling upwards. I took a deep breath and braced myself. A snake? A scorpion? A spider? Or some other deadly beast I hadn't been warned about?

In front of me, boots came in my direction. My rifle was at my side. I eased it over, ready to use.

I still had no idea what was crawling up the back of my legs, but whatever it was it had got to the top and was now negotiating its way up the cheeks of my arse.

The boots stopped less than three feet away and for one horrible moment I thought I had been spotted.

Suddenly everything became even worse.

'Time you took over,' the voice behind the tree said.

'Let me piss first,' the guy in front of me said. He unzipped his fly and I braced myself.

He was about to piss on my head!

On my arse was a scorpion. I could feel its legs pinching my flesh as it stood on me.

Even though dawn was just breaking and it was still cold I could feel beads of sweat gathering and running on my brow. I held my breath, screwed my eyelids tight and bit my lip as I resisted the urge to move and knock the little creature away. 'Sod off! Sod Off!' I repeated over and over in my mind.

The voice of the guy in front of me moved away as he turned and continued his conversation with the guy behind the tree. He turned back in my direction to finish urinating, but thankfully the pressure in his little jet had passed its peak and the last few spurts fell short of me and evaporated into the scrub. He zipped up his fly and cleared his throat again, only this time he spat it out. I heard it splat on a leaf somewhere up above.

I had no option but to wait it out: the sun was coming up and soon the little bugger perched on my arse would scuttle away under some rock and hide for the day. I just hoped it wasn't going to choose me as its rock.

I felt a drip on my head and just as I looked up to see what it was, I caught the rest of the gunrunner's phlegm full in the face.

The scorpion sat on me for a good five minutes and then disappeared back into the undergrowth; by then the phlegm had slid down my cheek and been absorbed by my skin.

We stayed in position for about two hours before we saw any other movement. Gradually the camp came alive. There were voices, but I couldn't make out what they were saying. I tuned in to their accents, trying to work out how many different ones there were. There were three clear ones, the Iron Curtain one I mentioned, an Oriental-sounding one and an American.

With the sun up the heat rose sharply and the patch of piss in front of me began to dry out and stink. When I could take no more of it I withdrew; backing up two or three metres. I found Doug and signalled to him that I was circling and he signalled back that he would follow. We both moved in a clockwise direction and remained close.

It took me until around mid-morning to get a good view of the goings on. I was at twelve o'clock to the camp, looking directly down it. It was apparent that in order to make themselves at home the occupants had blown away several trees, probably using plastic explosives, to make a clearing. They had done this carefully so as to retain coverage above them and then used camouflaged netting to make them difficult to spot from the air. But for Macca's sharp eyes the plan would have worked.

The trees remaining in the camp had made it difficult for me to see everything earlier, but the position I was now in allowed me to see an area where most of the gunrunners were congregating. I counted nine of them and I saw eight of them had AK47s.

The heat continued to rise. A faint breeze rustled the trees. The insect noises rose. By midday, having moved three times, I had still not caught sight of Shreela—that happened in the late afternoon when I had moved again. She was being held towards the centre of the camp and was chained up in a hole in the ground. I could just see the top of her head and assumed she was sitting down.

The sun was setting when a man taller than the others entered the centre of the camp. It was the first time I had seen him. He strolled through the camp with a purpose. I knew it was Koslov. He stopped to kick one of his men in the stomach. 'Get up, you slob,' he said.

He visited Shreela. I was too far away to hear the conversation, but I could tell it hadn't gone his way. When Shreela's food was brought out to her Koslov took the plate and tipped it in the dirt. He stood on it, grinding his toe on it like it was a cigarette butt.

When Koslov left her alone she stood up and took up some scraps of the food, cleaning off all the dirt she could before she ate.

Macca had been right: her lips hadn't changed. Neither had her almond-shaped eyes, or her forehead. Her hair was long, dishevelled and filthy from days on end sitting in the dirt.

By now I had become incredibly uncomfortable. My shirt was sticking to me, the undergrowth was digging in, I was tired, hungry and my bladder was full. The last hour, as the camp turned in for the night, was very difficult to cope with. We backed away and continued backing away for another thirty minutes before we rested and emptied our bladders into a jerry can that Doug had packed. We used the can so as not to leave any traces of our presence.

'How many of them did you count?' I asked Doug.

'Eleven.'

'I saw eight AK-47s, you?'

'The same. They also had a rocket launcher.'

I must have missed that.

'What about the girl?'

'Well chained up, if we can get the chains off we can get her out, no trouble. It's a ten metre dash for tree coverage from where she is. Did you notice the cam netting up above?

'Yeah, I did. It just means we can't drop in from above. We'll have to have sufficient numbers to surround the camp. We'll have to go in at night, get Shreela unchained and then let them have the good news.'

DOUBLE-CROSSED

Ramjit reported that twenty-five Indian troops plus Spaghetti and Macca would be flown in the following evening at 23:00, to a grid reference fifteen miles north of Tugagat, along the Road to Nowhere. He also told me his intention to move up the base at Port St. Peter airport to Haven Island. He justified it as a closer point for ferrying incoming troops and said it was nearer to our target area.

Doug and I packed away the radio and set off again. We knew our pace was going to be slow and that meant an immediate start if we were going to make the helicopter RV the following night.

I took another look at the map. 'We have twenty three clicks to make. We should make the most of the cool air now and rest in the main heat tomorrow. We'll reach the RV by tomorrow evening and that will give us a few more hours lying up before the drop.'

The prospect of meeting Jarawa was ever present and we did not let our guards down all day and night. By dawn the following morning my eyes were stinging, my body was knackered and my brain felt like it had been fried. Desperate for rest we put our Bergens on the floor and sat back to back.

It was another long day of fly-swiping, leech chucking and being eaten by determined ticks. We rested in the main heat then moved on, making the drop zone with time on our hands.

We recce'd the RV site, double-checking everything this

time, though with twenty-seven men coming, I had to hope that even if the Jarawa did attack again we would have more than enough fire power to cope with anything they could throw at us.

At just before 23:00 we were in position for the drop. At 23:15 I was getting fidgety. By 23:30 we were unpacking the radio in the back of Doug's Bergen. It took us twenty minutes to assemble.

'Romeo, this is Echo, we're at the RV. Site is secure, what is delay?'

A few seconds elapsed before Ramjit came back. 'Echo, please, this is Romeo, we have technical hitch. RV is good at 00:30.'

'Roger that, 00:30.'

At 00:30 we heard the low drone of the heli approach. Doug headed out onto the trunk road and gave the signal to the lead helicopter. I say lead helicopter because I was expecting three.

'What the hell's going on?' I shouted in Doug's ear as the solitary heli descended.

'Perhaps the others are coming up as this one leaves.'

Spaghetti was at the load doors. Doug flashed his torch to him from the bush. Macca stepped onto the road followed by Ali and two others in combat outfits. I stepped out of the foliage and shouted in Spaghetti's ear, 'Are the others coming in tandem?'

'There are no others. These two guys and us...that's our lot.'

'I don't believe this shit,' I said. 'And why the hell are you so late?'

'Ramjit! He didn't really believe you could avoid the Jarawa. He said he wasn't going to compromise soldiers to an RV he believed you wouldn't make. He was surprised when you contacted him. I told him you'd be here. I said you'd be knackard but you'd be here. These guys he's sent are the Indian equivalent of army cadets.'

'Why doesn't that surprise me?'

'Further intel from the Kremlin last night, they say that Koslov is shipping weapons through terror networks. They believe his organisation may be growing rapidly. New orders are to use any opportunity to gain further intel.'

We moved out immediately, but broke after thirty minutes to set up the Satcom so I could give Ramjit a piece of my mind. 'Where are the twenty-five men you promised me?'

'They are not available.'

'You promised me men at six hours' notice.'

'I gave you men.'

'There's a bloody big difference between twenty-five and two.'

'Why for bloody, bloody? You tell me Koslov has but only nine men. You have seven and the element of surprise. We are close to war over Kashmir. Only today there have been developments.'

I didn't reply to Ramjit. I'd had enough of him. Whatever he said he obviously couldn't deliver, so I decided it was best just to shut him out and spare myself the bullshit.

With the Satcom packed away we got moving. We had approximately twenty clicks to make before we reached the target area. I knew Doug and I had clocked up around one click an hour. What I wanted to avoid was reaching the target area during the day. I decided we would move throughout the night and break for rest at mid-morning. At that time we would be approximately seven clicks short of the camp.

Ali made up the seventh man in the troop. I had not expected him to come up with the heli. He came to my side. 'I cannot believe they are sitting right in a Jarawa settlement and the Jarawa have not killed them yet.'

'Is it possible that they might have made friends?'

He shrugged. 'Several years ago, a Jarawa boy fell from a tree. He was taken to hospital and treated and then sent back to his people. Now, sometimes Jarawa come into Port St. Peter. They come for medical treatment, sometimes for food, but people are wary. Making friends with cannibals is not very easy at all, but this story I have told you shows it is possible.'

We broke for a rest at mid-morning, after an uncomfortable ten hours of sitting and scratching and grabbing for weapons at the sound of the slightest rustle in the foliage. Two hours before sunset we moved on again. The aim now was to be within half a click of Koslov's camp by midnight. There we would establish a final LUP. Next Doug, Macca, Spaghetti and myself would go forward for the CTR, Close Target Recon, the final recce before our assault.

After the CTR we would then fall back to the final LUP. If everything was okay, we would get into our positions under the cacophony of the dawn chorus. From there, Spaghetti would extract Shreela from the camp while we lay in wait, ready to lay down covering fire if necessary. Once our objective was complete it was then down to the Indians to do what they liked with the rest. I certainly had no intention of compromising my unit of four for a task our allies were supposed to be taking care of and failing to deal with, but then perhaps that was their plan all along.

We were in place for the CTR just before 01:00. As I looked into the camp I saw no stag, no movement. I listened hard: no snoring, no heavy breathing. Nothing. After an hour we backed away about fifty feet. Everyone agreed the camp was empty. We headed back to the others and then moved everyone up before we moved in.

As night merged with day I inched into the camp, staying low. I headed in from the direction I had began my original recce in, from behind the tree, figuring it would offer me cover if we had in any way got the state of play wrong in the camp.

Looking into the camp now I could see half-eaten food on big green leaves, which I assumed had been used as plates. It gave me the impression that they had left in a hurry.

As I stepped forward I noticed the earth had been disturbed.

I froze.

I clamped my eyes shut, felt a chill run up and down my spine and tried to control my breathing.

In front of me I could see some other disturbances in the

earth, but that didn't mean that was all there was. Looking behind me I tried to work out to the millimetre where I had placed my feet as I had stepped into the camp and biting my lip I pirouetted and tiptoed out of there with the grace of a ballerina.

'Pressure mines,' I said. 'They booby-trapped the place before they left.'

We made a situation report to Ramjit, who said he was flying out to join us. Very carefully we made sure a small area of the camp was clear of mines: clearing away anything from a pin with a bullet on top with foliage spread over it, to a heavy duty land-mine. Next we cleared the camouflage netting above the camp for Ramjit to make an easy landing by fast rope. While we waited for him to arrive we looked for any evidence that might have suggested the direction Koslov had left in, a leaf with the sole of a muddy boot imprinted on it, broken cobwebs, snapped branches. We found no clues.

While we waited for Ramjit I sat down with Doug and discussed things. 'We can see they left quickly. They were probably still eating when Koslov had them put the mines in place. Then they scarpered.'

'And if that's true, you have to ask why.'

'You thinking that they were tipped off?'

He nodded. 'And that leads me to the question, who?'

Four hours later Ramjit arrived. A good part of the day had already slipped away and I was unimpressed with the casualness with which Ramjit brushed aside my frustration at the time it had taken him. 'No point to get angry if you do not know where he is gone away to,' he squealed at me as I launched into him on his arrival.

It took me a while to regain my cool.

We decided to back out of the camp and settle down for the night, splitting the unit up into two teams of watchers, each taking four hours of watch: half of each team was to watch for scorpions and the other two to watch out for the Jarawa and our gunrunning, kidnapping friends.

It began to rain after midnight and it stopped just after

sunrise. I was watching the earth billowing steam like weed in a smoker's pipe when Ali came to me. 'It is Ramjit,' he said.

'What about him?' I asked.

He was frowning and solemn as he beckoned me forward. I rolled out of my hammock, grabbed my gun and followed him.

He led me across our camp to a tree a few feet away from everyone else. Ramjit was propped up against the trunk, a damp cigarette dangling from his mouth and flies swarming around him.

I moved in closer. The dry blood on his shirt cracked as I touched his shoulder and examined the arrow sticking through his neck. I swallowed hard. 'The Jarawa?'

Ali nodded. 'But you should know that Mr Ramjit asked me to lead some people into the jungle several months ago.'

'What exactly are you telling me, Ali?'

'I believe the people I led into the jungle are the people you are now looking for. The Jarawa do not like these people.'

'And you know this because?'

'These people, white men, tried to make friends with the Jarawa. When it didn't go their way they shot some of them.'

I thought for a second. 'Ali, if the Jarawa recognise Ramjit and know he was involved with these other white men, then might the Jarawa believe that through Ramjit we are all connected?'

He thought about that one as it started to spot with rain again. 'Yes,' he said with a little more humility than usual. 'It is very possible that the Jarawa could believe we are all connected.'

BLOODBATH AT THE RAVINE

I woke the rest of the unit and brought them to where Ramjit sat with the arrow through him. I told them everything Ali had told me. Doug looked around us as though he felt someone close by watching us. Macca bent down and felt Ramjit's forehead and his wrist, like he was looking for a pulse. 'Judging by the heat of his body I'd say he was killed about three hours ago,' he said.

'And you can tell that irrespective of all the rain and temperature fluctuation,' Spaghetti said. 'Amazing.'

'It's body heat, not outside temperature,' Macca said.

'Oh, well, at least if it was a few hours ago we don't have to worry about them coming after us. They enforced their law and pissed off.'

'Enforced their law? What are you mumbling about?' Macca said.

'Obviously, according to jungle law smoking is not permitted and punishable by death. It's a very stiff anti-smoking campaign, but it certainly cuts down the burden on the health service resources and deters those too weak-willed or selfish to give up for any other reason. It hurts, but it works,' he said, grinning at his attempt at a catchphrase.

'Tosser,' Macca said, under his breath as he turned away.

The rain patted the foliage harder. Ali said, 'The seasons are changing. The monsoons are here.'

Doug was scanning the shrub around us. 'Stuff the weather,' he said, 'I want to know what you know about Koslov.'

Ali nodded. 'Koslov told Ramjit to make contact with the Jarawa. He tried several times, but was met by arrows every time. Koslov got impatient and decided it was a waste of time being friends with the tribe. He ordered his men to open fire on the Jarawa and drive them back. They not only attacked the Jarawa from the ground but from the air, from the same helicopter we used.'

Doug frowned at Ramjit and said, 'Now Ramjit's dead what can you tell us about his business?'

'Nothing,' Ali shrugged, 'I have told you everything.'

Without any rush or stress Doug reached over to Ali and grabbed him by the throat. 'Our lives are on the line here, Ali. The Jarawa might be back for us later. We trusted you. It's time for you to come clean.'

I slipped the safety off my gun.

'Okay. I will tell you about Koslov.'

Doug released him a little and I replaced the safety.

'Once there were many gunrunners and smugglers all working independently through Kali Pani, now Koslov owns the trade. He is developing Mayishmagar in north Kali Pani as his base, though he also uses Port St Peter and other places on other islands. It is known that the Indian government want to develop the islands, make them a tourist attraction. Only the Jarawa and the Coralenese tribes stand in their way of doing this. Recently they sent missionaries into the jungle.'

'Shreela Robert?' I said.

'Yes; she made friends with the Jarawa and for some time a kind of peace existed. Then the deforestation grew as the government found ways to make money from the islands. Next they bombed Coral Island killing hundreds of the Coralenese tribe. Then Koslov began killing the Jarawa. Miss Robert then withdrew her help and the Jarawa began attacking Koslov's camps. I understand that it has now been agreed that the Indian government will turn a blind eye to Koslov's business if he can dispose of the tribes. It seems that everyone in civilisation wins if this happens. Shreela Robert decided to stand up for the Jarawa. She met Koslov. She tried to appeal to him to stop the killing then she left the islands.'

'I don't get it,' Doug said, 'why doesn't Koslov just leave and find somewhere with less hassle?'

'It is the location,' Ali said. 'With rebels in many Asian countries he has demand all around him and a good shipping route from suppliers.'

'Do you know what kind of equipment Koslov has?'

'He is an arms dealer who works with the knowledge of the Indian government. I imagine he has whatever equipment he wants.'

'Don't fuck around. What equipment? What transport? What boats? Helicopters? Vehicles?'

'Yes, he has all of these.'

'Where?'

'He has big boats and motor boats in Port St. Peter and other boats at Mayishmagar.'

'Was Ramjit telling Koslov what we were doing here?'

He shrugged. 'I think he told him his camp was being watched and to move.'

I stared at Doug. He stared at me. 'We need to get out of here,' I said.

He nodded.

I nudged Ramjit's corpse with my toe. 'We're not going to bother burying him,' I said, 'the Jarawa can eat that pile of shit if they want to.'

'The Indians may not like that,' Doug said. 'We don't want them resenting us.'

I shrugged. 'Okay, if they want to bury him they can, but I want us ready to leave here in fifteen minutes. I suspect Koslov's departure from his camp yesterday had something to do with a message from Ramjit and I don't want to get caught hanging around here.'

We left it at that. I moved away from Ramjit's body; there were too many flies hanging around it now and I was getting fed up with swiping them away from my face. I asked Doug to wake the Indians and sort out the corpse and I headed back to my sodden sleeping area with the idea of re-evaluating our situation.

Rain tapped the leaves with the regularity of a metronome and puddles formed streams in the mud with dead foliage making dams. All around me steam rose, from the earth, from the trees and from my clothes.

The fact that I'd distrusted Ramjit from the start didn't make me feel any better about being conned by him. I also now believed Manisha Robert's theory that her daughter had been abducted to keep her quiet, but still I couldn't understand why they hadn't just done away with her.

Question after question poured like the rain: why had the Jarawa just taken Ramjit out? Why not Ali as well? Why not all of us? Were the cannibals keeping the rest of the meat fresh by taking us down one at a time? But there was the mystery: they hadn't devoured Ramjit's corpse, they had just left him pinned to the tree and that made me curious—surely cannibals didn't kill people to show how artful they could be with arrows, and they certainly weren't renowned for leaving their kill.

Answerless, I wiped the rain away from my eyes and ran my fingers through my sopping hair. The guys were moving in the camp; packing away gear. I began to do the same. My movements were slow as I continued to mull over the puzzle of Ramjit's death. Perhaps they were warning us to get out of the jungle, I thought, but I laughed at the irony that a cannibal would even know how to hint. It was just too subtle...too out of place for a primitive tribe who were threatened by civilisation.

And the questions continued to come: what the fuck were we doing getting involved in this problem? Why had the Indians asked us to help? Why did they keep letting us down? Why had the story of Shreela's abduction disappeared from the news headlines that morning when Antenna's call came in? Ramjit had been bought by Koslov. Who else? The media? The whole of the Indian forces?

I had to face facts: it was possible that all our Indian military friends could have been bought by Koslov in the same way Ramjit had been. The CO should have listened to me when I told him Manisha's theory. Doug, Spaghetti, Macca and I were alone on this mission from this moment on.

How could I regain some control?

I thought about that for a few minutes. We would set up

the Satcom later in the day and call the CO. He would have to listen to me this time.

For now, I felt like we were sitting ducks and needed to get out.

A noise came from behind me.

Something snapping.

A branch or a twig.

I made a quick head count.

Seven. We were all present.

Then what was the noise?

I gave three light whistles and had everyone's attention. I pointed at Doug and Spaghetti and made a walking gesture with my fingers and pointed to the trees. I signalled to Macca. He would cover them with the GMPG, General Purpose Machine Gun.

I watched the guys go forward, keeping low, moving noiselessly, nosing the foliage in front of them with their M-16s.

I squatted down by my kit, ready to add the weight of my gun as the rain continued to fall. It clogged my ears and I blinked droplets from my sticky eyelashes and continued to stare out at Spaghetti and Doug.

But a sudden noise from the other side of the camp startled us all.

A shout.

The snap of a single gunshot.

I hit the deck with a splat.

More gunshots cracked around me.

Shit, what was happening? I crawled through a puddle to get up behind a tree.

'Contact front,' I shouted.

Instantaneously, bullets whizzed and popped overhead. I cupped my hands around my head and kept it down as the bark erupted and showered me with fresh mulch. When the fire stopped I moved my hands, raised my head and peered under the low stumps of a shrub.

Out front, one of the Indian soldiers ran to grab his gun,

but before he had even laid a finger on it he was hammered so excessively in the guts that a hole opened up that I could see through.

To his left, the other Indian soldier was crawling, trying to find a position, but as he moved he drew fire and I saw his body shuddering as repeated rounds pumped into him.

We had to thwart the momentum of their attack or it would all be over in seconds. One, two, three of them were now visible on the edge of our camp, one hiding in the V of a small tree, the other two close together, low and bathed in the dawn sunlight. Both were holding AK47s, a good three hundred rounds a minute weapon. Both were coming towards me.

I was sure that the two Indian soldiers had drawn fire from my left flank when they moved, so somewhere close by I had company, but now the thudding AK fire was mostly coming from my right. Certainly it was pinning down Spaghetti, and I was sure Doug was still close to his side.

With the proximity of the battle and the volley raining down I knew I couldn't go it alone with my M-16 on automatic. The GPMG was the gun I needed most now, a thousand rounds a minute. Macca had it. Where was he? Why wasn't he returning fire?

Two rounds snapped close by, single shots. The two Indian corpses had been slotted again, just for good measure. They were getting close now. Too close. I had to do something.

My hands shook as I slipped a flash-bang out of my Bergen: it's an SAS-designed bomb that emits a blinding flash and a hell of a bang. Its purpose is to disorientate and I laid it by my rifle and worked out which one of Koslov's bastards I was going to slot first while they worked out what was happening.

Bang! The flash-bang went off.

Crack, crack. I hit the first man direct in the forehead, firing in pairs as we had been trained.

The second dropped for cover, but I stitched him up the trunk before he hit the deck. Crack, crack. Crack, crack. Crack, crack. The others would be bewildered but would recover sufficiently in a few moments to find their friend's bodies and unless I moved they would be able to guess at my proximity.

'Break rear,' a voice called. It was Doug who, had found an avenue of escape.

I grabbed my Bergen. Crouching and moving as fast as I could I scooted through the foliage, trees, undergrowth and low branches. Ten or twelve yards to my right, but obscured from my vision by the trees, there were other shots cracking in the smog. They weren't coming in my direction. It could have been Popeye or Spaghetti or Macca; it really didn't matter who it was so long as they were there. I hit the deck, rolled into a new position and began offering covering fire.

Right away fire was returned; it cracked over my head, flicked up the dirt and burst into the trees. Abruptly it stopped.

In front of me, not far away, the GPMG had thundered into action. Then it stopped. Macca was on the move. Then he was down about a metre to my side. 'Just what I was feared of,' he said. 'Bastards,' he roared as he opened up on them with great big beautiful covering fire. Tree bark flew off, branches were torn to tatters.

Doug was moving with Spaghetti. I saw them heading away, but suddenly fire opened from the trees in between us in both directions. They had driven a wedge between our two groups of two. If I now shot and missed the enemy I could easily hit Doug or Spaghetti. Effectively, they had stopped us working together.

Macca swung around with the GPMG and fired into the trees on his left. 'Go,' he called to me and I assumed he had recognised that we needed to split up and cover fire for each other.

It was really hot now—close fire on three sides. It was then that Macca did something that I could not believe. He rose up with me and moved out with me, leaving us open to fire and without cover.

The largest of all of us and carrying the largest of our guns he made the easiest and most desirable target. They zeroed in on him and rounds whizzed and whooshed beyond me. I heard the slice of the bullet entering his flesh and saw his body slam backwards into a tree.

He roared with agony as he crumbled to the ground. I got to him in a second and already blood was trickling out of him. He looked at me, his eyes clouded with pain. 'My chest,' he said, raising an arm limply. The bullet had entered his ribs and gone upwards, exiting his body just above his shoulder-blades. I grabbed his hand and stuffed his thumb into the hole at the front. 'Kath, Kath, oh, hen,' he was crying. 'The bairn. The bairn.'

Rolling over and crawling forward I grabbed the GPMG, let it loose in a ten second burst in an arch and dumped it. Snatching my M-16 up again and seizing Macca around the ankles I hauled him along behind me like a broken wheelbarrow as I burst through small shrubs and dodged low branches.

For a few happy moments I dreamed I'd knocked them all out with the GPMG, but then the return fire started and the rounds whooshed and pinged around me. I hit the deck, rolled over and loosened some aimless and manic M-16 rounds towards them. Picking up Macca's legs again I was off through the undergrowth.

I knew they would get me. It was just a matter of time.

I knew there were too many of them. I didn't know how many, just too many.

I knew I was now alone. Spaghetti and Doug's fire had disappeared. They could have been down, dead or injured.

I knew I was going to die, but I was going to do it fighting.

They were swarming around me. I could hear them beating the foliage, coming after me.

And that was when I fell—tumbling down, side over side, head over heels.

I crashed into trees and mud banks and had the wind knocked out of me on every landing. I came to a stop, face down in fly-ridden water. I put my hands down and tried to touch the waterbed. My head went down and I took in a mouthful. As I choked, my feet found the bottom and I was up, trying not to cough up a lungful of filthy mosquito-flavoured water as I stood in the ravine Doug and I had stumbled on two nights earlier.

The water flow was stronger now: no longer a trickling little stream, it was just below my knees and belting past. Macca was twenty yards to my side, halfway up the bank, wrapped around a tree that was growing at a forty-five degree angle. I waded out of the stream towards him, keeping my strides even and slow so as not to make extra noise. I was on the muddy bank beneath him and about to start climbing when I heard voices from above. I got low and hugged the bottom of the bank.

I was now directly below Macca, though I still had the bank to negotiate before I could get to him. I peered up and saw how open he was lying up there. Surely they only had to look down to find him.

My breath came quickly, in short sharp bursts so intense I could feel my nostrils flaring. I panic-gulped, trying to control it, trying to control my arms, my legs, my whole body as it convulsed with fear.

I listened as the voices came closer. I listened as they headed away from me, moving further and further away, inch by inch, but never far enough. Those seconds felt like minutes, or were they minutes that felt like hours, or hours that felt like days...whatever they were they were painfully slow, drawn out, agonising.

But as I listened I heard the birds resume their chorus and almost laughed...would nothing keep them from their chirping?

Then a voice, broken English, coming from along the ridge. 'Let them go, we get lost in here,' it said.

They came back in my direction. I could hear them beating through the undergrowth, snapping on dead foliage.

They were going to find me.

They were going to kill me.

They were going to find Macca.

Two shots snapped above me. Tentatively I looked up from my hiding place. It was Macca firing with a handgun.

There was movement in the trees. Something was thrown at Macca.

Bang!

I was knocked off my feet as mud all around me exploded with such force that I thought I had been hit. And it felt like just a moment later when I realised I was lying on my back in total silence, my eyes caked in earth. I rolled over and tried to blink it away, relieved that I could move.

My first thought was Macca. I looked up the bank towards where I had last seen him. I saw the red. As I looked harder I saw his camouflage jacket wrapped around a branch and then I saw fragments of his body, torn into tatters and spread across the river bed.

And that was when I heard it—the squish of mud behind me and then the cold, cold metal on the back of my neck. I knew for certain now that my brains were about to be blown out.

❧

Light flickered like a strobe. I thought I was having another vision, but there were no pictures, only the flashing light.

Pain burned in my joints, under my arms, as though every muscle fibre had been torn beyond its elasticated limits. My wrists and ankles felt like they had been separated from the bones in my hands and feet and I dreaded what was waiting for me on the other side of sleep.

I opened my eyes. The sun blinked through the trees, blinding me at secondly intervals.

I shut my eyelids and scrunched them up and suddenly I was back at our camp. The compromise...the blood on the leaves...the bark flying off the trees...Macca being shot...My body turned cold. The red river bank...Macca's body parts strewn in the ravine. I adjusted to reality. A hard, cruel reality with Macca gone and my unit lost. I had not known Macca long, nor had I got to know him well, but his loss, like any loss in action, had a demoralising impact. He was a part of my unit, a part of our Regiment, a brother, a father-to-be, and a husband.

The gun on my neck...Darkness.

I was moving now—swaying from side to side and facing upwards.

I tried to move my arm, but it was held by something. I tried to move my other arm, my legs. They were held together, wrist to wrist, ankle to ankle.

I wriggled.

I opened one eye and peeked out. I was bound to a wooden stake and being carried through the jungle like a snared animal.

I closed my eyes again and resigned myself to my fate. I had been left by Koslov's men and collected by the Jarawa. I was on my way to their settlement to be cooked on a spit, carved up and eaten over the coming days.

My thoughts were random and I was back with Macca, then the scars his death would leave on his family and then I was thinking of my own family...my son.

Would I ever look into his brown eyes again, ruffle his hair? Would I ever wrap my arms around him, hug him again? Would I ever see him grow up and become whatever man he would become?

Deep, deep regrets grew inside me rapidly at the thought of leaving him without making the significant mark that a father should leave on a son's life. I had not been an inspirational figurehead, a great role model. I had not been all that I had promised myself I would be to my child. I felt my stomach begin to ache, my body convulse, my cheeks puff out and the tears begin to flow.

But almost immediately I got a grip. I was a soldier, not a blubbering baby. I had to pull myself together. I could not allow my heart to break, show weakness in the face of the men who were about to eat me. I sucked my heartache back within and cried no more.

It was then that anger rose up, rising up to boiling point. I had failed him, failed myself, failed to meet my own standards. Bitter with the path my life had taken, enraged with the choices I'd made, I bore down on my jaw. I had been cheated by life, I had been cheating myself. I was a cheat. A wimp. A man who stood for nothing, not even his own shadow.

At the realisation of my own true character my head fell back. I groaned in disgust at what I had been...at what I was.

And then I opened my eyes.

I blinked, astonished.

I had been wrong.

I was not being carried by the dark little Jarawa pigmies. I was being carried by white men, Koslov's men.

Fuck! That was worse. What could be worse than being devoured by a cannibal? Being chopped up and having your soggy remains lifted out of a box by some poor, unsuspecting bastard in the mail room of the British Embassy somewhere, that's what.

There were six behind me, seven in front, more than we had counted in the camp on the recce.

I considered my chances of escape and knew almost immediately that it wasn't going to happen. Doug, Spaghetti and Ali had got away. I hoped that they had radioed for help. More soldiers would come, they would find me. I would go home.

The trek seemed endless. The pain in my joints and limbs was agonising. My throat burned for water, my stomach ached for food and my skin crawled with devouring, bloodsucking ticks and leeches.

My head had flopped back and I was watching the green bushes rush by when I thought I saw something within them. For a second I thought my eyes were playing tricks on me. A leaf hit me on the nose and I blinked rapidly and tried to see into the trees. I was sure I had seen a pair of Jarawa peering out from behind the foliage.

I was elated. I wanted to punch the sky. Federal Express wouldn't be bumping me on and off their vans and lorries. The Jarawa would hit us all with poisoned arrows and my death was actually going to feel more like the pleasant, drifting effect of a sleeping pill than some agonising body-chopping.

Maybe they would attack and I would escape. I checked the bonds around my wrists and ankles. They were thick and strong and as it dawned on me that I would not be able to break free another thought occurred to me: if the Jarawa did attack and didn't hit me with an arrow I might get cooked or worse, eaten alive like that graphic portrayal in the encyclopaedia back at the Roberts' house.

Gritting my teeth and scrunching my face with the agony that burned in my limbs I gawked into the bushes. Come on, I willed the Jarawa to attack. Come on. I may have been a piece of meat on a stick, a Kali Pani Kebab, so to speak, but I wanted them to attack. Come on. Come on.

I blinked away leaf after leaf with blinding regularity. Attack the bastards. Attack. Come on. Adrenaline was surging through me. The pain vanished. I might even be strong enough to rip away the bindings myself. Come on. Attack. Come on.

But suddenly my enthusiasm jolted to an abrupt end as our column halted without warning.

The silence in the ranks screamed with fear. I could feel the attack waiting, hiding behind a leaf, concealed by the trunks, hanging from the branches. Excitement and fear crawled across my skin and tiptoed down my spine. Come on! Come on!

Short and bow-legged with bulging narrow eyes, slicked-back greasy hair and lip in spasm an Oriental man passed along the column. A cross between Elvis and frog, I thought. And I almost burst out into terrified hysterical laughter as I imagined him standing on a lily croaking the words, 'You ain't nothing but a Hound Frog.'

He pushed and bumped his way along the rank. I had seen him earlier at the camp recce, but as I looked at him now, up close, I knew that I had come across this man before. I had conversed with him. Where did I know him from? The surroundings were familiar. A jungle. But where? Why? Here? Was it another vision? A mind trick? Was I really going crackers?

Elvis raised his arm and signalled that I should be put down. As he moved his arm I caught a glimpse inside his jacket. Resting on top of a dirty white t-shirt was a gun in a shoulder holster. But before I could think anymore about it, and as I was lifted off the front bearer's shoulder I saw something else, something flying through the air.

The bearer's body jerked. Stiffened. And as he grabbed at his neck and let go of the pole, I fell, banging my arse on the hard jungle floor.

'I've been hit,' the bearer cried out in English. 'I've been hit.'

'Fire,' Elvis shouted.

I saw another man clutch at his shoulder and another at his neck and then machine-gun fire started ripping into the bushes from all around.

After a thirty-second burst the man who had passed along the column waved two men into the bush to make sure the Jarawa were dead. 'Keep you guns ready,' Elvis croaked in broken English.

The men returned no more than a minute later dragging two black, bloodstained corpes behind them.

'Tie them to tree and slit stomach open. I want lesson for little bastard's brother and sisters.'

I wanted to warn him not to mess with the Jarawa people, but I knew the effort would only land me a kick in the head, so I spared myself the pain. I hoped he was satisfied with what he had done and I hoped he had been watched by a little pigmy somewhere among the undergrowth who would go and tell his friends.

I was staring at the commander with hatred because what he had done lacked honour: as a soldier you kill, but you don't humiliate the corpse!

Elvis grabbed me by the chin. For a moment I thought he was going to bebop me, but he just shouted his spit in my face. 'What you problem?'

I held my tongue as well as his stare. If the Jarawa didn't get him I would. He was staring me in the face, squinting like he knew me but couldn't place me, and come to think of it was more than the way he looked, it was his voice and the surroundings and more real than a vision. I knew him. I damn well knew that I knew him. He let go of my face and made as if to walk away and then swung back quickly and kicked me in the stomach. I would have doubled up at that moment, but the way my body was tied up made it impossible. The winding was painful.

'You careful how look me next time,' he sprayed.

I'd learned my lesson the hard way: in my training, when you're taken hostage you're trained to be subservient. Hostage takers don't like hostages who antagonise them, you keep your head down and your eyes low, especially when you've just been captured—it's in the first minutes and hours after your capture that you're at the greatest risk, tension is high, nerves are raw and one look, one word might be all it takes for them to slot you.

The sun had fallen and it was much cooler by the time we stopped again. We had reached a camp. I tried to count the number of men, but before I could I was thrown to the floor with my face held in the dirt so forcefully that my nose and mouth were blocked. As my head was pulled up by the neck I gasped for breath as a blindfold was wrapped around my eyes. They checked the ties around my arms and legs then pulled me up into a kneeling position.

If they were going to shoot me they wouldn't have carried me through the jungle. But why the blindfold now? What was the big secret? I didn't get the chance to analyze it any further. I was kicked in the stomach again.

I collapsed and was hauled back upright, coughing from the winding and gasping for breath.

'Name?' a voice said. It was male. I couldn't place the accent.

'Michael Edwards,' I spluttered.

'Number?'

I gave it.

'Rank?'

I gave it.

'Date of birth?'

I gave it.

'What are you doing here, Michael?'

'Under the Geneva Convention, I can't answer that question.'

Another kick in the stomach. This time it was harder and not so accurate. It caught me on the bottom rib. I curled up again, sure the rib was broken. Again I was hauled back up.

'Sorry to teach you the hard way that I do not care for the Geneva Convention. Now tell me, what are you doing here, Michael?'

'I can't answer that question.'

Two kicks, one from either side. I was badly winded this time, coughing and wheezing.

'Come on, Michael, we are both professionals, so tell me what you are doing here?'

'I can't answer that question.'

I braced myself for the kicking, but it didn't come—well, at least not until I had relaxed slightly, then it came and it came, and it came. I was like the tennis ball at a kid's playtime where the tiny round ball was used as a footie and the unskilled youngsters booted seven bells of turd out of it. I took it in the arms, legs and stomach and then when my head went down I was kicked there too.

There was a pause as they got their breath back. I was hoisted back to my knees.

'You are English?'

I delayed, not sure if I wanted to answer, but the answer was obvious anyway. I was wearing British disruptive patterned combat gear and had just replied to each of his questions in English. 'Yes,' I said, hoping to avoid another kicking.

'Thank you, Michael. See, it is not so bad to cooperate. Now tell us, what are you doing here?'

'I can't answer that question.'

This time I was hit on the head from behind and I collapsed on the floor. I felt the blood trickling through my hair and at that moment I wanted to cry, I wanted to shout out, run away. But they hit me again and again and again.

'I have had enough for now,' the voice said, 'we will talk

again later, Michael. We have given you something to think about. Please try to cooperate later.'

I was dragged, still bound and blindfolded, across the dirt. I heard a dull clunk, metal on wood: a padlock? Then I heard a scraping sound, a wooden gate being opened. I was thrown to the ground. A male voice said something which I didn't understand and then I heard him leaving, the sound of wood on dry earth again, then the metal sound.

I exhaled and felt my pain. A voice said. 'Is someone there?' It was a woman, a soft voice with a light accent which I though at first might have been American.

I coughed. 'Yes,' I wheezed.

'Did you understand what they said to you?'

'No,' I replied in a great deal of pain.

'They said they are going to piss on you when they bury you alive tomorrow morning.'

THE VOICE THAT WOULDN'T SHUT UP

'My name is Shreela,' the woman said.

Gritting my teeth to bear the pain and digging my heels into the dirt I forced my battered body backwards across the ground. I wriggled and struggled until I felt something solid behind my back.

I slid my shoulders back and forth and up and down to try to establish what it was. Gradually I eased my weight onto it. I wriggled my fingers and felt what I believed to be wooden slats.

Out of breath, head pounding, congealed blood cracking on my chin and up my nose, I raised my knees up to my chest and planted my forehead on top of them.

'I see, so you don't want to talk,' Shreela garbled. 'That's okay, I understand. I've had no-one to talk to for days. It doesn't matter. I was just hoping...you know...that we could talk. But that's okay, no, really, no, it's okay.'

It was at this moment that my training on the theory of hostage situations kicked in: she hadn't spoken to anyone friendly for days...her moral was low. I had no idea how long they would keep us together; I needed to get her talking, start to pick her moral up, give her some hope. I also wanted to get as much information as I could from her about her and my surroundings.

'Sorry,' I managed.

There was a pause. I heard scuffing; she was shifting the way she was sitting. A sniff. 'Sorry...sorry what? Sorry you didn't introduce yourself, sorry you are so rude, sorry I've been feeling lonely, sorry I've been kidnapped, pushed around at gunpoint—

what? What exactly are you sorry about, Mr Whoever-you-are?'

I toyed with a sarcastic response, but didn't have the energy to voice it or deal with any backlash I might have encountered.

'Are you blindfolded?' I struggled.

There was a pause. More shifting. A sniff. Was she crying? 'No, no, Mr Whoever-you-are, if you can't tell me your name I will not answer your questions.'

I began to draw in a deep breath. The pain seared through my chest. I coughed. My stomach felt like it was ruptured. 'I am Michael,' I wheezed.

Another pause. 'Oh, I see, you tell me your name now only because you want to get some information from me. Well, that's not how it works.'

I exhaled and it hurt. I swallowed and that hurt too. I wondered if she was always like this or if this was just her strategy for coping under stress.

A pause, a shift, a sniff. Her voice mellowed, 'Do people call you Mike or Michael?' she said, almost sweetly.

'If I like them they call me Mike.'

'So should I call you Mike?'

'Let's start with Michael,' I said. 'You haven't told me if you are blindfolded.'

Another pause. I assumed she was thinking up another pugnacious comment. She must have failed, as eventually she just answered that she was.

'Tied up?' I asked.

A shorter pause. No sniff, just a shift. 'Yes, and you?'

'Yeah.'

'Do you know where we are?'

'I only know we're somewhere on North Kali Pani. They blindfolded me yesterday, I feel like we headed north, but I don't know...I know we didn't cross water.'

'What happened to you?'

'I was kidnapped from near my parents' home. What about you, where were you kidnapped from? What have you done to him? Why are you here?'

'I can't tell you,' I said.

A snide laugh, one of those 'I can't believe this guy's such a prick' kind of laughs. 'Is it really such a big secret?'

'I can't see you, and if I can't see you I don't know who you are, so I can't trust you.'

'I am Shreela Robert. I'm blindfolded, tied up and in the same prison pen as you. I think we can safely assume you can trust me.'

'Someone could be listening close by. If I can't see, I don't know. I don't trust.'

'Man, are you suspicious. Lighten up. You're not going anywhere, neither am I.'

I didn't reply and we had a few seconds of blissful silence. She started up again. 'So what are you doing here?'

I ignored her.

The strain was back in her voice now. 'You know what...I thought I'd be glad of some human company, but then they put you in here. Quite frankly, an elephant's arse has more personality appeal than you.' She raised her voice and shouted, 'Hello, guards! Anyone out there? Please come and take this idiot away.'

'For Christ's sake, woman, shut your trap before you get us both beaten to pulp.'

'Hello! Anyone?'

'Look, for your own safety I can't tell you who I am.'

'Oh, go to hell. There's a hundred different ways I could die in this jungle and I seriously doubt that knowing why you're here is one of them. I mean, how dumb do you sound? I'll tell you how dumb you sound...really dumb, bordering on the ridiculous, that's how dumb. In future there'll be dumb and then there'll be Michael dumb, a dumb beyond normal dumbness.'

Her voice tone changed and I knew she was now mocking me, 'Oh, my...hero...I can't tell you why I'm here...It's for your own safety. Dumb, dumb, dumb. I bet the next thing that will happen is they'll come along and take the blindfolds off and I'll see that instead of you being some pompous English idiot, you're actually a gorgeous hunk in a combat uniform come to save me from the evil dark lord. Let's burst into song—Bollywood saves the day!'

I was considering telling her how accurate part of her prediction was when I heard a chain rattle and wood scuff on the dirt.

Hands grabbed me and I was dragged away.

'Are you there? Hey, Englishman. You, I'm talking to you. Answer me when I'm talking to you? Hey...ignorant human!'

Her voice faded away as I was dragged from the pen, feet flailing behind, bouncing over stones. We came to a stop. I was dropped face-down from about three feet in the air. The bridge of my nose exploded.

I was grabbed again and forced to kneel, with my face throbbing. I felt the blood running down the inside of my nose. I wanted to wipe it, but couldn't. It ran over my lip, trickled into my mouth. I tried to blow it away. Then I heard the same slow, correct voice I had heard before. Round two was about to start.

A chill ran down my sore spine.

'Michael Edwards, how are you feeling?'

I was slow to answer. 'I ache.'

'Is it because we beat you?'

I winced as I nodded my head, slowly—it was heavy and sore.

'Sorry, I can't hear you,' the voice said.

'Yes,' I said, weakly.

'That's better.' A pause. 'Are you hungry, Michael?'

'Yeah, a little.'

'When did you last eat?'

My thoughts gathered slowly. 'I don't know. I can't remember.'

'If you did know, what would be your guess?'

'Yesterday. Last night.'

'Shall I see what I can do about some food for you?'

'Yes, thank you.'

'That is my pleasure, but before I sort out the food,

Michael, I want you to please recap for me what you were doing in this jungle.'

'I can't answer...'

The voice cut in. 'I'm sure you can't answer, but if you could, how would you answer?'

'I can't say.'

'I see.' I heard him sniff. 'Look, I can help you, get you food and water and perhaps I could even get your blindfold taken off, but I do need just a little help from you.'

He didn't ask a question so I didn't say anything. He sniffed again.

'We killed a few of your friends back there, well-armed men, trained soldiers from India v

Britain. Were you out there just looking for Jarawa?'

Had they killed Spaghetti or Doug as well as Macca...both of them? Was he bluffing?

I swallowed. 'I can't answer that question.'

'The Jarawa are very dangerous people, they fire poisonous darts. We have lost many men. You witnessed an attack from them on the way here. You were taking a risk being in the jungle—whatever you are doing here must have great importance.' Another pause. 'What were you looking for, Michael?'

'I can't answer that question.'

'If you could tell me, what would you say?'

I gave the stock reply.

'Were you looking for smugglers?'

He met the same stuck record.

A sniff. 'I have a photograph here. It fell out of your pocket earlier while you were lying on the ground after we beat you. It is a picture of your daughter, yes?'

I stayed silent, kicking myself for being so stupid—I should never have brought that picture along, you never did that, for this very reason. You bring personal items and the enemy get them and they get the upper hand. They use it to twist the knife.

'Michael, I would like to rest, it's very late. I'm tired, we are getting nowhere. Help me and I will help you. I am being nice to you. I can get you...' His voice trailed off. I heard whispered voices. They spoke for five seconds or a minute.

I smelled cigarette smoke. A new voice, deep-throated, and an air of arrogance. 'Do you smoke?'

'No.'

Silence. 'I've just heard all about you, Michael. I'm particularly curious about this photograph. Tell me about this person. They must be close to you if you carry this with you.'

I didn't speak. I guessed this was now Oleg Koslov talking to me.

I swallowed again.

'I know you are British Services. I know you are SAS.' My chin was grabbed, my cheeks squashed. I smelled cigarette breath in my face. 'The British sent the SAS after me once before. My general, used to work with the Philippine police. He tells me he recognises you from that time. You cost me millions of dollars when you destroyed my camp in the Philippines. Now, I have you here. Perhaps this is a picture of your daughter, perhaps I can recoup a few of my losses in revenge. You know I can find your family. I assume you would not like me to do this, so I just need you to tell me why you are in my jungle.'

'I can't answer that question.'

At that point I was kicked in the head and I blacked out.

I woke up coughing when warm water was poured over my head. It puddled under my face. It tasted acid. It smelled of ammonia. I realised what it was. I tried to turn my head away, but the jet followed me until I was choking and gagging.

I coughed and tried to spit it out. My head felt like it was split, like someone had driven a three-inch nail through my skull. I was hauled back up, dizzy under the blindfold, with my throbbing eyes closed. I tried to wiggle my nose to clear an airway, but it was blocked with blood. My face hurt, my cheeks pulsated.

'We're not getting on very well,' Koslov said. 'Try to help me.'

'Okay,' I managed.

'Why you are in the jungle?'

The standard response.

'I'm not sure now, Michael, is it that you can't answer my question or is it that you just choose not to? I think you just choose not to. Think about this: I like families, I have a kind of fixation with them, but I'm not what you might call your typical family man, more of an anti-family man.' There was a cold edge to the voice now; impatience was setting in. 'Now one last time, what were you doing in the jungle?'

'I can't an-swer...'

I was kicked in the stomach, a real toe-ender. Crumpled up in a ball, I gritted my teeth and thought, that's it, my stomach's ruptured for certain. There was a few seconds' break and then my shirt was ripped off and just as I wondered what they were going to do next I heard a whoosh and felt the lash as it cracked across my bare back. I held my breath and tried not to yell out. Whoosh. It stung like nothing I've ever felt before. Whoosh. Whoosh. Whoosh. Whoosh.

They picked me up. Someone held me. A boot smashed into my face, my mouth exploded. I could taste the blood, but I couldn't feel where it was coming from.

Another boot to the head, this time the cheek. Repeated kicks, one after another, for time with no end, until I passed out.

❦

'Michael? Michael? At first I thought the soft voice was inside my head. I thought I was back at home, sick in my bed at my parents' home. I thought it was my mother calling me.

'Michael? Michael?' The voice was sweet. In the hazy, floating world inside my head it sounded angelic. Was I in heaven? Was this what angels sounded like, soft and loving?

'Michael?'

It was another dream. Someone was about to point another gun to my head. I returned to consciousness with a grunt.

'Oh, so you are there,' the voice said.

I opened my mouth to speak, but cried out from my throat as pain seethed from my lacerated lips as the wounds opened.

'Were you asleep? I was calling over to you, I could hear you breathing, but you didn't answer.'

'Erm,' I managed, in my throat.

'Where did they take you?'

'Er?'

'Are you okay?'

'Erm.'

'Michael, talk to me, I want to help you.'

'Erm.'

My ears started ringing, my head went fuzzy. I was sweating. I vomited. My head fell into my own puke and I blacked out again.

⚜

'Michael?' Someone was nudging me, their shoulder on my shoulder. 'Michael?'

'Erm.'

'Did they beat you?'

I could smell vomit. 'Er? Erm.'

'Let me try to help you.'

'Erm.'

She was quiet for a few minutes and then I started to feel very warm. I actually felt like I was glowing. I was getting red hot and I felt like the pain was numbing and in some places disappearing. My throat started to feel better.

I either fell asleep or fell unconscious. I woke and was aware that the heat continued to glow all around me. My throat felt clear. I opened my mouth slightly and felt the wounds open. 'What's happening? Why am I hot?' I asked, speaking through my throat like a contortionist.

'I'm healing you. Be still.'

Even in my numbed state the thought of being healed was bizarre. Healing? Bollocks! How could she heal me? She'd need hospital equipment and drugs, pain-killers, plaster casts, bandages and days for me to rest.

I drifted off to sleep again. I woke and slept on and off for I don't know how many hours, always aware that the heat still continued to penetrate me. It wasn't like a heat on the surface of the skin: it was deep within my core, like something was being sucked out by a vacuum and replaced with this magnificent glow. It felt uncomfortable, but better than the pain.

I finally woke when I heard Shreela give a huge sigh. 'I must stop, I'm drained,' she said. She sat quietly for a few minutes. 'How do you feel now?' she asked.

My body felt better. My nose was still blocked. My head still hurt.

'Not so bad. Thanks,' I managed.

She sighed again. 'I gave you my healing energy.'

I vaguely remembered her mentioning something about healing me, but it was so deep and distant in my memory that it took on an unreal quality.

'It's like when you get treated by a masseur or a hypnotherapist, they send healing energy through their hands to whichever part of your body needs healing.' She kept her voice low, whispered, and spoke with the occasional croak, as though she had a dry throat. It was a pleasant voice to listen to.

'I don't even have to touch you,' she went on. 'I can heal you just by focusing on you. It's something I learnt from my work with the native tribes. You would be amazed what they can achieve with the power and focus of their minds.'

'Any chance they taught you how to pick the lock with your mind?' I asked.

Quick as a flash Shreela retaliated. 'Mock me if it pleases you, mock my work and my knowledge. Mockery comes from fear. You know, it's people like you that drain the universe.'

We didn't speak for a while, then she surprised me. 'I think we might have quite a lot of time together and I think we might have got off on the wrong foot. I'm sorry if I came over as rude earlier. Let me speak the truth...I wanted you to talk to me. I've been very scared and very lonely.'

I warmed to her a little after that admission. 'I understand.

I'm sorry too,' I said, 'but if you ever talk to me like that again I'll crawl over to you on the cheeks of my arse and knock you over with the biggest nudge I can manage.'

She laughed, only this time her laugh was not derisive, but infectious. It sounded like a lot of nervous energy being released.

I laughed too but it hurt too much and I tried to stop myself. 'Shush,' I said, 'or they'll come back and beat me up again.'

Shreela laughed even more. When her laughter subsided, she said, 'I hope you can find your faith while you are here with me.'

'Why do you say that?'

'Because it's about your only hope of getting out of here alive.'

'Shreela, I was just starting to like you. Please don't start preaching to me.'

I heard a titter of laughter. 'Okay, I won't.'

Voices were heading towards us. The chains rattled off, the gate scratched the mud. I braced myself for the heavy hands to lift me away and thought that if they continued to beat me into a pulp they wouldn't need to Fedex me—they would be able to fax me.

But the hands never came. I heard scuffling noises inches away and then I felt something cool on my face, the lightest of breaths. 'Pray for my soul,' Shreela whispered.

The gate shut. The chain rattled and she was gone.

A LIGHT IN THE DARKNESS

During the hours I spent alone I wondered if anyone cared about what had happened to my unit. Was anyone back home trying to contact us, trying to contact the Indians to see where we were, why we hadn't made our Sitrep or was this why we had been sent...because we were dispensable, because we were expected to disappear.

And then I wondered about the news bulletin I had seen on the morning before I left. I was feeling quite positive now that the story had been killed. Why had it only been screened once? What was to hide? Did the Indian media not know to begin with that it involved Koslov? Had someone in India been threatened and told to lose the story...cover it up? Or did the British want to hide the fact that they had any knowledge of Koslov's whereabouts and want to hide that from someone else? I felt sure the Americans would be peeved if they knew the British had been this close and not taken this wanted man out.

And then I began to wonder why Doug, Spaghetti, Macca and I had been selected to come on this mission. It was clear we had all messed up in some way, but was that sufficient to warrant being sent on a dead-end mission? True, Doug and I had previous experience in the Philippines, but it just seemed ironic, that three of us were self confessed screw-ups and had all had run-ins with our Sergeant Majors' or in my case the CO. Perhaps by messing up we had just made ourselves visible and being visible made us the first names that came to mind for a mission like this. Whatever the case, it seemed immaterial now.

Shreela had been gone hours, but how many hours I didn't

know. What I did know was that beyond my blindfold the brightness of the day had vanished and that the sounds had taken on that muted quality you only get after dark.

I heard a rumble in the distance and guessed it was thunder.

I lay down on my front and tried to get comfortable with my head turned to the side, cheek pressed into the earth. A breeze chilled my back and I shivered.

I dozed. I was woken by a loud rumble overhead. 'Shreela?' I said, hoping they had brought my companion back to me. My question was answered by silence.

I wondered what had happened to her. Had she been released? Moved to another camp? Was she being questioned? Had they asked about me?

I was glad I had told her nothing.

Another rumble and the first spots of rain splattered onto my bare shoulder. I heard other drops on the floor around me and took one on the head. The tempo of the rain increased and within a minute it was lashing down.

Wind howled through the trees, rain lashed the foliage, and as the mud around me started to turn sticky I rolled over and raised myself up off the ground. Curled up in a ball, I shuddered and shivered against the pen wall for what seemed like forever and then I heard it, the chain rattling. They were bringing her back.

The gate scuffed the floor. Hands grabbed me painfully under my armpits. They weren't supposed to be taking me. Shreela was supposed to be coming back, but they dragged me away. When we stopped I was ready for the nosedive this time. I tucked my chin into my chest, but the impact just thumped my forehead this time and forced my mouth to close with such force that every nerve in my gums seemed to scream.

'Up, up,' someone shouted. I recognised the voice—my old mate Elvis.

I was pulled up to a kneeling position. Another familiar voice—Koslov's. 'I thought we would encourage you to co-operate. Out here when it rains this area of our camp floods.

Mosquitoes come. I think they might enjoy having your company. Also you are close to the trees, so the leeches will come and so will the ticks. Of course the sun will also shine tomorrow and the reflection from the water that pools here will ensure that you receive an even burning. Oh, and I forgot to mention...I also have access to an extensive supply of drugs and chemicals. If you have not been helpful by tomorrow night I will be injecting you, first with something which will loosen your tongue and then perhaps I'll arrange to give you a dose of something like the bubonic plague or anthrax. So, you see, you have a choice, we can do things nicely or we can do them with a mind altering substance and a horrible death. The choice is yours. We will discuss this tomorrow evening. As they say in America, "Have a nice day."'

He spoke to Elvis. 'If he gets uncomfortable and moves, beat him.'

I wanted it to be over. I didn't want drugs. I didn't want mosquito bites, leeches and ticks crawling all over me and I certainly didn't want sunburn or to still be in this position until tomorrow.

Within a couple of minutes my feet and calves were beginning to tingle. It was uncomfortable, like being spiked with a hundred needles in the sole of the foot and the back of the leg. Already I wanted to move, but I knew I'd get beaten.

I thought about Elvis's gun tucked away in his shoulder holster and I wondered if he was wearing it now. I thought about it for a while. I hallucinated—a scene where I reached out and grabbed his gun and then commended myself on the fact that I had been vigilant enough to spot his pistol, disarm him and then use it against him.

Still it rained. Still it thundered.

To take my mind off the discomfort I thought of Christian. I thought of the times we played together, the school work I helped him with, the bedtime stories, the walks in the park, hiding in the woods, me as Hook, him as Pan hunting me, the baddie. I also remembered his face when his mother and I argued, the nervous scratching he did on his belly, the hug he gave me before I left for the mission, football, cricket, Pan, Hook, Aladdin…

The rain continued. The thunder rumbled in the distance. I could hear the falling raindrops making their pool close by my side.

I wondered what life would be like for Christian if his mother and I separated. The way she scolded him bothered me, though it had bothered me less when I was away on tour. Perhaps it was because I always knew I would be coming back. Thoughts of leaving for good made the smacking different now…more important.

My legs were totally numb. My thighs, my back, my shoulders and my neck ached. Still it rained.

Light came up. The sun came up, burning away the clouds until the rain stopped. God, I was uncomfortable. My teeth were clenched, grinding. My shoulders hurt. My stomach groaned for food, my throat burned for water.

Voices came close. I heard a splash on my right side, no more than a few inches away. They were changing their guard. Elvis was off. 'Mosquitoes in water—don't get close. If moves beat him.'

I could see the brightness from the water's reflection now. It was close. I could almost taste it. Cool, refreshing, flooding down my throat and putting out the flames. I wanted it. I wanted to taste it. It was calling out to me.

I pictured Christian again, ran back through the memories and mulled over the future I wasn't going to have. The sun ate into my scars and still I wanted it. I could smell it. I could smell food, the flat, watery smell of plain boiled rice, like eating a warm cloud…. I felt twitchy. Hunger, thirst. I swallowed, hotched forward an inch. I breathed out, tried to focus on other things, but it was no good, I couldn't shake the smells. I couldn't shake the urge to quench my excruciating thirst.

I wanted it. I wanted it now. I wanted it like I'd never wanted anything before, ever.

Fuck the mosquitoes. Fuck the kicking this would cost me. I wanted water and without another thought I got it.

I lunged forward, face first. Splosh!

I gulped and gulped. I was in my own Evian Heaven! Buxton Bliss Paradise! Fantastic. I laughed in my head. I was smiling as I gulp, gulp, gulped.

I was grabbed by the arms and pulled out. It was inevitable.

I smiled to myself. *Bastards. I cheated you. I've won!*

Chaos was all around me. There was shouting coming from everywhere. But I didn't care. I didn't give a damn. I had had my water and I was the happiest one of the lot.

And then of all the voices I could hear, it was Elvis' that came through the loudest. He was doing his little fruitcake, really making the jailhouse rock. But I didn't care. I had lost the will to live and I was going to go out with a song, and at the top of my knackered lungs I sang out loud and proud:

'And now the end is near, and so I face the final curtain, my friend, I'll say it clear, I'll state my case of which I'm certain. I've lived a life that's full, I've travelled each and every highway. And more much more than this I did it my wa...y .'

On that note, with my mouth wide open, I was thrust down, crashing through the water's surface. My head was twisted back and forth, I took in muddy water, tried to cough it up and took some more in and then I was out, back in the fresh air. And I heard a voice, not Elvis, but Koslov, spitting and shouting in my face, 'You think you're very funny. You think you are very smart, British soldier.'

I was plunged under, pulled out and forced down again and again and when it stopped I was kicked in the stomach, the back, the legs and the arms. I wanted to cry out but my vocals now seemed stuck somewhere between my chest and my throat and were being pounded out of me before I could form even a proper wail.

They hauled me back up. My body was in seizure, shaking and shaking uncontrollably. My lungs forced out short, sharp breaths and I wheezed like a set of century-old bagpipes that had been set on by a horde of hyperactive kids.

It was then that someone's knee smacked me right on the nose, shattering the cartilage.

My head throbbed, tears ran over my cheeks, my body continued to convulse and for an age my breathing was erratic and desperate. Gradually it harmonised. My body still shook, but at least my throat wasn't so raw. I tried not to smile. I did it my way! The fucking hard way, but my way.

I was sitting up again now. I had to go through the pins and needles in my legs again as they went numb. My body itched all over. It could have been the ticks or leeches or the disease-ridden mosquitoes, but I was past caring, they could eat me alive now. I just wanted it over.

The sun burned deeper. I could feel my skin glowing, turning dry, shrivelling under the grill. It itched. I wanted to scratch it. I wanted to scratch all over. I felt like a crazed man—bites or burns, I didn't know. I didn't care. I just wanted to scratch.

It was the longest day I had ever known. Every bone was sore; every muscle was stiff and hard. I was parched again and hunger roared in my belly.

Voices. Another shift change. Fractured English—Elvis was back. Bastard!

Dizziness started as a mild swing as the day wore on, but soon it became impossible for me to control. I was swaying, gliding, floating. It was an incredible experience, as I no longer felt the pain in my body. It reminded me of a time when I was a young Para out on the town in Germany. That night in a club half a dozen Germans toppled over. As they fell they landed on my ankle, twisting it. It didn't matter, because I was so light-headed with their delightful local brew that I didn't feel a thing, at least not until I stepped on it in the morning.

I must have blacked out. I was woken by water being thrown over my head and my burned back and shoulders being slapped.

As I knelt up, Koslov spoke to me. 'How are you feeling?'

'D-dizzy. I hurt,' I slurred.

'We heard you laughing with the girl yesterday. Do you like her?'

I struggled to form the words. 'I d-don't like her. I t-told her I would p-push her over. After I said it, it seemed funny.'

'Funny? Why was it funny?'

'I'm b-bound up. That's why I laughed.'

'Yes it does sound funny. English humour, eh?'

'Yeah.'

'After you laughed with her did you like her more?'

He sounded like he was trying to be my buddy now, but I knew he was only doing it to manipulate me into giving him information. It was liked being quizzed by a jealous love rival—how long have you been seeing her? Where did you meet? Is she good in bed? I knew if I said I liked her more they would hurt one of us, most likely me. I said no.

'She is very pretty. We were thinking that if you were more co-operative we could remove your blindfold, then perhaps you would appreciate what all of us red-blooded males are appreciating, if you know what I mean.'

'I think I know what you mean.'

Someone pinched my hair. The voice was now in my face. So pungent was the smell of cigarettes and the stench of unbrushed teeth that even through my smashed-up nose I could smell his breath. 'The photograph is not of your daughter. Who is it?'

'I c-can't answer that question.'

'Where did you get this picture?'

When I didn't answer I was kicked in the chest, a sickening blow. I was on the floor again, coughing.

Another kick—this time to the back.

'You know what makes me think that the girl in the picture is not your daughter? It is the fact that at your home you don't have a daughter, but a son.'

I was sure he was bluffing, but further thought on the subject came to an instant halt as I was kicked in the kidneys and booted in the head. My body was paralysed, my head was spinning. In semi-consciousness I lay there for what seemed like several minutes.

They lifted me up and held me in place now.

There was a pause. I could smell the cigarettes again.

'As you looted my operation in the Philippines I thought it was only fair to consider looting your home, so I took the liberty of finding out a little more about you.'

He was definitely bluffing.

'His name is Christian, and your wife is Jodie.'

Shit! They might as well have kicked me in the kidneys again. Where did he get the names from? How? Who?

Shit! He had their names...The evil bastard had their names. He wasn't bluffing...

He was waiting for me to say something, show a reaction. I said nothing. I stayed as still as I could. He must have been observing me, watching for a flinch or a swallow. I tried to keep my face straight and not show him any fear or give him anything that might make him think he might have the upper hand.

Shit! He had their names.

Shit!

What could he do to them? Would he do anything to them? Could he really harm them? Kill them? Surely it wouldn't be worth his while, but the fact that he had managed to get their names in a relatively short space of time told me it would be easy for him to do if he chose to. What had I got Jodie and Christian into? They were innocent. Shit. My work was never supposed to have any effect on them. Shit! Shit! Shit!

Fortunately, at that moment the blindfold stopped him seeing my eyes; if he could have seen into them they would almost certainly have betrayed me, told him he had got it right and that I was scared.

The blindfold was removed.

The sun was directly in my eyes. Totally blinded, I had no idea what was coming until the boot caught me on the chin. It slammed my jaw shut, smashing my teeth together with such brutal force that I felt like my head had just exploded.

I might have passed out. I had no idea.

I was hauled back up. Dizzy and sick. I heard Koslov's voice again 'We could have someone pay your little family a visit or we could send you home a piece at a time, fingers and toes first...all individually.'

My eyes were adjusting to the sun, which was behind Koslov. I could now make out his shape, tall and broad-shouldered. I saw him draw on his cigarette and exhale. There was a man to his side, slightly shorter than Koslov, but his face was blocked by the light behind him.

'Let's stop playing games now and start communicating. Michael Edwards, you are an SAS soldier. You have a son and a wife at home. I'm sure you might like them to live.'

I was silent and I received the mother of all blows to the kidneys. 'Take a while to think. I know you are thinking now, you are thinking about innocent Jodie and Christian who you really don't want to get involved in all of this.'

In my mind I was screaming. I wanted to shout at him. You just don't do this kind of thing. You fucking low-life bastard!

He was waiting for his answer and rose up like a cobra about to strike its prey. I could see him more clearly now, bald head and thick hood of bone over his brow, a shadow hanging over me threatening to blot out my sun.

He drew in slowly, a permanent sadistic smile closing like a vice on his cigarette, his whole face sucking in, contorting with pleasure, then exhaled upwards, releasing the scarred lines of age from his leathery reptilian complexion. He lowered his gaze and flashed his amber eyes. 'Talk,' he hissed.

I said nothing.

He stepped forward and belted me in the face, almost toppling me over. 'You made a mistake,' he shouted. Then he swung at me from the other side. 'You came into my jungle and won't play by my rules.' He launched his boot at my stomach and thumped the wind from me. I could see him, his scummy top teeth biting down on his skinny bottom lip as he lashed out at me with everything he had, punching me with one fist them the other intermittently as he shrieked at me. 'I know why you

are here. I know it's because of the girl I kidnapped or because
of the gun trade I now run from these islands. I know.'

I ended up in the dirt after about the sixth blow. 'I'm
making big business and I think certain people don't like the
power I am creating,' he said, tapping my face with the toe of
his boot. 'People don't like the fact I can get powerful weapons.
I threaten them.' He toe-ended me on the chin, slamming my
mouth shut. 'What are you doing in my jungle?'

I closed my eyes.

'Bring me the drug,' he said to someone.

My mouth was full of dried mud, but Koslov hadn't finished
the beating yet. He grabbed me and pulled me up by my crushed
face. 'Today I have nothing better to do today except beat and
torture you. Today you are my toy. Did you know the British
army thinks you are a toy, the Indian army use you like a toy, a
cheap toy that doesn't matter? Today you are my toy, and I will
smash you and break you until you make friends with me.' He
dropped me and stood up.

Two guards put me back on my knees, shoved a pole under
each armpit and across my back so that I straightened.

There was a long silence. I knew by now that by now
Doug, Spaghetti and Ali had been given time to get away and I
wondered if there was any point in me keeping my mouth shut.
There was no value to it now. It was time to give up.

It wasn't like I was going to be telling him anything that he
didn't know already. It wasn't as though I was betraying state
secrets or anything, but I saw no harm in bending the truth here
and there.

I was kicked in the stomach as I thought about it.

I wanted to curl up, but they hauled me up by the pole and
held me steady.

Another kick in the stomach.

'What are you doing here?'

Another kick.

I leaned forward.

They pulled me up again.

The same question.

Kicked, pulled up, kicked pulled, the same question again and again and again. It was impossible to catch my breath, each kick compounded on the last, less and less air was going in, more and more was coming out.

'G-gun t-trade,' my voice spluttered and exploded from within the agony.

The beating stopped immediately. They let me go and I collapsed on the ground. My breathing slowed. They brought me something to sit on.

It was over.

'I was just about to administer the drugs,' Koslov smiled, holding a needle in front of his face. 'Food and drink and first aid will be brought to you, but first tell me about your orders.'

I just didn't want him thinking I was only there to get Shreela so I adlibbed a little. 'I—I am, am h-here t-to o-ob-observe y-y-your t-tr-trade. A-a-a f-few d-days ago I was t-told about, about, about Sh-Sh-Shreela R-Ro- Robert. I-I w-was a-asked to assist in her r-recovery.'

He drew on his cigarette again and exhaled slowly. 'I don't like lies. I have an associate who told me something different. I understand you are here for Miss Robert only.'

'You talking about 't-t-talk-a-load-of-bollocks-R-Ramjit,' our former m-military liaison? If you are d-did you know the Jarawa put an arrow right through his throat while he was taking a p-puff of his cigarette?'

He looked at his cigarette, then at me and laughed, a great big hearty laugh. His goons around me joined in, so I laughed too.

Big mistake. ·

He stepped forward, reached out and stubbed his cigarette out on my neck, next to my Adam's apple.

I clenched my jaw and suppressed my urge to yell as he held it in place until all the heat had died from it. Then he stepped away and flicked the stub in my face. 'Don't get too smart,' he said.

The worst of the pain passed quickly, but I could feel the heat of the burn searing away at my skin.

Koslov nodded to the men either side of me and I was dragged away and put back in the pen.

At least I wasn't concussed this time and they hadn't replaced my blindfold when they put me back. I could now look around the camp. I watched the men lock the pen and walk away. I tried to get myself into a position where I could watch the camp, but it was no good—I was in too much pain.

'Is that you, Michael?' Shreela asked. 'Did they beat you?'

'Yeah.'

'Are you hurt?'

She didn't wait for the answer. She came towards me and soon I began feeling that heat again. I dozed and woke and thought about home and Christian and Jodie and what I could do. If Koslov did send someone to take them out they wouldn't stand a chance. I had to speak to Antenna. I had to get a message home at the earliest possible moment.

I dozed again. When I woke I was thinking about escaping. While I had been blindfolded I had put all my hopes of escape on Doug and Spaghetti, but now they had given me my vision back I could take a look at the alternatives, but before I began looking I was asleep again.

When I woke Shreela had finished healing me. She was sat back quietly with her legs crossed and her hands out like she was meditating. A while later she spoke. 'Can you talk to me now? Can you tell me why you're here?'

'Let's not talk about that just yet,' I said.

'Can we talk about anything else? Can we talk about you?' She shuffled to get herself comfortable and I saw her smile. She was actually excited about doing this. 'Are you married?

I didn't like her question.

I looked out at the camp, weighing up the opposition for the first time: two of Koslov's men talking on the far side of the camp. They lit up a cigarette and I watched them take a drag.

'Yes,' I said, reluctantly. 'I'm badly married.'

'Do you have any children?'

'A son.'

She paused. 'Badly married...what exactly do you mean?

Do you mean the ceremony was poor or that your marriage has been awful?'

The two men on the far side of the camp chatted as they smoked. They were more engrossed in their conversation than watching the bushes. I checked out the distance from the pen to the jungle cover...twenty or thirty yards.

'The awful one,' I said returning to the conversation she was desperately trying to spark up.

'And what's so awful?'

I didn't like that question either.

'Everything.'

'Everything...surely not everything?'

'Everything.'

'If everything is awful, why be married at all?'

Good point. Very valid, very accurate...but I didn't like it.

'What's your life like at home?' she pressed.

A strange question, but I answered it nonetheless and then found myself saying more than I had meant to. 'Crap,' I said, with real passion. 'Really fucking crap. My wife sleeps upstairs with the local policeman, my son sleeps next door to them and I have the sofa, a bottle of brandy and the TV.'

In the central area of the camp, several men were sitting or milling around. They seemed relaxed, almost casual.

'Are you telling me your wife is having an affair?'

'Yep.'

'And you are sleeping in the same house? I mean, aren't affairs usually secret? You must be incredibly tolerant.'

'No, actually, I'm not at all tolerant. I'm a dumb fuck-up who wants to cut flesh off the bastard and feed him a slice at a time to a crocodile. I want him to watch his life being taken away a little tiny bit at a time. I want him to watch himself being devoured in the same way he's devoured my life. I want him to see another creature chewing up his life in the way he's chewed up mine. And then I want to pickle my wife, so I can watch her life decompose really, really slowly.'

Again the silence. I guessed she didn't approve of my vision for the future. For a second I felt a pang of guilt at having spoken it out loud. Then I felt shocked at how I had failed to guard my mouth. Then I just shrugged it off. If Shreela didn't like it, she could shove it. She was only a hostage. Her opinion didn't matter. I didn't care.

'You should bring both of them to India and have them disappear off the face of the earth, like I did,' she said.

Her reply shocked me. I swallowed my laugher. 'You know,' I said, smiling wickedly, 'this is exactly what my plan has been lacking, Shreela—an accomplice like you.'

She laughed quietly, a girlish laugh, the kind I remembered hearing in the playground at school, when two enemies discovered that they had a mutual enemy and they collaborated in the corner, bitching behind the hands that covered their mouths until they became the best of friends. It occurred to me then that excluding her eyes, hidden behind the blindfold, and ignoring her dishevelled, lank, greasy hair,—there was something kinda sexy about Shreela, a devilishly wicked streak that hid behind the persona of this holier-than-thou missionary—what I guess her mother had meant when she referred to her as 'a rebellious child.'

There was more movement in the camp. They were changing the stags. I made a mark in the dirt, to count how many times they would change in a day.

'Tell me about your wife,' Shreela said. 'What does she look like? Is she pretty?'

'Blonde hair, leggy, dancing blue eyes.'

'You still love her?'

'I don't know.'

She smiled, knowingly. 'A person usually knows when they're in love.'

I didn't like the questions or the smart-arsed smirk on her face. 'You're too young to understand,' I snapped.

'No, it's simple, when you love someone you want to be with them every minute of every day and when you're not with them you spend the hours apart thinking about them.'

'That's a pretty immature way of thinking. Like I said, you're too young to understand. What you're talking about is infatuation and that burns out, love evolves, deepens, supports, understands.'

I saw her hackles rising. 'So your love evolved, deepened and whatever and then your wife had an affair. Was that before or after the infatuation burned out?'

It was after, but I didn't want to admit that. She was blindfolded and for the moment I was happy that she was: it stopped her from seeing the expression on my face. I conceded the point silently and stuck my tongue out at her. Cow!

Neither of us spoke for a minute, then she said, 'Do you miss your wife?'

I didn't want to continue the conversation. I sighed. 'Sometimes,' I said.

'Do you miss what you have or what you had?'

'I miss what we had when we got started. Are you going to let up in a minute?'

She paused only briefly. 'What did you have when you got started?'

She wasn't getting the hint. What the hell...'Fun and laughter—it was great being together in those days.'

'What happened?'

'I don't know.'

I saw her mouth curl up into a smile, as if she was having some funny internal dialogue. 'Fun, laughter, really great being together—what does that sound like to you?'

I ignored her.

'Did you meet her when you were younger?'

'Yes, of fucking course I did. I couldn't meet her when I was older, could I?'

'How much younger?'

'We met nine years ago.'

'So you were how old?'

'Twenty-five or six.'

'Which were you, twenty-five or six?'

'I don't know.'

'Work it out, it's not like we have anything else to do.'

I took a deep sigh and worked it out. 'Twenty-five.'

She was smiling again. 'About my age…so you were much younger when you met and fell in love. I wonder if love meant something different to you back then?'

She had driven me into a cul-de-sac. 'Okay,' I said, 'you win. I was once as immature as you are now. I was infatuated by her and I believed our relationship should have evolved; it didn't. The rest is history. Are you satisfied now?'

We fell silent and my mind began to wonder back to the early days of my relationship with Jodie. For the first few years I had thought of her as the most incredible woman in the whole world. I wished I could turn back the clock to when it all started to go wrong…whenever that was. I wished I could tell her how much I loved her back then, how much I missed her now, how much I wanted to be with her and how much I wished we had done things differently.

But even though she had offered me the chance of making another go of it, I felt deflated, like the chance to do it right had gone now.

Except for Christian it was nine years wasted.

I looked out at the camp again. A small group had gathered in the centre. They were doing something—it looked like a game of cards. Occasionally they laughed lightly.

'What about you, is there a Mr Shreela?' I asked.

Her body stiffened.

So she felt uncomfortable. So what? She had asked me uncomfortable questions. I wasn't going to let her off the hook.

'I don't want to talk about it.'

'Hardly fair, is it? You just beat my story out of me and now you don't want to talk. Have it your way if you like, but I'm not talking to you again until you answer my question.'

An hour might have passed before she spoke. 'There is a man who thinks so,' she said.

'So tell me about him.'

'He's the one holding us captive.'

My jaw dropped.

'You're shocked. I can tell you're shocked. You should be shocked.'

'It does seem a bit of a mismatch.'

She drew herself in. Her head dropped. Her heart broke. I let her sob for a while and then suggested that it might help her if she talked about it.

A while later she said, 'I fell ill in Mayishmagar. I was walking towards the store to find drugs and stumbled out in front of his jeep. He said he could help me and took me back to his camp. I stayed with him a while. I was very ill while I was there. It was an illness that came and went, but not with nausea, just light-headedness, like I was up in the clouds.

'A man came. He said he was a doctor, but...I don't think so now. He said I needed to rest and should stay at the camp until I had been well for a few days. This went on for weeks.

'I liked Oleg then, he was very attentive.' Her voice tailed off as she drifted away into her own thoughts for a few moments. I asked her if she wanted to continue. She didn't reply immediately and then slowly she went on.

'He would come to me and talk late at night until I was asleep. One night as he left he leaned over me and kissed me. It woke me. I was startled, but it was nice. The next day he told me he had cared for me as he had never cared for another.'

I fought back a derisive laugh...Kolsov caring? 'You make him sound romantic,' I said.

Abruptly her manner changed. 'He is anything but romantic. My time with him was vile. He did the vilest, vilest, sickest things that could ever happen to any woman on the planet.'

'What happened?' I said, more as a response to her change of character than a need to know the details.

'Do I have to spell it out for you?'

'Well I...'

'No, I won't tell you. I don't have to tell you. Who do you think you are anyway, my doctor?'

'No I'm not. I'm just –'

'Don't bother to explain yourself. You're a man, how could

you ever understand? What would you know about being drugged to the point where you are willing to degrade yourself? What would you know about that? You sit there asking your dumb, stupid, pompous English questions and you know nothing...nothing.'

She pulled her legs up to her chest and rested her forehead on her knees, rocking backwards and forwards. She did this for several minutes. She wasn't sobbing, at least not that I could hear, though I suspected that a lot was going on inside her mind.

With Shreela, Koslov had been subtle: in the Philippines there had been none of that, jabbing needles into women's arms before he raped them. With Shreela he had shown more compassion, and I wondered why. I released my fingers and stretched them out as I had become aware that I was clenching my fists so tightly that my nails were digging into the flesh of my hands. I wished I had taken that shot in the Philippines. I wished I had taken the risk, even if it had meant despatching one of the hostages. I was sure now, in the long run, that that would have been a better option.

'I am ashamed,' Shreela said. 'I'm ashamed because all of this is against my morals. It was wrong. It's wrong. It's wrong. It's wrong.' Then the pace of her speech picked up and she began to ramble, but curiously she now told the story from a third-party perspective, like it was unfolding in her head as we spoke. 'He returns to her night after night. Every night she is all over him with her hands and in the morning she feels so, so guilty. Dirty.' Her lip curled with disgust.

'Over and over she sees the night playing around and around in her head. It's like it's not real, like she imagined it all. 'It's all right,' she tells herself, time and again, 'It's all right. It's all right.' But she knows it isn't all right. She has the bruises and the scratches and the pains in her belly that tell her it is not all right, but still she tells herself that it is all right.

'And then he comes again, only now she is not all over him and he can't understand it. He flies into a rage. Then she sees him looking at her drink, the poison he has been giving her night after night. "Why have you not taken your water?" he shouts. And she tries to back away, she tries to curl up, to disappear, but it is no good. It is no good.'

She paused for a while and then continued again, more slowly, and I noticed the change in tense again. 'She watched things the next day. A boat came in, a shipment of boxes. She walked to where they were unloading them. Guns, bombs. She was scared. Her mind was all crazy. She didn't know where she was. She wanted to leave, but she didn't know where to go. How would she survive? And then without thinking anymore she just ran. She ran and ran. A day later she stumbled in to Tugagat.'

'What happened to her then?' I asked.

She switched viewpoints again. 'I caught a bus and went to Port St. Peter. I spoke to the chiefs of the island, then the governor; no-one wished to know about him. They told me that the government had changed their policy on the Jarawa and were increasing the pace of deforestation. They told me that Koslov's trade was allowable. It was then that I left and returned to India, to Calcutta, to speak to the ministers.

'In Calcutta, I met with family friends in the police and the military, I researched old newspapers in the library and spoke to ministers. All of them told me of Oleg's reputation, an arms dealer with links to terrorists. I was warned not to cross him.

'I visited my parents with the intention of keeping my mouth closed about what I had discovered...what I had become involved with, and when I arrived I was bawled at hysterically by my father for days.'

'He had heard that you had been speaking to ministers?'

She nodded. 'His friends in the government had met with him, told him that I was confronting them, stabbing them in the back after they had helped me, helped him. My mother told me again and again that he would calm down and on the third day he suddenly did.'

She paused to compose herself, 'My father hugged me that day...he hugged me tightly and cried. For the first time in all of my life he told me he loved me. It was a very strange experience, as though he was full of regret or pain. It was like he knew he knew something was going to happen to one of us. He wouldn't let go of me.'

'That night it thundered and rained. Kalid, my servant friend, escorted me into the village. Thunder was cracking overhead, lightning was flashing across my nose. I had never felt such electricity in nature before. I wanted to go up the rocks, but Kalid was dragging me further and further into the village, telling me he had discovered a better place. I sensed danger. I tried to pull away from him, but he forced us on and on.

'Lights shone into my face—headlights, blinding headlights. I could see my feet, but I could not see the road ahead. And then as I drew closer I saw it, a lorry parked by the side of the road.

'It was an odd vehicle to be parked in the village so late at night. It was like a military lorry. It worried me instantly, but Kalid was with me. We were two, and although my nerves were jangling I thought that I was just being silly and that I was worrying for nothing.

'But as we drew level with the lorry I knew I was being watched from the cabin. As we passed I heard the door click, feet on the pavement, behind me and beyond. We were surrounded.

'He called my name and the sound of his voice paralysed me. I had become so scared of him, this arms-dealing, drug-user who had taken my body and who I had found out was friends with men of terror. I lost control of my bladder...that's how much he scared me.

'He placed a gun to the back of my head, told me I was a troublemaking, lousy lay. He told me if I squeaked or squealed I would never breathe again.'

Her story made me hate Koslov more. Repulsion at his acts, the fear and the degradation he subjected her to churned inside me like a razor blade in the pit of my stomach. A deep, despising wave of disgust rose inside me, disgust at myself, at my employers and at all of the authorities and intelligence-gathering services everywhere who had failed to take this man off the streets.

We were quiet for a while, then Shreela said, 'Sorry if I touched a raw nerve earlier about your wife. I didn't mean to upset you.'

'I suppose I don't like admitting stuff,' I said.

'That's just your big macho ego.'

'Yeah, I suppose it is.'

'Do you think you'll divorce her?'

'It's a lot of wasted years.'

'What would be worse: to leave now after wasting a few years or to waste a few more and then leave? She's committed adultery, most guys wouldn't think twice about leaving.'

'Adultery': the word shook me. It was the first time my wife's actions had been narrowed down to a single, cruel word.

'It's not that,' I said. 'It's my son, Christian. I want to be there with him, but in my line of work I'm hardly at home and I'm scared I might never see him again. Jodie's promised that she's going to end the affair while I'm out here. She asked if we can make another go of our marriage when I get home.'

'And you want that?'

'I'd like my son to grow up in a normal family,' I said, persevering, knowing I was now sounding like a right idiot.

'You, her, him and the memory of the affair?'

'She's my son's mother,' I said, my voice almost pleading for her to shut up and let me off the hook.

There was a pause. 'You really think she'll end it before you get home?'

I snapped, 'I don't know. What the hell do you think?'

She thought about it. I couldn't believe she was actually mulling it over. After a minute she said, 'I'm not sure, perhaps if I lived in your Western culture...I wouldn't end the affair. I might wait until you got back to make sure you were still worth it. If I liked the other guy I might want to keep my options open, but then what do I know...I'm just an immature woman.' She paused and then went on, 'I do know one thing, if she does end the affair and you do try again, you're going to spend the rest of your life looking over your shoulder, waiting for the next guy. Do you really want your life to be controlled by that?'

I thought about that and understood that she was probably right; after all once a person has had an affair once they always think they can do it twice. I knew I needed to take back control of my life, but the question was how did I find the strength to pull away from my wife and child?

She broke the silence again. 'My father has had many women. My mother knows and has to allow him to have these affairs. It is humiliating for her to know he does this, yet she cannot divorce him in the way you can divorce your wife.'

'Surely she could walk away.'

'She tried that once. The servants told my brothers, my brothers told my father and my father beat her within an inch of her life. He only stopped when I hit him with a chair. My mother knows if she tries to leave again she will be met with the same violance, so she stays, blaming herself for not being womanly enough for my father. It is an awful way to live. All the time I tell her she is a wonderful woman and that it is my father who has the problem. I have told her if ever she decides to leave I will help her.'

That night, as I sat against the pen walls I noticed Shreela was restless and uncomfortable. After all the healing she had done for me it was the least I could to let her rest her head on my lap.

In the moonlight that penetrated the jungle cover I looked down at her and smiled. She was very pretty, a simple, kind woman who possessed so much mental resilience.

It was as I was sitting there that it hit me what a mug I had been over the last few months. That all the nastiness of wanting to walk in on Jodie and the sleeping policeman's sex life, be around and needle him when Jodie was in another room, pressuring for money from the property—it was all a waste of my life. There was so much more I could be doing.

Shreela turned her head to look up at me. Sleepily, she whispered, 'I have no idea why you are here, Michael, but I'm glad you are with me.'

Her words comforted me. I wanted to say something nice back to her. I dived into my well of compliments only to discover a bucketful of cheesy lines. I ran through them in my head, only to find that the moment had passed: her body fell limp and her breathing turned light and rhythmical.

A strand of her dark hair had strayed across her cheek and stuck to the corner of her mouth. If I'd had a hand free at that moment I would have eased the hair away, put it back in its place.

I lifted my head up and gazed out into the camp. I looked at Koslov's men, some sleeping, some on stag, some playing cards. But as I looked along the tree line a sudden movement in the foliage thirty yards to my right startled me. My eyes strained through the blackness until they watered and stung and I was forced to blink. I was sure a blackened face was looking at me through the scrub.

KARMA

Shreela slept soundly on my lap. When she woke she smiled up at me and stretched. I particularly enjoyed the stretch, as she was still blindfolded and I was able to admire her figure with a lecherous freedom seldom enjoyed by a man.

'Hi,' she said. 'Did you sleep well?'

'No, but you did,' I replied.

She sat up, raised her feet off the floor and spun herself around on the cheeks of her bum. 'Your turn,' she said, suggesting that I now lay my head in her lap.

'Not just now,' I said, 'later...perhaps tonight when it's dark. I don't want to upset Koslov if he has a thing for you.'

'Okay,' she smiled brightly.

'What happened when they took you away a few days ago?'

Her body slumped. 'First he asked me to give him locations for every Jarawa camp. I refused to help. I know his intention is to murder them. Next, he asked me to give myself to him.'

'What do you mean? As in sex?'

'I refused, but that didn't stop him.'

'He raped you?'

She chose not to answer the question directly. 'It no longer hurts my spirit,' she said.

'Yeah, right,' I muttered under my breath.

'He broke my spirit the first time he forced himself on me, my first night in his keeping. I think he enjoyed the struggle so now I don't even give him the pleasure of that. I just let my body go and allow my mind to go with it. Koslov likes the victory. He can have that, but he's not having the soul.'

As we talked of the serpent he slithered across the camp, chatting to a couple of his men, kicking another who was lying on the floor. He reached the pen and bent down to look in through the wooden slats. 'For your information, Mr Soldier, the British government is not aware that you have been captured. I intend to keep it this way. Also, your friends will be joining you soon. I will of course check their stories against yours when they arrive. After that, your deaths will easily be explained on this island. There are many ways a man can die here.'

Although my heart sank at the thought that he had caught Doug and Spaghetti and although they had been my main hope of escape it occurred to me at that moment that Koslov himself looked devastated. It was as though my very presence there bothered him, as though it perturbed him greatly. He had mentioned not wanting more British soldiers...the thought worried him! The bastard was scared we were coming after him!

I wanted to laugh. What if the guys had got on the Satcom and told Antenna that I had been caught, that Macca had been killed? What would happen then?

Of course, he could still carve me up and Federal Express me from Calcutta or we could all do as he had suggested, mysteriously disappear in the jungle. But it was enough for my moral just then to know that the bastard was scared that someone out there might just be coming after him.

After he had slithered away Shreela said, 'What is this about, "Mr Soldier and the British Government?"'

It was time to confess. 'I am a British soldier, sent to find you and help the Indian military round up Koslov. Unfortunately, Koslov bribed an Indian soldier and we were ambushed. Two of my men, Doug and Spaghetti got away.'

'I think Koslov has bribed more than one Indian soldier. You may well find he has bribed almost every commander. He has grown very powerful in these parts and appears to have a great deal of influence with the government.'

'I want to fucking kill him,' I said, under my breath.

Shreela's head snapped up. I immediately apologised for my foul mouth.

'Your mouth may be crude, but your morals are even cruder.'

'I said sorry. What more do you want?'

'Forget sorry. You express a will to kill someone and then apologise to me for swearing, you epitomise the senseless times we live in. You cannot kill another human being.'

I ignored her. I was glowering at Koslov across the camp as he talked with Elvis.

'Do you know the harm that wanting to kill someone causes, let alone saying it or even doing it? Do you know the darkness that causes, in your soul, in your environment, in the earthly vibration? Do you know? Do you have any idea? Well? I'm talking to you.'

I looked at her getting worked up, throwing herself around like crash-test dummy. She certainly was passionate about her subject.

She changed tack. 'You know what disgusts me about weapons and you Westerners? You manufacture arms and make them available on the open market for Tom the Terrorist, Dick the Arms Dealer and Harry the Heretic. You take no responsibility for the pain you cause and your only interest is in the amount of money you make. Money over suffering—that's what it comes down to—money over life, money over the environment.'

As she spoke it occurred to me that I would love to take a look in Koslov's ships or storage facilities and seen what his weapons were and where their origins lay. I bet a good batch of them had come from the West, British or American made, and no doubt that once used they were shipped on and sold second-hand. It remained me of a story about the fifty-four countries who supplied Iran and Iraq during their war. Apparently, twenty-nine of those countries had supplied arms to both sides.

'It's ironic, but not funny, that you Westerners make these weapons and ship them outside of your own country for profit... for profit! And then after you've made hundreds of millions from shipping the stuff out, it gets used back on you in wars, in hostage situations, in terrorism and by people like Koslov. They call it karma and your countries deserve it. It's stuff the environment, stuff morals, stuff long term safety and stuff the security of the millions. The priority is now personal gain, big profits, market shares, and Hi, I'm the CEO of a corporation that sold billions of pounds' worth of death equipment, but come and look at my new house and my adorable car and my spoiled kids that I send off to private school. Meanwhile, some poor children a few thousand miles away have had their father or mother blown away and watched their brother or sister torn to shreds by automatic gun fire. It's not fair. It's not right and I bet you all still have the gall to complain about it.

'Today it may be guns and rocket launchers, but one day I'm sure that some idiot is going to do the same thing with something much more deadly, probably sell some of those chemicals that the Americans and Soviets make in their underground labs. Get a strand of that stuff in the wrong hands...Where is the responsibility? Where are these people's morals? Why aren't they making something constructive? What do they think people want to buy chemical death for?'

It occurred to me that Koslov had already threatened me with anthrax or the bubonic plague. I wondered for a moment if this stuff was now readily available. Karma, I thought, and I laughed; what is the woman talking about? I was just thinking that if she ever got out of the pen and made it to safety I would buy her a return ticket to London so she could go on a demonstration, when thankfully she shut up.

Bliss.

Then...'As a soldier, how do you find inner peace?'

I didn't answer her question.

'You must have accumulated so much bad karma. And then when you're not soldiering and fighting you go home and fight with your wife.'

Now I was grinding my teeth.

'To even think of killing...'

'For God's sake,' I roared at her. 'Shut the fuck up.'

My voice echoed through the camp. Every head turned towards me.

Elvis marched across the camp. He unchained the gate and came in towards me. I knew I was going to pay for the outburst. I was dragged out of the pen, my head was bashed against the wooden uprights by the door, and I was thrown to the floor and it felt like every one of Koslov's men came and laid the boot in.

Tossed back inside the pen, I had learned a hard lesson. I lay in the silence until Shreela broke it. 'Their souls will be damned for that,' she said as though it would make everything better.

'I still want to kill them,' I said. 'They just made me want it more now.'

'You know, you're the same as all of the other idiots. They want to own you, so you want to own them. That's what wars are all about—control, power and dominance. And to think I was starting to like you. My goodness, you're as bad as them. You're just another macho nutter.'

'I'm a trained soldier, doing a policeman's job on nutters around the world. I'm nothing like Koslov.'

She laughed at me. 'The day we all love ourselves instead of fearing what our neighbour might do to us will be a great day.'

'And until that day, the world has men like me.'

'No, people like you have to change first. I wish that you would think of your soul. I wish you could see the bad karma that you have accrued. The bad karma you send out for your town, your country.'

'Shreela, I've killed a few men, another one or two aren't going to make any difference to my soul now, are they?' I turned my back on her and scurried into a corner of the pen using my heels and the cheeks of my arse to get away from her.

Why the hell was I arguing religious points with this woman? Why the hell was she opposing me when all I was trying to do, save her life? Missionary my arse...More like a religious hindrance.

After some time I heard her laughing.

'What's so funny?' I asked.

'Life,' she said. 'Do you believe it can reflect your own thoughts back at you like a mirror?' Here we go again, I thought, more mumbo jumbo. She continued. 'It reflects your greatest thoughts and your greatest fears. It gives you what you dwell on. Kali Pani for many years has been an island that reflects the negative thoughts of the universe perfectly. As well as working with the Jarawa to clear their karma I have spent time contemplating how I will change this island and bring its spirit to rest. Already it is awakening with a new, gentler spirit.'

That was it. I had decided—she was a total fruit cake, a loon, a crackpot. I had no idea what she was going on about. She was mad and it didn't matter that she was making no sense at all.

But it did matter. It did make sense. It mattered and it made a load of sense. The conversation with Macca, his fear of a gun battle with Koslov...Spaghetti's fear of spiders...what Ali had said to me about my dreams...I could see how all our fears had come to pass on Kali Pani and God, did that feel uncomfortable.

Shreela continued, 'My fear is that the Jarawa will lose their land or that they will perish because I fail to help them integrate. Life has put me in this pen to help me change my thoughts.'

'Are you saying I should be considering why I am here?'

'Would such reflection harm you?'

I thought for a moment then barked off the first answer that came to me. 'I'm here because I got caught, not because I need to change my thinking.'

'If you had changed your thinking before you got caught, would you be here now? Being here is a part of your karma. The universe has sent you to Kali Pani as a wake-up call because you are constantly ignoring her other calls, the more subtle ones.'

'Oh please...' I said, feeling so uncomfortable about what she was saying that I just had to challenge her. 'I'm here because I'm a soldier who had the shit luck of being captured on a mission to find and free you.'

'You will not be set free from here until you have changed your mind about killing people. It is a lesson. Maybe you also need to consider your thoughts about your son. Concentrate on thoughts of having him live with you, rather than you live without him.'

'Jesus, you really have had all the tools stolen from your shed haven't you?' I said. 'I can't believe that you really think things can change so easily. Getting out of here is no way as simple as that and if I want Christian to live with me, first I have to get past his damn mother, then if that doesn't work the courts...and the courts will never give the legal rights to a guy like me.'

'Why not?'

'They just won't. In the reality I live in, things just aren't that simple...change the way I think and off we trot...it's ridiculous.'

'I think you need to change the reality you live in and try something new. Your reality is very harsh, very difficult.'

'It's real.'

'It's the real that you make it. I believe if I adjust my thinking and trust with all my heart that something will happen to make my leaving here possible. Do you believe this can happen?'

'No.'

'Please start thinking about how we can do this.'

I almost shouted again. 'I'm locked in here. My friends are either dead or caught, how the hell do you expect me to think I can ever get out of here?'

'You are only exploring one possibility. Be more creative. Whatever way we get out of here it must be in a way that will not bring bad karma. Your soul is troubled enough, Michael.'

Fucked up and flowery was my conclusion of Shreela. But I couldn't help asking. 'If I saw bad karma what would it look like?'

'A bad relationship, inner pain and conflict, abuse brought to bear on you, things you love being stripped away from you, one piece at a time. Your friends being shot.'

'Are you telling me that killing people is what is causing me a bad relationship?'

She thought for a moment. 'I don't feel it helps you.'

I glared out at the camp with all my creativity. I looked at each of the men guarding us and tried to find a misfit in the outfit or a weak link, a man who might make a mistake or be manipulated, someone who might just give us that hope of escape. The problem was finding such a man and working on him without a clue as to how long we actually had before Koslov killed us. The problem with working on a man I viewed as a weakness too quickly was the fact that he was more likely to get a sniff of what I was trying to do and if that happened I could easily end up in bigger trouble than I was in already.

I watched the way they guarded us, their mannerisms, moods, routines. I searched every one of them for complacency. As I watched I mulled over Shreela's thoughts about the spirit of Kali Pani reflecting your thoughts back at you and remembered what Ali had said about my dream involving a woman and my yearning for the purest kind of love. He told me they had used this to prey on my weakness, so they could harm me. From there my mind went on the rampage, thinking of Macca, Spaghetti, Ali, Manisha, Shreela, Jodie...but when my thoughts turned to Christian and I considered my chances of leaving Kali Pani alive, a lump grew in my throat and I admit tears welled in my eyes.

For some time I replayed Macca's death over and over in my mind. I recalled the way I had killed Koslov's men in the Philippines and could no longer shut out what I did for a living. I had always thought that I was doing something good. I still believed it, though I no longer believed it with all of my heart. Something had changed. I didn't know what, I just knew that my conviction in the belief about what I did had disappeared for ever.

Shreela said, 'Why did you become a soldier?'

I blinked away my thoughts. 'I wanted to escape from home when I was sixteen and the army was a good excuse.'

'Was it something about your parents that made you want to escape?'

'They were angry people when they were younger. There

was always tension around them. Sometimes I hated being in their company. I enjoyed my early teens because they let me roam the streets until late at night.'

'What did you do when you roamed the streets?'

'I pretended I was in the army, creeping up on the enemy. I used to climb over people's walls and hide in their shrubs. What about you, why did you come to work in Kali Pani?'

'My path, according to my father, is only to find a good husband who will take care of me. I believe my father is wrong. My mother agrees that my destiny is very different.'

We were interrupted as our food came, cold, congealed rice. They untied our hands and then tied one arm up to the pen wall. We ate in silence and I thought she had forgotten my question.

She lowered her head. Her shoulders slumped. 'I find it hard to talk about my home,' she sobbed. 'For the first time in my life I'm missing it. My mother will be worried. I can see her crying. I think she will be very lonely, very scared of losing me.'

I could sympathise with her feelings a little. She was missing her parents in the way I was missing my son. I tried to reconnect her, give her something she could believe in. 'Your mother seemed very strong when I met her. She seemed to be keeping her faith.' I mentioned the photograph her mother had given to me. 'I've never seen such blind faith before,' I said.

'Her faith is not blind,' Shreela corrected me. 'Blind faith is faith without sight or belief. The faith my mother has is absolute.'

Leaning up against the slats of the pen I snoozed away the best part of the afternoon. Dusk was falling by the time I came alive again. My body ached all over, partly because of the hard floor and the way I had been leaning up against the pen, but also because of the bruises Koslov's cronies had given me the day before.

In the fading moments of that day I watched her as she sat silently in the middle of the pen, her crossed legs stretched out in front of her, her back straight in a perfect posture. She looked to be at incredible peace with herself and I wondered how she could find such tranquillity in the circumstances.

She had shown me her frailty when I arrived in the pen, yet she seemed to have few fears, just an acceptance of her circumstances and a willingness to let it all happen because she had such absolute faith that it was all happening for some higher purpose.

As the orange sky disappeared and darkness fell the rain returned, with a harsh wind and thunder. It lashed, howled, flashed and rumbled for hours. We sat back to back, shivering and trying to retain as much heat as we could between us, our heads nodding forward with exhaustion and our legs and arms twitching with tiredness.

But it was during that night that I saw something that gave me hope.

I saw it moving in the foliage — a hand waving slowly. For a moment I thought I was hallucinating again. I wondered if it was just a leaf flapping in the wind or just the way rain was sticking to my eyes, but then, as the lightning flashed, I saw the hand curl up into a fist and the middle finger extend.

I laughed and cried silently to myself. One of my unit was watching over me. I was going to get out. I was going to go home.

LIGHTING UP THE NIGHT SKY

Doug inched from the foliage, low to the ground and slow. I shifted myself across the pen to the side closest to his approach and a few seconds later he was perched at my side, speaking to me through the wooden slats. 'What took you so long, dickhead?' I said.

'Don't get cocky, shit-legs. We've been watching for two days, loved the rendition of My Way, we were pissing ourselves in the bushes. There's seventeen of them, all with AKs.'

'How many do we have?'

'Two, Spaghetti and me; three when you reach the foliage.'

He grinned at me, like it was all a game, like we were back at Stirling Lines, sharing a joke before practicing a hostage simulation in the Counter Revolutionary Warfare Wing.

I stared at him. It was a big moment. I knew he wasn't going to leave me behind, as I wouldn't have left him. But extraction was sheer bloody madness, absolute suicide. The keys success in hostage situations are: speed, aggression and surprise. Even with the element of surprise, the odds would be stacked way too high against us. We knew how to be aggressive, but with seventeen of them against Doug and Spaghetti, how much aggression did we have?

'He nodded to the other side of the pen. 'Tell me about the gate.'

'It's chained and padlocked, hinged on the inside, you can burst in from your side with a couple of well-placed kicks.'

He shook his head. 'Not an option. I need to be under cover, ready to lay down fire as you escape. You need to get out when they open the pen door, preferably at night time.'

Shreela shuffled over to us on her bum cheeks. 'Use me as a distraction,' she said.

I looked at her for a second then turned back to Doug. 'We're bound at the wrists and ankles.'

'We'll slip you a knife for that. We just need some action that doesn't cause a big disturbance, but gets them to open the pen.'

Shreela piped up again. 'I can ask to speak to Koslov, tell him I give in to him.'

Doug looked at me. 'What do you think?'

'We'll need to work out a plan so as Koslov doesn't get suspicious about a sudden change of heart—something that doesn't get her too far in the shit.'

'Right, you sort that out. We've got some prep to do, but we'll be ready to go tomorrow. Go to it any time after dark. Once they've got her out, I'll bring you a knife, cut yourself free and charge them when they return. We'll cover you.' He patted me on the shoulder and was gone.

'Tell me your plan,' I said to Shreela.

'I'll tell him that I agree to help him.'

'So tell me the locations of the Jarawa settlements?'

'What?'

'That's the first question he's going to ask you.'

'So what do I do? Do I make them up?'

'You could, but next he'll probably tell you that you are going to lead him there.'

'What do I do then?'

I thought for a moment. 'I doubt he's going to trust you...at least not until he's checked out the settlements. He might take you with him for that.'

'But we just want him to take me out of the pen for a few minutes and then put me back.

Taking me to the settlements doesn't fit with that.'

I thought it through. What if he didn't bring her back, but took her straight off to the first settlement? 'Doug and Spaghetti could follow, but it puts them at a hell of a risk when he realises that you're lying. We need to come up with something else.'

She thought for a moment. 'What if I tried a different scenario, something perhaps a little closer to home, more believable? What if I told him that I was attracted to him before, but was scared off by his lifestyle and the drugs he gave me?'

'You forgot something.'

'What?'

'That he's a murdering bastard and wants to kill the people you want to protect. He wants their grid references, their addresses, then he wants to go and knock on their settlement doors and do the job he's been given to do.'

'I see,' she said, frowning above her blindfold. 'I'm not very good at this, am I?'

'No, you're doing fine. We're just exploring possibilities... 'being creative' as you put it!'

'What if I told him the attraction and the lifestyle part and said I wanted to work a compromise out over the Jarawa?'

'What sort of compromise?'

She frowned, thinking hard. 'That I work with them to ensure they leave his men and warehouses alone and that he leaves them alone.'

'What about the Indian government? Correct me if I'm wrong, but they have given him licence to run his business from here so long as he rids the islands of the Jarawa, right?'

Again she thought about it. 'What if I told him that the Indian government plan to throw him off the islands once the Jarawa are gone? What if I suggest to him that he delays and delays and never does the job, but in the meantime I help him to create peace so he can go on trading?'

'Then the government will just throw him out anyway.'

'Yes, but he knows they will do it and he can plan for this and make maximum use of the islands in the meantime.'

'That might work. It sounds more believable. You're getting good at this.'

'Thank you.'

'So what if he says okay and cuts off your ropes?'

'Then I'll tell him no. I'll tell him that we have to learn to trust and trust takes time. I'll tell him that first he needs to recall all of his men who are out looking for Jarawa and until then I stay in my pen.'

'Sounds bizarre, but I can't think why he wouldn't go for it. What then?'

'I'll tell him when his men have returned I'll go and speak to the Jarawa and tell them his plan. From there I'll tell him I have done all I can and it is up to him to maintain peace with the Jarawa. I'll tell him if he does that then there might be some future for him and me...I mean continuing our relationship.'

'I wouldn't say that at the end.'

'Why?'

'Because he might not want to continue a relationship with you.'

'Why wouldn't he? He took the time to drug my water so I would have sexual intercourse with him, so why not?'

'Shreela, we're dealing with a guy who just takes what he wants one way or another. If he wants sex with you he'll take it. He's already proved he's not interested in your consent. But telling him you fancy him will do his ego good. It might gain you some favour.'

❧

The following day, right into the afternoon, Shreela sat quietly and incredibly still. Her calm amazed me when I considered what lay in front of her.

I had always perceived Koslov as an emotionless man and doubted he would ever be capable of any romantic notions. My perception was that he was all business, business and more business. And that led me to believe he wanted Shreela more for the information about the Jarawa than the sex he was taking from her.

I wondered what it would be like for her, lying to him, and I wondered what Koslov would do if he suspected anything. I knew it was a massive risk for her to take, but I knew that we had no less risky alternatives to consider.

For a while the words, speed, aggression and surprise kept going around in my head. I knew we were up against it and I knew my speed in getting us out of the pen was going to be the key to life or death for us.

'How do you do it?' I asked her, as the afternoon sun blazed through the trees, 'How can you be so unmoved by what you have to do today?'

'Because I am not focusing on what I have to do later,' she said.

'So what are you focusing on?' I asked her, wondering what else she could possibly be focusing on all day long.

'Gratitude for what I have at this moment,' she said.

'But you have nothing. You are stuck in a jungle –'

She cut me off. 'If you are not truly grateful for what you have at any moment, how can you dare ask for more?'

'But you're being held by an arms dealer who drugs you...It doesn't get much worse...You can't have much less.'

'I have my breath. I have my limbs intact and my brain. I have a friend for company and at this moment I have all the love and freedom I desire.'

'Freedom? Are you nuts?' I looked around me at the seventeen armed men in the camp, in particular my own pet hate — Elvis.

'Am I being disturbed by any of these men right now? No. Therefore I am enjoying all the freedom I require at this moment.'

'Shreela, we're planning an escape. You need to focus on the task ahead. You should be running things through in your mind.'

'I did this once earlier and I have trust that things will come right for us. Now if you don't mind I want to focus on what I want from this moment, not what I want in the future.'

❦

Shreela called Elvis over at dusk. 'Thank you for considering the alternatives,' she said to me, as we waited for him to return across the camp to collect her.

He called to one of the guys resting in the centre of the camp to join him and they both came to the pen.

I wondered if there would be two of them when they returned her later. If there were, would I be able to take both of them out?

The pen was opened. 'You, out,' Elvis said.

As they led her away I closed my eyes and wished with all my heart that she could pull it off without any harm coming to her. An unbending fear that something awful was about to happen to her swept over me; panic set in. Would Doug make it across the camp to me with the knife? Would it all be in vain?

The guys that were playing cards wolf-whistled and laughed as Shreela was dragged in their direction. A gangly man rose from the communal area and walked slowly over to Elvis. He stepped in front of them and groped at Shreela's breasts. She tried to step back, but Elvis held her firmly. 'Come and try,' Gangly called out to his friends.

A pony-tailed, bearded type with torn trousers rose and joined his friend. He fumbled the soft flesh of her rear artlessly as he undressed her with his eyes, then grabbed at her with such vigour that I saw her rise to the tips of her toes as she yelped with pain.

The cry of pain brought another man forward. He grabbed at her face then slapped her cheeks lightly with his fingertips and leered into her face before ripping open her blouse.

Others remained in the communal area, laughing and calling encouragement. I glared at them. No fertile imagination was needed to guess what was on their minds: one woman alone in the jungle, surrounded by a pack of drooling hyenas...taking her a piece at a time, warming up before they finally took her. What had I encouraged her to do?

I scanned the perimeter of the camp looking for their weaknesses. All the men on stag carried Ak-47s and had been distracted by the commotion going on at the centre of the camp. The ones resting, playing cards or lying down kept their guns by their sides, though the ones circling Shreela right now were unarmed.

'Take your hands off,' Shreela shouted, but the sound of her voice had the opposite effect to the one she desired, and more of the guys leapt forward.

It was at that moment that a tall figure appeared at the far end of the camp. His men saw him and backed away. Koslov made his way to Shreela, grabbed her by the arm and led her away.

I looked at the foliage for what seemed like several long minutes. When I saw nothing I hotched around the pen: where was Doug? How long did he think we had? Come on, I thought to myself as I checked to see if there was anything happening in the camp to stop him coming forward.

Come on!

And then I saw him, low and hunched. My heart was thumping. *We were going to get out. We were going to get out!*

I heard Shreela yelp.

Focus, I told myself. Focus on what you have to do. Immediately my mind went back to Doug.

'No,' I heard Shreela shout. I heard her crying.

I heard a slap and then a yelp and then an almighty shriek that broke the night apart.

Doug was at my shoulder. 'What the fuck's happening to her?'

'Something must have gone wrong,' I said. 'The plan seemed good.'

'I'm passing you a pocket knife, get your ropes cut and get ready. If you don't go for the guard, we'll lie low and wait for another opportunity. Good luck.'

I put the knife against the ropes on my wrists and slowly, with what little flexion I had in my wrists, I started cutting.

Shreela's shriek, though now minutes old, continued to scream inside my head. An occasional yelp carried across the camp to me. I heard noises further up the camp, laughter, a whoop of delight. More laughter, jeers. Whatever was going on it was the most fun they had enjoyed since I had been in the camp.

Suddenly two figures were heading my way. Were they coming for me? Where was Shreela?

For a second I froze and stared across the murky camp, then I realised that it was Elvis and Shreela coming my way. The ropes had been removed from her ankles and although she was moving her feet she was lolling all over the place like a rag doll. Her appearance shocked me and for a second I forgot about the knife and stopped cutting.

How could I escape with her in that condition? Speed was the key and now she was a liability that was going to hold us back. It wasn't safe for us to go. I couldn't just think of Shreela and I escaping. I had to think about the additional risk I was putting on Doug and Spaghetti shoulders.

But this was our chance; in a few seconds the gate was going to open and I either had to go for it or forget it.

I had to choose now.

With one more cut my hands came free. All I needed to do was free my feet, get past Elvis and we were on our way.

The key went into the padlock.

My heart was pounding. Sweat was pouring off me. This was it.

Come on, come on, you want to go home, you want to see Christian, I was saying to myself, biting down hard on my bottom lip as I hacked at the rope around my ankles.

The lock came off the pen door and the chain links ratted around the wooden slats and clattered onto the floor. I looked at Shreela: my God, what had they done to her? Her head was down, her hair hung forwards, but I could see her eyes, wide open, rolling upwards and vacant. Her mouth hung open. Was she going to make it out of the camp? Would I need to carry her? Would it slow us down?

I chopped away at the last frayed strands of the rope. It fell from my ankles. I was free.

Elvis hauled open the gate and shoved Shreela back inside. He came in close behind her, obscured from my view.

My eyes scanned the camp. There was movement at the top end: they were returning to the centre of the camp after their fun. The stags were chatting and slow. It was not ideal, but it was our chance to go. It had to be now.

Slowly and so as not to catch Elvis' eye I raised my hands up onto my knees and opened my palms wide so that Shreela could see that I was free and for one memorable moment her expression changed. She smiled, the kind of smile I'd seen by the possessed in horror movies, and in one quick movement she banged down her sandal heel on to the arch of the Elvis'—foot and hit him in the sternum with her elbow.

The knife clenched between my teeth I rose up, and in one stride I reached Elvis. He was still doubled over from Shreela's strike. I cut upwards with my punch and made a perfect strike on his chin. His mouth smashed shut and his head flew back with such force that his body flipped over.

It was game over for him before he even hit the deck.

I reached down and grabbed his gun from his shoulder holster.

There was a call from further up the camp. Someone had spotted us. 'Hey,' they shouted, 'the prisoners!'

I grabbed Shreela by her bound wrists and hauled her out of the pen. She was slow, her balance was uncoordinated. She was struggling. In one swift movement I threw her limp figure over my shoulder and ran.

'The girl is escaping! The girl is escaping!'

'Don't shoot her!' I heard Koslov shouting, 'Don't shoot her!'

I didn't look back now. I didn't need to. I could hear the noises behind me and just knew we were about to be chased.

Shots were fired at the ground around my feet, warning shots aimed at making me stop. I pointed the gun behind me, towards the calls, and without looking behind I fired off every bullet in the gun's chamber.

I expected Doug to be returning fire by now, but instead I saw a hand and then an arm outstretched in front of me, opening up the foliage as I made the final metres.

Inside the bushes Doug thrust an M-16 into my hands. 'Follow Spaghetti,' he ordered, his voice raw with panic. 'Stay right behind him. Don't deviate from the path he takes you. Go! Go!' Spaghetti was in front of me, already backing away. He turned and trotted off through the thick undergrowth.

Single gun shots suddenly became automatic fire. Tracers flew around me, bullets ricocheted and tore shreds off the trees.

Doug couldn't hold off this kind of attack on his own. He needed help, but as I began to lower myself to dump Shreela on the ground and turn back the camp erupted with one bang after another. The noise shook my body and throbbed inside my head until I felt as though my eardrums would burst. Flashes lit the sky above the trees and there was a glow through the foliage in the camp.

As the explosions died away confused, panicked shouts echoed from the camp as the men rallied, calling instructions and trying to regroup and give chase.

I got Shreela loaded back properly onto my shoulder and set off again.

Spaghetti was a couple of yards ahead, beckoning me on.

Whoosh!

Bang!

An explosion fifty yards ahead. Orange flames lit the jungle, fire spread over the branches from tree to tree and rushed along the ground.

Spaghetti didn't pause. He kept us moving, right through the flames.

Fifty yards, sixty yards, seventy yards.

Eighty yards, ninety yards. He stopped.

'What the f...'

'Okay, rest. Give her to me, wait here for Doug, cover him.'

I paused, doubting if this was the right thing to do.

'Come on, Mike,' Spaghetti said, prising away my fingers from the back of Shreela's legs. 'Come on. We're losing time.'

What the hell was I waiting for? What was I thinking

about? I released her and helped Spaghetti hoist her up over his shoulder and watched them head off.

Fire inched across the jungle. Gunfire echoed through the trees. It was coming closer. Quickly I considered what Doug's plan might be, to back off to me and then run a relay down to Spaghetti. Then Spaghetti would pass Shreela to Doug and he would run on with Shreela and so on. Only a few seconds passed before I saw Doug's head pop up from the foliage. He dashed a few feet and was down again, firing.

'Keep running,' I called to him, adrenaline now pumping.

'Hold here,' Doug shouted back, 'the fire will have them cut them off in a matter of moments.'

I laid down my first shots as a gentle breeze blew through the trees and the fire inched halfway across my vision.

I laid down more cover, which was returned with aimless shots. With the aid of the fire we would get the better of the situation now. We fired sporadically through the flames. Just enough to keep their heads down, stop them from fanning out or surrounding us.

I was up. 'Move, move,' I shouted. The fire was sweeping in all around us, we had to move or risk being enveloped by it. We backed off quickly now, putting down only the occasional shot. We found Spaghetti laying in wait. Return fire was now intermittent and distant.

Boom!

The ground shook under my feet and the jungle lit up.

'Told you we had a little prep to do. Remember those mines we dug up?' Spaghetti asked with a grin. 'Well they left them behind at the old camp so we put them to good use.'

Boom!

The jungle shuddered to a second blast.

Doug said, 'The situation is that we have no support, no radio and little food. Ramjit was moving the ops centre to Haven Island, so that's our target.'

'How do we get across the water?' I asked.

'We stole some wood from a place near the coast and

stashed it in a cave. We only need to bind it together. It will take a couple of hours.'

Gunfire had started behind us again. It was way back and not an immediate threat, but all the same I looked at Doug, 'Take the lead,' I said, 'get us out of here.'

ESCAPE

Strong winds and cold pelting rain slowed our progress, especially where it puddled and streamed on the jungle floor. I focused on our route as we escaped and thought of Christian often, especially the pleasure on his face as Pan slipped a penalty beyond the grasp of Captain Hook's good hand or as Aladdin bowled out Jafar.

Also holding up our escape was Shreela. She had not been able to coordinate her legs at all and her movements were so sluggish that we had been forced to pass her between each other and carry her on our shoulders.

Owing to her sluggish behaviour I was convinced Shreela had been drugged again, but what with and how much I had no idea—I just hoped that it wore off quickly as carrying her was taking its toll, but at that point the main thing was that we were safe and had gone the last few hours without hearing a single gunshot behind us.

We pressed on until just after first light and the last drop of rain, coming to rest on a volcanic rock just big enough for us all to perch on. Doug took Shreela down from his shoulders and stood her on the ground. She swayed uneasily from side to side and we both reached forward and grabbed her just in time to catch her fall.

Doug passed round the water and the ration of one biscuit each.

'Tell me about food supplies, munitions and comms,' I said to Doug.

'We have five biscuits left and this,' he said, showing

me a third of a 500ml water bottle. 'I also have three full magazines.'

'I've got the one in the M-16 you tossed at me,' I said.

'And I've got two,' Spaghetti added. 'Comms were lost when Koslov made the assault on our camp. We went back to look—burnt to fuck.'

We sat there shattered and not talking for some time. 'They have the edge,' Doug said. 'At that camp they outnumbered us by around six to one, but we checked out another camp at Mayishmagar. We counted around forty guys there.'

'Not only that,' Spaghetti said, 'he's got other resources that we don't have: jeeps and boats and we saw a helicopter.'

Doug said, 'How important is Shreela to him? I mean, will he follow us?'

I explained how she linked with the Jarawa.

'He could sort the Jarawa out without her though, right?' Doug said.

'Yeah, I suppose, but the fact that he's kidnapped her and brought her back here seems to suggest she's pretty important to him.'

I turned to her. 'Shreela...Can you look up at me?'

No response.

'Shreela, I want you to look up at me.'

Nothing.

'Shreela, look up at me.'

She raised her head. Her eyes were still drooping, her hair dishevelled.

'I want you to answer a question for me. Is there a reason, other than what you have already told me, that might make Oleg Koslov come after you again?'

Her eyes dropped down. She was thinking, recalling events, assembling her thoughts. I repeated the question again, slowly, pausing between each word, giving it a chance to sink into her consciousness, giving her the chance to think.

'Ch-child,' she struggled.

'Child?' I said, confused.

'Guard told me.'

'Guard told you what?'

'Koslov wants me to have.'

'Koslov wants you to have his child?'

Her head dropped.

I turned away to Doug. 'There's a good chance she's already pregnant with his child. I gather he's been forcing himself on her often. He uses drugs.'

'Sick fuck,' he said. 'Would he really chase after her for a kid, though?'

I turned back to Shreela. 'Did he kidnap you because of the child or the Jarawa?'

She shook her head. 'Last time he came looking for me. I found Jarawa I had worked with. They helped me. Jarawa chief drew etchings in the dirt. Told me if I helped Koslov he would lie and continue killing Jarawa. He would bring more corruption to the island. Jarawa cannot fight him, cannot stop him. The chief told me to run. He showed me help coming if I ran. Are you my help?'

'Yes,' I said, without even being sure what she was rambling on about.

I felt a strong urge to move away from Shreela. It was nothing that she had said or done, just an overwhelming push towards my own counsel. I closed my eyes and took a deep breath and felt the strangest sensation I have ever felt. It felt like my mind was being sucked through a black tunnel into another dimension. Images flashed through my mind, so bright and vivid in colour that they were more than real. It came on with such intensity that I jolted back from it instantly and tried to shake it off.

I blinked and breathed out. I shook my head. I tried to work out what I had seen without closing my eyes again. I had seen fragments, but they had been there so briefly and vanished so quickly that I was struggling to hold onto them. Move, a voice in my mind shouted at me. Without a second thought I turned to the others. 'Let's go,' I said.

I had no idea why I had such a strong impulse to leave our resting point so abruptly. Perhaps one of the fragmented images I had seen got stuck in my subconscious or something. I had no idea. But what I had leaned just now, besides his idea of starting a family with Shreela, was that she was Koslov's key to peace with the Jarawa, a peace that would allow him to bring greater evil to the islands.

We stayed alert to the possibility that the Jarawa were following us or watching us. With the risk that Koslov's men could be behind us, moving up from the camp as well as in front of us, moving down from Mayishmagar, the last thing I wanted was a shoot-out with the Jarawa that alerted Koslov to our position.

I called another break at midday. Doug unfolded the map. 'We made about ten clicks since last night,' he said. 'That means the trunk road is another fifteen clicks away. We'll be close to Mayishmagar then.' Doug glanced at Spaghetti and Shreela. 'I doubt we can keep this pace up, especially with Shreela.' Doug bit his lip and frowned. 'Are you sure she can manage all of this?' He lowered his voice. 'I mean look at her.'

I took a look: lack of military training, poor diet for over a week, plus whatever drugs Koslov had pumped into her the night before. Remembering how feisty she had been when I first arrived and how determined she had been once before when she escaped Koslov in Mayishmagar. I stepped over to her. 'We have a long way to travel and we need to cover ground quickly. It would help us if you could walk now,' I said. 'Doug is concerned you might not be able to make it. I think you can make it, but I want to be sure, what do you think?'

She raised her head, frowning at me as though her thoughts were full of pain and confusion. 'If I can't, what happens to me?'

I glanced at Doug, 'Well, we won't go on without you,' I said.

'You mean if I slow you down it will endanger everyone else.'

'Something like that.'

'So what are we waiting for?' she said. Pushing between us she began leading the way.

Doug looked at me and smiled. 'What a great woman,' he said.

❦

An hour later than I had hoped, tired, hungry and drenched in sweat, we reached Mayishmagar. 'It's a town of grass huts and a store on the corner of two mud track streets, one of which leads down to the quay,' Doug said, referring to his previous recce.

We spent three hours taking another look before we made a decision on what we needed to do. 'Food and water,' Spaghetti said.

'I looked at the quay,' Doug said. 'There's six motor boats and something bigger, a tug. There's a warehouse, I didn't want to go in unless you thought it was worth it. My guess is he'd keep the arms for shipping in there. We could break in and stock up a bit, blow up his boats and take out his warehouse.'

'There were five or six goons hanging around at the quay. The warehouse was busy when we were last here. I vote we just grab what is essential and bugger off ASAP,' Spaghetti said.

Although I would have loved to have taken out Koslov's warehouse it wasn't a part of the op. Taking the boats out...well, I could see the logic in doing that as it might offer us better protection for our crossing to Haven Island. The problem with that was twofold: first, it alerted Koslov to our presence and second, he would question why we had done it and he would almost certainly get the hint that we were going to attempt a crossing.

I told the guys we would move on, but before we did we visited the local store. There was little subtlety to our call there. We marched straight in the back door, banging it open. The owner, a man with a turban and bad dentistry, shouted at us aggressively in Indian. I didn't understand exactly what he was saying, but guessed it was something like please mind the door, I had to pawn my twenty children to buy it and right now I don't have any more children to barter with.... something like that! All credit to him though, when he saw Doug and Spaghetti follow me, recognised our disruptive pattern military outfits and took a closer look at the M-16 in my hands, he shut his mouth quickly.

As we grabbed a few things off his rickety shelves, Shreela wandered down one of the three isles in the poky shop. The store owner beamed his best come-hither smile at her.

'Namaste,' she said.

'Namaste.'

'Aap kaiseh hain,' she said.

'What are you saying?' I asked.

'He said you are European ransacking pigs and I said he was correct.'

I looked at her and she looked at the bottle of water in my hands, the water in Doug's hands and the sweets and tins of food in Spaghetti's. Sarcastically, Spaghetti said, 'You said all that in so few words...that was amazing, Shreela.'

'Ask him how much.' I said.

'Kitneh hai?'

'And tell him to send the bill to the Indian army.'

Shreela stared at me as if I was a turd under her shoe. 'Tell him yourself,' she said as she turned away.

Spaghetti grinned inanely. 'Discount,' he said, 'discount, discount, always discount, you give me very good price—cheapest price,' he said, taking the piss.

I tried the usual thing we English do when someone doesn't speak our language. I shouted, pointed, shrugged and left the shop with the view that he was the ignorant one.

On the step outside the back door of the store I stood next to Shreela. 'What was all that about in the store?' I asked her.

'He is a poor man and you have just stolen two weeks' profit.'

I felt momentary guilt. 'Then go and give him your father's name and arrange some credit,' I bit back. I opened the bottle of water and passed it to her.

Brushing me aside she went back into the store. A minute later she was back out. 'Koslov's close. Let's move,' she said, waving us forward.

Spaghetti almost choked on one of the sweets.

Doug dribbled water from his mouth. 'I think we have a new Patrol Commander,' he said, watching her disappear into the dry swaying grass like a pissed-off member of Mayishmagar's vigilante movement.

❧

It was 06:00 when we emerged from the trees again after another night of stormy weather. We walked out into brilliant sunshine, onto fine grains of golden sand and a dazzling reflection from the sea. We had begun a recce of the beach when Shreela's patience gave.

'The stupid cow's going to compromise us,' Spaghetti said. 'She'll get her tits blown off and our bollocks shot to shit.' He didn't wait for orders and stormed down the beach to where she washed herself with more vigour than I've ever seen from a woman cleaning herself. It might have been the days of dirt that had been ground into her flesh or the itchiness of all the bites she must have sustained, but I suspected that she was trying to wash away something more than dirt.

Spaghetti waded into the water. He waved his M-16 at her. 'Out,' I heard him say as he grabbed her by the arm.

She tried to pull away from him, but he slung his rifle over his shoulder and used both hands, dragging her to begin with then, when she rose up to confront him, he slung her over his shoulder and marched her up the beach, as she punched his back and protested.

Spaghetti dumped her on the sand and pointed his gun at her. 'If you ever do shit like that again I'll put a fucking bullet in you myself.'

'Who the hell do you think you are?' Shreela said.

'I'm a guy who is saving your arse and who doesn't want to die in the process, you silly cow!'

I stepped between them before it got any nastier. 'Back down,' I said to Spaghetti.

Shreela stared at him, bit her tongue and turned away.

'Before you go swimming or do anything we need to secure

the area,' I explained. 'What you just did could have got us all shot. As long as we remain on these islands you stay back until we tell you it is safe to move forward. It's for everyone's safety.'

We got moving again pretty quickly. To cover our tracks we walked along the sea-line for a while, but continuing that indefinitely would have been too dangerous. The ocean was reacting like a mirror with the sun and with the heat our skin would cook or the sun beating down on our heads would bring on sunstroke. After thirty minutes we headed up the beach and walked in the shade of the trees.

We continued south, on a heading which would bring us to a peninsula, Kali Pani's most western point. It was there that Doug had stashed the wood that he intended to construct into a raft for the crossing to Haven Island.

'It's only a couple of clicks,' Doug said.

I knew that making a raft overnight was going to be a tall order for Doug, but I had little choice at that point other than to ask him to perform the miracle. The fact that we had to stop while we built the raft left us susceptible to attack and I didn't want our situation to remain like that for a moment longer than it had to.

I made a spear and fished. Shreela collected dried wood. We built a fire and placed the fish one at a time into the only dishes Doug and Spaghetti carried in their Bergens. I cooked in silence over crackling flames.

Sitting cross-legged next to me, Shreela placed her hand on my leg and rubbed my knee. Her touch startled me. It was unexpected and pleasant. 'Thank you for doing what you've done,' she said softly.

The fish in the pan sizzled. I turned it. Blushing at her gratitude I shrugged the compliment away. 'It's my job,' I said. I glanced at her as she looked up at me. Firelight danced in her liquid brown eyes. A quick smile softened her fraught expression. 'I know this might be awkward for you to talk about, but what happened to you back there, before we escaped?'

She bit her lip, shook her head and looked out across the bay. The tarnished sun setting in the moody sky turned

Haven Island to a ghostly silhouette. 'Will we escape from here tomorrow?' she asked, ignoring my question.

'I hope so,' I said.

As the sun dropped into the water I felt the joy of peace in my heart. I smiled inwardly at the joy her thanks and the slightest of physical touches had brought to my life.

A toughened soldier on the cusp of mush, I stared into the flames and swallowed hard. If Koslov or the Jarawa caught up with us before we made it into the water or if the sharks in the bay ate through our raft as we crossed to Haven Island I knew I would die a more contented man.

THE CALM AND THE STORM

After we had eaten, Shreela curled up in a ball with her head on my Bergen and fell asleep. I headed outside the cave and found myself an observation point a few yards along the beach, where I could see most of the shoreline and look out across the ocean. I contemplated our crossing to Haven Island, dwelling especially on the sharks that infested the sea and wondering if dolphins really did scare them away.

I was about to try a prayer, but as I looked above me I saw that the sky was already lined with foreboding clouds. It gave me another reason to be cynical, another reason to ridicule faith in anything I couldn't see or touch. I laughed inwardly, because there within was the irony—even the things I could see and touch, people whom I cared about and trusted and put my faith in, had seemed bent on ruining my life.

A gust of wind swept in from nowhere, wafting across the beach, rustling the leaves in the trees behind me and sand-blasting my skin. And as I stared up at the black sky I mulled over my home life.

I had no idea how long Jodie's affair had been going on. She told me that the day I came home early from the barracks and caught them in bed together was the first time they had ever slept together. I found that difficult to believe as I had caught them first thing in the morning, less than two hours after I had left for work, just twenty minutes after Christian had gone to school, and only four days after I had returned from tour— quick moves and a quite unnatural time of day to say, 'Come on, honey, let's get it on,' for the first time.

There were two noticeable differences that morning in

both of our behaviours: usually I would shout up to her at the top of my voice as I came in the door, while she would usually be blasting the radio as she tidied from room to room. But that morning I didn't call up to her and the radio, though it was on, was much quieter than normal. I had the idea of sneaking up behind her and making her jump with surprise...which I guess I did achieve, though not quite in the way that I had intended.

I knew she was in our bedroom; the music was seeping through the crack in the doorway. I heard her giggle. I assumed something funny had been said on the radio. I eased the door open and saw a uniform on the floor that didn't belong to either of us. A badge number PC 666 or something. I remember the confusion in my head and the sickening realisation of what was behind the door. I pushed it open a little more. The sheets on the bed were ruffled and moving.

I opened the door fully and just froze, standing there like a man who had been shot and was waiting to fall.

Jodie was on top of him, breathing in the way she used to breath with me, grinding her hips in a way she used to do with me, saying what she used to say to me. And then I caught his eye over her shoulder and the smile evaporated from his mouth and he blinked and blinked.

She leaned over him, 'Come on, stud,' she giggled as she kissed his neck and stuck her tongue in his ear.

He wriggled away from her.

'Did you climax already?' she asked.

He shook his head and nodded towards the door. She looked over her shoulder.

I knew if I hit either of them I wouldn't stop hitting them. Doubled up, with my stomach tied in knots, I backed out of the room in what must have looked like a very apologetic posture.

'Oh shit,' I heard Jodie say, understating the damage.

Reality forced its way back in as I felt raindrops on my head, but I was numbed. The memory hurt me even now. I tried to convince myself it didn't matter, that it was all over, that it was in the past, that it would one day be as though it had never happened, but I knew that would never be the case. I knew that day, that scene, would always haunt me.

Still, I tried to convince myself it would be fine.

But everything wasn't going to be fine. Rationalisation was not going to work. I had seen too much, experienced too much and knew too much now to ever be able to put it out of my mind.

I held my head. Everything was not fine—I was going crazy.

Then I remembered what Shreela had said about life or the island or something reflecting life back at me.

Thunder rumbled in the sky, but my mind was racing like an out-of-control Formula One car that was no longer driving on the track. My relationship with Jodie was my fault. She hated me because I doubted and discouraged her in the same way I doubted and discouraged myself—she was a reflection, a mirror of what I was. My marriage collapse was my fault. It was *all* my fault. And if it was all my fault, could I repair the damage? Could I go home, accept responsibility for my behaviour and accept that her affair was due to my actions?

Was it worth it? Did we ever have anything, except for Christian, that was worth salvaging? Could I ever be happy with her again? Trust her again?

What did I feel when I opened the bedroom door that morning? It wasn't so much the shock of what they were doing, it was the realisation that it had been on the cards for so long and I had done nothing to stop the inevitable from happening.

She was a flirt. Men liked her. She liked men. It was going to happen. Maybe it had happened more than the once I knew about.

The sleeping policeman deserved a beating. Jodie deserved the nastiest words in my head, but I had been such a wimp... allowing them both to humiliate me in my own home that day.

I decided there and then I was going to take control of my life. Trust no one but myself. Clear away the people who took vows too lightly—find people of substance who stood for something...

A voice from the cave interrupted me. 'Are you just going to stand out there in the rain?' Shreela called.

'I need to keep watch,' I replied.

'That's very noble of you,' she laughed. She climbed over the rocks and walked out towards me.

'You should stay in the dry,' I told her.

She shook her head, 'No, I love storms. I was out in a storm with my friend Kalid before I was kidnapped and brought here.' Sadness passed across her eyes. 'Do you know what happened to Kalid?'

I took a deep breath. 'I wondered if you might ask me that. I'm afraid he died, Shreela.'

'Koslov killed him, didn't he?'

I felt the anger in her voice. I wished I could have said yes, but I shook my head. 'It was one of your father's servants.'

A drop of rain ran over her furrowed brow. 'I don't understand—why did that happen?'

'Because he helped the men who took you.'

She shook her head again and looked up at the dark sky. Her tone of voice changed. 'How? How could he help them? He was thrown to the floor and held down while they took me.'

I shook my head. 'Koslov let Kalid go. A shop-owner and Kalid were paid to help Koslov catch you.'

'Kalid was my friend,' she bit back. 'No, no, he would never do that. I can't believe what lies you are telling me.'

'Shreela, I heard what Kalid did. He said it right in front of me.'

She flung her arms out and raised her voice. 'No. No, no, no. You are lying. I cannot believe you. Kalid was my friend; he would never betray me like this, never.' She turned and walked a few paces away from me then swung back, frowning painfully. 'How did he die?'

I really didn't want to tell her, but I knew she would persist. 'He was decapitated,' I said.

She doubled over as though she had just been punched in the stomach. 'And you saw this?' she asked.

'Yes.'

'And you did nothing to stop it?'

'Shreela –'

She was standing up again, coming back towards me, 'You let them murder him.'

'No –'

'You saw them do that and you didn't even lift a finger to help him.' She stamped in the sand.

'Shreela, your father's servants were holding him, he slipped away from them and ran. I went after him, calling my unit to help me, but the store was on fire, there was a big crowd and so much noise that my voice got lost. Kalid ran away before I had a chance to stop him and then someone on a motorbike came along and...'

She had turned away again. I left her for a few moments, until she had wiped away her sniffles. 'The thing that hurts about Kalid is that no-one liked him, not even the other servants, they were all cruel to him. I tried to be kind, but now I think about it I never quite trusted him. I kept pushing that feeling away and kept trying to believe in him.' She paused to dry her eyes. 'I should have listened to my inner voice, but I ignored it to give him a chance. Everyone told me to stay away from him, but I was insistent that he was good. I hoped by sharing some kindness with him that I could make his life happier.' She paused to look at me. 'You know what hurts me now? It is that I went against my own feelings and my association with him has now cost him his life.'

'Don't be so hard on yourself,' I said. 'You offered kindness, nothing more. He did the rest.'

She went on, 'Because of what others said I always made sure I always had someone else with me when I was with him. The week before I was kidnapped he complained and said we didn't need the others. "They are spoiling our fun," he said, and he promised and promised me he would look after me and never let any harm come to me. He called me his princess and I called him Monkey Boy, because of his big eyes and wiry arms. He was so adamant and even though I felt my inner voice saying 'don't' I decided to try and believe in him. I was such a fool. I left the chaperone behind. All this time I felt he wanted my virginity, but all he wanted to do was sell me?'

'Are you disappointed at his trade-off?' I asked.

It was a totally artless comment that just came out before I even thought about it. The moment I said it I was cringing. I mean, here I was making cruel sex related comments to a woman who I knew had been repeatedly drug-raped.

She glared at me. 'A trade-off? How dare you? You are so insensitive!'

'I'm sorry,' I said, 'I didn't mean –'

'Do you have any idea what it feels like to wake up in the morning and know that the night before you were all over someone...to feel like it was just a dream...a very bad, disgusting dream...that made you feel like a whore...do you...do you have any idea?'

'I didn't–'

'Do you know, I had a dream of falling in love...giving myself to a man I love...a man who stood for something...a man with conviction, sensitivity and dreams...Just who do you think you are, asking me such questions?'

She stepped away from me with tears welling up in her eyes, frowning.

'I'm sorry,' I said, 'I really didn't mean anything offensive. It just kind of slipped out before I thought about it.'

She turned back to me. 'You might as well just call me a whore!'

'I was trying to understand whether you were attracted to him, that's all.' I was bullshitting now, trying to cover my tactlessness.

'You are a rude, ignorant man. Leave me alone.' She marched away from me, kicking sand up with her furious feet.

'Shreela, I'm sorry,' I called after her.

'Keep your sorry, you ignorant Englishman,' she shouted over her shoulder.

I called after her three times and then Doug was standing next to me. 'We're nearly there with the raft,' he said. He looked at Shreela stomping away. 'Did you upset her by any chance?'

'Why, aren't we observant tonight, Sherlock? I better go after her, make sure no harm comes to her and try to smooth things over.'

'Okay, lover,' Doug said.

I began heading away.

'Mike,' he called after me. I swung back, expecting more sarcasm. He pointed down at something leaning up against a rock. 'Your gun, mate. Think you better take it with you.'

'Oh yeah,' I said, feeling foolish that I could have walked away and made such a basic error.

'I Wouldn't go five paces on this island without my gun,' he said, taking his M-16 off his back. 'Go on, I'll take over. If Koslov or any of them hungry cannibal bastards show up I'll give them the news,' he winked.

DARK PLACE OF HOPE

Droplets of water hung from my nose as I pushed back another branch, the millionth of the day, and as my cold wet shirt pressed against my skin I shuddered as goose bumps prickled across my flesh.

Listening between the cracks of thunder and tuning my ears in to the noises beyond the frequency of rain patting leaves I headed back inside the jungle. Those eyes were around me once more, peering through the trees, like a thousand tiny drills boring through my bones looking for weaknesses in my soul again. I knew they were there this time. I knew what they wanted and I swear I could see ghostly figures as the lightning fractured the night.

'Shreela?' I said as I heard it, soft and stuttered, sniffing and sobbing.

There was no immediate reply.

I eased back branch one million and one and stepped beyond it. Was it Shreela crying or was it one of them again, one of those spirits?

'Shreela?'

I was moving back inside the creepy-looking jungle when she spoke from right next to me. My heart slapped the underside of my throat. It fell back into place, beating like a crazed rock drummer. 'Leave me alone. Go back to the cave. Just leave me alone.'

'Look, I'm really sorry for what I said. It wasn't thought through and it was really insensitive.'

'Just leave me alone.'

'Shreela,' I said, reaching out to touch her.

'Don't patronise me.' She pushed my hand away from hers, 'Go! You really think that I'm upset because of some pathetic little question you asked.... Don't flatter yourself. I've got bigger problems. It's so degrading. Humiliating. I don't even want to talk about it.'

'Talk about what?'

'Koslov, and that stuff he made me do.'

We were silent for a few moments.

'With all that's happened to you Shreela, I know a lot has happened, and with all of that–'

'Just spit it out.'

'Have you considered that you might be pregnant?'

'I'm not pregnant.'

'How can you be sure? You even said it yourself—that you might be pregnant.'

'I know. A woman knows. Do you have any idea what it means to be pregnant where I come from, when you are not married? It means being cut out, being beaten, kicked and punched, humiliated by everyone, even my own flesh and blood. You probably think I'm just making all this up, but just think back to Kalid.

'That's what it's like living in my village. You just don't know how bad it's going to get. They won't stop to think, that's poor Shreela, the girl who got kidnapped and raped. No they'll just look at me as some whore who gave herself up. There is no way I can be pregnant.'

I didn't respond immediately, but when I did I wished I hadn't. 'Just as long as you're sure that you're not...you know... pregnant. Then again, if you are, I suppose you could always have an abortion.'

She made to slap my face, but I caught her arm. 'Two insults in one night. You really know how to treat a girl, don't you? Let go of me!'

She struggled against me.

I held her firm.

'Okay, I understand it might not be the done thing in your

culture. I was suggesting it as a method used where I come from.'

She wriggled and turned but I still held onto her arm.

'Do you really think I would care for the lives of people like the Jarawa and the environment and then just abort a life like that?'

'Look, I'm sorry, okay? I'm going to let you go, just don't slap me.'

'Okay.'

I released her.

She raised her hand again, but backed off. Turning away from me she disappeared into the trees.

'Shreela, we need to go back,' I called after her.

'Then go,' she said.

'There could be Jarawa...snakes...It's not safe in here.'

'If it scares you, leave.'

I began to head after her, but pulled up short when I realised she had disappeared. 'Shreela?' I turned three sixty degrees. There was no sign of her.

Lightning flashed. Between two trees I saw what looked like a handful of steps. Surely she hadn't gone down them.

I went towards them. Cautiously I scuffed at the dead, slippery foliage and felt stone under my boots. Gripping onto roots that jutted out from the side wall I began to descend.

I cursed her on every step; she was one of those dopey heroines who led the hero into danger, screamed out at the wrong time or knocked the pot of paint on the baddie while hiding overhead. She was really pissing me off now, leading me into dark depths I didn't want to be in. Why couldn't they make kidnap victims like they used to? Why couldn't she just do as she was told?

Something crunched under my foot. I felt around with the toe of my boot. No more steps, just hollow-sounding things, like sea shells that you blow into...only football-sized.

'Don't come here with negativity and fear,' Shreela's voice echoed.

'We need to get back,' I said. Lightning flashed overhead.

The trees, high and hanging, loomed over us as though they were straining to listen to our conversation, and like snakes slithering down the pit walls their damp roots hung, waiting to entwine us.

'They can find your weaknesses. If they do they'll attach themselves to your negativity and mess you up for good.'

'Yeah, right, look we don't have time for this, Shreela. I've heard it all before anyway and we need to leave right away. We need to get back to the cave.'

I could hear the strain in my own voice as I tried to persuade her to leave with me, but still she ignored me. 'You're standing on once sacred Jarawa ground that was desecrated by the Japanese. Bad spirit doesn't have to look for you now. *You* just found *it*.'

I stepped forward to grab her.

Crunch, crunch!

I stood still.

'You just broke someone's face,' she said.

At that moment lightning lit up the pit. I stepped back, shocked at what I saw. I thought for a moment I had imagined it, but another flash up above made me realise it was no trick of the eye. With real force I said, 'We're leaving right now.'

'You can leave when you are ready. I'm staying until I'm done.'

My eyes had adjusted better to the deep darkness now and I could see what looked like a stone construction behind her: steps leading up to an altar, ancient pillars badly made, a weather-beaten roof.

'They're here,' she said, looking up and around her. 'I can feel them.'

I heard the whispers, the same spine-tingling whispers I'd heard in the hangar in Port St Peter.

The hairs all over my body stood on end as the voices seemed to gather over my head. This time there was nobody to accuse of rigging up speakers or throwing objects.

'Protect yourself,' Shreela said.

I took my gun off my shoulder.

She giggled at me. 'I don't mean with your gun. You can't protect yourself from bad spirit with that. It has to be with strong, positive thoughts. Shut your eyes and imagine you are stepping into a bubble. When you're inside nothing bad can get to you. Say to yourself that you only want to communicate with the highest entities.'

She was outlined by a faint glow, though there was nothing there to illuminate her, and I could just make out the slight movements of her head as she listened to whatever was speaking to her. Beyond her I could see what looked like piles and piles of skulls and bones. I didn't want to communicate with any entity. I wanted to drag her back to the LUP, giving her a piece of my mind all the way.

But I felt a force bearing down on me, stopping me from moving, an unseen force, like some massive hand pressing down on my shoulders.

'Quickly, quickly protect yourself,' she said.

I imagined the bubble and asked for the high stuff. When I opened my eyes everything still looked the same, I still heard the voices, but the pressure around me had vanished.

'They only want the settlers,' she said. 'The gunrunners, arms dealers and the smugglers, they won't leave the island until all of the bad has left. The settlers hurt them, destroyed their number. They are angry with the white man and with the bad trade that he brings to these islands.'

'Right, okay. Can we go now?' I reached out for her arm and she moved away from me.

'They say you are a friend. They say that by helping me you are helping them. They want to offer you proof that they watch you. They say they diverted the Jarawa arrow into your rucksack. They were watching you when that woman came into your dreams. She was a bad spirit, a whore who made trade from British soldiers and spread diseases among them. She hates the British. She has been dealt with.'

'Okay, great, now come on. We need to leave.' Again I made to grab her arm. Again she moved away.

Shreela tilted her head. 'They are telling me we will be safe when we cross to Haven Island. We are not to be frightened when the time comes to get in the water.'

I thought about the sharks and then I thought that there was no way we would be getting into the water.

'They say we will be helped. They say you already know you will be safe, you just believe that you don't know. They say it is safer for you to believe.' A moment later her shoulders slumped. 'The energy has gone,' she said. 'We may leave now.'

I backed out of the bone site slowly, Shreela walking towards me. I helped her up the steps, certain that I could still hear the chanting. As we stepped back onto the beach dawn was breaking. The blue skies in the distance melded with the blues of the sea and red and orange merged with the dark clouds that hovered over our heads. Thunder still rumbled in the distance and the last droplets of rain fell on the beach.

'Do you think you'll always be a soldier?' Shreela asked.

'I have thought of leaving the army, but I don't know. Why do you ask?'

She stared at me for a moment then shrugged. 'You've been through so much, but I sense you are searching for more.'

'I've been wondering what life is all about since I caught Jodie in bed with the sleeping policeman, if that's what you mean,' I said with a sad, ironic smile.

'What if you could look down on your life from above? What would you see? What changes would you make?'

'I'd probably see a disgruntled guy wanting to leave his relationship.'

She was frowning at me. 'You know, Mike...sometimes I think you see it, sometimes I think you even feel it, but your ego traps you. It stops you from doing the necessary. Take the situation with your wife—she is an adulteress, humiliating you in your own home, in front of your son and you've thought about leaving her, right?'

'Yeah.'

'But what is really stopping you from freeing yourself from this situation? Is it the stigma in your community surrounding divorce or is it the fear that others around you might somehow think you have failed as a man? Do you stay in the hope that someday you will triumph over all the odds and be able to say you are a bigger, better man, a better lover than the other? What if you knew no-one would judge you in that way? What if you knew no-one really cared what you did so long as your soul found happiness? What action would you take then?'

'Well, I'd leave, of course.'

She continued, 'It's your ego that keeps you in that relationship, but it's your soul that says you must leave. If you stay your soul will weaken, eventually you will be ill. Then you will be calling out all the doctors and none of these men of science have knowledge of how to deal with a broken spirit. You will be at death's door, and at that point you will have to decide either to leave your life by dying or to stay in this life by beginning with a new path.'

'How do you know all this?'

She paused for thought then answered my question very indirectly. 'You will find out all the answers yourself when you begin to listen to your inner voice. Since you came to India, especially since you came to this island, you have been given experiences that show you that there is more than you can see.'

At that moment I felt a real urge to get back to Doug. We had been gone too long. I had allowed Shreela to distract me. I looked back towards the cave. Doug and Spaghetti had the raft on the sand. Doug was shouting something but I couldn't hear him over the waves crashing on the shore. He was waving us to him in a big, 'Come on, get your arse over here' kind of way.

'Oh no,' Shreela said.

'What?'

She pointed across the bay. In the distance figures moved quickly along the beach. There were more than a dozen of them. White men. Koslov's men. Within a matter of minutes we would be in their gun range.

Without hesitation I took Shreela's hand and tugged her. 'Run!' I said. 'Run!'

BLACK WATER

Doug and Spaghetti were heading away from us with the raft. It seemed an illogical thing to do. Why not put out to sea directly in front of the cave? Surely it was better just to get out there and get away. But as I ran I saw Doug's logic.

The cave was just off the centre of the bay. The bay curved inwards. To have put out into the water at that point would have narrowed the distance our pursuers would have needed to travel in order to bring us within target range. Setting out into the sea from that point also meant we were putting out immediately into a stronger current—reducing the time that we would be sitting ducks bobbing on the water, begging a bullet.

Doug and Spaghetti crossed some rocks and dropped out of sight. A minute later we were clambering over the same rocks. I looked behind. Koslov's men had gained.

Shreela stood at the top, 'Look,' she said, jabbing her finger in front, 'further up the beach.'

I looked. 'Holy shit!'

Little dark shadows swarmed towards us. Already they were close enough for me to see their bows and spears, but running out in front of them was a sight that forced me to look twice—the tattered remains of one of our camouflage jackets, no more than a strand of material around the shoulders and chest with sleeves. But even more shocking than that was what he carried in his hands—a pole with a figurehead, a ginger-haired figurehead—Macca's skull.

It wasn't fair. It wasn't right. It wasn't how a man in my unit should end up. 'Noooo,' I shouted, 'you bastards.' I flicked the safety on the M-16, but was stopped by the hand on the end of my gun.

'I can talk to them,' Shreela said.

My heart pumped like machinery on an oil field. 'Talk?!' I spat at her. 'What the fuck are you going to talk about? You can't spread a blanket on the beach and parley with them.'

I lowered my gun as I saw Doug putting out to sea. With our way blocked from the front and the back he'd had no option.

Shreela stopped on the shoreline and looked at the Jarawa hurtling towards us. 'I know some of these people. I can speak a little of their tongue.'

'Get to the raft,' I rasped, taking hold of her arm.

Doug and Spaghetti, now waist-deep and unsteady, were taking a battering from the incoming waves. I grabbed hold at the back of the raft and helped take the weight. It seemed to balance better now and we headed out until we were at chest depth. 'Lower it,' I shouted.

Spaghetti, exercising his instincts for his own survival, clambered on board. Doug and I hoisted Shreela up to him. 'Get the paddles going,' I said. 'Doug, help me, kick from the back.'

Spaghetti took a knife from his belt and slit the vine that held the paddles in place. 'What about sharks?' he asked.

'Right now the sharks are the ones with guns,' I replied, 'now paddle.'

Without further question he dipped his paddle in the water and began calling out a rhythm to Shreela. 'Pull, pull, pull.'

There was a shout behind us on the beach.

The first shots of automatic fire thudded.

Doug swung round.

'What's happening?'

'The Jarawa are fighting them. Koslov has good cover from the rocks. It'll be over in seconds.'

'Let's make the most of it,' I called back. 'Come on.'

My thighs burned, my arms ached, my neck hurt, my

breathing was laboured, but I continued to kick, swallowing water, gasping and spitting.

'I must go back to shore,' Shreela said.

'Don't be fucking ridiculous,' Spaghetti shouted. 'Now pull.'

Shreela stood up on the raft. 'Those men are going to be slaughtered because of me. I cannot allow it.'

She moved to the edge of the raft, about to jump into the sea. Spaghetti grabbed her round the legs, rugby-tackle style and pulled her down. We drifted for a few seconds as he wrestled her to the deck, then Doug and I were clambering up, grabbing the oars and paddling.

'Let me go,' Shreela shouted.

He covered her mouth with his hand, wrapped his leg over hers to stop her wriggling and spoke firmly to her. 'They'll kill them anyway and then when they've finished with them they'll come after us,' he roared at her. 'If you go back we'll all die too.'

Shreela was still struggling when the fire on the beach intensified. I glanced back to shore and saw a tall figure rise up from the rocks, distinguishable by his reptilian features. And from his hip he fired three hundred rounds per minute from his AK-47, massacring the Jarawa.

He yelped with delight and jumped down from the rocks, loosened a few more rounds into the air just for good measure before he began wading out into the sea towards us.

Panting like a dog on heat I rolled onto the deck of the raft. My freezing cold fingers fiddled with the safety of my gun. Unbalanced by the swell of the waves, I found him in my sights and let him have a burst.

My shots fell short. He stretched out his arms and laughed. He was showing me I couldn't reach him, showing me he didn't fear me, showing his men his bravery, ridiculing my effort to take him down.

We were now fairly and squarely in the pull of the outgoing current. Spaghetti was back at the paddle I had vacated. Shreela was by my side, kneeling up with her arms hanging loosely at her sides, and staring blankly back at the beach. 'Their death's allowed us to escape,' she said.

I ignored her. I didn't care about the Jarawa. They could rot as far as I was concerned. I cared only about the way my colleague's corpse had been treated. A bullet was one thing, the explosion another, but what they had done to him...taken his remains to pieces, like a written-off car at a scrap dealer's.

I blamed Koslov. I hated Koslov. I hated the way he just stood in the waves and just smiled. I hated his big nose, his snake-like skin, the smell of his fucking cigarettes and most of all I hated the way he had eluded me yet again.

It was then that I heard the low thud of helicopter blades in the distance. Above the trees on the main island it appeared as a metal glint in the sky.

I glowered at it. 'If that bastard does a flyover it's gonna get the news in the form of a 40mm grenade,' I said.

I shoved an oar in Shreela's hand. 'Help me paddle. Let's make the most of the raft while we have it. Doug, call out what's happening and get ready to lay down fire. Spaghetti, get your grenade sorted.'

From the corner of my eye I saw Shreela matching me stroke for stroke. Her effort and energy were inspiring. We dipped the oars in unison, like a desperate Mohican couple paddling downriver to escape the cavalry. I dug deep. 'Arghhhh,' I groaned as I heaved the oar back, pulling hard and long. I grabbed a breath as I lifted it from the water. 'Arghhhh.' I plunged it in again. My muscles burned and my shoulders felt like they would pop with the strain. The rough wood of the oar bore deep into the flesh of my hands as I heaved and heaved and heaved.

'Heli is over the beach,' Doug said.

I looked at Haven Island, so near yet so far. Even with the head of steam we had built up it was still going to be untouchable for some time to come.

The incoming fire started a distance away from us and came towards us in two parallel lanes that cut through the waves.

Shreela shrieked and paddled harder.

'Contact rear! Contact rear! Warning fire! Warning fire!'

'Keep paddling! Keep paddling!' I roared at Shreela. 'Hold your fire,' I shouted at the lads. 'Bring it in close, make your shots count.'

Seconds later the helicopter blasted overhead. It passed with such violence it almost rocked us right off the raft. It swung back in towards us, dropping and hovering, blocking our path and buffeting us with wave after wave from its downwash.

It dropped and hovered twenty feet away, blocking our path.

'Let 'em have it boys,' I shouted.

Spaghetti fired.

Whoof!

Bang!

The heli seemed to hold for a moment then it was all over the place, dipping and swaying. Its rotors were down, just above the surface of the water. Smoke was billowing out of the back doors. It was coming right for us.

Whoof!

Doug fired.

Bang!

We were thrown to the deck by the blast. Fragments of helicopter splintered and flames poured out of the craft.

A wave hit the failing rotors. It toppled over. Its rear arm swung high and then it just came down, straight on top of us.

Horror-stricken, Shreela watched the heli bringing death towards her. She had less than a second of life left in her before the rear rotors stripped the meat from her bones and blended her flesh into tomato pulp. I launched myself across the raft to save her, knocking her into the water.

Our lungs filled with water as we tumbled, swallowing and choking. Still holding onto her I kicked upwards and away until we broke the surface of the water, and we gasped and barked for air like a couple of winded dogs.

Doug waved to me from across the other side of the wreckage. Spaghetti was grabbing a piece of raft that bobbed on the surface and swam it over to us.

Doug did the same. At my side, he opened his mouth to speak and took in a mouthful of wave instead. He coughed it up.

Spaghetti rocked on the waves. 'Hours of fine craftsmanship stripped to shit at the ocean sawmill,' he said.

'Anyone manage to hold onto their guns?' I asked, ignoring him.

They both shook their heads.

Shreela's driftwood bumped into mine. She reached out and touched my hand. 'Remember what the spirits told us,' she said.

I saw the faith in her eyes and wished I could believe as she did, but drifting in shark-infested waters, a one-hour swim from shore, I remembered the fleet of speed boats we could have knocked out in Mayishmagar and wondered how long we had before they came bounding around the peninsula towards us.

CIRCLING SHARKS

We swam clinging to drift wood, with sunburned faces and skin so tight that every slap of salt water bit deep and painfully. Slowly, painfully slowly, we inched towards Haven Island's coast.

We had expended vast amounts of energy on our escape. I knew that the days of poor diet and beatings and traipsing through the jungle steaming in thirty-one degrees and eighty percent humidity while being bitten by one insect after another were catching up with us all.

Back at home the SAS have something called Selection which weeds out the ones who may be 'excellent' but not 'elite' soldiers from those who are the best. We run for miles, up mountains, down mountains, we run through forests, are deprived of sleep and food, we're made to sit in stress positions and undergo interrogation, with everything aimed at breaking those who don't have the intestinal fortitude to operate effectively when their bodies are swollen, aching and exhausted.

Selection usually starts off with around a hundred hopefuls on day one and over the weeks it gets whittled down to just a few. It's a tough process, with the success rate only about as high as ten percent. If you crack it, you know you can hack almost anything else that life can throw at you.

We had now been on the move for almost thirty hours, had little food and been exposed to the elements. My body was shaking, my head felt dizzy, my arms tingled and I puffed with every movement. I knew I was out of condition before this mission had begun, but I knew now that my survival came down to one thing—my next kick, then the one after and the one after that. There was no point looking any further ahead or thinking about anything else, I just had to focus on that next kick.

One kick at a time I pushed myself on. I had done this in selection, I had done it in training, I had done it on other missions—I could do it again now. This is what I had been trained for, no way on this earth was I going to quit.

Shreela, on the other hand had never gone through any of our training and had shown enough guts to put most guys to shame. Like me, she was now at the outer limits of what her body could take, but she lacked something that I had, something to reference the pain and the feelings with—the benefit of Selection, SAS routines, discipline and training. For her, perhaps the thought of giving up would soon become a preferred option.

Wearily I turned to look back over my shoulder towards Mayishmagar, just checking to make sure nothing was behind before I started to kick the water again.

The Indian navy, in port less than twenty clicks south, might have heard the gunfire, but almost certainly would have heard the explosion of the heli, and yet there was still no sign of a rescue or even a heli to see what was going on.

'Shark!' Spaghetti shouted. Dizzily I swung back to look at him. He was pointing along the coast of the island.

I stared out in the direction he had shown me, saw a grey fin and instantly lost the will to live. I didn't have the strength to fight off a cold now, let alone a shark.

'It's a dolphin,' Doug called back.

'It's a sign,' Shreela said weakly.

'Let's keep going,' I called to everyone. 'It's getting nearer.'

I was just beginning to believe we could make it when Spaghetti announced yet another twist of fortune.

This time he had seen a shark, but at the same time Spaghetti was getting my attention so was Doug, but for a different reason. He was pointing behind us, scared out of his wits and no longer able to form his words.

Three boats dotted the horizon, one a good distance ahead

of the others, and they were not coming from the south, where the ops Centre was located, but the north, Mayishmagar.

'Kick,' I called, 'kick hard.'

As I kicked I changed the angle of the raft wood that had been my float. I was no longer interested in keeping my balance; now, all I was interested in was defying the laws of water resistance, being as aerodynamic as possible and cutting through the water like a torpedo. At a base level, outrunning the shark was impossible, but outrunning my colleagues to ensure it reached them first was another matter. It was now a case of survival of the fittest.

Spaghetti saw what I did and followed suit. The skinny git was out-paddling me, Shreela and Doug were easing by. I could feel my initial burst of energy failing, the others passing me by, life slipping away before me.

But then automatic gunfire revived my senses in a way that only automatic gunfire can. The shots landed nowhere around me and I guessed they must have fallen short. I kicked and kicked and tried to stay focused on the trees. I surged past Doug and sailed beyond Spaghetti. And that was when I saw it.

It came right at me, parting the ocean on either side of its fin.

My stomach dropped. Oh fuck!

I was going to die. Teeth were about to clamp around my torso. My stomach was going to be torn open, my limbs torn to tatters.

The distance to the shore no longer mattered. I was dead already.

And then I realised that it wasn't cutting through the water; it was porpoising. I saw its eyes, its mouth and its teeth, two hundred and fifty shining white teeth, and then it rolled over onto its belly and swam backwards alongside me, making that clicking sound that only dolphins make.

Still thrashing the bejesus out of the sea, I almost cried and laughed at the same time. It was only a dolphin and the dumb bloody animal wanted to play...now!

It rolled over and I grabbed its fin. I had no idea which way this ocean-cruiser dolphin was going but I jumped on board.

There was shouting from behind me, but we were already dipping and rising through the waves. I tried to look back, but as we submerged, with my eyes and mouth wide open with exhilaration I swallowed and choked and blinked away a gallon of salt water.

I couldn't see behind, couldn't hear, couldn't breathe and couldn't give a toss. I had been a moment from death and found a pleasure cruise—I no longer gave a shit about anything or anyone else. I was going to survive.

Minutes later my feet brushed against something underneath. Was it the shark darting beneath me? My heart sank. Then it happened again and again and then I knew it wasn't the shark but the sea bed. I let go of the fin and put my feet down.

Doubled over and breathless with exhilaration and strain I looked back at the others. Dozens of dolphins lined the waves and all of my unit and Shreela were hanging onto their fins. I waded across to Shreela, the shortest person in our group, and dragged her onto the beach.

'Fucking Man from Atlantis,' Spaghetti said, as he jogged out of the water.

Back out at sea the lead motorboat had stopped. Someone was being retrieved from the water. Whatever had happened out there I really didn't understand. I didn't care—we were on dry land and, for the moment, safe.

It was vital for us to keep the momentum of our escape going. 'Single file. Doug, set the pace, Spaghetti fall in behind Doug, Shreela, in front of me. Let's move it out.'

It was good that we did not delay a second longer. I could hear the boat's motor, I could hear them shouting. They were closing in.

Suddenly, rounds pinged and whooped off the trees and exploded in the foliage around my feet. I didn't need to tell Doug to get a shift on as he was sprinting already, but I roared at him all the same. If one of us took a bullet now, that would be it. None of us would go on without the others and that pact would seal our fates. Koslov wasn't going to mess around with three SAS troublemakers. We'd all have bullets in us by the end of the day.

Driven on by pure fear, we crunched through the dried undergrowth, skipped over fallen trees and ran straight through cracking branches that whipped across our faces. Haven Island was sparse compared to Kali Pani, more like English woodland in autumn, only with tropical trees and blazing sunshine. Losing the enemy was going to be difficult now, and without any weapons we had nothing to deter our enemy from coming on to us. We got as deep into the woods as quickly as possible.

The incoming stopped, but still we pressed on at a suicidal speed and it was then that our luck hit rock bottom.

Shreela stumbled. I almost ran straight into her. I bent down and took her arm, 'Get up,' I shouted as though she was one of my unit. I grabbed at her arm and tried to heave her back to her feet, but the arm was limp, her head was down. I grabbed her by the chin.

Her eyes weren't focusing. 'Doug, Spaghetti, problem,' I called. They swung round and came back. 'She's had it,' I said.

Doug looked at our surroundings, 'The shrub's thicker over there,' he puffed.

'Okay.' I heaved her up onto my shoulder and jogged into the thicker area. I returned her to the ground in full view.

'What you doing?' Doug said.

'Don't fucking argue,' I said. 'Get the fuck in to that shrub over there. I go there, Spaghetti, there. They come for Shreela, we hit them, get their guns and fuck off.'

'That's fucking suicide.'

'Do it,' I snarled.

It was desperate plan, a crazy idea, but our only real hope now was to trick our enemy.

'Shreela,' I panted, 'you can't go on, we have to set an ambush to get guns. You have to be our bait. Please just sit there and this will all be over in a few seconds.'

'Go,' she said, waving her arm like a drunk. 'Go.'

I dashed to the bush, thinking I had just fucked up big time. My heart was racing at Mach 2. It was an idiotic plan, but it had to work.

It was then that I heard dry twigs and foliage snapping. A few seconds later I saw them. They stopped dead in their tracks when they spotted Shreela.

There were four of them and they approached with caution. If they had been good soldiers they would have fanned out and covered the surrounding ground as well as the area they were moving into, just one of them would have gone forward. These guys were crap. They played straight into our hands.

The first of the men was within five metres when Shreela looked up at him. It was Elvis. She held out her hands. 'Help me,' she said pathetically.

He stepped further forward. 'Where are men?' he said.

'I tripped. I am injured. You frightened them and they have run away and left me.'

The idiot laughed. He looked back at his cronies and they all laughed. 'English soldiers,' I heard him say. I saw two of them lower their weapons and relax, the other, obviously a brighter, more qualified idiot moved out towards where Spaghetti was hiding. I could just see Spaghetti and Doug. Slowly, and so as not to draw attention, I held up my fist and shook it three times, our signal to go.

Spaghetti jumped up and dragged the guy closest to him into the bushes. I could hear him bashing the wind out of him.

Doug piled in.

I hit the guy closest to me with everything I had left in me. He sprawled to the floor, gun out of reach, and with a couple of well-aimed punches and knees I had the better of him.

'Dat will do,' Elvis shouted. His voice was cracked, his body language jittery.

This time he stood well back from Shreela, with his AK pointing at her head.

'You will move back,' he screamed at us. His head twitched from one of us to the other.

'Fuck off,' Spaghetti said.

'You won't hurt her,' Doug said.

'If you touch her your boss will kill you,' I added. 'You know, dead, dead.'

I saw confusion on his face. He had the gun and the girl and he knew he could not kill her. He had two choices either grab her and back out with the hostage or wait for his friends.

I didn't wait to find out his choice. I took a step forward. 'I shoot you,' he shouted.

As he shouted he moved his gun away from Shreela's head and pointed it towards me. Shreela rose up and knocked the gun away. Doug leapt for a gun on the ground close to him, but Spaghetti already had that covered. He opened up and Elvis was taken down.

We had wasted enough time. The occupants of the other boats were now going to be close. They would have heard the shots coming from our direction and be on their way. We grabbed the guns and frisked the prostrate figures for spare magazines and food. I slung my new gun over one shoulder, the weak and spent Shreela over the other and with no map moved out in the only direction I knew...away from Koslov.

BEGGING AND STEALING

My earlier recce over Haven Island had given me a general knowledge of the island—the only place of habitation was the Bengali settlement, the same location as the new ops Centre Ramjit had set up. The Island was no more than about ten clicks wide and thirty long and the settlement, at a guess, was about twenty-five clicks to the southwest. We struggled throughout the day, carrying Shreela between us in skin-grilling temperatures. By mid-afternoon our condition was dire and although Shreela did occasionally walk for a few minutes at a time we were all swaying and staggering.

By nightfall continuing was no longer an option—Spaghetti, Doug and Shreela all just came to a complete standstill. While they dropped to the ground I forced myself to take a brief look around, just to make sure we were safe. I discovered we were up on a level, not particularly high up, just higher and close to a ridge. I went to the edge and looked over and there to my amazement was the settlement I had been aiming for.

With the aid of moonlight I could see clearly into the valley. There appeared to be three tracks in and out, small dwellings, grass huts and one building that stuck out above all of the others. Further on I could see a jetty with several small boats moored around it.

'Guys,' I said, scrambling back to them with tired excitement. 'We just stumbled onto civilization.'

They forced themselves up. Exhausted, hungry and dehydrated they followed me to the ridge and lay on their bellies to stare down on the moonlit town.

'Where's the navy?' Doug said, his voice wooden, distant.

'Where the fuck is the navy? There should be a boat down there, an ops centre, a tent or something, with soldiers around. We're supposed to make our RV and they're not there?'

Spaghetti slumped, his face in the earth, his voice a dull, listless monotone. 'We got stitched up. This whole op has been one big stitch up.'

Doug said, 'We're no better than those convicts they used to keep on theses islands, a thousand miles across shark infested water and basically alone—no boat, no radio and rampant with hunger...the bad news in this place just keeps on coming, hits you over and over.'

'We have one advantage,' I said. 'We've been trained for this shit and we have some ammo left. We just have to be resourceful.'

'I'm all resourced out,' Spaghetti said.

I lifted my head and sniffed as though I were in a Bisto commercial. 'I swear there's cooking going on,' I said.

'Don't be stupid,' Doug said, looking like he could dissolve. 'You can't smell a thing from up here.'

Spaghetti took a long hard sniff, 'No, I reckon he's right. I can smell spices.'

'Yes,' Shreela said, scrambling to her feet. 'Yes, I can smell it too, onions, garlic, ginger, peppers, come on.'

'Hold on,' I said, reaching up to grab her arm. 'We don't just get up and charge.'

'I bet it's coming from that big place,' Spaghetti said. 'We need to go there.'

'No,' I said, 'I don't give a damn how hungry you are—we're not going to storm it.'

He scratched his head with both hands, looking like a deranged monkey. 'Well, we have to get food from somewhere. There has to be some food down there.'

I looked at Doug, 'You think once we've pinched some food from somewhere that you can hot-wire us a boat with a motor?'

'Can a dog shit on the pavement?' he said, without a smile.

I thought for a second then gave them the plan.

With Shreela holding on to me we crept down from the ridge. At the bottom we paused to get a feel for our new surroundings. Most of the homes in the settlement were grass huts, a few were brick, some had corrugated roofs. I guessed the area was not one where money and personal possessions were a priority and it looked like these people were in life just to survive. I didn't feel the area offered too much for us to worry about in terms of confrontation, but as ever we would proceed with due caution.

At the roadside Doug tapped me on the shoulder and pointed out of town. About two hundred yards away was the jetty. We skirted the back of the settlement, dodging between the grass houses and huge trees at the far end of the village. We paused as we reached the cover of the last house.

Inside, a television blared with English voices, cockneys arguing; it had to be one of our old soap operas. There was the occasional sniff or mumble from the occupant.

Outside, the only sound was a dog barking. The yapping came from the big building, a guest house, according to the sign outside.

'See, I told you that's where the smell was coming from,' Spaghetti whispered.

'Bloody hell, you don't let up,' I replied.

Doug's eyes twinkled. 'The dog's gone quiet. You think they're cooking it?'

I held my finger to my lips before anyone laughed or said any more.

Out at sea, it was dark except for where the moonlight glistened on a ripple. I beckoned Doug over, 'Go and find us a boat,' I said.

He headed across the dirt track, over a ridge, down into the water and disappeared from sight.

The dog yapped again, there was a yawn from inside the grass hut, voices from further up Grass Hut Avenue.

A few minutes passed, then Doug's head popped up from the bank. He climbed up and came back across the road. The thumbs up told me we had transport.

I pointed over to the tents, which I assumed were occupied by day-trippers like the ones I had seen getting off the boats and walking along the jetty during our helicopter ride. We set off towards them, keeping low and moving quickly.

Thirty feet from the first tent, I held up my hand. 'Hang back here,' I whispered, 'I'm going for a close-up on the tents.'

I left everyone lying on their bellies and crept forward. I stopped to listen a few yards from the tent and when I heard nothing that disturbed me I moved right up next to it. A gas lamp was burning and I could see the shadows of two figures sitting down. I moved to the opening and eased back the flap just enough to see inside. A man and a woman, white and middle-aged sat around the lamp; they didn't look threatening, so I just went straight in.

They both recoiled at the shock of seeing me. The man jumped out of his seat and almost fell over himself. Thankfully, neither of them shouted or screamed. I made a gesture of eating. 'Food,' I said.

They both nodded. The woman looked inside a box and pulled out a single slice of bread.

I shook my head, 'Friends,' I said, gesturing outside and then hugging my belly.

'You English, mate?' the man said.

I glanced at him, recognizing his northern accent.

'We're from North Yorkshire,' the woman said and handed me the whole loaf of bread.

'Christ, what do you want to come to a place like this for? You got any drinks?'

'Bloody 'ell mate, don't want much, do ya?' the bloke said.

I swung the rifle in his direction. He shut up and held his hands up.

'I'm a travel writer,' the woman said. 'The Indian tourist board want to develop this island, make it into something like the Maldives and the Seychelles. They're sponsoring our visit. We just have a little water, will that help?'

'Whatever you have will be fine. Did they mention the cannibals on the other islands to you?'

'Yes, yes, they did, and if I can get a picture of them I'm going to put that in the article. Have you seen them?'

I nodded. 'They're not photogenic. The ones I've seen look like their eyes have been dug out and most of their teeth have been smashed up.'

'Oh,' she said, looking disappointed.

'You might want to investigate what the government are doing to those people so they can commercialise the islands. Check out deforestation and the reclamation of the land from the native tribes, oh, and you might fancy checking up on the arms shipment trade.'

She handed me the water and seemed to relax. 'I have some lovely mango jam for the bread, do you want some?'

I almost laughed; I was being offered bread and jam for information! 'Thanks,' I said. 'Do you have a spare knife as well?'

She dug around for a minute in a bag and then handed me a stainless steel, Sheffield knife. 'It wasn't the story I was intending to write, but what you say might be very interesting. I'll dig around a little. Thank you.'

'I wouldn't mention the arms dealing to anyone connected with government—might get you killed.'

I felt like I was involved in a comedy sketch as I backed out with a loaf of bread, a flask of water, a knife and jam! 'Thanks,' I said, 'I hope I didn't frighten you. And good luck with the travel writing. I don't expect to read about our meeting in an article. If I do...'

She tapped her nose with her finger. 'Secret's safe with me. Thanks for the info.'

'Enjoy the rest of your visit to Haven Island.'

I got out of the tent, scuttled across to the others, gave them a slice of bread each and told them what had happened.

'So when do we get the rest of the bread, the mango jam and a drink?' Spaghetti asked.

'Let's get to the boat and get the hell away from here first then we'll have a midnight picnic out on the ocean under the moonlight.'

'You're fucking crazy,' Doug said, laughing lightly.

'No,' I replied, 'fucking crazy would be going into the next tent and demanding wine to go with our meal. Now let's move out.'

At the dirt track, by the last grass hut we paused to check the road and the jetty were clear. Doug turned. 'The tide is in, water is thigh-high, mind your bollocks,' he said dryly.

He crossed the dirt track and went over the ridge into the sea first. I went next, easing myself down. I waved Shreela over and helped her down. Spaghetti came last.

The jetty was up ahead; on the far side of it was a boat. It was a little bigger than a speed boat and had a canopy. Doug said, 'I'll loosen the moorings and then you lot come forward. Once you're all in I'll hot-wire it and we're out of here. Piece of piss. Wait for my signal.' He eased himself lower into the water and swam without splashing.

The settlement fell silent. The only sound now was Doug's smooth strokes parting the water. When he got to the boat he peered over the side. He turned and gave us the signal it was clear and Doug swam to the front of the boat to remove the mooring. Shreela headed towards him, Spaghetti followed on.

With the packet of bread in my mouth, the bottle of water and the knife in one hand and the mango jam in the other, I eased down into the water and moved forward.

Spaghetti was aboard now and Doug was at the back mooring, waiting for me to arrive before throwing off the rope. He gestured for me to get in and then waggled his index and middle fingers in a gesture that I understood to mean he was going to swim the boat out.

I dropped the bread into the boat and Spaghetti came to take the jam, the water and the knife. As I passed the stainless steel knife to him it slipped through his fingers and clattered to the deck.

The metal clattered on the wood with the same vibration as a drummer hitting a small cymbal. It echoed in the bay.

There was no delay in any of our reactions.

'Get in,' Doug said. I hoisted myself out of the water with

Spaghetti's help as Doug threw off the rope and began steering us out. Shreela, proving her worth as a team member—she found two oars under one of the bench seats and passed them to Spaghetti and me. We both dipped them in the water and helped Doug.

We were level with the end of the jetty when a door squeaked open at the guest house.

A shout.

'Get in and hot-wire this bastard before the guy's whole family jump in after us,' I called to Doug. I handed Shreela my oar and told her and Spaghetti to give it some welly as I hoisted Doug in.

The guy from the guest house was running towards the end of the jetty, now some fifteen metres behind us. Lights were going on at the guesthouse and people were coming out of their grass huts to see what was going down.

The guy from the guest house raised something to his shoulder. 'Everyone down!' I said. A second later his gun erupted.

It must have missed us by a mile. I didn't hear it hit anything, didn't even hear the bullet whoosh or ping.

'Get this thing started,' I shouted to Doug. 'His aim might get better.'

I didn't think it was a particularly funny thing to say, but Doug began to chuckle. I think more than anything it was just a release of tension, but as he tried to control his laughter and hot-wire the boat he farted, and at that moment we all ended up howling on the deck of boat.

Another shot: this time it deflected off something metal. 'Missed,' Spaghetti shouted and we all laughed even harder.

I would have liked to have seen what the Bengali settlers saw that night, our boat drifting out into the ocean, the owner shooting at us, and us on the floor doubled up in fits of laughter. With tears streaming down his face, Doug broke the casing around the ignition unit, but he was still laughing too much to connect the wires.

I risked a look over the back of the boat. On the end of

the jetty the guy was loading up for another shot. I slipped the catch off my stolen AK-47 and let the jetty have a dozen rounds. I saw bodies disappear, some to the ground, others diving back into their homes, one into the sea.

The engine spluttered into life and we began heading away from the shore at a nice speed. Doug took the helm and jokingly welcomed us all aboard. Spaghetti and Shreela got off the floor and I picked the offending knife up from the deck and sat with the loaf of bread on my lap. 'So,' I said, trying to act like a mother out for the day with the kids and a picnic, 'Who's for bread and mango jam?'

There were four rounds of bread each. I spread the jam on thick and it lasted until the last slice. We washed it down with a mouthful of water each.

After eating I moved to the back of the boat and sat on the bench seat. Shreela got up and followed me. Before she sat down she said, 'You were all fantastic today.'

'Heeey,' Spaghetti returned, triumphantly. 'We have an admirer at last.'

She went on, 'Today you have continually saved my life. You also provided food and made me laugh in a way I haven't laughed in a long time. Thank you.'

She sat next to me with her arm behind my back and cuddled into me. 'Today I learned what it means to live. I faced death and was turned away from it by you all,' she whispered up into my ear. She reached up, pecked me on the cheek and nestled into my shoulder.

'Thank you,' I said.

'What, for a kiss of gratitude?'

I smiled down at her. 'Yeah,' I said, 'it means a lot to be appreciated.' I took a deep breath and felt the breeze on my skin. I let out one long breath and relaxed. 'No Jarawa, no Koslov, no scorpions,' I said. 'What a blissful feeling.'

The sky was clear, the stars were bright, the moon was shining; what could possibly go wrong for us now?

At that moment the engine spluttered and conked out.

WHEN THE WORLD IS AGAINST YOU...

The engine whirred as Doug turned the ignition. He tried it again and got the same result. Slapping the wheel he turned towards us and threw his arms up in the air. 'Typical, just fucking typical, it's out of fuel.'

'Christ,' I said, as I got up from the back of the boat, 'do you ever feel like the whole world is against you? Are there any fuel cans lying around?'

We searched the deck, but there was no fuel.

'Let's not waste any time,' I said, 'We've already had one swim in this sea. Let's get the oars in the water. I don't want us to have to defend ourselves out here against a Bengali flotilla.'

Spaghetti and Doug got to it. After the engine noise the tranquil swishing of oars in the water took a bit of getting used to. I swapped with Doug after a while and then a while later he changed with Spaghetti. We kept it going like that right through the night.

During one of my breaks I sat at the back of the boat with Shreela. 'I was thinking about what you were saying earlier, about the whole world being against you, is that how you feel?'

'Sometimes I do. My marriage is a perfect example.'

She smiled kindly. 'My teachers told me that when I am on the right path all things go well and fall into place and I am easily happy.'

I shook my head, 'Life going well and fitting into place... sounds weird. My life has never been like that. It's been one long battle.'

'You mean you rushed out of home at sixteen, joined the

army, met Jodie, the first girl you ever fell in love with and married her.'

'What's so wrong with that? I mean, none of it felt wrong at the time. I even felt happy for a time.'

'But did you...when you really think back, did you really feel happy? Think back to the days before you got married— were they happy, romantic days that all went well or did things go wrong that made you feel anxious, frustrated and annoyed?'

'My tie broke on my wedding day, oh, and someone took the groom off the top of the wedding cake and pushed it through the icing, head first; oh, and we had a row the night before, silly thing over something her bridesmaid said. It spiralled into a right slanging match: I hate your bridesmaid, I hate your best man, your sister's a bitch, your brother's two faced. It just went on like that.'

'Did you stop to think about what you were doing?'

'I asked myself if this was what married life with Jodie had in store for me, if that's what you mean, but I just shrugged it off as pre-wedding jitters. I told myself the wedding was all planned, suits were ordered, guests were coming, the meal was paid for. I also wanted to show my parents that I had made something of my life.'

She looked out to sea. 'In my culture many girls are married before they are women. Their weddings are arranged very early in life and they have no choice in the man. Some of these arrangements work out, but there are many stories of shackled disharmony. In your society those shackles are created by your choice...' She paused as though thinking about something then looked up at me. 'You didn't answer my question; did you believe that this behaviour was an indication of what married life with Jodie had in store for you?'

'We argued on many occasions before I had even proposed to her, but more so after I moved out of the barracks and into her place. I guess I knew it was going to be stormy even then.'

'So why did you go ahead with the marriage?'

I shrugged. 'Like I said, it was all arranged.'

'No, I mean before that, you argued a lot, why didn't you

just leave and move back into the barracks long before all the wedding plans were finalized?'

I thought about the question and then had to admit to Shreela that I found it impossible to answer.

We sat silently for a minute and I thought over the questions she had asked me and my answers. 'There's a pattern in my life,' I said. 'Arguments, things going wrong...but I guess that's just life.'

'I understand that things go wrong from time to time. Couples can work together and become stronger if they choose to rise to the challenges. Sadly, for others problems cause conflict and the conflict turns to disharmony. Do you back off from your problems and see them objectively or just carry on to the bitter end? You see, how you handle things is crucial. How did you resolve your differences?'

'She shouted, stormed away from me and slammed doors. Occasionally I got a slap across the face. When she left the room I'd try calling after her, but she would put her hand up and just dismiss me. I'd end up on the couch flabbergasted and fed up.'

'Who do you perceive is the strongest, you or your wife?'

'I think she must be the strongest. I was always the one to back down from the arguments. Christ, sometimes I even called myself a wimp.'

She gazed at me, smiling. She touched my hand. 'You're a very wise man. Your wife may have won the arguments, but you allowed for that to happen.'

I laughed at her. 'You call that wise? I thought wise was winning. She actually backed me into a corner most of the time, tied me up in argumentative knots and got pretty aggressive.'

'They are all weaknesses in spirit.' She explained, 'You were the one who retained the control over the situation by remaining flexible to the circumstances, by not lashing out. You were wise because you rationalised. You were strong for this reason.

'Something I have come to understand from my parents is the power struggle. My mother acts as you do; at times she may seem weak. My father is like Jodie, the aggressive one. He has to have what he wants in order to be proved strong, my mother has what she has and is content.'

'You're speaking in riddles. I don't understand.'

'What happens is one person wants the other's strength to fill their weaknesses and they achieve this through creating conflicts and then winning the battles.'

'I'm still not sure I'm getting this. You're telling me Jodie used to set up conflicts so she could win?'

'Yes, because her weak spirit needed strength and you had strength in abundance. You have to be mentally strong to be a soldier. She wanted to overpower you. She had to overpower you to win...to survive.'

'Sounds bizarre.'

'Maybe a little, but think about it, I bet you argued most when she was having a bad day, perhaps a dispute with one of her relatives, a problem at work, your son answering her back or questioning her or perhaps when she was under the weather, most probably at the time of her monthly cycle.'

'Sometimes I didn't want to argue. I'd shut myself in a room or go in the kitchen.'

'Did she follow you?'

'Always!'

'Is that when she hit you or walked out slamming the doors?'

I thought about it. 'Yes,' I said, 'almost every time.'

She paused for thought again. 'Some couples have recurring arguments, things they throw at each other when they have nothing much to argue over; they niggle at each other. Did you have these?'

I mentioned my work and that Jodie wanted me to leave the service.

She looked at me as though questioning something.

'What is it?' I asked.

'Have you considered that this affair is just a continuation of the same theme?'

I shook my head.

'You said that she wants to end the affair and that you two get back together...is it conditional? Do you have to leave the army?'

'She's said both of those things, just not in the same sentence.'

We didn't speak for a minute then Shreela broke the silence with another question. 'How soon did she back down from arguments?'

'After I had spent between ten minutes and an hour convincing her she was right and that I understood what she meant and that I was just being a total idiot.'

'So when your strength flowed into her in sufficient amounts to give her the strength she needed the argument ended?'

'Yeah, I suppose.'

'How did you feel when you argued?'

'Weak.'

'And when you were trying to convince her?'

'Strong,' I paused and then corrected myself. 'No, I felt like I was running on fuel reserves—I felt exhausted, but somehow strengthened, what we call a second wind—usually I'd just collapse in a chair. Sometimes I'd even fall asleep.'

A knowing smile stretched across her face, 'So why didn't you leave her and return to the barracks?'

I was about to tell her she had asked me that question already when a new thought occurred to me. 'To be honest I was used to all the arguing—stormy is what I'm used to. I've never been far away from a fight, either with my parents or my occupation.'

'So even though you were unhappy it still felt natural?'

'Yeah, but there was more. I never moved out, because I felt she needed me.'

'She made you feel like that?'

'Well...I don't know, yeah, maybe. She didn't always seem like she could cope. She would cry or get annoyed over little things and then I would feel bad. Going away with the Regiment was the worst, everything seemed to go wrong before I left and sometimes I wished I could just phone in and say sorry, I can't make it, but in the army you can't do that. I always felt awful leaving her. I don't know if she tried to make me feel guilty or if I just felt like that because I knew I could help if I was there.'

'That is spiritual violence. I understand it happens in relationships all around the world. I understand it isn't usually meant, but occurs when there is an imbalance between two people's emotional/mental abilities. The weaker will usually start to absorb the stronger unless the stronger is aware and knows how to stop it. Of course when people find someone from their soul group, a twin flame, the balance is very even.'

She took a deep sigh and leaned back, looking up at the stars. I stared at her in bewilderment—here was a twenty-four year-old spinster telling me the way the world worked. 'I can't believe you know so much,' I said.

'I may look twenty four, but I'm really thousands of years old.' She grinned and tossed her hair over her shoulder. 'I have had many previous lives. We bring the imprint from those lives into this one and we can tap into the knowledge from those lifetimes. We are more than just the body. I have learned this from the teachings of several religious men.'

'Is this the kind of stuff you teach as a missionary?'

She shook her head. 'The Indian government may have dubbed me a missionary, but in truth I was just trying to twist people into civilisation under the banner of religion.'

'I'm surprised you could get that close to them, especially that Jarawa bunch.'

She smiled painfully. 'If you understand how cruel civilisation has been to them you would get a sense of compassion towards them. The Jarawa are very spiritual people. They have ways of healing, as I demonstrated on you, inner knowing, hunting, but their existence and identity has always been threatened by outsiders. Killing the outsiders and devouring them is their way of possessing their power, overcoming them.'

I started laughing. 'Now you're making my wife sound like a cannibal.'

Shreela laughed too. 'Both behaviours come from the fear

they feel of the external world. This is their shadow, their belief.
They saw me for what I was immediately, a woman of love
who was not there to threaten them. When they saw this they
trusted me. From there we began to build bridges.'

She slumped. For a woman who could be so tough, I was
amazed to see such a stark change in her posture. 'My kidnap
is all about a power struggle too, similar to you and your wife's
and to the Indian government and the Jarawa, similar to the
wars you fight as a soldier. Koslov wanted me to do something
I didn't want to do and he has used every grain of power he has
to make that happen, bullies always try to win, but when there
is no fight –'

She smiled at me and looked at me for longer than usual. I
saw a twinkling in her eyes and began to fight the temptation to
reach forward and kiss her.

At that moment Doug called to me, 'Your turn, Mike.'

I patted Shreela on the shoulder and went over and took
the oar. As I rowed I thought about the power struggles we had
talked about and remembered the countless arguments I had
endured with Jodie. I wished I had left the marriage before. I
wished I had walked away before life had become complicated,
then I wished I was no longer a soldier. More than anything at
that moment I just wanted to be me, not a job, not a husband,
nothing, just me.

I wanted my life back. I wanted to get back in control.
I had to do something, rid myself of all my troubles, live for
myself again...enjoy life. For a few precious seconds I imagined
myself already there...living in this wonderful dream of
freedom, without nagging and abuse. And I was smiling, feeling
somehow lighter and so very happy.

The thoughts all sat right with me at that moment. For the
first time I accepted the pain I was going to have to go through
by leaving my work, Jodie and Christian. It was all necessary in
order to free myself and regain my happiness and my identity.

During my time at the oar, dawn broke, and we caught the
first sight of the landmass which we hoped was southern Kali
Pani. If it was Kali Pani we would swing east and travel along

its coast for about twenty five clicks, then we would turn at its most western point and head south another ten clicks before hitting Port St. Peter.

I looked forward to tucking into a beef curry, chicken or seafood...I didn't care what, I just wanted food. With my mouth watering I dug the oar in a little deeper and pulled a little harder.

'Hey, what's going on?' Spaghetti said. 'Why are we pulling your way?'

'I'm dreaming of food, a soft bed and a beer,' I said.

He laughed, 'Oh well in that case so am I,' and he began to pull a little harder.

'Chicken Korma,' he shouted as we pulled.

'Beef Madras,' I replied.

'Prawn Phall.'

'Naan bread,' Doug piped up.

'Chapati,' Shreela joined in.

'Chutney.'

We were all smiling, the boat was cutting through the water faster and I was just hoping that for once...just once...we could manage to get somewhere without complications.

LAST LEGS

Dawn broke as we paddled between north and south Kali Pani. On both sides of us lush green trees overhung white beaches where the turquoise water foamed.

Shreela woke looking pale and drawn, and almost immediately she was leaning over the side of the boat.

'You okay?' I asked.

She didn't reply, at least not verbally. She vomited into the water. I stopped paddling and turned to her even although there was nothing I could do for her except offer her my presence. She retched again and again, straining every muscle in her neck until they stood out. With little food in her belly there was hardly any end result.

'Is it sea sickness?' Spaghetti asked.

'No,' I said.

'Shock or something?'

'No.'

'Food?'

'No.'

'What else could it be then?'

I flashed my eyes at him.

'Oh,' he mouthed across the deck, then he looked away.

'Sorry,' Shreela said, wiping her mouth with the back of her hand and dropping down onto one of the bench seats. 'Perhaps it is seasickness or relief after all we've been through.'

I stood up straight, hands on hips. 'I think you know what it is, Shreela.'

She shook her head. 'No, it can't be. It's too soon.'

'When did Koslov first drug you?'

'Only a couple of weeks ago.'

I shook my head, 'We've been on this mission for two weeks.'

She shot me a look. 'Well, it was just before that.'

'You told me you were in his camp for some time and then you escaped, spoke to a Jarawa chief, returned to Port St. Peter and then went back to India. Then you met with government officials and returned to –'

'What happened to me, happened to me. It's none of your business. Who do you think you are, my father?'

I held up my hand then stepped away, leaving her to chew it over for herself. A while later I gave Doug a shake and told him it was time he took over. As I stretched out at that back of the boat Shreela came and sat next to me. 'You really think I'm pregnant?' she asked.

'I don't know, maybe I'm wrong. For your sake I hope I am.'

Her shoulders slumped again and she looked down at her feet. She dabbed her eyes and sniffled. I wished there was something I could do for her, some way I could comfort her and make it all go away.

'Well fuck me,' Spaghetti shouted from up front.

'What? What is it?' Doug called back to him.

'Indian navy, dead ahead.'

The vessel came into vision as the coastline dropped away and opened up into a cove. It was kind of parked up around the corner, hidden. We steered in towards it and a few minutes later our boat clunked against its hull. Several of the crew were leaning over the railings and I shouted up, 'We are British soldiers. We need to speak with your captain.'

While we waited for the ship's captain Shreela got a good shower of compliments and winks from the sex-starved crew. The numbers leaning over the railing swelled and they were just starting to get a little rowdier and more daring with their comments when we were told we could board the ship. Spaghetti, Doug and I struggled up on to deck without any assistance, but when Shreela got within the last few steps ten guys suddenly became perfect gentlemen, helping and welcoming her aboard.

We were led through the boat by more men than was really necessary, four in front of us and at least six behind. 'Big escort,' I said to Doug.

'It's certainly not for our benefit,' Spaghetti said. One of the sailors in front was jeered by his colleagues as he almost fell over himself because he was looking at Shreela instead of where he was walking. 'I can't believe these guys are so obvious.'

'Different culture,' I shrugged.

'Yeah, but I wonder if all the attention works.'

'Try it when we get back to Hereford,' Doug said, without any apparent humour.

The passageways and steps went on forever, but eventually we came to a briefing room. 'The captain, he will come soon,' one of escorts told us.

The clock on the wall read eight thirty-five when we sat down; at nine fifty-six the captain walked in. We all stood up. With his long jaw line and layers of fat under his chin, his features corresponded to Ramjit's in such an uncanny way that I wondered if this was the dead liaison's twin brother. The one marked difference between the two was the captain's teeth. Unevenly spaced, with black gaps between twisted teeth, his mouth resembled work carried out by a cowboy resurfacing road-crew who had been overzealous with the jackhammers and sloppy with the tarmac.

The resemblance to Ramjit made me wary.

The captain's bloodshot eyes lingered on Shreela. 'Why are you on my boat?' he scowled.

'We are part of the joint Anglo-Indian mission to retrieve a woman...'

He waved his hand and cut in, still staring at Shreela, 'I know about this mission.'

'I am Mike Edwards. Patrol Commander with the SAS.'

He stuck his finger in his ear, and twisted his face. After examining the wax he ignored me and spoke to Shreela. 'You are kidnapped woman?'

She nodded.

He continued looking at Shreela, his focus mostly on her breast area. He smiled leerily and rocked back on his chair. Coming forward again he turned to me. 'I have heard you are dead in the jungle.'

'It appears your information is incorrect, sir.'

'Incorrect information gives me problem.'

'How?'

'Because you are dead.'

'Who says we are dead?'

'You have been found dead.'

'Obviously a load of bollocks,' I said. I was about to tell the captain what had happened but suddenly I felt like I didn't want to tell this man anything else. 'I'd like to speak to my Commanding Officer in the UK, can you arrange this for me?'

Pushing his chair back he got to his feet. 'I will see about calling Commanding Officer. Wait.'

I stood up too. 'We'd like to get some air. We've been stuck down here for over an hour. I want to wait on deck or on our boat.'

He shrugged and opened the door 'As you wish,' he said, before he disappeared.

We headed back onto the deck and I told everyone we would wait on our boat. Spaghetti protested, 'They must have some breakfast we could eat. You could have asked if we could wait in the mess hall, that would have been better...bacon and eggs and fried bread or something...anything.'

'Look,' I said, leaning into Spaghetti's face, 'I didn't like the captain. We're getting off.'

'So what...we have to go and wait down in our boat and miss out on breakfast because you have a personal prejudice?'

Doug said, 'Mike's right. I didn't like the captain either and I really don't trust our situation here.'

I headed towards the ladder and climbed down. Doug and Shreela followed readily, Spaghetti came but still wasn't happy.

'Let's be ready to cast off at a second's notice,' I said as we settled back into the boat.

'We'll never out-paddle that ship in this,' Spaghetti said.

'We only need to get ourselves on land,' I said.

'You make it sound like we are going on the run again,' Shreela said, looking worried.

At that moment one of the ship's crew started coming down the ladder. I told Doug to push us away from the boat, just out of reach.

'Captain says girl must come with us,' the sailor said.

'And what about us?'

'He says you can go.'

I looked at Doug. He shook his head, 'Something's not right with that.'

'I'm stopping with these men,' Shreela shouted up.

'Start paddling,' I said, to Doug and Spaghetti. They eased the oars back into the water and moved us further away.

'Girl is coming with us,' the sailor's voice echoed as we rowed away.

We rounded the ship and I pointed ahead. 'The land sticks out over there, we can get out of sight and then ditch the boat. We'll watch out until nightfall and if they leave us alone we'll get back in and head to Port St. Peter. If they come after us we'll leg it through the bush.'

'Aren't you overreacting?' Spaghetti said. 'They only wanted Shreela to go with them.'

'I didn't trust their motives.'

'Stuff their motives. Our job was to find and free her. We've done that. I vote we turn her in now and head home.'

'Their behaviour's odd. Considering this is supposed to be a joint British and Indian mission. Plus Ramjit was on Koslov's payroll...I just don't know how many others in the services he's recruited.'

'Stuff that, we have orders and they were to get the girl.'

'Exactly, Spaghetti, they were to get her. No-one said we had to turn her into the Indians.'

'I still think you're overreacting. We need to take her back to the ship.'

Spaghetti was becoming irritated and his irritation was fast becoming mine. 'What the fuck's got into you?' I blasted.

'We should have left her there. Our mission would be over now. I'm tired, I'm fucking sunburned and I'm hungry. I itch like fuck and I'm fed up with all of this fucking cloak and dagger shite that's not our fucking problem.'

It was during Spaghetti's outburst that I realised how much trouble we were in. If he could lose his sense of humour then he was on the road to ruin...we all were. It had been a long few days and the stress on our bodies was now taking its toll. It was inevitable that any of us could and probably would crack now.

A few minutes later, out of sight of the ship, we dragged our boat onto a narrow strip of beach. We knocked the canopy down and slid the boat into the trees. We picked up fallen branches and swept the beach to cover our tracks. We had just reached the trees again when we heard the sound of a motor approaching.

There were two boats and I counted five sailors in each. As we watched them pass, Spaghetti said, 'So what does that prove?'

'Nothing,' I said, 'but I still don't trust anyone.'

'So what now? Another day, another shite night without food and water, and then what?'

'Let's start heading to Port St Peter,' I said. I got to my feet.

Spaghetti grabbed me. 'And then what? If we can't trust Ramjit and the navy, who the fuck we gonna trust back in Port St. Peter?'

I prised his fingers off my arm. 'We don't have to trust anyone. I need to make a phone call to the CO and discuss an RV and a way out.'

'This is fucking ridiculous.'

'That's the way it is, now get your fucking arse back in line and let's use what we have left in us to get home.'

We got moving and started making our way through foliage again. It was another long, uncomfortable day in the heat. 'This jungle is fucking suffocating me,' Spaghetti said time and again.

On one occasion he threw himself on the ground and refused to move. We all knew how he felt.

We rested while he threw his tantrum, then Doug kicked him. 'Come on, you skinny sod,' he said dryly. 'Let's get cracking again.'

Late in the afternoon we emerged from the trees and once again found the only road through the whole of Kali Pani, the Road to Nowhere.

'It goes to Port St. Peter,' Shreela said weakly. 'Jarawa rarely wait along this section, they stay mostly in the north island. We should be safe to walk along the roadside.'

We did as she suggested, ready to jump back into the bush at the first hint of a vehicle coming toward us.

By dusk our situation had become desperate. Doug led us, scuffing his feet. Spaghetti lolled from side to side like a rag doll. Shreela constantly stopped for breath. My vision was blurring, my legs were trailing and my head was pounding. I stopped walking and sat on the roadside.

'Get up,' Doug said.

'No,' I replied.

'Get up.'

'I can't go on. We need to flag down the next vehicle that comes along. I'll walk out and do it, just cover me in case it turns nasty.'

'Do it,' Spaghetti said, 'I want food, and fast.'

An hour and a half later I heard an engine coming our way and staggered out into the road. The headlights dazzled me and I had no idea what was coming until it slowed and halted and I more or less tumbled onto its bonnet.

A door slammed. A man stood by the side of the vehicle.

'I need a lift.'

Through stinging eyes I could make out that this man was a local or an Indian. I had no idea which. I noticed he had a gun.

'Michael?' he said.

He knew my name!

'Yeah.'

'It is me, Ali.'

I lolled on the bonnet and laughed. 'Ali,' I said. I stepped forward and hugged him as though he was the long-lost friend that I hoped he was.

LOOKING OVER MY SHOULDER

As we bounced along the Road to Nowhere, Ali said, 'You may stay at my home.'

'We just need some food and a telephone,' I said. I wondered how much trust I could put in Ali. His connection to Ramjit still made me wary.

'You may eat and rest at my home. I can take you to a telephone.' We drove on in silence for a few minutes, then he said, 'I know you do not trust me. I don't blame you, but you should know that the Indian Military want Miss Shreela only to return her to Koslov. He has paid everyone. Police are watching Port St. Peter for you, but you *will* be safe with me.'

I looked in the back of the jeep, hoping for a nod of approval or something from Doug or Spaghetti. I was met by vacant stares and lolling heads.

'I have one simple favour to ask in return for my help,' Ali said, 'when you leave Kali Pani you take me with you. I want to go to London. You must understand that by helping you I am endangering my life.'

I said nothing. I knew in my mind that a decision like that didn't rest with me, but I didn't have the energy or the ability to form the words to express this to Ali. I was, by that time, incredibly weak and felt more passive than I had ever felt before. I wanted food and fluids. We all needed them. Nothing mattered any more. It was basic survival time.

We didn't discuss our immediate destination any further. Ali drove us straight to his home. He parked the jeep next to a mashed-up kerb line, walked us past a row of shops with corrugated frontages and around the side of a building. I struggled up the steps to his apartment with shaking legs, gripping onto the handrail for balance.

We headed along a balcony. People were smoking out of their windows, leaning over the balcony, standing on thresholds, all staring at us.

Going to Ali's place no longer felt like a good idea, but by now I was too weak to raise any protest or consider any alternative.

Ali's flat was a compact square, a tiny hallway, a bedroom cum sitting room, a bathroom and kitchen. 'Make yourselves at home,' Ali said, as he collected dirty dishes from the floor. It was a sparse place: no carpet, no curtains and no table. It had only one chair, a huge armchair, and only one bed, queen-sized. In the corner was a television screen, twenty-eight or thirty inch, and a stereo with the biggest speakers I had ever seen. Apart from these luxuries he appeared to have nothing.

Shreela lay on the bed staring ahead, Spaghetti lounged in the armchair gawping at the walls, Doug leaned back against the wall looking up at the ceiling.

Ali returned to the room with a bottle of water and some cups. He poured it out for us. The cup felt heavy and I barely had the strength to drink. He brought us some sugar cane and a bowl. 'It is very good,' he said, 'very sweet. It will help you. Chew it and spit the cane out then rest and I will cook up some food.'

The water and the sugar cane helped. It took away the bleariness I had been feeling, but there were so many things wrong with me, with all of our bodies, at that point. I ached so much I could easily have cried, I itched from all the ticks, leeches and mosquitoes and I had less will to live than I had had when I had been at Koslov's mercy.

Ali cooked, we slept. It was not a restful doze and I had no idea how long it lasted, but I do remember being woken by a violent shake.

The room spun as I opened my eyes. I had no idea where I was to begin with. Someone was standing above me: swarthy skin. *Bollocks!* I scrambled to my feet and into action and reached out for my gun.

The bastard had double-crossed us.

My gun was gone.

Aroused from a deep sleep and shocked, I struggled to work it all out. Doug was standing in front of me too. He leaned forward and put his hand on my shoulder. 'It is okay, Mike,' he said. 'Ali's just got us some food ready.'

My heart beat like a bass drum at a heavy metal concert. My eyes couldn't focus properly. I felt heat rising up through my body. I felt sick.

'It is only onions and garlic and ginger and tomatoes with a little bread, very simple, but very good for you,' Ali said.

Doug sat back down. His movements seemed heavy and stiff. Spaghetti was hunched over his bowl, spooning it out like a possessed food-taster. Slowly Shreela broke her bread into smaller pieces and scooped out the red mixture. She glanced in my direction and managed a smile.

'Try,' Ali said, passing me a bowl and bread.

I tore the bread in half and dipped it into the tomatoes. 'It's hot,' I said.

'Yes, it's very good. Eat, eat,' Ali said.

'No, I mean it's hot.'

'Yes.'

'Ali, it's fucking hot.'

'Yes.'

'Ali, it's burning my fucking mouth.'

'Eat a little more sugar cane.'

'Water! Not fucking sugar cane!'

'Here,' he said, laughing at me and shoving sugar cane in my mouth. 'Sugar cane is better. The sweetness takes away the fire.'

I grabbed all of the remaining sugar cane from the bowl and stuffed my mouth full of it.

He was right. In seconds the sweetness of the cane had been released into my mouth and the burning sensation had disappeared. 'I can't eat that,' I said, shoving the bowl across the floor as though it was shit.

Spaghetti leaned forward. 'You mind if I have it then?' he said.

'Help yourself, but leave me the bread you, greedy bastard.' I grabbed it from the plate as Spaghetti tried to take everything from me.

Ali said, 'I have nothing else to offer you.'

I held up the remains of the bread. 'The bread is good,' I said. 'Best meal I've had in the last twenty-four hours.' It wasn't much of a compliment.

We slept until morning. I woke with a big headache. Shreela was sick and everyone complained of aches and pains. Ali shopped and returned with mangoes and bread. We ate again. As the morning wore on I began to feel better.

In the bathroom, as Shreela wiped vomit away from her mouth she said, 'I have decided I don't want to be returned to India. It is not safe for me.'

'What happens to you needs to go through our CO and I think immigration might have a say. I'll mention it for you.'

She returned to her vomiting and I returned to lounge on the floor. We watched satellite television for a while and as with most TV it bored the life out of me. Later, Ali got out his music tapes and blasted out some of his favourites, mostly music that was over a decade old. After an hour I was fed up with that too and turned it down.

Doug sat next to me for a while. 'I bet satellite television doesn't come cheap in these parts.'

'So what's your point?'

'I think he makes money on the side.'

'You're saying that you think we're sitting ducks?'

He nodded.

'Antenna,' I said, referring to the CO, 'is the only person who's going to get us off the island.' I glanced at the AK-47 next to me. 'One way or another Ali is going to take me to this telephone today so I can call him. If he makes a fuss I'll slot him. We can take his jeep and get the fuck out of here. Alternatively,

if he makes life easier I'll give him the benefit of the doubt and
hope he continues to be useful.'

A few minutes later Ali entered the room. I asked him
about the telephone. 'We have a telephone at the tourism
office. You cannot go there in the daytime. People will see you.
I will take you in the dark.'

❧

Ali shook me at midnight. 'Now is a good time,' he said.

I rubbed my face and got up. I gave Doug's foot a kick so
he could keep watch once we had gone. 'Look sharp, mate,' I
said.

He nodded and got up.

Ali headed down to his jeep with a portable stereo in
his hand. He pulled the hood over the interior of the car and
cranked the engine. I followed about a minute behind him. As
I headed along the balcony people were still smoking. I noticed
one guy in particular, a young wiry boy, certainly no more than
twenty. He nodded his head at me in acknowledgement. I
nodded back, but as I passed I felt a deep feeling of distrust
towards him. I looked over my shoulder as he flicked his
cigarette butt over the balcony and smiled at me and waved.

In the jeep Ali blasted the music from his portable stereo.
'What's this in aid of?' I asked. 'I don't want to get noticed.'

'It is always best to play loud music and cover the jeep
when you travel in Port St. Peter at night time. First, the ghosts
cannot hit you with bricks and second, it makes it harder for
you to hear them.'

I didn't protest.

We headed into town. I kept down low in the back, happy
to be out of the way.

He unlocked the door to the Tourism Office and I followed
him inside. He went to flick on the light, but I grabbed his arm
and stopped him. 'We don't want anyone to see us.'

He waited in the front of the office while I dialled the
number in a back room. After speaking to three people I
eventually got to speak to Antenna. 'What the fuck is going

on?' he blasted me. 'They told me you failed to show for an RV. I haven't had a sitrep for days. We were preparing our own search and rescue team.'

'Sir, the Indians are doing bugger-all over here. They have not supported us through any of this.'

He cut in. 'What the fuck are you talking about? You had a liaison. They told me they supplied you with troops.'

I told him about Ramjit double-crossing us, that we had only two soldiers to help us against Koslov's men, the RV at the ops Centre on Haven Island that never existed and the episode on board the Indian navy ship.

He was silent for a moment. When he spoke again his tone was less accusing, more concerned. 'Where are you now?'

'By chance, our original guide, Ali, picked us up on a road. I am at his office.'

'Is he a friendly?'

'I can only hope so, sir.'

'Where is Miss Robert?'

'At Ali's flat with Doug and Greg.'

'What about McNamara?'

'He died, sir, when we were ambushed.'

He must have turned his mouth away from the phone. I heard him swearing repeatedly.

'Sir, one other thing. Oleg Koslov knows my home address. He knows I have a wife and a son.'

'How the fuck did he find that out?'

'I just gave my name and rank, the Geneva Convention stuff. Also, sir, his right-hand man liaised with us in the Philippines. He worked for their police. Maybe the MOD has a leak somewhere. Maybe someone filled in the details for him.'

'Fuck me, what next? I'll despatch some of the boys to babysit your family.'

'Thanks, sir.'

'Edwards, we are going to get you out. Hang tight, call me again at the same time tomorrow.'

By the time we reached the apartment again I felt drained

and as I pushed open the door all I wanted to do was fall asleep, but a new situation confronted me.

In the hallway Doug was standing over a body, with his foot on their back and his gun pointing at their head. 'What's this?' I asked.

'This nosy bastard decided to come in and take a look around.'

I raised his head from the floor and looked at his face. It was the guy who had flicked his cigarette butt over the balcony when I went out.

'My neighbour,' Ali said. They jabbered to each other for a minute. 'He says he was curious and wanted to see what we were doing here.'

'Do you trust him?' I asked.

Ali shrugged.

'Do you guys usually just go in and take a look around each other's apartments?'

He shook his head.

'Is he living with anyone else...wife, kids?'

'No.'

'Does he work?'

He shook his head again.

'Okay then, as no one's going to miss him, we tie him up, gag him and stick him in your toilet for safekeeping.'

'Are you sure you should do that?' Ali asked.

'I don't know this little bugger from Adam. He might have been paid by Koslov. I'm not compromising my unit and our subject. You have a problem with that, Ali?'

CO-ORDINATES FOR A PLACE WORSE THAN HELL

Day two at Ali's place was very much the same as day one, except we had our hostage banged up in the toilet—which made for interesting viewing when Shreela dashed in without notice to puke.

After a second night of rest we were all recovering well. Spaghetti whipped up breakfast, omelettes and bread and a pot of tea, with ingredients Ali had pinched from his neighbour's flat.

I became better acquainted with the surroundings. Ali's lounge/bedroom overlooked a court, a square formed by other flats built in the same fashion. It was a concrete mess, littered with papers and rubbish and patrolled by a scrawny dog. I went into the kitchen and spent some time looking out from behind the blind. 'Outside is the main road into Port St. Peter,' Ali said, before he headed out to his workplace.

The front window gave us a good view. All the buildings opposite were one-storey affairs. Most had flat roofs and were built on a slope that gently rolled upwards so that each row of dwellings was slightly higher than the one before.

'Drivers seem to honk their horns over everything and nothing,' Doug observed. 'And the locals speak to each other at maximum volume. It doesn't seem to matter whether they're standing right next to each other or at opposite sides of the street.'

We'd noticed one local in particular. He leaned against a wall down in the street, opposite the apartment. By all appearances he fitted with the neighbourhood, dark skin, white beard, turban, no shirt, but what aroused my suspicion about him was the amount of time he lingered there. On Ali's return I asked him if he had noticed the guy before. He shook his head. 'Do you want me to ask him why he is there?'

'No, Ali, that's the last thing I want you to do.'

He shrugged. 'Perhaps it's his day off.'

A pensive frown furrowed Doug's brow as he looked at me. 'You think he might be working for Koslov?'

I nodded slowly.

'We can't just take him off the street; that might cause his associates to question his absence.'

'We'll just have to observe him,' I said. 'See if he moves or speaks to anyone. Try to build up logical reasons for his presence other than the fact he might be observing us. If we go after him and miss and he is working for Koslov then we have a bigger problem than if we stay hidden and make him think we're not here or haven't seen him.'

Doug was still frowning, 'You mean we're hanging tight and hoping nothing happens before you speak to Antenna?'

'I don't see we have much option. We'll see what his plans are and then we'll decide what we need to do. If we are compromised before then we head to the dock and meet up there.'

Shreela had come into the kitchen for a glass of water. Doug and I moved into the small hallway to allow her some room. 'We need to leave here by tomorrow evening,' she said.

'What makes you say that?' I asked.

'A very strong feeling that something bad will happen to us all.'

With that, the toilet door burst open and the hostage rushed out and headed for the front door. Spaghetti was leaning against the wall with his arms crossed. In a casual reflex he stuck out his leg. The hostage fell, his hands slapping the tiled floor. It all happened so quickly and Spaghetti was so relaxed about it all that it looked comical.

Calmly he took his AK-47 off his shoulder and pointed it at

the hostage's head. The neighbour jabbered something quickly. Doug said, 'I think he's thanking you for introducing him to the tiles.'

Staring at the man's spread-eagled form, Spaghetti gave the faintest grin, 'And there was me thinking he was just demonstrating freefall technique without a parachute. One thousand, two thousand, three thousand...splat!'

We all had a laugh, a healthy sign that things were getting back to normal. 'Okay, tie him up this time,' I said to Spaghetti.

A few minutes later he stood at the kitchen door and beckoned me to him. 'What'd you think?' he asked as he stepped proudly away from the toilet doorway to let me see inside.

I looked open-mouthed into the room. 'Doug, come and take a look,' I called.

When the bewilderment vanished from his face he walked away shaking his head. 'I don't believe you,' he said.

Spaghetti grinned boyishly. 'Isn't that what you had in mind?'

'When I said tie him up, I didn't mean to the U-bend and I certainly didn't mean that you should do it in such a way that his head would end up down the pot.' I slapped him on the back. 'No, really, mate...nice one...very creative.'

'There was nothing else solid enough in there,' he said. I didn't know if he was still making a joke of it or trying to offer me a legitimate excuse.

I raised an eyebrow. 'The sink stand?'

'Oh, yeah...shit...why didn't I think of that?'

'Because you're a tosser,' Doug guffawed from the kitchen.

I was at Ali's tourism office by midnight and got straight through to Antenna.

'We are arranging extraction for four, including the girl.'

I looked at Ali, standing in the front office, just out of earshot. 'Five, sir,' I said.

'Why five?'

'I'm including our guide, sir.'

'What's the fucking deal with the guide?'

'Because he helped us. His life is in danger, sir.'

A pause. 'Explain yourself.'

'The situation we are holding in was being watched today, sir. We observed a native watching our LUP for nine hours.'

'I can't bring your guide out on that basis.'

'Sir, the native we observed might have looked like a local, but did not behave like one. He spoke to no-one and was not spoken to. He watched our LUP all day.'

'Has your guide been threatened?

'No, sir.'

'Shot at?'

'No, sir.'

'Then we are not responsible for him. The Royal navy have a taxi in the Arabian Sea, currently on a course to Thailand. It will make a detour and send a chopper. Your RV will be tomorrow midnight. I repeat your RV will be tomorrow midnight.' He read off the map co-ordinates and I grabbed a pen and any old slip of paper I could lay my hands on.

When I put the telephone down I gave Ali the map co-ordinates and he looked them up on a map on the wall. He stood back. 'Hum,' he said, scratching his chin. 'This might be a problem.'

'Why?'

'The co-ordinates are for Coral Island. Do you remember I told you about the Coralenese? I'll tell you about the Coralenese. The Coralenese make the Jarawa look like angels.'

❧

'So what happened?' Doug asked as I slammed a mug down on the counter in Ali's kitchen.

'RV tomorrow. Midnight, Coral Island. It's ten clicks south out of Port St. Peter.' I poured out some water and missed the mug. 'Shit.' I brushed at my slacks. 'There's another tribe of cannibals on the island.'

Doug shrugged. 'We dealt with the Jarawa.'

Ali was by the door. 'Let me make this clear,' he said, narrowing his eyes. 'The Coralenese are not like the Jarawa. Not like the Jarawa at all. They are much less friendly.'

Doug scratched his head. 'Can you explain how someone does less friendly than a cannibal?'

'As I have told you, some of the Jarawa are civilised. Sometimes these more civilised ones can influence the others not to kill you. With the Coralenese there is no such person who is civilised among them.'

Ali walked the length of the small kitchen and stood at the far end with his arms folded and his legs crossed. 'Although Coral Island is small there are more than a thousand of the Coralenese remaining. I suggest we arrive at the rendezvous at the very last possible moment.'

We talked through our plans for the following night and then settled down for some sleep. We alternated the stag between the three of us at three-hourly intervals. During my turn I contemplated our situation again.

We were all regaining our strength and another day would probably see us almost back to normal. The bruising and injuries inflicted on me at Koslov's camp were healing and disappearing quickly with the exception of my nose, which throbbed at times. I knew that it had been broken and I knew that the bones would be fusing back together. That was making my breathing difficult because they were not fusing properly.

My main concern was Shreela. She had not eaten during the days of our escape and since we had been at Ali's she had vomited several times each day. We made sure she took in plenty of fluid, but I knew her body must now be paying the price of days without food and water prior to the onset of the sickness.

She had been quiet for the last two days, sleeping mostly, with very few smiles or words. I was concerned about her overall health and I knew when we escaped the following night that one of us would inevitably end up carrying her.

Sunrise brought a very similar routine to the previous day: watching out of the windows in shifts and occasionally checking on our hostage. While I sat in Ali's only armchair I was facing up to the facts about my personal life: for one, even staying put in Ali's apartment had more appeal than going home. I guess I hoped the feeling would pass, but I knew that when I got home I really needed to take action to sort out my private life.

'Guy's back over the road,' Spaghetti said. I got up and headed into the kitchen and took a look out from behind the blind. 'What the hell's he doing? You don't just spend days on end standing in the same place.'

I said, 'What do we do? A recce and then a final recce, just to make sure things haven't changed before moving in. If he'd just been around yesterday, I'd say he was waiting for something, but as he's back again today my guess now is that he's definitely looking out for something.'

'He's so obvious, though. You really think he'd do a reece like that?'

'Don't just think, mate, I feel it.'

'So what do you feel surrounds the man?' Shreela asked me, clutching the frame of the kitchen door. 'Just tell me the first thing that comes into your head.'

'Danger,' I said.

'Now tell me what sort.'

I shrugged. 'Gunfire, explosives.'

'When?'

'Bloody hell, Shreela –'

'We must know—what time?'

'I dunno.'

'First thing that comes into your head.'

'Eight...no, nine o'clock...between eight and nine.'

'Now remember that as you plan the rest of the day and our escape,' she said. She turned and shuffled away.

Doug came in behind Shreela, 'Right then, we'll be all squared away and ready to jump ship by 20:00.'

Spaghetti was now sitting on the counter in the kitchen. 'That's too early. Ali says it's five minutes to the dock once the traffic dies and then fifteen to twenty minutes to the island by boat. We can't wait on Cannibal Island or whatever it's called for three hours.'

'We need to work out what we do once we leave here, but we are going to leave by 20:00,' I said.

Spaghetti leaned towards me. His nostrils flared. 'I agree that the guy over the road might be up to something, but 20:00 is way too early.'

'It's 20:00,' I insisted.

He slipped off the counter and disappeared into the other room.

Doug stepped towards the window and peered out. Smiling, he said, 'I see you're getting your act together at last.'

'And your point?'

'Well you haven't exactly been captain bloody invincible lately, have you? I mean look back right to the point where the CO bawled you out for your lack of training, the way that you handled yourself at home and the way you handled things right up to the point where you were captured and held with Shreela.'

'Look,' I said stepping towards Doug as though to grab his jacket. 'I may have been pathetic at times, but that's my shit.'

'Fine,' he said. He pushed my hand away. 'I was just observing.'

'Well don't.'

'I was meaning it as a compliment—a yardstick for how far you've come.'

'Gee, thanks...now fuck off.'

He looked at me and then changed the subject. 'You really feel Antenna will come through for us?'

'Yeah, course he will, why wouldn't he?'

He shrugged. 'Just we've been let down by everyone else on this mission. It's been bugging me and I never got around to asking you, do you really think that news story you saw got squashed?'

I lowered my voice, 'Manisha Robert's theory was that Indian officials wanted to shut her daughter up.'

Doug frowned. 'So why not just take her out? Why kidnap her and bring her back here?'

'I've asked the same question. It seems to me that she has formed a strong bond with the Jarawa. She had a relationship with Koslov, one he manufactured, but...there's something missing from the picture, something I just can't put my finger on.'

Doug shrugged. 'I guess it's all pretty irrelevant to us anyway. We got the job done, all we need to do now is get to the RV. It's just that I hope Antenna comes through for us.'

The guy across the street stayed there until 18:00, but by 19:30 he was back at his place by the wall. 'What the fuck's going on?' Spaghetti said.

I joined him at the window. 'I don't like this.'

Doug stood in the doorway. 'Where is Ali? He's usually back here by now.'

'Get Shreela ready,' I said.

A minute later Doug was back in the doorway. 'Shreela's stirring. She doesn't look good.'

I sighed and went through to her. She was sitting up with colourless cheeks looking like she might vomit at any second. 'We're going to be leaving in the next thirty minutes,' I told her.

She acknowledged me by raising her eyebrows.

I went to the rear window of the flat. So far there had been no sign of anyone watching us from this angle, but I noticed someone across the concrete square that I had seen the previous day, though only briefly. He was leaning over a balcony opposite us.

I told Doug. He came to cover the window. Something made me get Shreela out of bed then and move her into the toilet with our hostage. 'It's just a precaution,' I said, trying not to alarm her. I left her sitting on the edge of the bath, still looking pale.

'Where's Ali?' Spaghetti said. It was now 19:40.

'Doug,' I called from the kitchen door. 'If Ali's not here in ten minutes we have to go.'

'OK,' he said, 'but how do you propose to get us to the docks without being spotted in combats?'

'Easy, mate, you borrow some of Ali's clothes, go into town, hot-wire us a taxi and pull up out front.'

'One flaw in your plan...my skin colour is all wrong.' Suddenly his tone of voice changed from joking to urgent. 'I've got movement at the back,' he said. 'Our man's talking to someone. They're looking in our direction.'

I went to look. One of the men walked away. He had a purposeful stride and I suspected he was someone in authority. 'Bollocks,' I said, as I saw a movement at a window across from us.

'That's a fucking rocket launcher pointing at our window,' Doug said.

'Be ready to move out,' I called as I jogged through to the kitchen. I grabbed one of Ali's big knifes from a drawer and took it into the bathroom. I cut the neighbour free from the U-bend. 'Out,' I said, waving the AK-47 in his direction. In the hallway I pushed him to the ground. 'Stay there,' I said, letting him feel the gun on the back of his head and my boot in the centre of his spine. 'How are we looking at the front?' I shouted to Spaghetti.

'Situation static.'

'OK, we have our hostage at the door. We are exiting via the front door. Move up to the front door now and stand by for my, go. We're heading along the balcony to the bottom of the steps and then we're gonna double-time it to the docks.'

Spaghetti exited the kitchen and Shreela stood at the bathroom door.

'Incoming rear! Incoming rear!' Doug shouted. He ran a few paces and launched himself into the hallway.

'Hit the deck. Hit the deck.'

Instinctively, I pulled Shreela through the bathroom doorway, threw her to the ground and covered her as best I could.

Glass shattered.

Bang!

The building shook. It trembled for several seconds as plaster and brick and glass fell all around. My ears were ringing, my vision was obscured by brick dust, my brain was fuzzy, but we had to get out.

'Go! Go!' I shouted. I was up, hauling the neighbour to his feet, flinging the door wide open and forcing him out.

I grabbed Doug as he climbed to his feet. 'You're next,' I said, shoving him towards the front door.

Spaghetti was up, his face covered in dust. 'A1 condition,' he said, slurring his words and looking shaken.

Doug had eased out; bent low, using the balcony wall as cover, he ran to the end of the balcony. He checked the stairwell and waved Spaghetti up. At the end of the balcony Spaghetti headed down the stairs. He would relay to Doug that we were clear and then we were out.

We waited for the signal to come from Doug.

Still my ears were ringing. Still I felt dizzy and disorientated. I could hear the sound of my own breath. I could hear my heart beating as though it was inside my brain.

I held Shreela's arm as we waited at the door; she was shaking uncontrollably. 'Keep low, keep moving. Only stop when I tell you,' I said, speaking right into her face.

She nodded.

Still we waited.

'Any second,' I said, coughing up sand and cement and thinking, 'What the fuck is happening?'

Doug looked at me and gave me the OK.

'Let's go,' I said, hauling her forward.

Bang!

We were thrown to the floor for a second time. The building seemed to shake forever. Rubble was falling all around us. There were screams from neighbouring buildings, voices in the street below us.

I was up again, spitting out dust, shaking my head, stumbling over ankle-twisting bricks.

Then I saw him, the neighbour, at his door, with a knife in his hand and coming towards me. I could tell from the way he was holding it—like he was about to jab the end of it into the arse of a Bombay Duck—that he had not been trained in the art of kitchen utensil weaponry, but even so, I was dizzy, hauling Shreela and needed to get out of there before smaller guns got firing at me.

Doug had him spotted.

'Drop it,' he roared.

The neighbour paused, then lunged towards me.

Crack, crack! Crack, crack!

Two in the knife-holding arm, two in the leg. He staggered and collapsed onto one leg and then to the floor, but still he looked at me and still he held the knife.

I moved forward now. Standing on the hand that held the knife I heard his bones crunch under my shoe, as though they were another piece of glass or rubble that was strewn across the landing floor.

At almost every doorway along the balcony there was movement now. Still there were frightened screams and shouts and angry voices. I looked back and saw a woman in a sari running towards us through the smoke that billowed from Ali's flat. She paused by the body lying on the landing. Crouching down, she gestured and hurled insults, but she was silenced by the thud of machine-gun fire from across the street as it stripped mortar from the walls above my head.

'Move, move,' I shouted.

At the bottom of the stairway Spaghetti charged across the street as incoming pounded into the tarmac behind him.

'Contact right,' Doug shouted.

His eyes darted manically from left to right. He edged along the wall to a point where he could lay down fire as we crossed the road. Spaghetti would have us covered from the other angle.

'Go,' he called.

Shreela and I ran, hurling ourselves into a brick wall on the far side of the street.

A second later Doug was with us again.

'We should get off the main drag and use the back street buildings as cover,' Spaghetti said.

I knew we were short on rounds and was about to agree with him, despite the fact that I was concerned we might get ambushed. It was the lesser of the two evils, I thought, but then I saw something that gave me hope.

Heading down a road almost opposite us was a familiar-looking vehicle. It slowed and began a three-point turn and suddenly Ali was beckoning us forward.

'Across the street,' I said.

Doug sprinted across the road first, while Spaghetti and I covered. He rolled onto his belly and signalled for us to follow him.

'Road of death,' Spaghetti grinned, wild eyed. 'Ladies first!'

I grabbed Shreela and ran across the road. To my amazement, and just like Doug before us, we took no incoming fire, but seconds later, as Spaghetti followed us, he took it every step of the way. I believe the only reason he made it to us was the fact that he was an incredibly fast sprinter.

In a matter of seconds we were aboard Ali's jeep. 'Where the hell were you?' I shouted at him, as he accelerated away.

'I saw men with guns coming into the town three hours ago and stayed back and watched them. I guessed they planned to attack you. I saw you from the top of this road one minute ago and came to your rescue. Now please, you must get me away from this island or I will die for certain.'

SNIPER OR VIPERS

Being alive is something you might take for granted until you come close to death. In the Regiment, being close to death is an occupational hazard, and as Ali's jeep bounced us up the hill and away from the action we all managed smiles.

I suspected the action was far from over, and so did Spaghetti. Already he was pointing his rifle out of the back of the jeep, ready for the first sign of any pursuit.

The roads were still busy with the most unserviced, dirty-looking traffic I had ever seen. Ali slammed his foot to the floor and shot into the middle of the road, hitting every pothole as he constantly honked at his horn.

As I sat in the back of the jeep I wandered if our enemy had covered the possible escape routes from the island. It was conceivable that they had been complacent enough to assume that we would be taken by the surprise of their rocket fire, but I couldn't bank on it.

The obvious escapes routes were Port St. Peter harbour and the airport and I wondered if they knew our plans, like they had known we were at Ali's flat.

I looked at Ali as he shifted the gears, gunned the engine and took us past all the old Austins on the inside lane. I still wondered whose side he was on. Was it possible he had sold our plans to Koslov? I called across the jeep to him, 'I want you to know that I will slot you without a blink if you cross us, Ali.'

'I want to leave Kali Pani,' he said, keeping his eyes up front. 'You are my ticket. I will look after you.'

Still there was no sign we were being followed. Although it was great not to be shot at whilst in transit, the lack of pursuit did strike me as unnatural. Ali dropped down the gears and the jeep lurched forward. The revs shot up and we accelerated past an old bus that looked like it had been in service since the first days of Ghandi.

'How many rounds do we have?' I called to the guys.

'I have thirty rounds,' Spaghetti said.

'I have about the same,' Doug said.

Ali swung us around the bends, bounced us over a ramp and squealed to a halt at the quayside. 'My boat is over there.' He pointed across to half a dozen boats bobbing on the swell in the port. 'We will row out,' he said.

We jumped down from the jeep.

A pensive silence hung over the dock; not even the sea dared to lap the quayside with any passion. I eyed the area quickly: old buildings, colonial in style, run-down and probably unpainted since the British handed the islands over in the forties. There was no movement and the only sign of life came from the one Indian navy ship in dock.

We jogged along the jetty to the rowing boat. Ali untied the mooring. He threw it into the boat and climbed aboard. Doug followed him, holding out his hands for Shreela to board. It had been no more than thirty seconds since we left the jeep. Everything seemed to be going smoothly, but not quickly enough, I felt like we were ants trying to clamber out of a treacle pot.

The sun was fading fast, warmth I had felt a few minutes earlier had now turned to a chilly breeze and I shuddered as I scanned the area a second time.

Still the silence.

I didn't like it. It was as though we were being watched again, like someone was waiting until we were at our most vulnerable, waiting to pounce.

Without any warning Spaghetti removed his Ak-47 from his shoulder and stepped in front of me. 'On the roof,' he said, his gaze fixed upwards.

A single shot reverberated.

From the corner of my eye I saw Doug dropping onto his

belly in the boat. 'Man down,' he called. At first I thought it was him that had been hit, but in front of me Spaghetti was down and writhing on the jetty.

'Contact front. Sniper. Top of the white hotel adjacent to the jetty. Conserve your rounds.'

A second shot cracked from the roof.

It ricocheted right between Spaghetti and me, less two inches from my foot.

Spaghetti cried out in agony as he edged towards the boat on one hand and his arse.

A third shot.

'Cover me,' I roared at Doug as, crouching down, I moved towards Spaghetti. Blood oozed out from between his fingers. I grabbed hold of him under the armpits and dragged him towards the boat.

Doug sent a series of single shots up to the roof, enough to keep the sniper's head down and stop him from shooting at us.

Ali helped Spaghetti down and into the boat and took the oars as I cast us off with the biggest push I could manage.

Spaghetti's blood pooled on the deck. He bit into the collar of his shirt and kept his cries of pain to a whimper.

I took over from Doug and he tore away part of Spaghetti's trouser leg. 'It's his shin. Bullet may have lodged in the bone,' Doug said, doing his best to cut off the blood supply just below Spaghetti's knee.

'Fuck the description,' Spaghetti spat through gritted teeth. 'Just wrap it up.'

Adrenaline pumped through my veins quicker than fuel to a Formula One car engine. I roared at Ali to row faster. He responded, but I continued to roar at him to make sure he kept up the momentum. We were totally vulnerable: Doug doing Spaghetti's leg, Spaghetti wincing with pain and me putting up the occasional shot to the roof.

We were moving away from the hotel, out of the gunman's range. My shots must have kept him pinned down as we took no incoming heading out to the boat.

'We have company,' Ali said, nodding back towards land.

A jeep sped along the quayside with five, six, seven bodies packed into it. Including the gunner on the roof and, discounting Spaghetti, who was out injured, we were outnumbered, eight guns to two. Once the jeep pulled up and the men were in position to fire we were in serious trouble. At a guess we now had around sixty or seventy rounds between us. Their eight guns would spew three hundred rounds a minute down on us.

The next few moments were to prove crucial.

Ali rowed us alongside his speed boat. He wasted no time leaping out from one boat to the other and starting the engine.

It was a precarious time. With the odds stacked against us, the last thing I wanted to do was transfer one casualty and one sick woman from one bobbing boat to another without covering fire. It's the kind of situation you dread being in, but you just have to do it and block the rest of it out.

Doug and I began to move Spaghetti. The key to our success was balance—if we shifted our weight too quickly the boats were going to wobble. If the boats wobbled we were going to lose precious seconds and become target practice.

Doug and I shuffled forward and made a bridge between the two boats, one foot on the deck of each. Shreela, to her credit, shifted to balance the boat with what little weight she had on her bones. Spaghetti hooked his good leg over the speed boat and between us we clamped the boats together.

We were a helpless bunch at that time and our lives depended on the keenness of our pursuers.

A fourth shot pinged off the rear of the boat close to where Doug was standing.

We wobbled unsteadily.

'Focus,' I snarled, aware of the temptation to look up and waste more vital seconds. No way was I going to die here. Not now, not after everything we had gone through together. We were going to make it.

We heaved Spaghetti's across and more or less dropped him into the well of the speed boat. He landed with a thud and a cry of pain.

On the quayside the jeep squeaked to a halt. Bodies

emptied from inside like ants from a hill being attacked with boiling water. They trotted towards the end of the jetty. From the end of the jetty they were only a hundred metres away from us.

Spaghetti hauled himself across the deck of the boat. 'My gun,' he shouted.

I chucked it over to him.

'Cover us,' I shouted to him, just as incoming from the jetty began whizzing and pinging around us.

I hurled for cover. The landing knocked the wind out of me, but still I crawled along the deck. I nodded at Spaghetti and we raised our heads as one and returned fire.

Behind us, Doug was still straddling the boats together. We were swaying us all over the place as Shreela lunged across and Doug threw himself across the deck.

Incoming zipped overhead. Curled in a ball, I knew it was over as strips of wood splintered from the boat. In less than a minute our boat was going to become a tea-strainer.

Suddenly our engine gunned. We surged forward with such power that Doug rolled into Spaghetti and he rolled into me.

As the boat swung we all leaned over the rear and we let the jetty have our remaining rounds.

The guys on the jetty scattered; some jumped into the water, others threw themselves on to the ground while another ran back for the jeep.

We had done it. We had escaped. Ali, who had been squatting as he steered us out of the port rose to his feet and took the helm. Spaghetti slumped, and Doug crossed the boat to finish attending to his wound.

I coughed and wheezed and looked at Shreela. Her breathing was rapid, like she was about to have a seizure, but she forced a relieved smile and flopped her arm in my direction.

Coral Island appeared from out of the dusk fifteen minutes later. 'We have just over three hours to kill,' Doug said.

'We're out of mags,' I said. 'We can't go there now.'

'And we can't stop on the sea in case they come looking for us,' Doug said.

I could make out another island in the darkness. 'Let's head there,' I said to Ali.

'You do not want to go there,' he said hysterically, 'that is Venom Island!'

'I'd prefer that,' Spaghetti grunted. 'I don't fancy clubbing slipper fuckers to death as opposed to out running cannibals.'

But other than Coral Island I could only see one other island out of the supposed three hundred that existed and that was way off in the distance. 'We have to go there,' I said.

Five minutes later we dragged the boat into the line of trees on Venom Island. We sat back to back, very still. Time dragged. Darkness fell slowly, the slowest I could remember.

In front of us a snake slithered across the sand. No one moved, but I sensed that every one of us was ready to leap up and do it some damage if it gave so much as a hint of turning in our direction. I doubt it would have stood a chance with the three of us clubbing it with the blunt ends of rifles.

That one passed without giving us any trouble, but I sensed that the long grass behind me was alive. It might only have been the wind whipping up from the open sea or it might have been snakes slipping into formation ready for the kill. I had no idea which was the case...and I had no intention of finding out.

'A storm's brewing,' Ali said a while later.

Surrounded by snakes, with cannibals a five-minute boat ride away, Koslov somewhere behind us and no rounds to fire, the last thing I needed was a storm that would jeopardise the helicopter coming in for us.

Within minutes of Ali's storm warning rain was falling. As it patted the sand the beach around us came alive. Snake heads rose from the sand, necks extended, and then reburied themselves. It was at that moment I realised how precarious our situation on the island was.

In the distance the first flash of lightning zig-zagged across the distant sky. Judging the distance by counting the gap separating the light from the rumble it was still some twenty clicks away. Every second on that island dragged. I closed my eyes and wished that it was all a nightmare...but when I opened

my eyes I was still sitting in the same place. I told myself
everything was going to be fine, but I knew that it wasn't fine.
There was no way a helicopter was coming to us in this storm;
we were stuck on Venom Island, surrounded by snakes and with
nothing left but the butts of our AK-47s to protect ourselves.

We were such a desperate bunch then, sitting in the rain.
Shreela was without wisdom, Doug without ideas, Ali had
become a desolate soul, staring at the dark sky while Spaghetti
was devoid of humour, slipping in and out of consciousness.
But despite the atrocious weather we still had to be at the RV
in case the heli came. At 23:00 we dragged the boat back down
the beach, ready to beat any snake that so much as glanced in
our direction.

Out on the sea the rainfall accelerated from drizzle to skin-
lashing torrent in a second. We were soaked and a puddle was
building up rapidly in the bottom of the boat.

For our own safety from the Coralenese we stayed off
shore and took the full storm as it came overhead at 23:30. We
were crouched down, shivering and waiting as the slow seconds
passed to midnight.

'You think the heli's coming?' Doug said.

'I hope so,' I said. 'If it doesn't, we have no communications,
no food, no water.' My mind raced on to the next day and then
the next and I considered the prospect of heading back to Port
St. Peter and calling Antenna again.

Spaghetti was still losing blood. He whimpered or grunted
occasionally and his sense of humour had long gone. I wondered
how long he would last if the heli didn't show.

At 23:55 we edged in closer to shore, close enough to jump
from the boat and run to the heli if it came. We remained
vigilant for a Coralenese welcoming party and hopeful that on
nights like this that their lust for flesh might dwindle.

At almost exactly 00:00 I heard the thudding of helicopter
blades in the distance. At first I thought it was my ears playing
tricks with me, but it grew louder. The heli would be coming
in with no lights on. Spotting it would be very much a last
minute thing, like picking out a dark shadow against a black

background. I knew for sure the pilot would have night vision goggles on and I just hoped he could pick us out on the boat.

'I can hear it,' Doug said. 'It's coming in.'

The thudding of rotor blades came closer. I checked the dark sea for a sign of Koslov. I checked the dark island for the Coralenese. Our way out was clear.

Above us lightning forked and I caught a three-second glimpse of the heli. The pilot must have spotted us at the same moment because I saw it alter course slightly and begin to drop down. It hovered for fifteen seconds or so just above the sand and then descended the last few feet.

I called to Ali to hold the boat as Doug and I went forward. We needed a stretcher for Spaghetti and wanted to hurry it up before the locals got curious about all the noise. Doug and I waded in and waited knee-deep in water for the loadie to come to us.

The loadie ran towards us and made his ID I told him about Spaghetti. We followed him back to the heli and then ran out to retrieve Spaghetti on a stretcher. Doug brought Shreela.

We rolled Spaghetti onto the stretcher with Ali's help and began carrying him through the water to the heli. It was then that our luck changed again.

Running towards us across the beach was a group of black figures. I called to the guys to hurry up, but it was no use—my voice was lost in the sound of the heli blades thumping overhead.

At the head of the stretcher I moved faster, bounding through the waves to the shoreline and the safety of the heli.

We slid Spaghetti inside and I jumped in, roaring in the loadie's ear that he should tell the pilots to get us up. I hauled in Shreela, then Doug and Ali.

A spear flew into the cabin and slid along the heli deck.

'Up, up,' the wide eyed loadie was screaming at his pilots as he began to close the doors.

In a second we were rising and swinging up and out into the darkness.

Crack. Crack.

Two gunshots from the cockpit.

I ran through. Standing on one of the skids was a Coralenese and one of the pilots was leaning out of the window shooting at him.

Through the green glow of the cockpit lighting, out in the darkness, with his long, black, curly hair flying in the wind, there was an evil look about the tribesman. He was banging at the front window of the heli with what looked like some sort of prehistoric hammer, a rock at the end of a lump of wood. The glass shattered. Another shot from the pilot, then another and in a second the windscreen of the heli was sprayed blood-red and the native was gone.

I headed back into the rear of the heli and the loadie pointed to a spare headset. I put it on. Through it the pilot spoke. 'Strap yourself in and expect a buffeting. We have monsoon conditions all over the Indian Ocean. This is going to be one hell of a ride.'

I buckled up and leaned my head back. We were away from Kali Pani now. I was going home to Christian, Aladdin and Pan, football and cricket. We were going home. For the first time in weeks we were safe. We were safe and going home...safe...

The pilots reeled off heights and speeds in the background, 'Eight hundred and fifty feet,' one of the pilots said.

'Fifty knots.'

'That's holding eight hundred and fifty feet, fifty knots.'

'Eight hundred and...what the hell?'

The heli swayed as though it had been hit by something, something like anti-aircraft fire. My stomach rose, like the feeling you get in a lift as it drops.

'Eight hundred and ten feet.'

'Thirty knots.'

The rotors strained as the pilot increased the thrust.

We swayed again. The whole helicopter seemed to be screaming—the rotors, the engine, Shreela, the loadie, Doug, Spaghetti and me.

'Seven hundred and eighty-five feet.'

'We can't make this,' the pilot's voice said clearly. 'The wind is swirling all over the place.'

The co-pilot reeled off latitude and longitude co-ordinates.

Our altitude dropped again as we were hit again. I could see the pilot trying to hold us steady against the wind, but it was no good, we were swaying all over the place.

'Affirmative, delta seven zero, we have that fix.' The voice of his controller, I assumed.

'Confirm best alternative flight path.'

'That's negative delta seven zero the weather is unstable in a three hundred mile radius of your position.'

We had just been told there was no other route out of where we were.

The pilot said, 'We have to land. Control, confirm intention to land.'

Above us the rotors were whirring, not the normal whirring of a heli, but the kind machinery made when it was just about to die.

'Delta seven zero, control confirms your intention to land.'

'I have an island in sight,' the co-pilot said. He read off more co-ordinates.

'Six hundred feet.'

'Twenty-five knots.'

'That's six hundred feet and twenty-five knots.'

'Holding five hundred feet.'

'Were going to settle down on the beach,' I heard the pilot say.

No, my brain said. Not Coral Island, not the Coralenese. Please. Fuck, no.

We hung in the air, dropping carefully, swaying slightly as the wind caught us or the pilot corrected his landing.

We touched down and the rotors slowed.

I grabbed Ali and marched him through to the cockpit. 'Where the hell are we?' I shouted.

The co-pilot pointed at the map. 'Here, I hope.'

'Is it safe? Is it safe?' I said, shoving Ali forward to look at the map. The pilots were staring at me like I was a care in the community case who had not been taking his medication.

'We are south. This is Smith Island. It is quite friendly here.'

I relaxed my grip on his clothes.

'Only thing on Smith Island is the volcano, but this has not erupted for six months now.'

At that moment I didn't know whether to laugh or cry.

THE MOMENT OF TRUTH

The rotors continued to turn. The communication between the heli and the controller was constant. Doug paced the heli. 'I'm worried about Spaghetti,' he said. 'He stopped wisecracking and grumbling ages ago.'

I went back to the cockpit.

'We'll get back up as soon as we can fly safely, but until the worst of the storm is over we're stuck.'

'Why can't we fly around it?' I asked.

'Too risky and too far,' the pilot said before he returned to his radio. 'Delta seven zero, go ahead control. Negative, we're parked up on the beach. Negative, there is no better place to hide. The island is mostly trees. That's affirmative control, confirm we will be visible come daybreak. Control, we have a casualty.' He proceeded to detail Spaghetti's injury.

The pilot swung around in his seat and looked at me. 'Weather forecasters predict that this will continue for three or four hours. Control is concerned about our visibility come daybreak. This is a hot zone for the Indian navy. If we get spotted here without their authorisation...'

Doug was behind me, looking worried or pissed off or both. 'No-one was joking when they said these islands were the worst place on earth, were they?' he said.

I forced a grin at him. 'Sod all we can do about that now,' I said.

The pilot was back on the radio again. When he had finished he spun around to me. 'I've been ordered out of here by first light whatever the weather. I have agreed an RV with control.' He read the co-ordinates back to the co-pilot to make sure he had them right.

⌘

The wind had abated a little when we took off again three hours later. The large gusts had given way to a constant battering. It was still raining heavily. I watched over Spaghetti during the flight. His face was contorted even as he slept. His wound was still weeping and he needed us to get to the ship urgently now.

The wind died away as we headed further and further south and then we were dropping again, only this time we were landing on a ship.

'Thank God for that,' I said.

Doug was on his feet, ready to grab the other end of the stretcher. We swung Spaghetti round and the moment the doors opened we moved out. 'Let's get this ugly bugger down to sick-bay then,' Doug said as the load doors opened.

Spaghetti waved an arm and beckoned us towards him like he wanted to speak. 'Fuck you, wanker,' he said.

Doug and I smiled.

⌘

We steamed to Thailand in what appeared to be no time at all. I slept for most of the journey. There were no spare beds on board so when I was not sleeping I was mostly looking for somewhere to sleep. Invariably I ended up just grabbing any bed available until its owner returned and turfed me out. Doug was bed-hopping too, while Shreela and Spaghetti enjoyed the comforts of sick-bay.

I was looking forward to seeing Thailand, but my hopes were dashed when we were flown into the country by helicopter and out by plane an hour later. It was all rather rushed and disappointing.

As we waited to leave the ship I headed down to Spaghetti and Shreela. Spaghetti was asleep when I arrived, but there was a tray full of empty dishes next to his bed—evidence that he was recovering quickly. As Shreela saw me coming through the sick-bay door she gritted her teeth and heaved herself up into a sitting position.

I fussed over her for a moment, helping her with the pillows so she could get comfortable, and even though her cheeks were gaunt and her eyes were red-rimmed, I told her she was looking brighter.

She smiled her thanks at my flattery and patted the bed, 'Pull up a chair,' she said. 'Sit with me. Spaghetti is so drugged up that I'm starting to feel about as lonely as when I first met you in the camp.'

'Does that mean you're going to give me a hard time again?' I joked.

She held out her hand to me. I took it in mine, shocked at how bony it felt. I knew she had been slim when I first saw her in Koslov's camp, but the days without proper food and the sickness had really taken their toll.

'I want to live in London,' she said. 'It solves my problem. If I am pregnant...I do not have to have my father's interference and the abuse from my family. For my father it is all about family image and what he calls 'good breeding.' It is not about individual people in the way your society is shaped. If I am pregnant and have a baby out of marriage, I will be labelled a whore. My own brothers will be tarnished. No woman will want to marry the brother of a whore, no matter how much gold he has. I will be an outcast and beaten, my baby will be known in my village as the bastard.'

'London is an expensive place to live. There are other towns or cities,' I said, trying to be helpful.

'No, I want to live in London. In India the government can try to force me to work with them, manipulate me, shut me up if they want to, but in London I might be able to make a bigger impact.'

'How?'

'I'm not sure at the moment, but if anyone can find a way...' She smiled for a second then her eyes narrowed. 'Kali Pani has such a terrible past. The British, the Japanese and the Indians created this hell on earth and must accept responsibility for righting those wrongs.'

'And you really think the governments will do that?'

She shook her head. 'The Indian government have shown me resilience. Maybe if the British got involved or if the Japanese helped—I don't know—I have a lot to think about.'

'Well, if the governments don't help and you are based in London you will have other opportunities.'

'What do you mean?'

'In London there's a huge commercial network. All you need is one philanthropist with a truck-load of money to burn...'

She mulled that one over. 'You know, I might just look for such a man.' She squeezed my hand. 'Thank you, Michael, that's a great idea.'

'Shreela,' I said.'

'Yes.'

'You can call me Mike now.'

⁕

Shreela was thoughtful and distant on the flight from Thailand to the air force base at Cyprus. She sat apart from us all and made no eye contact. I closed my eyes and pictured her smiling and laughing and remembered a few of our moments together. The warmth of the memory made me not want to part from her.

Cyprus airbase was a stopover. It gave us a night of rest and rehabilitation. Spaghetti hobbled around on crutches. We knew his pain must have been subsiding because he moaned that the food was shite and said he wanted to find a bar where he could have a few beers.

We drank to Macca, my first drink in three weeks. We talked about him as though we had known him for years, though in truth none of us really knew him that well. We turned to lighter matters: Spaghetti. With his shot-up shin resting on a chair, we got stuck into new nicknames for him. To begin with the names were not very original and not even funny, but I liked one of Doug's suggestions, Long John Pasta.

I stuck with just two beers as opposed to the bottle of brandy a night I'd been used to before flying out to India and despite calls of 'lightweight' from the guys I turned in for the night.

In the morning they complained of feeling groggy and blamed it on rough Cypriot brew. 'Long John Pasta didn't even get into his bed last night,' Doug told me.

Spaghetti giggled, still a little drunk.

'He fell out of bed and was still lying on the floor this morning when I whipped him with a towel and tried to wake him. All he did was grunt when I stung him.'

I looked at Spaghetti. 'And you called me a lightweight?'

He stuck his tongue out. 'At least I have an excuse. I lost a lot of blood back there and that means when I down my usual ten pints that the blood to alcohol ratio, which I normally abide by, is all wrong. Perhaps my limit is now eight pints.'

'Or perhaps just the four you drank last night,' Doug added.

I left them slagging each other. As we waited to be taken out to our aircraft I chatted to Shreela. She dabbed her eyes with a tissue as she saw me approaching her. 'I spoke to my mother and told her I was okay. She wanted to know when I was returning to see them. I told her I was heading to London. She was very upset.'

'Has that changed your mind?'

She shook her head. 'I need to be strong. It is a difficult choice I have made, but a correct one. Although I know what would face me if I went home to India, it doesn't stop me missing my parents.'

I was aware of the tears gathering in her eyes. 'Just because you don't intend to go back home today it doesn't mean that you won't go home ever. It's just temporary. There is always tomorrow.'

She looked up at me and let her tears roll down her cheeks. For several moments she gazed into my eyes. Gradually I saw her pain drifting away and her eyes relaxing and brightening. She leaned forwards and touched my cheek with her hand. A light touch, then she smiled.

Choking on happiness she laughed, 'Mike, you have an amazing ability—you live in intolerable situations and somehow make light of them. In the camp you made me smile many times, you even made me laugh and you did all this not knowing if you or I would die or live another day.'

I blinked. I drew in a breath. Her words rang so true and it all seemed to fit together—to sit right. I did live in intolerable situations, whether those situations were as a result of sitting at the top of my professional tree as a soldier or living in the wreck of my marriage.

Shreela's words sank in as we headed to the C-130 Hercules that was going to fly us in to Northolt Airbase. It dawned on me why I had become such a master at making the best out of shitty situations—because I lived in them so much of the time. And as I delighted in Shreela's revelation I remembered my moment of truth in the jeep, not long after we arrived in Kali Pani—the moment when I realised that I habitually ignored the very things I needed to deal with, the things that trapped me.

❧

The air was cool and damp as we landed at Northolt. A Home Office official was waiting for Shreela and Ali and our time to say goodbye had come. Spaghetti and Doug perhaps sensed something in the air: a quick handshake, a peck on the cheek and they trotted off to the waiting Augusta for our transfer back to Hereford.

'What are you going to do now you are home?' Shreela asked.

'I'm going to enjoy seeing my son today. Then after a good night's sleep I'm going to tell my wife our marriage is over and get a divorce. I might even get a discharge from the service. I know there's lots of jobs for ex-SAS guys, body-guarding that sort of stuff– I need to think that through though.'

She took me by surprise. She reached up and hugged me

and whispered into my ear. 'When you start your new life, look me up,' she said.

I wasn't sure what she meant by looking her up. Did she mean for a relationship, for a friendship...or just a catch-up? Confused, excited, hopeful, I let it go.

She kissed my cheek and I moved back, still holding her arms. I forced a smile. 'You'll be okay?'

'Yeah,' she nodded unconvincingly, 'I'll think about you and the way you made me laugh a lot.' We hugged for a second time. 'I learned a lot from our time together.'

'Yeah,' I said, 'Me too.' I was already missing her compliments.

She stepped back, saluted me and smiled. I laughed, and with a final squeeze of my arm she turned and headed away with the Home Office official.

As I strode across the tarmac to the Augusta life seemed to come to a standstill. I didn't feel the rain or the downwash from the rotors. I only saw the loading doors and the loadmaster waiting next to them. Even Spaghetti's jabbering sounded muted. 'Thank God for that,' he said as I climbed on board the helicopter. 'You've been gone so long I've got pins and needles in my arse.'

I wasn't in the mood to joke. I had been saying goodbye to a woman I had grown to like and was now going to say hello to one I had grown to loath.

The loading doors slammed shut. The heli took off.

HELL'S REFLECTION IN MY HOME

SAS operations are carried out under a blanket of secrecy, though with the press coverage these days, at times that secrecy is blown away. Orders are given on a need-to-know basis and are not common knowledge. It was no surprise then that on our return to Hereford we were not greeted by a welcome committee, a marching band, flag-waving family or someone of royal blood saying, 'Bloody good job, chaps.' But there were a few guys wandering around and they hailed us with homely regimental greetings such as wanker, dickhead and shit-legs.

Hereford felt cold, safe, and...strange—more like an illusion than familiar territory. Not even my car's failure to start or the humour of a couple of 'salt of the earth' guys helping me to bump-start it in the frozen car park felt real.

My mind was relaxed as I drove home, coming and going as it pleased: drifting from the swish of passing cars to Jodie in bed with the sleeping policeman, from Shreela's smiles to people posting letters in post-boxes, from dogs barking to Kalid.

And as I turned into my street I was no longer hurt by Jodie's affair, no longer angry towards her for all of the arguments and the hurtful things she had said. I was no longer resentful about all of our wasted years. Quite naturally and passionlessly I had come to the conclusion that it was over. But for the moment, out of a sense of obligation and an unwillingness to barge straight in and immediately turn everything on its head, I had decided to get the evening over with, see Christian and then sort things out with Jodie in the morning.

Christian was out of the front door before I got out of the car. He ran at me and threw himself into my arms as he talked about a walkie-talkie his mum had bought him. He talked non-stop until we were inside the house and I knew then that leaving home was not going to be as easy in reality as it had been in my head.

Jodie stood in the hallway, nervously scratching at her wrist as though she was meeting me for the first time. Stiffly she pecked me on the cheek. I smelled her perfume, my favourite one, the one she had stopped wearing over a year ago because she knew how I liked it. It still had the same impact now, it jabbed me in the back of the knees and made me think of doing things to Jodie that I no longer wanted to do.

'What do you think?' she said, referring the dress she was wearing. I had once told her how hot she looked in it and reeled off a string of things I'd like to do to her when it came off. She had never forgotten that and worn it a few more times. Then I remembered one time when I had suggested she wore it again and she refused point-blank. Now, hands on hips, she was twirling in front of me and smiling in it.

'It still fits!' she said.

Right away she was fishing for a compliment, pushing me into saying something that I didn't want to say to her. Immediately she was attacking me right in the heart and breaking down all the barriers I had erected. In sheer defiance I wanted to tell her that the combination of her and that dress were well beyond their use-by date, tell her that the perfume and the dress were just cheap seduction tricks to delude me into being attracted to her again.

But I couldn't say it. I couldn't be that cruel. Even after everything she had done to me I couldn't knowingly say something that would break her fragile, volatile world. 'It still looks good on you,' I said, hating myself for saying it.

She giggled. 'Don't just stand there, come in,' she said, grabbing me by the hand.

She pointed at the dining table. 'Look, we made you something.'

Half-heartedly I turned and saw a buffet big enough for the whole street to have eaten and there in the middle of it all was a cake. As I read the words I choked. It said, 'Welcome home, we both love you.'

I had been in the house less than two minutes and already I felt like a complete bastard for ever contemplating leaving my family. What had got into me? Of course Jodie looked good in the dress, her perfume smelled great, she was a kind, loving woman who would never do anything to embarrass or hurt me. Her affair was just a genuine mistake that I should forgive.

My wife and son were both happy to have me home; what more could I ask for? Get on with it, I told myself. And forcing a grin I pushed myself back into reality.

'Thank you,' I said.

Jodie leaned into my ear, 'He's gone,' she whispered. 'You can relax. I told him to go last night. Come on, sit down. Sit down.'

Told him to go last night?

The words knocked me back out of reality. Our conversation had been almost three weeks ago and she had waited until last night, when she knew I was returning home, before she dumped him.

I couldn't believe it. Then I couldn't work out why I couldn't believe it—it was just so bloody believable...even Shreela knew what was going on in my own wife's mind better than I did, and she had never even met her!

Ever the diplomat, I said, 'I appreciate all this, but I'm a little jet-lagged. I'll just have some pizza, a brew and small slice of cake.'

She leaned against the edge of the dining-room door with her head tilted towards it, swinging her leg backwards and forwards like a bored teenage girl at a family party trying to tease her uncle. The dress rode up her thigh a little; she still had great legs, but was that enough of a reason to forget everything else?

She had caught me eyeing her legs. I saw her smirk as she turned towards the kitchen, flicking her hair.

'Sure you don't want a beer, or a brandy?' she called.

'Narrh, just a screw.'

Oh shit! Shit! Shit!

A screw?

'A brew,' I said, recovering quickly. 'I meant a brew. A brew...A brew!'

Shit! Where did that come from?

'Whatever you say, darling,' she replied in a nonchalant manner that neither confirmed nor denied that she had heard the slip of my tongue.

Christian plonked himself on the chair next to me. He stretched his neck and looked hard into my face in a way only kids can get away with. He beckoned me closer and leaned towards me. 'Daddy, she gave kisses to him last night at the door and told him she would see him tomorrow.'

My mouth fell open.

I stared at Christian.

A million questions all at once...was Christian that perceptive? Was it true? Yesterday...tomorrow...he was a child and that meant by nature he had no perception of time...but had he got it right this time or had he got it mixed up with another day when she kissed him off on the doorstep? Was Jodie going to continue this behind my back?

Bitch!

Would she do that? How could she do that? Why did it matter if I was going to leave her anyway? Would she really do that?

Bitch!

'Just because you can't see –'

'Or hear or because you don't believe, it doesn't mean stuff's not there.'

'How did you know I was going to say that?' Christian asked.

I shrugged. 'I feel like I've heard it a million times.'

I heard her feet clonking across the kitchen floor on her way back into the room. I couldn't confront her now. I couldn't say, 'Christian said you didn't dump him.' That would land him in trouble, get him a smack or get him sent to bed. We'd have a massive row, one of the brutal ones, one of the ones where she threw something at me.

She came back into the dinning room. 'You two conspiring?' she said, smiling uneasily and easing her hair back behind her ear.

'B-boy's talk,' I said, still bewildered. 'We...we are just...just catching up.'

I ate silent pizza and noiseless cake and drank quiet tea then headed over to the sofa that had been my bed for a few months before the Kali Pani mission. I picked up the cushion that I had hugged every night and the blanket that had been my warmth and started to settle down.

'Why don't you go up to our room?' Jodie asked.

The suggestion shocked me. I blinked at her. I blinked at her for several long seconds.

'It's your house too,' she said with a shrug that was meant to suggest she didn't care. She rose from the table and began tidying the plates and giving Christian a list of instructions.

I knew what she was trying to do. I could see through the veil now...I knew how the game worked...the perfume, the dress, the food, acting as though nothing had ever happened... as though she had never slept with the sleeping policeman and as though I had made it all up in my mind. I felt like I was back in my childhood, in hospital with a horrific head injury, and people bringing me grapes were saying shite like, 'There, there, it will all be better soon.'

Was this real life...my life...or was I working as an actor, playing the part of the patient in a psychiatric drama about a guy I knew intimately? Had I imagined the affair...the arguments...the twisted gut at knowing she was with another man? Had I really slept on the couch or the lounge floor? Had I really drunk myself within a gnat's bollock of being tossed out of the Regiment?

I raised an eyebrow at what seemed like a pleasant enough idea and shuffled across the lounge floor and upstairs.

The floorboards gave a familiar groan and the bed its usual creak. I flicked the switch on the bedside lamp and it snapped on in exactly the same way I remembered it always snapped on. I picked up a pillow and sniffed it. It was fresh, ironed and still smelling of the same old fabric conditioner. I looked at the carpets and curtains and the furniture: none of it had changed, none of it had been moved.

Apart from the drive home, the time in the bedroom was the longest I had spent alone and awake for weeks. I had held it together for all that time...and the months before it, but I couldn't hold it together a moment longer. My mind flashed back through the images: Kalid, Macca, the beatings Koslov had administered, Spaghetti getting shot, Jodie bobbing up and down on the policeman, the men I shot in the Philippines.... My body began to tremble, my teeth began to chatter and my head began to feel like it would explode.

But it was the bedside table that tipped the balance. It pushed me over the edge. It should have been changed. It should have been thrown out with him. It had lost the right to be there. It was a traitor. It had changed sides, collaborated with the enemy. I hated it.

I lashed out at it, punched it, punched it repeatedly, punched it until my knuckles throbbed, kicked it until my toes hurt. I grabbed it and dragged it across the floor, all the time chuntering at it, 'Turncoat, Judas, stab me in the back, would you? I'll show you.'

The lamp crashed to the carpet. I opened the window and with one big heave I lifted the cabinet onto the ledge and pushed it out.

Drawers opening and clothes tumbling it crashed down into the garden.

Gritting my teeth and snorting I turned to see if there were any other takers amongst the unwelcome, unchanged, gawping bedroom furniture. Why hadn't she changed it? The curtains, the carpets and the bedding...why hadn't she redecorated the whole dumb, fucking bedroom?

It was then that something broke inside of me—an involuntary noise that squeaked out of my throat. I collapsed backwards onto the bed and I started to cry silently, using a pillow to muffle the noise.

I have no idea how long I cried; all I know is that at some point Jodie slipped into the room and sat next to me. When I noticed her she was stroking my leg.

'This feels weird,' I said some time later.

Her reply was slow, her voice caring and low. 'Why do you say weird?'

I wanted to be evasive. I changed the subject. 'They've given me a couple of days' leave,' I said. Immediately I regretted telling her that. I knew from the flash in her eyes she would try to organise the days for me.

'We need to get you some help. You need to see a doctor or a psychologist.' She patted my leg and stood up to help me into bed. I rolled into the covers like a child and curled myself up in a tight ball.

'It's good that you have a couple of days,' she said, drawing the curtains. 'Once you've rested we can spend some time together.'

I scrunched my eyes tightly and began rocking myself to sleep, thinking that I'd rather spend the days on Kali Pani.

❧

Morning came too quickly. I was woken with a kiss and handed a breakfast tray full of more food than I was ever going to manage to eat. Jodie had been out already to take Christian to school. She slipped off her jumper and jeans and slid into bed beside me. Her feet and legs felt cold as she nuzzled in and helped herself to some of the food.

She nibbled toast and I could feel the vibration of her jaw on my arm as she leaned on me and chewed. I sipped coffee. The sunlight coming into the room seemed filtered and dulled. It appeared to be bright outside and I couldn't understand why. I leaned forward to see if the windows needed cleaning. They seemed okay.

'This room seems dark,' I said.

'We could decorate it in a lighter colour,' she said.

'No, I mean it seems darker than I remember it. I remember the sun coming through the window.'

'It is coming through the window,' she said.

I picked the tray up and got out of bed.

'Where are you going?' Jodie asked with a mouthful of toast.

'I've got some things I want to sort out.'

'What things?'

'Stuff.' I pulled open my wardrobe and grabbed a fresh shirt.

'Can't it wait?'

'No.'

She breathed out slowly, raised an eyebrow suggestively as she pushed the covers down to reveal breasts hung in red lace. That same playful method had worked wonders on me in the past, but not any more, not now. Too much had happened between us and it wasn't going to just evaporate with a romp.

'I've made you breakfast, couldn't you at least stay for a while and just eat with me?'

I knew where this was heading—manipulation first—if that didn't work the temper would flare up. I decided to stick it out—I had to. I was going to do what I needed to do.

'I'll get it later,' I said.

'Mike, you can't go out in your frame of mind.'

'I'm fine.'

'You call throwing bedside cabinets out of the window fine? You just don't do that. I know everything that's happened in the last few months must have hurt you, but –'

'What makes you think it's about that? You don't know what I've been through over the last few weeks. You don't know how lucky I am to be alive. You haven't had one of your mates exploded and seen his guts and limbs all over the valley, seen some kid's head lopped off, had your head bombarded with visions you can't understand.'

'And this is exactly the reason why I want you to leave the service.'

'Oh, here we go again. It didn't take you long to start that old record up.'

'I'm just sick of the way you get screwed up every time you come home.'

'It's not every time. Every time is different.'

'Keep kidding yourself if you want to. I'm prepared to help you. I'm prepared to help you see someone, go to marriage guidance, whatever it takes. All I want you to do is say you'll leave the service.'

'I'll leave. Happy now?'

She shook her head. 'Look, just come back to bed and let's talk about what we can do.'

'No!'

She threw the remainder of her toast back on the plate as though I had just told her that the bread was buttered with shit.

'I'm trying, Mike. I'm trying really hard for us.'

'I can see that,' I said, standing in the middle of the bedroom in my underwear, clutching a t-shirt. I turned to the wardrobe for slacks.

'You're acting like you don't care.'

I whipped trousers off the hanger. 'I just can't sweep everything under the carpet like it never happened, Jodie.'

'I understand all that. I was thinking about what you said last night, about feeling weird. I wondered if it was just because we hadn't got ourselves properly reacquainted.' She moved the blanket down to her midriff. I could just see the frilly lining of her lace panties. 'I want to try, Mike. Come on.' She lowered her eyes and beckoned me towards the bed.

I looked at her semi-naked body and slumped on the bed with a pair of socks in my hand. For a moment I imagined turning round and getting back into bed. I knew that it wouldn't work. I knew when I told her that I wanted to leave she would say I had just used her for sex. It would be a good excuse for her to get angry.

She moved the tray away, lifted one leg out from under the covers and slid across the mattress. Curling herself around me she kissed and stroked my bare legs. 'I saw the way you looked at me last night when I stood by the door. I know you still want me.'

'Look,' I said, moving away to the far side of the room like I'd been stung, 'it's not about getting reacquainted. It wasn't that kind of weird that I meant—it's like I shouldn't be here. This actually feels like someone else's room and I'm the one sneaking in to have the affair.'

She recoiled like a snake that had just been donked on the head. 'You're being ridiculous, Mike. This *is* your room. This is *your* home. I'm trying to make things work. Why can't you just go with the flow?'

'I am going with the flow...my flow. Maybe we just have to face facts—you and me...it just isn't going to work out.'

'Why not? Why can't it work out? I just made my boyfriend leave because I wanted to be with you. Doesn't that mean something to you?'

'He should never have been here in the first place.'

'And he wouldn't have been if you had listened to me and got yourself a proper job where you could be at home more. Do you understand what it's like to be a single parent for eight or nine months of the year and then having some crazy lunatic walk into your home?'

'You're not a single parent and I'm not a lunatic.'

'I might as well be a single parent and you are. You don't know what it's like doing everything alone, being in love with someone you can't get close to.'

'How can you say you're alone? You have Christian! And we were close.'

'No we were not! And you try communicating with a sodding six-year old day in day out. And how can you say you're going with your own flow? What exactly does that mean anyway? And how can you say this can't work? You haven't even tried yet. We're supposed to be making a go of it again, aren't we? Do you remember?'

'Jodie, we've tried it. We've been married for years and it's been shite.'

'You're the one who always harped on about how great things were.'

'Yeah, well maybe I was trying to convince myself...but really it was just a few ordinary years and two completely shit ones intermixed with a few brilliant moments. I mean, isn't that why you really went off with another man, because our life together was shit?'

She was kneeling up now. Tears were rolling down her cheeks and the bed was bobbing to the rhythm of her voice. 'Is that what you think? Is that why you think all this happened? Christ, don't you ever listen to me? I had an affair because I hated the loneliness and because I believed we'd never end up doing that thing that married couples should do, growing old together, spending time together.'

'So you decided to do something that would ensure it would never happen?'

'Yes...I mean no...It wasn't meant to be like that...it was just –' She threw her arms up in despair. 'Look, can't you just come here and we'll try to make all of this right.'

'Sex doesn't do it. Sex is hiding, making...manufacturing, forcing it out. I want fulfilling love, the kind of love you don't just hump out...pure love, the kind that you and I have never had.'

I had done it. I had done what I didn't want to do. I saw the hurt on her face, the frown, and more tears welling in her eyes.

'How can you say that?'

I reached out to her, but she swiped my hand away. 'I don't hate you,' I said. 'I just don't want this life with you anymore.'

'Oh great, just great. So what, you think you're just going to leave? Is that it? And what's that based on, two shit years and my fling? You have to work at a marriage, Mike. That's what I want to do, work at this with you, but you...well...now you can't be bothered.'

I headed for the door, but at the threshold I turned back, 'Jodie, I want a divorce. I don't want to spend the rest of my life living like this with you.'

'And that's it?'

'Yeah.' I didn't know what else to say. 'I'm sorry.' I flapped my arms and left the room, pulling the door closed behind me.

As I headed downstairs I heard the bed creak, the floorboard groan and the bedroom door opening and thought, *here we go again.*

She went back into the bedroom. I could hear her moving around and anticipated she was pulling on her clothes. 'You want a divorce? I'll give you a fucking divorce. I'm glad I had an affair. I'm glad I got some satisfaction rather than waiting for your miserable face to come home from another sodding tour. And if you think you're getting any money from this house you can think again, arsehole—I've seen a solicitor and you're not getting a fucking penny.'

I pulled on my boots without doing up the laces, wondering when she had seen the solicitor. But more immediately I thought about what might happen next. I knew she wouldn't have a problem flinging open the front door as I got in the car and letting the whole street know about our differences—she had done that one before, on several occasions.

I had to get out quickly.

I grabbed my car keys, hid her door-key under the lamp-stand and was out of the house, locking up behind me.

I unlocked the car door and shoved the key in the ignition as I watched the front door of the house. I could see her through the frosted glass window, swaying from one side of the hallway to the other, throwing her arms around as she looked for the key.

The engine fired.

I laughed at the childishness of locking her in. Suddenly she was at the front window bawling at me, 'Where are my fucking keys? What have you done with them, you prick?' I backed off the driveway quickly as I saw her trying to climb up and out of the window.

I turned into the street and headed towards the main road. Almost as soon as I was in it I was aware of a police car behind me, flashing its lights and pulling me over. So the sleeping policeman had pulled a few strings and sent his mates to bother me: nice one.

I wound the window down.

'Morning, sir.'

'Morning.'

'Just a routine check.'

'Right.'

'Can I ask where you were going?'

I looked down at my disruptive pattern uniform to give the officer a gentle hint. He ignored it and raised his eyebrows as he waited. 'Jesus Army,' I replied. 'Just off to the high street for a spot of preaching.'

'Jesus Army?' He nodded and then started scribbling on his notepad.

Dickhead, I thought. 'I'm heading to Stirling Lines.'

He frowned. 'I'm confused, sir, you said Jesus Army and then Stirling Lines, which is it?'

I gathered my strength. I shouldn't have been sarcastic, that was just inviting trouble. I took a deep breath. 'Stirling Lines,' I said.

'I see, and where were you coming from?'

'Home.'

'I see. Would you mind stepping out of the car, sir?'

I opened the door and got out. 'Is there a reason why I've been stopped?'

'Like I said, sir, routine, sir. Would you mind blowing into the bag?'

'It's nine o'clock in the morning,' I protested.

'I'm aware of the time, thank you, sir. The bag please, sir.'

I did what he wanted. Negative. I thrust the bag back at him. He took it, then circled the car, checking the tread on the wheels. The officer thanked me, wished me a nice day and wandered back to his vehicle. I stood by my car, chewing my lip. I knew what this was all about. I knew why I had been stopped. I couldn't let him go without a word. I wandered over to him and knocked on his window. He opened the door and got out.

'You might like to let your mate know, if he wants my wife now he can have her without the fucking provocation.'

'Sorry, sir,' he said. 'I'm afraid I don't know what you're talking about.'

I stepped away from his car and shouted at him. 'Make sure my message gets through. You know your Chief Constable is a mate of my CO, don't you? You know what happened last time you provoked one of us.'

I got back in the car chuffed to bits and knowing that one word from the CO to the Chief Constable and they would be in it up to their neck. Occasionally they harassed us, but the CO was known for picking up the phone. The 'last time' I referred to was a time when one of their guys harassed one of our guys in a pub. The next thing we knew the boys in blue were on the phone and apologising. They even had a whip-round and sent us thirty quid, in case they had spoiled the evening.

I called my solicitor and made an appointment to begin my divorce petition. I thought about what that would mean for Christian and me. I wanted him to live with me and I knew that would involve changing my work. I could leave the Regiment, but I doubted that I could convince his mother that the best place for him was with me. There had to be a way of making it happen.

I had to be more creative.

I drove around for a while and asked out loud in my car for help from anyone who was listening. 'Help me find a way to have Christian living with me,' I said.

It was then that I felt the urge to drive home. At first the urge started with a wish to be at home before Christian got there, otherwise he might experience his mother and me at our worst again. But the urge grew and grew and I squeezed my foot further and further onto the accelerator.

As I turned into my driveway and got out of the car I felt unsteady. I looked around for something, as though I didn't know what I was looking for. I pushed the key into the door and entered, and then the weirdest sensation enveloped me.

I felt like I had been in this exact same scene before. The

house felt cold and I could see through the lounge doorway to the open windows and the blinds that were tapping against the frames.

I took a step toward the lounge and stopped. I looked upstairs. I heard a thump on the floor above and then a yelp.

I leapt up the stairs two at a time.

Noises were coming from the bedroom, like wrestling, breathing, laboured and grunting, struggling.

I pushed open the bedroom door, half-expecting to see a rerun of Jodie on top of the policeman, but that wasn't the scene I burst in on.

It was worse.

MAN OR MOUSE...

.

For a second I froze and just watched. Was it really happening again?

Jodie was on the bed. Someone was on top of her, fighting her, her hands were all over him. And then I saw it. I saw what he had in his hand: a gun. I ran into the room, dug the palm of my hand into his shoulder-blade and yanked the gun-holding arm back until the firearm fell from his grip. Pulling his arm back I took him around the throat, and with a knee in his back lifted him from Jodie and shoved his face into a wall.

'On your knees,' I roared at him, punching him in the kidneys. 'The gun, the gun,' I called to Jodie.

She was shaking too much to apply herself, fumbling around the bed blindly, breathing like she was the one I had just winded.

Suddenly there were more voices shouting, men rushing through the bedroom doorway, fully armed, bullet-proofs, guns, boots, the lot.

'Stand down. Stand down,' one of them shouted at me. 'We have him. We have him. Stand down.'

Guns were pointing in my general direction. I put my hands up and eased away.

My heart was pounding.

I recognised the eyes of one of the guys. I recognised his voice too, but at that moment I was damned if I knew his name.

'She needs sedation,' the voice said. 'Get her an ambulance and get him out of here.'

They bundled the intruder down the stairs and I followed

them. 'Where the fuck were you?' I blasted the nearest soldier as I reached the hallway.

'About ten steps behind you.'

'What took you so damn long?

He looked up at me and whipped his balaclava off. Whitehead, his name was Whitehead, I remembered it now. He made a beckoning motion and I followed him towards the lounge.

As I passed the front door I could hear voices outside as the guys sorted our intruder out. 'Right, get down, you bastard. Kneel. Hands behind your head. Move.'

Whitehead eased the door closed. 'Your wife confused us. She was climbing in and out of the windows...we didn't have a damn clue why...she left them open. He came out of nowhere and climbed in. The problem was we had been told in our brief that your wife...well...that she was...well...you know...'

'She was having an affair.'

'Yeah, and God knows why, but we thought he might be climbing *in* the window too, but then one of the guys at the back of the house said he saw a gun. By that time you were pulling up at the front. You got out of your car and were heading for your front door before we could react. He could only have been in the house a matter of twenty seconds before you arrived.'

I kicked the sofa. Hiding the keys like that, what an idiot!

Then something occurred to me. 'Were you watching my house the night before last?'

He thought about it, 'Erm, yeah, I was actually.'

'Was there a guy coming and going?'

There was a pause. 'I remember I saw one guy, it was raining, raining and cold. He's always had a hood up. I couldn't see his face—that's what threw us this morning. You see, we don't know what your wife's lover looks like.'

'No, no,' I said, 'I wasn't asking for that, I just wanted to know what was going on. What did you see?

Another pause. 'It's coming back to me now,' he said. 'The guy came around two in the afternoon, left around four, came back at eight and then left in the early hours of the next morning.'

'Any sign of any arguing, disagreeing?'

He shook his head, but glanced away from me. It occurred to me he was holding something back. 'What is it, mate?'

'I shouldn't tell you really.'

'I'm a big guy.'

A pause. 'It's not the kind of thing that a guy really wants to hear.'

'I can handle it.'

'Well, all I can say is they didn't argue. They looked like a normal couple on the doorstep wishing each other goodbye.'

'Kissing, you mean?'

'Yeah, that kind of thing, hands all over her and...'

'Right. Thanks. That's enough,' I said bundling him out of the lounge.

Christian's tale told it all. He hadn't been doing six-year old shit-stirring, he had it sussed out and had called it, spot on. Jodie and her bloke were deceiving me. She was feathering both nests.

I made a telephone call to Christian's school. They told me he was happy and enjoying himself. I told them there had been an incident involving his mother and I would be collecting him soon. I put the telephone down and ran upstairs, threw some of his clothes in a bag and then went into my room.

A soldier was sitting with Jodie and rose from the bed to leave as I entered. I held up my hand and he sat back down next to her. I headed for my clothes drawers. I slid them open one by one and emptied them. On the second drawer, Jodie said, 'What are you doing, Mike?'

'I'm going to stop with my parents.'

'What about me?

I continued to stuff my bag with clothes.

'You're not still going to leave me after all this. You can't just walk out. A man just tried to kill me.'

'The ambulance crew are going to sedate you. Call a friend, call your parents, call your lover, I don't give a shit.'

I looked at her, sitting on the bed, hair matted to her face, mascara on her cheeks, blouse torn. Could I really do this? Could I really leave her now, like this? If I didn't, what faced me...more years of the same unhappy, unfulfilled marriage?

'You heartless bastard,' she shouted. Her voice had so much force that her body bounced on the mattress.

She was right; it was heartless to leave there and then, but I had to leave—I had to stick to what I knew was right for me. She was the one that had been playing me for an idiot, had an affair and lied about ending it. And if the money and the house and all the material shit really mattered to her so much that she wanted to fight for it she could have the sodding lot. I wanted nothing.

'I can't believe you can leave me like this,' she howled. 'What am I gonna do? I can't stop here on my own.'

'I presume the sleeping policeman has a home, go and stay there.'

She stopped crying instantly and glared at me. 'We broke up, you arsehole. I broke up with him for you.'

'Who are you trying to kid? You were seen kissing him on the doorstep yesterday morning.'

I saw her expression change. 'I was saying goodbye. Letting him down gently.'

I spewed with sarcasm as I rammed the empty drawer back into the cupboard. 'Christ, you know, I can see that, now you mention it. He came after work in the afternoon. You screwed before Christian got home. He left then came back again after Christian was in bed and you screwed again. He stayed the night, you screwed. He got up for work the next morning and left before Christian saw him. Then you kissed him goodbye on the door in your underwear, while he groped your arse.'

Her mouth dropped open. 'How could you...'

'How could I know? The house has been watched, you were seen kissing him on the doorstep. I made the rest up. You were going to fuck around behind my back until I went away again then see how it went with him for another nine months.

Cheers, Jodie. You were really gonna take me for a ride.' I threw the bag over my shoulder.

'You bastard,' she said, flying at me. I caught her arm and eyed my colleague to help restrain her. He held her as she screamed and flailed at me. I could understand how she would feel upset with everything that had just happened, but I needed to follow through now, come hell or high water.

Two people in white smocks were at the door now. They came into the room. One helped my colleague wrestle Jodie to the bed while the other opened a case and took out a needle. I didn't stay to watch.

I headed downstairs and out the front door. I told Whitehead I'd speak to the CO tomorrow and headed down to the school to collect Christian.

In the car Christian questioned me: why was I early? 'Where are we going? Is it someone's birthday? Are you taking me out for a treat?'

I guess they were normal questions for a kid whose routine had just turned to ratshit.

'I'm just taking you to your Nan's,' I said. 'You're going to have a few days there.'

He seemed to ignore me. 'I was painting at school. I liked that. Will Nanny let me paint?'

I settled him in at my mother's house. She took him off to the kitchen for a drink and to make some cakes. I hung around by the windows, waiting as if I expected a visit from someone. In the late afternoon I pulled up a chair in the darkness and stared out into the blackness until it was Christian's bedtime.

I tucked him up in bed, into sheets that were well-pressed and pyjamas that came right out of the packet. I stroked his brow and hugged him and stole from the room when his breathing struck the rhythm of sleep.

I was feeling shivery and sick as I wandered onto the landing. I took a blanket out of the airing cupboard and sat cross-legged between my mother's bedroom and the room Christian was in. If I had been followed by Koslov or one of his associates and they were going to come after my family again I wanted to be in the way.

I shivered and shivered with cold sweats throughout the night. Several times I had to run to the bathroom to hunch over the toilet bowl and puke. I put it down to shock or trauma, but in truth I had no idea what it was. Occasionally I napped, but never for long.

In the morning I ached all over, threw up again. Still feeling sticky with sweat I made my way to see the CO.

With me standing in front of his desk he got straight down to business. 'You look like shit,' he said to me.

I told him the symptoms.

'Bollocks to trauma, you arsehole. You have fucking malaria. See the doctor when we've finished.' Then he continued. 'Koslov made what seemed like a ridiculous threat to make thousands of miles away in order to get information out of you, but he obviously meant to carry out the threat to you and your family.'

'I've screwed him twice and he knows it. I want to finish the job, sir. I want to go back and finish him.'

I was shuddering like a mid-winter arctic wind was blowing behind me.

'Sit down and shut up,' Antenna told me, without a drop of sympathy. I sat down slowly; every muscle and bone, every nerve in my back pinched and ached. 'Police detectives say the guy sent to your home was supposed to take you out. Apparently your wife got in the way. The Chief Constable has arranged a safe house for you and your family.'

'I'm issuing divorce papers. I need alternative arrangements for me and the wife.'

Antenna blinked. He wasn't a man easily lost for words.

I filled the silence. 'I want to take him out, sir. I want you to give me a special mission to finish him off. We were well and truly stitched up over there. I want to go after him—finish the job.'

'Your mission was a success, Edwards. You did the job you were sent to do. You will focus on that.'

Still quaking with fever and with a sickening headache growing, I argued, 'Koslov can't just be left out there, sir.'

'It's not your concern.'

'Macca's dead and my wife almost got her brains blown out!'

His eyes bulged and his fist came down with a bang. 'Edwards! What you don't fucking understand is that Koslov is on Indian soil and the Indians will not permit *us* to spill his blood on *their* soil. It's political. Do you understand?'

'Sir, if I may speak frankly,' I spluttered, 'can you please explain the fucking politics to me?'

He glared at me for a moment. I was expecting to get bawled out of his office, but his eyes dropped and he took a seat and stared blankly into the corner of the room for what seemed like several minutes.

'The word of intel...some Indian politicians are in support of Koslov. He provides trade, they say he runs a legitimate business. They say if someone makes arms for general sale then he is nothing but a wholesaler and for that reason they choose to turn a blind eye.'

'And what about the kidnapping and the killing of children like we found in the Philippines and like just happened in India, there has to be something we can do, these are humanitarian issues.'

'The official word in the Philippines regarding our operation two years ago is that only two hostages were recovered. Their reports say nothing of the mutilated corpses you reported in your debrief and not one word of their report relates to a connection to Koslov.'

'The Philippine policeman,' I said, and then I gave him a full explanation about Elvis. 'You know they turn a blind eye, sir, and you know why? Because they agreed with Koslov that he would rid the islands of a tribe known as the Jarawa. Without them in the way the Indian government can get on with their plan of deforestation and tourism—there's billions to be made from that.'

Antenna rocked forward in his seat and leaned on his desk.

'According to intel, Miss Robert became a thorn. Her family are wealthy and well-connected. An insider reported that her father met with Indian officials and was horribly embarrassed by the noise his daughter was making over the rights of a few hundred natives, their land and the deforestation taking place. He was told to shut her up and it was decided that she would be removed, but not killed.'

'Her own father arranged it?'

'Her own father.'

'So why the hell did we get involved, sir?'

'You have to understand the network of family in Indian culture. Our insider's family grew up with Miss Robert's mother and felt compelled to do something on the mother's behalf. His brother-in-law is a politician, his brother-in-law's brother-in-law works for the media...'

I cut in, shuddering the words out of my mouth. 'I heard the story on the morning news, the day you called me in on the op. Macca heard it too, the others missed it.'

He nodded. 'That's because the story was jumped on. The powers that be wanted Miss Robert out of the way. She could have just disappeared, been held captive by Koslov and no-one would really have known, and usually in India no-one would have cared. The problem the Indians had then was that the kidnap story got out via the mother's brother-in-law's brother and the Indians then had to be seen to be doing something.' He pointed at me.

'So we got involved to make it look like India was making an effort.'

'It was a political move; if ever the name Koslov was mentioned in connection with the incident, they had to look as though they had done something, but while you could retrieve Miss Robert, you could not touch Koslov. In the meantime, we have knowledge of where Koslov is and we will now put some pressure on them to remove him.'

Antenna stood up, came around towards me and sat on his desk. 'For the time being however, Koslov is protected property—protected by the Indians. He ships military toys to anyone, from your run-of-the-mill terrorist group right up to Saddam. I imagine some Indian ministers who support Koslov got pretty nervous when the story broke. They knew that some people wouldn't like the loss of a reliable supplier. There could have been reprisals if that had happened. The Indians above all else do not want to be drawn into a war involving terrorist states.'

'Meantime they fuel it.'

Antenna held up a hand to silence me, but it didn't work.

'Are you justifying their management of this, sir?' It was a bold question to ask the CO. He was not renowned for cooperating by answering questions and had already told me far more than I had ever anticipated he would.

'No, Edwards. I'm telling you this because selling arms is legal, selling arms on the free market is acceptable and because the world no longer cares about its people, it only cares about making money—a fucked-up set of values if you ask me. I'm also telling you because I'm leaving my command here soon. As you know, we usually only give information on a need-to-know basis, but I'm speaking to you off the record here. I feel you need to know what just happened so you can make an intelligent decision about your future.'

'My future, sir?' The headache and the shivering were worsening. My head felt like it was about to burst and spill onto the floor. 'Were we sent on that mission because we fucked up?'

'Fucked up? Fucked up? What are you talking about?'

'You told me before I left that if I didn't pull my shit together I'd be RTU'd. I understand Doug and Spaghetti had been trouble too.'

'Edwards, you did fuck up, but I picked you and Cooper because you had the right experience. Fielding was available, so was McNamara. You were never sent on a mission because you fucked up. You, Edwards, are a dickhead who I hold in high esteem and because of that I want to arrange something for you.'

'Arrange something for me, sir...what's that, sir?'

I was bewildered.

'It's no marching band, but I think you'll like what I have in mind.'

He told me his plan. When he had finished I staggered from his office and spewed up.

HEALING THE WOUNDS

The thing with some strands of malaria is that it comes and goes.
After the initial onset it can disappear for a day or two and then
return. This is exactly what happened to me. Two days later I
couldn't say I felt as right as rain, but I felt a lot better when I
got into the back of the hire car and slammed the door.

'Jammy bastard,' Doug said from the driver's seat. 'You get
more holiday and get more days with Shreela.'

Not really sure what to say I shrugged and smiled.

'I was shocked to hear your news. You're okay, though, I
mean...you're holding it together?' He was examining me in the
rear view mirror, with that look of 'I know there's something
wrong with you and you haven't told me.'

I nodded.

'How's the kid?'

'Fine.'

'He with your mum?'

I nodded.

'And you're fine?'

'Yeah.'

We drove on main roads for about an hour before turning
onto a dirt track and bumping through potholes and puddles.
A mist observed me from the fields and murky grey clouds
watched me from the sky. Everything was scrutinising me.

We swung into a courtyard housing a worn red brick
farmhouse. It had tiny upstairs windows that stared down on
me. It had half-drawn curtains that looked like questioning
eyes and a roof with a bow in it that looked like a frown. To the
side was a derelict barn with its burned rafters pointing into

the mist; it looked the way I felt, like it had caught fire and was waiting for repairs.

Doug was peering at me between the seats with a cheesy grin. 'How will this do you for a few days' R&R?'

I grunted, reluctant to make the best of yet another crummy location.

He produced a box of chocolates from the front passenger seat and handed it to me. 'She doesn't know you're coming. Thought you might like to cheer her up, the guys think she's such a miserable moo that none of the other cows on the farm want to graze with her.'

It was quiet and still inside, except for the creak of the old floorboards below the threadbare carpet. Already I was getting a sense of the stagnant air in the house; no wonder Shreela was miserable.

I pushed open the door at the end of the hallway and entered a room with thick thermal curtains blocking out the daylight. I slipped open one of the curtains and poked the weak fire. I added more wood and waited for the flame to catch. I knelt down beside her and listened to her breathing lightly.

Her appearance was a shock—she looked no more than a bag of bones in a blanket, but I felt happy and comforted just to be at her side. I wanted to send her the same kind of healing energy she had breathed into me. I focused on her and felt myself drifting towards her, surrounding her, enveloping her.

A minute later, or an hour, I heard her catch her breath. She blinked her eyes open and looked at me. She tried to sit up and take it in.

'I'm hallucinating,' she said.

I touched her arm and was surprised at the heat exuding from her. 'No, this is real, Shreela.'

She relaxed back into the pillows on the sofa, 'I was just dreaming about you, there was a huge light around you and you were healing me.'

'That's what I was just trying to do for you, like you did for me on the island.'

I leaned forward and hugged her. I told her everything

that had happened at home. After we had finished talking I was staring blankly at the wall when I heard her sniffle.

I took a tissue from the box by her side and passed it to her. 'I feel so bad,' she said. 'Your friend that died and your wife that also nearly died...'

'Nobody knew all this would happen,' I said. 'Macca was a soldier, we're all aware of the risks. What happened to my wife wasn't expected.'

When she calmed down she told me the doctor had been to see her. 'I have Rickettsia,' she said. 'Brought on by tick bite and poor diet, I'm told. Some days I will be better, other days I will be worse.' There were a few moments of silence, then she burst into tears. 'The doctor confirmed I am pregnant.' Her voice cracked as she spoke. 'And now I can't go home. I can't see my mother. So long as I only thought I was pregnant I could cope. I had a little hope, but now...now I know...now I know, I cannot go back home.'

I held her as she rocked back and forth and I wondered what it would be like for her, bringing a child into the world with no support from her parents or the child's father. I wondered how other single parents coped. I wondered how I would cope if Christian ever did come to live with me. I also wondered how a mother would answer her child when it asked about the dad it had never seen. I wondered if you would tell it what its father was. I knew she was going to have many tough days ahead of her, many issues, many heart-breaking moments.

Emotionally, it was a heavy day for both of us, and by late afternoon we were drained. I suggested we go for a walk. We wrapped Shreela up warm and ventured out into the courtyard and meandered through the overgrown garden. We found a spot we both felt comfortable with, a little patio where the bushes receded and opened into a view of the surrounding meadows and I felt the fresh air restoring my energy.

The sun set and dampness fell. We headed back inside. She asked if I would help her wash her hair and I obliged. Doug visited the local town and returned with a take-away and Shreela and I sat in front of the fire to eat.

We took a long time over the food as we began to talk about some of the situations we had found ourselves in during our escape from Kali Pani. Doug's fart and the whole episode of stealing the boat from Haven Island were amongst our brightest memories. We felt much better for having laughed and it warmed me no end to see her smiling. ·

I suddenly remembered the chocolates and passed them to her. She was taken aback by the surprise and told me I was kind. I had to admit to her that it was Doug who had thought of the gesture to help cheer her up.

'I've spent the nights here in England wishing I had gone back to India. I even wished I was with my father again and began to think that his abuse might even be an acceptable alternative. It has been awful here on my own.'

The chat with Antenna flashed through my mind. I knew I couldn't tell her about her father. It would break the code I had been trained by. I also believed she would find it hard to understand that her father had betrayed her.

'I love being in your company,' she told me, looking at me with liquid brown eyes. 'I missed you very much.'

I looked at her sitting there in the firelight, in a brown V-necked jumper two sizes too big for her. She had lost so much weight. The food and the fresh air had done her good.

'I just realised,' I said, 'it's the first time I've seen you with clean hair.'

She smiled and ran her finger through it: shining and bouncy, it curled on her shoulder. I thought about kissing her; the temptation was strong.

'Mike,' she said. My pulse was racing. I looked up. 'Your government seems to think I should change my identity and disappear.'

I shook myself from my thoughts. 'After what Koslov tried to do to my life, I wouldn't blame you,' I said. 'He's seen my face, and that means that for the rest of my days I'm going to be looking over my shoulder for him. In disguise, he could be one of a hundred people on every street, and every stranger could be part of his organization. He's going to be in my sleep, following me down alleyways and hiding behind trees. There's going to be bombs under my car when I want to drive and explosives behind the door when I return home. When I'm asleep his people could be out looking for me, they could be in my street. We already know we've got a leak in the MOD. They'll have my picture in no time and be looking me up wherever I go. It's going to be a long life of constant paranoia. If he finds out you have a child...'

Shreela ignored the implication. 'Why does he want to kill you?'

'A few years ago I was responsible for killing some of his men. We found his hideout in the jungle, released his prisoners and ruined his trade for a time. Now I've blow up his helicopter and recovered his prized asset, you.'

'I bet you wish you had killed him.'

'If it had been in my orders to do so then I would have done my best to do that.'

She touched my arm and looked pained. 'I'm sorry for all this.'

'You did nothing wrong. You were fighting for what you believe in, the same as I do. They are different fights, but they come from the same ideal, to save those who are overpowered and threatened and who have no voice. To free and liberate from oppression.'

Shreela twirled the noodles with her fork then looked up. 'I had never thought of all the things you said, how this man can make people feel, what he does to their lives.'

'And yet he was doing many of those things to you before you even knew he was there.'

'You mean he was watching and following me, before I was taken?'

'Maybe not him, but his people were. Are you going to take the new identity?'

She shook her head. 'What would I stand for if I did? Cowardice? I am going to continue to stand up to the government policy. I'm going to take the fight right back to them.'

I looked at her and smiled. The food and the heat of the fire had left me feeling lethargic and I felt my eyes becoming heavy. I knew it was the kind of tiredness that I wasn't going to be able to fight off indefinitely, and even though I wished I could chat with Shreela all night, I knew I had to give in. 'I'm going to turn in,' I said, getting up.

I was at the door when she called my name and eased herself up from the carpet. 'I'm going to get some rest too, please come and lie down with me. I haven't slept properly at night since I've been here and I'm sure if you were at least in the same room it would help—if that's okay with you.'

'I don't mind,' I said, 'we can talk until we fall asleep.'

We headed up the stairs, but I hung back a little at the bedroom door, 'It's okay,' she giggled, taking my hand, 'your virtue *is* safe for tonight.'

'But what makes you think yours is?' I smiled.

She flicked on the light switch and led me inside. 'If you knew what I'd caught from Koslov you wouldn't even consider me as a lover,' she said.

THE BOTTOM OF THE RIVER

It was still dark when I peered out from behind the curtains the next morning. I paid a visit to the bathroom, emptied my bladder and then inspected my face in the mirror. I looked awful. I had not showered or shaved since we left Kali Pani. My hair was a mess and my eyes were red.

I picked up the toothpaste by the sink, put a dollop on my index-finger and gave my teeth a quick going over. I looked at the bath and thought that I would become a social outcast unless I made the effort to have a proper wash.

The water nipped the backs of my legs and my bum as I settled in. I was not properly awake, staring, yawning, scratching and rubbing. It was probably because I was still feeling so out of sorts that I forgot to lock the bathroom door.

I had just found the soap and was slowly lathering it in to my hands while staring at the tiles, when the door crashed open, startling me. I whisked my hands across my privates and sat bolt upright.

Shreela couldn't hold it back. The noodles from the previous night splattered into the pan and the smell of stomach acid and Chow Mien wafted across to the bath.

'You okay?' I asked, staring.

A minute passed. She wiped her mouth and flushed the toilet. 'I'm never having Chinese again,' she said. Another minute passed. 'How are you today?'

'Just tired,' I said. I rubbed my eye, not realizing my hand had soap residue on it and Shreela laughed as I splashed and swore and tried to rinse it out.

'If you want to shave off your beard there's a razor on the shelf. I used it for my legs yesterday, I don't mind if we share.'

She shut the toilet seat, flushed and left.

I washed, wiped away the condensation from the mirror and took her up on the offer of the razor. With such long hair on my face it was a painful shave, like tearing off a layer of skin. I was sure I would feel better after the redness had gone down and the cuts had healed.

I got dressed and headed downstairs. Spaghetti had arrived and was hobbling around the kitchen. 'Nice razor burns,' he said. 'There's some extra bacon cooked up. Help yourself to bread if you want to make a butty,' he grinned, before stuffing food in his mouth.

I was just opening the plastic wrapper of the loaf when Doug came in, whistling and rubbing his hands. 'Parky out there this morning. Let's get a brew on.' He flicked the switch on the kettle and turned to me. 'Just been speaking to...fuck me...you had a shave. I was expecting to be talking to a yeti. Anyway, as I was saying, I was talking to Antenna. We're on the move this morning. We're off to London. Soon as you've got your food down your neck, get your girlfriend ready. We need to hit the road in about forty-five minutes.'

'What are we going to London for?' I asked.

Doug shrugged. 'Don't have a clue.'

'New pastures for Shreela at a guess.' Spaghetti chuckled like a schoolboy.

Doug grinned at the continuation of the cow jokes, 'We got any milk grazing around here?'

※

The sun burned off the hazy layer of fog as we headed east into London. Spaghetti grinned at us through the front seats like a little boy. 'We're slightly ahead of time so we'll give Shreela a quick tour of our great city shall we?' he said.

And it was a quick tour. Doug whisked us past Buckingham Palace, down past St Paul's and Parliament and up to St. James.

A while later we were drawing up in an underground car park in Greenwich.

'We're booked into a hotel,' Doug told us. 'It's an adjoining suite, so we'll all be nice and cosy together.'

The day was spent in a hotel bedroom looking out through the net curtains and lounging on the bed. In the afternoon I was so bored I ended up watching an American chat show about forbidden lovers. 'I could be on there,' Shreela said, sitting up.

'I'm not sure it's that kind of show,' I said, 'I think they're just thriving on the conflict. You need to have someone to shout at in order to get on there.'

Twirling her hair, she looked at me. 'Do you think you and I will ever be lovers?'

The question was a shock. 'You mean after the antibiotics have worn off?'

She hit me with a pillow. I hit her back. She hit me harder. I hit her again and we fought and laughed for the next few minutes.

I wanted to say yes. I knew I could fall in love with Shreela, but I had so many other issues to sort out and so did she. Logic told me it wouldn't work out now, so I shied away from any talk of involvement and just enjoyed the pillow fight.

She stopped laughing and looked up at me. 'There's one thing I haven't told you,' she said. 'When I went to Kolsov the night we escaped he told me my father had been involved in my kidnapping. He told me that the Indian government wanted to do away with me. He told me that my own father knew about the plot and said he would allow them to kidnap me, even help them. He said my father told them to go to the shopowner and Kalid and that they would lead me to them.'

I stared at her.

'Did you know this?' she asked.

'It was only a possibility,' I said, trying to soften the lie.

'But you knew.'

'Only after we returned to the UK.'

'You know why I really came to the UK? I came here because I cannot face my father. He set up my downfall and killed Kalid to make it look like someone else had plotted my kidnap. He did this because I embarrassed him amongst his friends, because I fought against them for the rights of innocent people and their land. I am going to return to India one day with thousands of people and millions of pounds backing me, and I'm going to change the state of the island and the plight of its people.'

I looked down at her and smiled. 'I believe you,' I said and I meant it. 'If anyone can do it, you can.'

'Enough of that,' Doug said, as he wheeled in the dinner trolley and saw me pinning Shreela to the bed. 'Antenna's been and gone. He left his orders with me and I'll feed you the details as and when it is appropriate.'

We ate dinner and then settled down for the evening. I lay next to Shreela and watched her as she fell asleep. It was the most peaceful I had seen her yet. Her skin reflected the dim light that stole in from the adjoining suite. Her mouth made a perfect O as she breathed. I snuggled up beside her, eased back a strand of hair that had fallen across her cheek and kissed her gently goodnight.

Though I didn't know it then, it was the last time I would be seeing her.

❧

I was dreaming when the shaking began.

'Bugger off,' I said.

The shaking continued, my arm swiped heavily in the air and connected with nothing. A hand pressed firmly over my mouth, so firmly that my head was forced back into the pillow.

My eyelids flew open and I stared wildly into the dark. A shadow stood over me, and a second shadow behind the first. 'Get up,' the one with his hand over my mouth whispered, 'be quiet, and don't wake the woman.'

Muddled panic. Who was telling me to do things I didn't want to do at this hour? Had Koslov found me? How about Doug and the guys?

'Where's Doug?' I asked.

'Shut up. Don't ask questions. Get your shoes on and stick this over your head.'

Something was thrust into my hand...A balaclava. What the hell was going on? Why the cloak and dagger? What about Shreela?

Nauseating spurts of adrenaline spattered and gurgled through my tired veins as half my body tried to fire me into action while the other half slept on. I groped on the floor for my shoes. Found them, fumbled them onto my feet and fumbled the balaclava over my head.

They grabbed me and strong-armed me out of the room into the adjoining suite. My eyelids were heavy, but I stared into the darkness. Bodies shuffled across the small room in quick, quiet organisation. Almost as one, they stopped moving.

'What's going on?' I asked.

'Shut the fuck up.'

A voice close to me spoke, 'India one ready to go mobile, over.'

A crackled voice on a radio confirming.

'Stand to.'

Silence.

The radio crackle...a voice.

'Roger that. Go.'

The door opened an inch and a shaft of light stole in. I could see the man by the door as he stuck his head out into the hallway and checked in both directions. He slipped out. A dark figure I had not noticed before slipped into the place vacated by the man who had just left the room. Fifteen seconds and the same happened again. Fifteen seconds more and the procedure was repeated.

'India one is mobile.'

The radio crackled...the voice on the other end.

My arm was grabbed and I lunged towards the door. At the door, the man who had my arm raised his index finger to his lips. 'Not a fucking word.'

Suddenly I was out in the cool of the hallway, being swept along. The fire-escape door opened as we reached it, held by another man in a balaclava. I shivered with the cold blast of air. It woke my senses. I was thrust down the first of the metal fire-escape steps. Our boots clanked, but the noise was not enough to have been heard inside. On the ground, a car rolled down the hill. The driver was looking up at us.

The back door opened and I clambered in over the back seat to sit on the far side. The door thudded behind me.

I could hear the grit on the road under the tyres. The engine engaged.

'India one, Romeo is rolling, over.'

We came to a standstill at the street corner, pulled out to the right. The car picked up speed, up through the gears, smooth, natural, not your Hollywood wheel-screeching.

'Keep the balaclava on and get down,' I was told.

'Who are you?' I asked the driver.

He ignored me. I felt the sway of the car. A tight bend, a pause, a junction. Another turn. Up through the gears into fifth. A main road.

'Mind telling me what's happening?'

'Keep your head down and your mouth shut,' the voice returned. There was something familiar about it.

Down through the gears, fifth to third, second, a left-hand bend, third, fourth.

Who did the voice belong to? Where were we going? What about Shreela? Who was the driver? The doubts played with my mind. I was a blind child, being led to its death. I wanted to shout, 'Stop!' or scream, 'I'm not playing any more', but I knew this game was going to finish, whether I played it or not.

I had to let go—let it happen.

The car slowed.

Thunk. Thunk. The central locking closed.

I pulled myself up between the two front seats. 'Right, tell me what the fuck is going –'

I was thrown into the back of the seat as he hit the accelerator. In front of us was a barrier, in front of that the river Thames.

'Hold on.'

Thump. We hit the barrier. My arms were stretched out in front of me, but the impact almost threw me over the seats in a somersault.

For a second, everything seemed to be frozen in midair. Then suddenly everything came back up to speed. I heard the engine roaring. We tilted. We were heading down.

Smack. The front of the car landed. Smack. The back of the car landed. My head hit the ceiling with the first impact; my arse broke the seat springs with the second.

The car bobbed and rocked backwards and forwards as we wallowed in the Thames. The engine raced, spluttered and died.

Glug. Glug. Glug.

We were sinking.

The bubbling was slow to start with, but it quickened as we took on water. Front, back and sides, the river was all around me. Water dripped in through the seal on the door.

The driver was scrambling around in the front seat. 'Get your shoes off,' he yelled.

'Tell me what the fuck is happening.'

'In case you hadn't noticed, we're sinking. Your oxygen is going to run out in a matter of minutes. Do as I tell you. Now, get your fucking shoes off.'

I didn't delay a second longer. I had to trust that the voice in the front was one of my colleagues. I whipped my shoes off. I had no socks.

'Pass me your shoes,' he said.

'What?'

'Your fucking shoes! Now!'

The foot-well was filling rapidly. I splashed in the cold water as I moved my feet.

We were sinking faster now, heavy with water. It was trickling through the sides of the windows and the air-vents in the front. All the time the pressure around us was increasing.

I passed my shoes to him and he put them in a bag.

'Right, balaclàva next,' he said.

I whipped it off and shoved it to him. He did the same

with his and stuffed them both in the bag. He was covering his tracks, making sure no one knew we had been there...but why crash the car and then sterilise it?

The water was already knee-deep.

I recognised his face as he passed me a scuba mask over the seats.

Whitehead.

Confident now, I dipped the mask in the water and swilled it about. I spat in it and smeared the screens.

The water was creeping up my legs. Pouring through the vents, the seals, any crack. It was cold and I shuddered.

Waist-deep, and the early morning light was disappearing as the water lapped up the windows. Sound was muted. My ears were blocking. I equalised, pinching my nose and blowing as though I was clearing my sinuses.

'Pull down the rear partitions,' he told me, pointing at the back seat. I did as he said, while he pulled off his top layers revealing his wet suit. He stuffed his shirt and jumper in the bag and waded between the seats.

As the partition came away in two parts, more cold water flowed inside.

Frenzied and fumbling in the dark, I pulled the oxygen tank out of the boot, turned the supply on and slipped the straps over my shoulder. I checked them for tightness, pulled them tighter and buckled myself in.

The water was chest height. I felt short of breath, like my breathing was restricted. We were sinking faster now.

Shoulder height. I grabbed at the fins that floated on the surface with hands that were numb with the chill of the water. 'Put them on outside,' Whitehead said.

River water lapped my chin. I felt like I was suffocating. I put on the regulator, checked it and started to breathe with it.

The car jolted as it touched the river bed. It floated up a little, bobbed for a second then rested.

Thunk. Thunk. The central locking released. 'Need your help outside,' Whitehead said. 'Follow me.' He opened the rear passenger door, allowed a small rush of water to fully submerge us, then glided out of the car.

The only noise now were the bubbles from our regulators.

Out in the river I exhaled every last drop of air from my lungs and sank down to the river bed. Sitting down, I pulled my fins over my feet.

I followed Whitehead. He was at the rear of the car, easing open the boot. He pointed at a bag which lay across the rear section and mimicked a carrying gesture to me.

We raised the bag out of the boot, closing the boot behind us. The bag was around six feet long, with a zip. It reminded me of a body bag. We swam it slowly towards the front of the car and unzipped it.

It was a fucking body bag.

A blank, dead face with blue eyes stared up at me. Its hair flapped gently with the current. I recoiled, taking in water through my regulator and mask.

Whitehead had taken over now, lowering the stiff corpse into the driver's seat, easing the door closed behind him, making it look like the guy from the body bag was the driver.

I cleared my regulator by blowing out hard. I tilted my mask and blew out through my nose.

Through the murky water he gave me the OK. I returned it and he beckoned me towards him. I clasped my hands together and held them under my body, close to my abdomen, and began swimming towards him. His eyes were scanning the water above us and I rolled over on my back and glanced up.

A blue light was flashing on top of the bank. The hull of a boat was approaching, its propeller unsettling the river.

We swam along the river bed for some time. The water was freezing. My movements were getting stiffer and shorter; my body was beginning to feel like it had been anaesthetized. All the time I was thinking, how much longer? I want to get out of the water. Why are we doing this?

Whitehead pulled up abruptly and gestured with his thumb that we were going up.

If you rush the assent you can get nitrogen poisoning or

burst a lung, both nasty experiences by any account, so I'm told. We took it slowly.

Suddenly my face broke the surface. 'We're heading to the Grand Lux warehouse,' Whitehouse said, pointing.

We swam to the water's edge and got out. It had been cold in the river, but out in the air it was even colder. As soon as the breeze hit me I shuddered uncontrollably. Quickly, I whipped the fins off and ran up into the warehouse.

Inside, Whitehead lit an old gas heater. I stripped down to my underwear and shivered in front of the heater as he disappeared.

He was back in a matter of seconds with two Bergens. He dipped his hands into one and took out a pile of neatly stacked clothes, a towel and a pair of shining shoes. I whipped off my kecks and got dried and dressed as quickly as I could.

Whitehead lit a burner and got a brew on. As we sat down to drink he passed me an envelope. I opened it and slipped out the contents. It confirmed everything that had just happened, explained why and instructed me as to what would happen next.

A BETTER FACE

The Bed and Breakfast was a North London dive next to the Jubilee Line. It stank of stale fags and mould. The carpet was hard enough to have been original M1 concrete and sticky enough with beer stains to have belonged to the busiest pub in the West End. Still...in accordance with the prophecy as declared by Shreela, I had turned the intolerable situation into something bearable.

I blanked it out.

The building shook to the thundering vibration of the first tube of the morning. It was just after 05:00. It wasn't the most pleasant way to be eased into a new day, but you can't have everything in life. I sat up in bed, sheets wrapped around me, eased back the scraggy curtain and looked out of the condensated window.

It was a gloomy day if ever I saw one. I stretched. I'm alive and free, I thought.

And I smiled at the irony of where I was at: fallen from the pinnacle of an illustrious career, marriageless and reduced to a room that was smaller than my childhood bedroom. I reached over to the bedside lamp and flicked it on then fell back on to the spongy mattress and laughed to myself as the headboard tapped the cheap walls and the pictures shook for the second time that day.

I wandered along the corridor to the bathroom and showered. The water ran cold as I lathered my hair. I rinsed myself quickly, got out and shivered my way back to my room, with steam rising from my body as I headed along the freezing landing again.

I dressed, grabbed a handful of magazines that I had bought the day before and headed towards the smell of fried bacon and eggs that drifted up from the kitchen. I endured the bullshit chatter of the tubby owner as she took my order of water.

'Oh, you can't eat this morning, can you?' she said, way too cheerfully for her own good.

I leafed through the pages of my magazines and detached myself from the superficial conversation of other guests as they greeted me. I smiled ironically at what I was doing that day and thought fondly of old girlfriends, even Jodie, as they flicked through pages of male models, show biz stars and pop idols, praising their smiles, bums and bone structure.

I had decided on my new nose and jaw-line long before my cup of hot water came. I poured slowly and enjoyed.

⚓

The surgery was a tube station and a five-minute stroll away: a three-storey building full of angelic receptionists with perfect noses and no wrinkles. I took the newspaper in the waiting room and browsed the headlines.

My death made page five. It was a pictureless story, thank God, and told how the soldier had lost control of his car on the banks of the Thames and plunged to his death. It gave the sob-story of the perfect wife and mentioned only in passing the six year-old son who was left behind. Although I knew it would be a year or two, I knew I would see him again. It did pain me, but I knew I had to apply my soldier's resilience to my thinking — I had been long periods without seeing him before and I knew I could do it again.

A slim, 36DD Barbie blonde called me in to see the doctor, who grinned at me with a cute Ken smile. He documented, discussed, measured and escorted me to a bed and told me to wait.

It was a long wait, interspersed with Barbie checking my pulse, blood pressure and potential medication.

The plastic surgeons greeted me with shark-like, menacing smiles and I could almost imagine them in theatre with their fins fitted outside their smocks, tossing my freshly-cut bones back and forth and laughing at my request for a smaller nose and a squarer jaw.

They marked their cuts on my flesh with felt-tip pens and discussed me as coldly as though I was a piece of meat that was deaf and emotionless—by comparison, the anaesthetist was a dreamboat, who chatted easily about the previous weekend's footie as he prepared to administer the injection.

I hardly felt the needle enter my vein, though I was aware of the coldness flowing up my arm. I was thinking of Koslov and all the beatings, and smiling at the fact that when I woke up my face would be on the way to a better state of repair, while Koslov would still be an ugly duckling.

I stared at the light bulb above my head and drifted away.

❧

I woke in the late afternoon in pain. I woke mid-evening in pain. I woke in the middle of the night in pain and every time I was glad of the needle that brought me relief.

I woke in the morning to the familiar face of the CO standing above me. 'How do you feel, shit-legs?' he asked.

I tried to open my mouth. It wouldn't move. It was stuck solid and hurt like hell. 'Course you can't talk, can you, arsehole,' he said. I saw the twinkle of humour in his eyes.

He disappeared for a second or an hour. Next time I looked he was standing over me with a mirror he'd taken off the wall. 'Not sure if I should call you the invisible man or a mummy,' he said, forcing me to look at my reflection. 'Anyway, get up, arsehole.'

Barbie helped me dress. She passed the medication to Antenna and he wheeled me down to the car.

Buildings streamed past me in a blur of nausea. Traffic lights and street corners were unwanted jolts. Potholes were shooting pains.

I was helped back to my bedsit shit-hole, made as comfortable as possible and left in the hands of Tubby, the hotel owner.

I drifted in and out of consciousness, maybe for hours, maybe for days, never quite sure whether the sickness and the pain were caused by the malaria or the surgery.

I heard trains during my periods of wakefulness and drank water through a straw. I had hardly been awake for more than half a day before I was back at the surgery with the nurses removing my bandages and dabbing my scarred tissue with cotton wool. I saw my new face, a battered apple that had been used as a playground football; I looked like I'd spent another night in Kolsov's camp, with all the cuts and bruises and swelling. The doctor sat on his desk. 'You had some fairly major work. The swelling will go down quite quickly now. The bruising will take a little longer. The scar tissue will take about six weeks to heal.'

Outside, the winter wind bit into my wounds. I wanted to clench my teeth but the pain made me cry. I stopped my taxi at a newsagent and sent the driver in to buy me coke and fumbled through my pockets for my drugs. Through the tiniest gap in my lips I poked in my medication.

☙

My recovery progressed. The sickness subsided. I began to walk, a few minutes the first day progressing into hours by the second week. I began to jog lightly and bought a video player and a yoga tape. My weight was down by twenty pounds. I liked the lightness and decided to maintain it.

My new career loomed. I familiarised myself with my new credentials. Thirteen weeks after my death in the river, I stepped out from a train and onto a platform at Portsmouth Station. I had a new face, new physique, new ID, new sports bag and new clothes, all paid for by me. I got a taxi and rode to the training site.

At the security post I gave my name as Peter Thompson and whistled annoyingly as the guard looked for my name on the list of delegates. He released the security bolts on the gate and I was in.

I grabbed a hot chocolate from the vending machine in

the waiting area and attempted to play the spy game with the other three delegates, peering out from behind my newspaper every few minutes, detailing their movements in my mind, memorizing everything about them from the cleanliness of their shoes to the colour of their eyes.

Leafing through the paper, only glancing at the articles haphazardly, I found something of interest, a photograph of Shreela and an article written about the Indian government opening the island up into a tourist haven. First it waxed lyrical about the beauty of the corals and the dolphins, then it got stuck into the plight of the natives and their land.

I smiled at her picture with a sense of pride that I had helped save her and that she in turn might help save others. While I was still staring at her picture, my long wait came to an end.

A door flew open behind me and a familiar face came in. 'Thompson,' he bellowed. He looked around the room as though he didn't know me. As I stood, he turned without a word and walked away, expecting me to follow him.

He led me to a small room. Sat me down and looked me in the eye. 'Now I've settled in to my new role I thought I should take a stroll down from London and welcome you personally,' Antenna said.

'Thank you, sir.'

'Also wanted to bring you up to speed on things.'

I frowned.

'Good news and bad. First, I asked the MOD about your face. I asked if they would pay for the work you had done. They said they would have paid for your nose to be straightened on the NHS and your jaw to have been wired. They said if you needed a new look they would pay for your hair dye and a pair of glasses, but as you wanted things straightening and altering they told me to tell you to fuck off. That's the bad news.

'The good news is that your wife has had a nervous breakdown. She has recently been admitted to a psychiatric unit. Your son has been taken in by Child Welfare and funnily enough your name is top of the list for fostering. Once your training with the Secret Intelligence Service is complete you will be shipped overseas to a new home; a nanny will be arranged and your son will be flown out to join you.'

He talked about the Official Secrets Act and I listened in stunned silence. He pushed documents across the desk and told me to read and sign them. I tried to take in the wording, but my brain was too jangled with excitement about Christian and thinking ahead. I was going to see him sooner than I'd thought. He was going to live with me. We were going to have a nanny. We were going to live abroad!

THE MAN TO BE

Life had turned sweet. The next six months flew by. Dead-letter boxes, disappearing ink, vanishing paper, building contacts with informants, debriefing them, tests for our abilities to build and maintain cover: it was all brilliant stuff.

I couldn't wait to get the training out of the way and get it all put into practice. James Bond, here I come, I thought to myself every morning as I stood in front of the mirror.

I thought about Christian every day. I wondered what was happening to him. I hated the fact he was away from his mum in Child Welfare care, but I knew the day was coming when everything would turn out well for him, for us.

❧

In my spare time I had been reading books on successful parenting. I had found three good titles and studied them thoroughly. I knew that when my time to be with Christian came again I was going to be the best-prepared parent in the world. I knew from what I had read that I didn't need to smack him in the way his mother had. I knew I could do more though love, through giving him time and space and by encouraging him to be responsible for his own behaviour.

I'd been saving all my spare cash up. I wanted to make sure Christian and I could have some days out, have some real fun together. I also wanted to start involving him in decisions about things we did or didn't do. My books had told me that this was important.

I couldn't wait to see him. I couldn't wait to get started on our new relationship.

The day came. The paperwork had all been done weeks before, and I was to meet him at a hotel. Child Welfare would bring him into reception and then leave. I arrived early—found the best seat where I could watch him arrive.

The minutes dragged.

I heard a child. My heart jumped and I leapt out of my seat. It was a boy, about Christian's age, but not him. I sat back down and tried to calm myself.

He was late. I checked my watch.

It wasn't time yet.

I fiddled and scratched and pretended to read things in newspapers that didn't interest me. Surely it was time now.

I checked the watch again.

No, it was still early.

I'd been wondering for weeks what he'd look like now. I'd wondered how much he'd grown. I'd wondered if he was still interested in the same things, if he still remembered me.

I saw a car draw up outside the foyer. I heard the door close. I saw the woman walking with the child. I knew it was him. I knew it instantly. His hair was cut short the way mine had been when I was in the army. He walked with his shoulders back, more confident than I remembered.

He had changed so much. I had missed so much.

They headed to the hotel desk. 'I'm looking for Mr Thompson,' the social service woman said. 'Is he here?'

'I'm behind you,' I said.

She spun around, forced a smile and backed away as she had been instructed to do.

Christian stared at me, cold, for a few moments. Confused.

'Dad?'

I swallowed the lump in my throat, put my arms out, grabbed him and swung him around. When I stopped he pressed his head into my shoulder and I felt his little body trembling.

'They told me you died,' he said, with tears running down his face.

'I did,' I told him. 'I had a very bad accident.'

'So how come you're here? Shouldn't you be in a grave or something?'

'Yes,' I said, laughing and crying in one go. 'I should be, but I'm not.'

He frowned at me. 'You look different.'

'My nose and chin...I had to have them fixed.'

'Did the accident break your face then?'

'Yes,' I smiled, keeping things simple for him. 'So what are you into now? Still like Pan football and Jafar cricket?'

'Narhh. That stuff's for babies. I play proper football now. I hate cricket.'

'Good job I've got tickets for the England game next week then,' I said.

'You have...cool! Are we near the front?'

'Yeah, right behind the dugout.' He was smiling all over his face. 'Come on then,' I said. 'Let's go and do some shopping.'

He twisted his nose up. 'Shopping? Why do I have to go shopping?'

'Because we've got to buy you a new bedroom.'

He looked at me with a furrowed brow, as though he expected me to answer no. 'Can I have a TV, and a video player in my new room?'

'Today, Christian, you can have anything you want.'

Do you feel obligated to the things you do

finances   relationships

or

family   career

do you feel freedom because they're totally YOU?

It's your life. Make it worth living.

Life Purpose Programmes

www.unstoppablelife.com
0800 781 3816